A MOST UNSUITABLE COUNTESS

SCANDALOUS REGENCY WIDOWS, BOOK THREE

AMY ROSE BENNETT

COPYRIGHT

A Most Unsuitable Countess

Copyright © 2023 Amy Rose Bennett
Editor: Emily EK Murdoch
Cover Artist: Erin Dameron-Hill

ISBN Print Book: 978-0-6450505-4-7

PRAISE FOR AMY ROSE BENNETT

"Amy Rose Bennett is a fresh new voice in historical romance with a flair for historical atmosphere."

— ANNE GRACIE FOR *HOW TO CATCH A WICKED VISCOUNT*

"Amy Rose Bennett is a charming new voice in historical romance."

— ANNA CAMPBELL FOR *HOW TO CATCH A WICKED VISCOUNT*

"A sweet and spicy read full of sly wit and rich with delicious details that pull the reader into the scene. A delightful confection of ballroom banter and bedroom seduction."

— SALLY MACKENZIE, *USA TODAY* BESTSELLER FOR *HOW TO CATCH A WICKED VISCOUNT*

"The perfect blend of sexiness and humor... Amy Rose Bennett has created a lush, vibrant love story, her characters sharing a fabulous sensual chemistry that fairly scorches the page."

— CHRISTINA BRITTON, AWARD-WINNING AUTHOR FOR *UP ALL NIGHT WITH A GOOD DUKE*

ABOUT A MOST UNSUITABLE COUNTESS...

A match most unsuitable. A love that's undeniable...

Catherine, the widowed Lady Rosemont, is considered a most unsuitable countess by polite society. Whispers about her checkered history follow her wherever she goes. Was she once a courtesan? Is her young son really the late Earl of Rosemont's child or a by-blow? And worst of all, is she a murderess? Despite the scandalous rumors, Catherine navigates high society's treacherous waters with her head held high. For the sake of her beloved son, Louis, she must never sink. But when she receives threatening letters and young Louis's life is endangered, she desperately turns to a past paramour for help...the man who once left her heartbroken. The far-too-honorable Earl of Dalton...

Adam St Clair, Lord Dalton, has always been one to adhere to family duty no matter the cost. Five years ago, he set aside his all-consuming desire for his mistress, the beautiful and mysterious Catherine Delacourt, and took a conventional ton bride. Now, newly widowed, fate decrees he should cross paths with Catherine once again. When she shares a stunning secret and implores him for protection, Adam is torn. With danger lurking around every corner, keeping Catherine and her son safe is undoubtedly the right thing to do. Nevertheless, Adam must decide whether he'll risk his reputation—and his family's —for the only woman he's never been able to forget... The one woman who might just steal his heart...

DEDICATION

For my very own hero, Richard. I love you always.

CHAPTER 1

Winthorpe House, Mayfair, London
October 1811

"Catherine, you cannot be here." Adam St Clair, the Earl of Dalton, ran a hand down his impossibly handsome face, his expression caught somewhere between exasperation and despair.

At least, Catherine hoped it was despair. Because that was the emotion churning about inside her heart and making her throat tighten with the effort not to cry. That, and a good dose of apprehension.

"I know." Her voice was so hoarse, the words came out as a croak. She licked dry lips and continued. "But...there's something I need to tell you." Her trembling hand fluttered downward over the skirts of her lilac silk ballgown to her belly.

Adam blew out a sigh as he raked a hand through his tousled light-brown hair. His pained gaze darted to the French doors leading to the crowded, chandelier-lit ballroom of Winthorpe House, then back to her. Oh God, he *was* frustrated with her.

"We said goodbye a month ago." His deep voice was low yet tinged with an unmistakable undercurrent of urgency. "I thought you understood. You being here tonight... It's too..."

Dangerous. Inconvenient. Pitiful? The bitter words hovered on Catherine's lips but somehow she swallowed them down along with her tears. How could she tell her former protector—the man she loved with her entire foolish heart even though he couldn't possibly love her in return—that she was with child?

His child.

"I know," she repeated uselessly. "I know I shouldn't be here." It would be futile to remind him that he had instigated the parting of ways, not her. Men discarded their mistresses all the time, and it was Adam's prerogative after all.

But he was going to be a father and she had to tell him, come what may.

The sound of merrymaking—laughter, chatter, and the strains of a small orchestra—traveled clearly on the damp cold night air, filling the taut silence stretching between them. Lord and Lady Winthorpe's ball was in full swing but the October night was so chilly, the stone-flagged terrace was deserted...except for her and Adam.

"How did you gain admittance?"

Adam's gruff question cut Catherine to the bone. It was to be expected, but nevertheless, it hurt. Narrowing her eyes to mask her pain, she fired back, "I didn't slink in the back door like a common sneakthief, if that's what you're implying."

"Of course not—"

She raised her chin. "I came here with Sir Louis Fortescue."

Adam nodded. The light spilling through a nearby window revealed a muscle pulsing in his lean jaw. A flash of jealousy in his eyes? His reaction gave her courage. But not hope. She dared not hope he would change his mind about her and a longed-for future that was well-nigh impossible.

Noblemen didn't fall in love with whores and then marry them—especially bastard brats who'd grown up in the gutters of revolution-torn Paris. It was simply the way of the world. And hadn't he once told her that he didn't believe in the idea of love? That romantic love made both men and women lose their minds? Caused them to make foolish decisions and take rash actions? That he would never let himself fall victim to such a senseless, volatile emotion that often ruined hearts and lives?

But he has a right to know I'm pregnant, doesn't he...?

Before she could drag in a breath to say what she needed to, Adam spoke again. "God help me, Catherine," he muttered through clenched teeth. "I'm trying to do the right thing here."

She shook her head, bewildered. *Right thing for whom?* "I don't know what—"

She got no further as Adam seized her, crushing his hot mouth against hers. He pushed her into the dark velvet shadows up against the cold brick wall, his strong arms crowding her in, trapping her so she couldn't escape, even if she'd wanted to. The kiss was rough, brutal.

Desperate.

His teeth nipped, his lips grazed, his tongue invaded her mouth and lashed against hers. And she loved it. Welcomed it. Clinging to his wide shoulders, she kissed him back with equal ferocity.

Yes, her heart sang. *Remember this, Adam, Remember us. Don't cast me aside. Don't abandon me.*

His hands were in her hair, gripping the back of her head, then cradling her jaw. At her throat where her pulse pounded. On her breasts...

Then all at once Adam dragged his mouth away. His wide chest rose and fell with his jagged breaths. He shook his head and released her from his embrace, his hands clenching and unclenching at his sides as he stepped back toward the French doors. "This is madness. I..." A wash of bright candlelight illuminated his piercing blue eyes as they locked with hers. "I can't do this."

"But why not?" She reached out a hand but let it fall when Adam took another step away from her. "You want me. I know you do. And besides—"

Another emphatic shake of his head. "Wanting isn't enough. I have responsibilities. A duty—"

"Adam? What on earth are you doing out here?" An attractive, fair-haired young woman appeared in the suddenly open doorway. "I've been looking everywhere..." Her sharp gaze slid past Adam's broad shoulders and landed on Catherine. "I don't believe we've met," she said in a voice dripping with icicles.

With a jolt, Catherine recognized her—it was the daughter of the house, Lady Sybil Gower. She couldn't have been older than twenty. A mere slip of a thing. *A debutante.* A ripple of unease passed over Catherine's skin, making her shiver.

Adam moved toward the scowling younger woman. "Sybil, Miss Delacourt is a former acquaintance of mine. And a friend of Sir Louis Fortescue's," he said in a voice so smooth, Catherine blinked in astonishment.

How could he be so calm, so urbane when only a moment ago a wild storm of passion had consumed him?

"I see." Lady Sybil turned her attention back to Adam and reached for his arm. "Come, my darling. Papa wants to make the announcement after the next cotillion finishes."

My darling? Announcement?

Catherine's stomach pitched as sharp realization slapped her in the face.

I have a duty...

"You're getting married," she whispered through numb, frozen lips.

Adam turned back to her, his expression wooden. "Yes."

"Yes, indeed we are." Lady Sybil stared up at Adam with such adoration, Catherine thought she might lose the contents of her stomach.

How could he do this? Of course, Adam needed to marry someone from his own class, but why choose someone like Lady Sybil? Someone so young and inexperienced? He'd grow bored with her within the space of a few weeks. She just knew he would.

Wouldn't he?

Surely Adam hadn't fallen in *love* with Lady Sybil. Not when he was so cynical about that particular emotion. Or so he'd always claimed...

Unless he simply can't love you, Catherine...

A sob gathering in her throat, Catherine swallowed hard and somehow made her voice work as she stepped out of the shadows. At times like this, she was grateful she'd inherited her mother's gift for acting. "Then may I be the first to offer my congratulations, Lady Sybil?" Plastering a false smile on her face, she blinked away her tears and forced herself to look Adam in the eye. "Lord Dalton."

Lady Sybil's expression was a combination of smugness and a civility so false it matched her own. "Why thank you, Miss..." She trailed off then affected a small laugh. "Goodness, I've already forgotten your name."

"Delacourt," Adam supplied. He offered a gentlemanly bow and another smooth smile. "Thank you, Miss Delacourt. Your good wishes mean a great deal to me."

Lady Sybil shot him a suspicious look but Adam ignored it. Tucking her gloved hand into the crook of his arm, he inclined his head in farewell again before escorting his haughty betrothed back inside.

Catherine staggered backward toward the edge of the terrace. Gripping the white marble balustrade, she closed her eyes as dark anguish engulfed her. *Adam is to be married. I've truly lost him. I didn't tell him he's going to be a father. And now he'll never know...*

Burning tears welled and this time Catherine let them flow unheeded. Their child would forever be tainted by the stain of illegitimacy. It was a stain she knew all too well.

"Catherine, my dear. Are you all right?" Sir Louis Fortescue appeared at her side. His graying hair shone like silver in the moonlight.

Catherine dashed at her eyes with her gloved hand. "Yes." When the baronet raised a dark eyebrow in disbelief, she shook her head. She'd never been able to hide the truth from Sir Louis, not in all the years she'd known him. "No. To be perfectly honest... I don't feel quite myself at all."

Sir Louis's brows plunged into a deep frown. "What's happened? If Dalton has hurt you—"

"No. No, he hasn't. Well, not on purpose." Catherine drew a deep, shuddering breath. The cold air hurt her lungs but nevertheless, it cleared her head a little. "You were right to caution me about coming tonight. I have just been informed that Lord Winthorpe is about to announce his daughter's betrothal. To Adam."

"Ah... That explains why everyone is assembling in the ballroom."

"You knew Adam might be announcing his engagement, didn't you?" There was no accusation in her voice. Sir Louis had tried to dissuade her from coming but she'd insisted on accompanying him when she'd learned he had received an invitation.

After pressing a linen kerchief into her hand, Sir Louis

gathered her close and dropped a kiss on her forehead. "My poor darling girl. Dalton was bound to become leg-shackled to one of the *ton's* chits at some stage. But I suspect knowing that doesn't make it any easier for you."

"No... No it doesn't."

"And we both know the real problem. Lord Dalton is too noble for his own good."

Catherine nodded. Sir Louis was right. Adam wasn't the sort of man who would be able to countenance keeping a mistress if he'd sworn fidelity to another. She supposed it was one of the qualities she loved about him so much. He was indeed, noble.

And wary of scandal.

Lord knows, someone like her would never make a suitable wife for someone like him. He'd said he had a duty. *Responsibilities.* No doubt to his family and the all-important Dalton legacy. But understanding that didn't make things any easier when she and her child were the ones being cast aside.

But deal with it she must. Just as she'd always dealt with any obstacle thrown her way. She might not be a Lady, but Catherine Delacourt would not be defeated by any of life's slings and arrows, no matter how much they pained her heart or wounded her spirit.

She stood quietly for a few minutes, her head resting against Sir Louis's shoulder until the baronet's chest rose and fell on a deep sigh.

"I'm sure you wish to leave, my dear, but I have a small...business matter to take care of first. I won't be long. Five or ten minutes, at the most."

Catherine lifted her head and wiped away the last of her tears. "That's quite all right. Do what you need to do. I shall wait here." It might be cold outside, but she didn't think she could face returning to the ballroom. To see Adam with his

7

glowing fiancée, to hear the congratulatory toasts and good wishes offered by other guests, would surely be her undoing.

Sir Louis drew back and studied her face. "Are you sure?"

"Yes. I'm sure. *Absolutement*." Catherine forced a smile. When the baronet's frown deepened, she gave him a little push. "Now go. I promise I will be fine."

She watched Sir Louis disappear through the French doors. For a man who was nearing sixty, he held himself well. In the nine years she'd known him—he'd been her late mother's first well-to-do protector—he'd always been scrupulously kind to her. In a way, he was like the father Catherine had never had. She would always be grateful that the baronet had provided his French *émigré* mistress, Madeleine de la Court, with a generous income and comfortable rooms in an affluent part of London during the three years they'd maintained their arrangement. It was far better than the hand-to-mouth, often-times fraught existence she and her mother had endured before that point.

It would be an understatement to say the streets of Paris and the brothels around Covent Garden—and even the Drury Lane Theater where her mother and Catherine had worked for a time—had never felt safe. Much to her mother's disappointment, however, Catherine had ultimately followed in her footsteps. At the age of eighteen, she'd styled herself as the sophisticated and alluring courtesan "Catherine Delacourt." Aside from a natural facility for flirtation, Catherine's linguistic adeptness had also allowed her to adopt a refined English accent; she'd reasoned that to appeal to a wider number of "gentlemen of means," she should "Anglicize" herself. And her reasoning had paid off. Catherine's wealthy upper-class protectors—she'd only had three including Adam —had not been the least bit stingy. Particularly Adam. In fact, he'd provided her with a generous allowance and a stylish townhouse in Russell Square which she could easily sell if she had to. At least her child—their child—would want for nothing at the beginning of its life.

Well, nothing except a father.

On a heavy sigh, Catherine retreated to the farthest, darkest corner of the terrace and tried not to listen to the excited hum of voices and tinkling laughter, then the portentous hush right before a man—probably Lord Winthorpe—began to speak. Wrapping her arms about herself, she inhaled a bracing breath of cold night air and studied the pale moon as a surge of applause and cheering erupted through the French doors. Like a musket shot, the sound shredded her already broken heart all over again.

Yes, she really shouldn't have come.

The next fifteen or perhaps twenty minutes were spent alternately pacing about the terrace or taking refuge beside a brazier that contained weakly glowing coals, but when Sir Louis didn't reappear, a nagging foreboding began to tug at the end of Catherine's already frayed nerves. She was no longer alone on the terrace. Lord Winthorpe had completed his speech and now several courting couples had wandered out, no doubt looking for their own dark corners to make mischief in.

Catherine really didn't want to go back inside to look for Sir Louis, but she supposed she must. The night air was growing chillier by the minute and her silk gown afforded her no protection whatsoever from the icy breeze that suddenly whipped through the garden and along the terrace, catching her skirts and making the coals splutter and spit.

Sliding a mask of practiced serenity over her face to hide both her heartbreak and apprehension, she entered a side parlor then slipped into the still crowded, brightly lit ballroom. Keeping to the fringes, she made a full circuit of the room and quickly ascertained Sir Louis was not to be seen.

Of course, Adam and Lady Sybil were there—they were

conversing animatedly with Lord Winthorpe, his wife, and several other couples near the entrance to the drawing room. Thankfully, neither Adam nor his betrothed noticed her, and she headed for the billiards room and adjoining card room—not that she expected to find Sir Louis there, or in any of the crowded and noisy rooms where most of the guests gathered.

He'd said he was attending to a small business matter, which meant he may have decided to avail himself of a small parlor, Lord Winthorpe's study, or even the library.

If he wasn't in any of those rooms and could not be found, Catherine decided she would simply ask one of the footmen at the front door to hail her a hackney cab. She really didn't have the emotional fortitude to linger in Winthorpe House any longer than she had to. Maintaining a calm visage in the face of Adam's happiness was taking its toll. Not to mention she was the proverbial fish out of water in a *ton* ballroom. She might be draped in a *haute couture* gown with expensive jewels at her throat and ears—past gifts from Adam—and she might possess impeccable manners, but she was, after all, only a whore. A well-paid, sought-after whore of course, but she was well known in certain circles, and she really didn't wish to be recognized, and then accosted, by any of the gentlemen here. Or worse, their wives.

As far as she was concerned, her whoring days were now well and truly over.

Dragging a fortifying breath into her lungs—her chest currently felt as though it had been clamped in a vise—Catherine asked a bored-looking footman for directions to the library.

Within a minute she was pushing open the paneled oak door into a lavishly appointed, distinctly masculine room. Firelight danced over the floor-to-ceiling bookcases of dark wood and equally dark oak and leather furniture. But at first glance, there was no sign of Sir Louis or anyone else. As the library door snicked shut behind her, one of the heavy velvet curtains on the other side of the room billowed in a strong gust of wind. The fire crackled and spat, and Catherine caught a glimpse of the townhouse's moonlit garden. It appeared someone had left the French doors leading onto the terrace open.

And that was when she heard a deep groan.

The skin at her nape prickling, Catherine turned toward a pair of free-standing bookcases on the other side of the room. And then she gasped. The flickering shadows revealed a figure —a man—slumped on the polished wooden floor between the shelves.

"Louis!" Catherine rushed across the room and fell to her knees beside the baronet. He moaned again and his eyelids fluttered as he attempted to raise his head. He was half sitting, half prone on the floor, his back against the shelves and his legs curled at an awkward angle beneath him.

"Cathy..." he whispered. "Must...leave...danger..." He clutched at his chest. "Make..."

"What is it? Are you hurt?" Catherine's heart cramped with horror as she lifted one of Louis's hands to reveal something protruding from his chest. An inky black stain marred his cream satin waistcoat. The unmistakable coppery scent of blood filled the air.

Oh, God. Had Sir Louis been stabbed? Terror beat about Catherine's head like dark, suffocating wings. She couldn't breathe. Her head swam and her stomach roiled. *Oh, no. Please, God, no.*

Before she could even think to do anything at all to help her friend, Sir Louis grasped her arm with bruising, desperate force. A trickle of blood slid from the corner of his mouth as he rasped again, "Please, go... Not safe..." He exhaled shakily, his next words barely intelligible as his grip loosened. "Tell you...make...peace..."

Dear Lord, is he slipping away? "No, Louis. Everything will be all right. I'll get help." Something—an unexpected movement—at the edge of Catherine's vision made her turn her head. Had someone come to offer assistance? She had the fleeting impression of a tall man in evening dress. His arm was raised. And then blinding pain flashed through her, swallowing her whole.

CHAPTER 2

P ain pounded through Catherine's skull and her cheek was pressed against a strange sticky wetness. Her gloved fingers curled against hard floorboards and she moaned as she shifted her weight, trying to lift her head. Prizing open an eyelid, she watched a pair of black leather shoes traverse a Turkish rug until they disappeared from her line of sight. Moving her head again, she caught a glimpse of a shadowy form slipping behind the ballooning velvet curtain.

Her assailant. And quite possibly Louis's attacker.

Awareness sliced into Catherine's addled brain and icy fear penetrated her heart anew. Now more than ever, she needed to get help. Where were all the servants? The other guests? There was a ball in progress, for heaven's sake! Why hadn't someone else walked into the library by now?

Pushing herself up to sit, Catherine was hit by a wave of dizziness and nausea. Her head throbbed and her vision blurred for a few moments. Had the attacker really gone? Or was he watching from behind the curtain, waiting to strike again? He'd be a fool to stay here surely, risking discovery.

She needed to stand but she felt dull-witted. Not quite

right. Blinking, she passed a hand over her eyes. Her white satin gloves were stained with blood. Was it her own or Sir Louis's?

Oh, God, Louis. Catherine forced herself to look at her friend. His mouth hung open, his eyes were sightless. One didn't need to be a doctor to know Sir Louis had gone.

Grief and horror gripped Catherine's throat and her vision grew hazy again—this time with tears. She tugged off one of her soiled gloves then reached out to touch Sir Louis's still warm cheek with trembling fingers—

A choked scream pierced the silence. "What did you do?"

Catherine's gaze whipped upward to meet the wide, terrified eyes of a young housemaid.

"Oh, thank God." Catherine reached out for the maid's hand but the girl backed away. "Someone stabbed Sir Louis— a man. I-I saw him leave by the French doors. You must raise an alarm."

The maid shook her head and stumbled toward the oak door which was still ajar. "You butchered 'im, you did. You're covered in blood!"

"No. No, you're mistaken." What was wrong with the girl? How could she possibly think that? "He's my friend and we've both been attacked. I was hit." Catherine winced as she touched the back of her head and then showed the maid her bloodied fingertips. "See?"

The maid shrieked and bolted for the doorway. But then a footman appeared, barring her exit.

"Polly, keep it down," he hissed, closing the door firmly behind him. "What's all the hullabaloo for? Lord Winthorpe will be livid if you kick up a stink about nothing again."

"It's not nufink, Roper," snapped Polly, hands on her hips. She jerked her head toward Catherine. "She's just offed someone. I saw 'er. Her 'and was on the knife. Just look at all the blood!"

"Bleedin' hell." The young footman, Roper, advanced farther into the room, his eyes peeling wide open and his jaw dropping when he saw Sir Louis's body and Catherine's disheveled state. Catherine might have laughed at his choice of words if the situation weren't so dire and she wasn't so gripped by grief and terror.

"No. No, you don't understand," she began as she clambered to her feet, using the bookcase for support. The room tipped and swayed again but somehow she managed to stay upright. "My name is Catherine Delacourt and Sir Louis, the victim, is my dear friend. You see there was a man— another guest here. When I came in, Sir Louis had already been stabbed. Then the man struck me on the back of the head."

The footman glanced about the room then fixed his wary gaze on her. "I don't see no other man."

"Well after he attacked me, he ran off." Catherine pointed toward the velvet curtain with a visibly trembling hand. "He escaped onto the terrace. Look. The door is open."

The footman strode swiftly across the room and jerked the curtain back but the French doors were shut.

Catherine shook her head in confusion. Between the pounding pain in her head and her churning stomach, she could barely think. "It *was* open. He must have closed it when he left."

The footman drew closer, his gaze suspicious. "I don't see no weapon. What did he hit you wif?"

Mon Dieu, these servants were exasperating in the extreme. Catherine wanted to scream and cry in frustration. But that wouldn't do any good, so she forced herself to inhale a calming breath. "I-I don't know, it all happened so quickly. But it hardly matters. P-Please. You have to alert Lord Winthorpe and Lord Dalton, straightaway. Make a hue and cry. Summon the Bow Street Runners! Someone needs to find the perpetrator and apprehend him before he gets away. I'm sure he must have blood all over him."

"Wha'? Like you, miss?" scoffed Polly. "You've been caught red-'anded. Lock 'er up, I say. In the storage cupboard behind 'is lordship's desk. The key is always in the jib door."

"What? No!" Catherine cried. She could try and make a run for it out the French doors, but a fresh wave of dizziness was already assailing her.

Ignoring her protest, the footman nodded grimly at the maid. "Lord Winthorpe will clear this up."

Before Catherine could even blink, he gripped her tightly about the arms and began to drag her across the room. She writhed in his uncompromising grip and pleaded with him— even mounted a scream—but it was to no avail. She was no match for such a tall, strong man and she was still woozy from the blow to her head.

When the maid unlocked the cupboard—the jib door was neatly concealed in the oak paneling behind the desk—she caught a brief glimpse of a small, cramped space between shelves stacked high with ledgers, books, and papers, before the footman thrust her inside. Then the thick door slammed, leaving her in the cold, musty darkness and suffocating silence.

The key turned in the lock and Catherine sank to the wooden floor. Bending her knees up to her chest, she tugged off her other ruined glove then rested her still throbbing head on her arms. A wave of burning tears stung her eyelids.

Poor, poor Louis. Who could have taken his life so brutally? And why? If only she'd looked for him earlier, perhaps the killer wouldn't have acted. Whoever had murdered her friend was ruthless. Evil beyond measure. And clearly concerned about being identified. Why else would she have been struck down? Indeed, she and the babe growing inside her were fortunate she hadn't been killed too.

Despite the maid's accusations and the footman's suspicions, Catherine was certain common sense would prevail when Lord Winthorpe arrived. Level heads were needed in a situation like this. And she trusted Adam would vouch for her good character and the fact she and Sir Louis shared a close, longstanding friendship.

Yes, Adam would help her. In no time at all the matter would be sorted out, and after the Bow Street Runners had taken her statement, she'd be back at her Russell Square townhouse, tucked up in bed with a nice cup of tea and a hot compress pressed to her aching head. Although her heart would still be weeping.

Poor Louis.

~

"Christ."

Adam glanced at his friend Phillip Latimer, Lord Maxwell, as he muttered the blasphemous curse. The Scottish earl's face was pale as he stared down at Sir Louis's body, and when he wiped a hand across his mouth, Adam noticed the man was shaking.

Adam felt rather shaky himself. He'd witnessed the aftermath of death before—almost six years ago he'd sat by his father's bedside as he'd slipped from this world—but it hadn't been like this. So visceral. And vicious.

He didn't want to believe Sir Louis Fortescue had been stabbed to death—*murdered*—but the metallic smell of blood mingling with other, more unsavory bodily odors put paid to the notion it was all some bizarre dream. A nightmare which didn't make sense.

To prevent any accidental eavesdropping by the two young Bow Street Runners currently examining the slain baronet, Adam turned away and addressed Maxwell in a low voice. "Catherine Delacourt wouldn't have done this, despite what the servants think they saw. You and I both know she and Sir Louis were very good friends. In fact, he was like a father to her. She'd sooner cut off her own hand than hurt him."

"Yes..." Lord Maxwell's attention traveled to the French doors where Lord Winthorpe was conversing in hushed tones with another Runner who was obviously the senior officer. "I'm glad Winthorpe is reluctant to make a fuss. My gut tells me this business has something to do with the intelligence I passed on to Sir Louis but an hour ago. In this very room. With the Runners' permission I'll check Sir Louis's coat pockets, but I suspect the papers I gave him are no longer on his person. Which means one of Winthorpe's guests tonight is a spy for Old Boney. A traitor to King and country. I'll need to inform Lord Castlereagh, and then of course, Sir Louis's brother, Lord Rosemont, will have to be notified." He grimaced and cursed again.

Adam nodded. Maxwell worked for the Foreign Secretary, and he knew better than to ask too many questions about the "business" of espionage. "In that case, Catherine most certainly has nothing to do with it. Of course, she's French by birth, but I *know* her. She's not a spy. She has a good heart. This is not something she'd be a party to. I'd stake my life on it."

Maxwell sighed. "I trust your opinion. The problem is, whoever did this is undoubtedly long gone. Yet the Runners will still insist on questioning Miss Delacourt and they'll take her away to Newgate if they believe she's a murderess. I'll speak with her too—she might know something useful—but I might not be able to do anything to help her until morning."

"Good God." Horror squeezed Adam's chest as he envisioned Catherine being dragged off to such a hellish place as Newgate Prison. Although duty had forced him to part ways with her, he wished her nothing but the best in life. If she were labeled a murderess and locked away in London's worst jail—even for just a short while until the matter was resolved —it was a fate that didn't bear thinking about. Not only would she be subjected to torment from hardened female prisoners, the turnkeys would also view someone like her as an easy target. Someone to take advantage of. Physically abuse.

A shudder passed through him. He couldn't let that happen.

Maxwell looked about the room. "Where is Miss Delacourt, by the way?"

Adam frowned. "Winthorpe told me she was 'being held somewhere safe.' Whatever that means." He nodded toward the French doors. "But I suspect we're about to find out."

A stony-faced Lord Winthorpe with the senior Runner in his wake crossed to his desk on the far side of the room. Rather than addressing Adam or Maxwell, the marquess shot a glance at a young footman who stood guard by the library door. "The key for the storage cupboard if you would, Roper. We need to speak with this woman."

The footman approached. "Of course, my lord."

What? Hot anger flared inside Adam as he marched toward Winthorpe. "My lord, please don't tell me Miss Delacourt has been imprisoned in a cupboard."

Lord Winthorpe cocked an eyebrow as he took the proffered key from the footman. "You know her, Dalton?"

"Yes," he said, his voice rough with emotions he should conceal from his prospective father-in-law. But then again, he also couldn't pretend Catherine was a stranger. He wasn't that cruel or mercenary. He'd never throw her to the wolves. So he offered an explanation that approximated the truth. "She's a... a former paramour of mine."

The marquess's expression hardened as he inserted the key into the lock of a barely visible jib door. "Really? Former, you say?"

Adam hesitated for a heartbeat before admitting a truth that hurt more than it should. "Yes."

The senior Runner, a middle-aged man with a ruddy face and graying untrimmed whiskers, smirked. "Word around Town is Miss Catherine Delacourt is a nothing more than a well-heeled whore."

Adam's knuckles cracked as he balled his hands into fists, but then Winthorpe pulled the door open. And his heart clenched.

Catherine was sitting on the floor in the tiny space, her fair head resting on her knees. She looked up and blinked dazedly before wiping a trembling hand across her cheeks. "Oh, good," she said in a voice that was clearing husky from crying. "It looks like you've finally called the Runners. Have you raised a hue and cry?"

Winthorpe grunted. "Get up, Miss Delacourt. These men have questions for you."

"Y-Yes. Yes, I'm sure they do."

Adam took a step forward, barely resisting the urge to sweep Catherine into his arms. "Are you all right?" he asked, searching her pale, tearstained face.

She arched an elegant eyebrow then winced. "No," she said, before using one of the shelves to pull herself up. It was then that Adam noticed the dark stains—bloodstains—on the pale purple silk skirts of her evening gown. "One of my best friends has just been murdered and I have a thumping megrim after being whacked on the head. And I've been unceremoniously locked in a cupboard."

Lord Maxwell's gaze sharpened. "You were attacked as well? Did you see the perpetrator?"

"The answer to both questions is yes." Catherine pushed a loose lock of hair behind her ear with bloody fingers as she turned to regard Maxwell. "But it all happened so quickly, I only caught a glimpse of him. Unfortunately, I have no idea who he was."

Oh, God. Catherine could have been killed as well. Adam's blood froze in his veins but it appeared Winthorpe didn't believe her account, judging by his derisive snort.

"It seems Miss Delacourt is not only a whore but a practiced liar." The marquess shifted his attention to the Runners. "Gentlemen, the evidence of this woman's guilt is smeared all over her person. But I'll let you deal with the matter. Suffice it to say, I want her and that man's body out of my house. As soon as possible, and with minimal fuss. I don't want my family nor my guests to learn about any of this. At least, not tonight."

Catherine raised her chin as she took a step forward out of the cupboard. When she spoke, her voice shook. "I did *not* kill Sir Louis Fortescue. He was my friend."

Lord Winthorpe's mouth twisted with a scornful smile as his gaze wandered over Catherine's body in blatant appraisal. "Yes, I'm sure he was...right up until the moment you plunged a knife into his heart."

A growl gathered in Adam's throat but then he felt Maxwell's hand on his shoulder; his friend was obviously trying to prevent him from acting on his own murderous rage, triggered by Winthorpe's slight.

Catherine, on the other hand, didn't refute Lord Winthorpe's insult. Although, it was clear she was not the least bit cowed. "No, I didn't. I *wouldn't*," she countered with a vehemence that bordered on righteous fury. Her eyes glittered with tears. "You don't understand. There *was* another man here. When I found Sir Louis, he was still alive. He tried to warn me I was in danger and urged me to go. But then the man—the actual murderer—struck me and I lost consciousness. Look." She bent her elegant head forward and parted her blood-matted blonde hair, exposing a sizable egg and a small gash.

"Sweet Jesus." Ignoring Winthorpe's censorious glare and the grumbles of the Runners, Adam gently clasped Catherine's slender arm and led her away from the box of a cupboard to settle her on a leather wingchair before the fire. Pulling up a footstool, he sat and then held one of her cold hands. "I believe you, Catherine. Can I get you anything? A brandy? A compress?"

Catherine shook her head and slid her hand from his. She threaded her fingers tightly together in her lap, the knuckles standing out starkly beneath her pale, delicate flesh. "No. I just want to go home."

Adam frowned at her rejection. However, he had to grudgingly acknowledge she was right to do so, considering he had been the one to end their...arrangement. And he was engaged. To the daughter of the house within which they sat. Aloud, he said softly, "I wish I could make it so, Catherine, but I think the Runners will want to talk to you."

His attention drifted to Maxwell. He was now kneeling beside Sir Louis's body and talking in hushed but urgent tones to the gray-haired Runner. Winthorpe continued to glower at Catherine from across the room. He prayed his friend would be able to convince them all that Catherine spoke the truth. That she was innocent. That this wasn't a crime of passion but something else entirely.

"Tell me again what happened, Catherine. My friend here, Phillip Latimer, Lord Maxwell, may be able to offer assistance if you can provide more information."

She nodded and related her story a second time. "It's infuriating that Lord Winthorpe and his staff won't even consider that it could have been someone else who stabbed Louis. Or believe that I was attacked too." Her mouth twisted with the approximation of a wry smile. "But then I suppose whores make for convenient scapegoats, don't they?"

Catherine wasn't wrong. But that didn't make it right. Unfortunately, there wasn't much Adam could do about the judgmental views of others right now. All he *could* do was try to help in practical ways. Tamping down his sparking indignation on Catherine's behalf, he said, "Do you have any idea what the man used when he struck you?" He hadn't noticed any other weapons lying near Sir Louis's body. But then the room was dimly lit and no one had conducted a search. "It sounds like it must have been heavy. The poker perhaps? A candlestick?"

Catherine's forehead knitted into a frown as she gingerly touched the back of her head. "I really don't know."

"Just give me a moment." Adam checked the fire irons on the marble hearth, but there was no sign that any of them had been used as a weapon. It was the same case with the silver candelabra on the mantelpiece. Crossing to Winthorpe's desk with one of the candles, he spied a small brass statue of an elephant sitting atop a haphazard pile of papers...and it appeared to be smeared with something dark and sticky. Blood?

He didn't touch it but called out, "Maxwell, you might want to see this."

His friend blew out a low whistle as he bent down to examine the statue. "Your Miss Delacourt is telling the truth."

"Of course she bloody well is," muttered Adam. "I take it the papers you gave to Sir Louis are missing too?"

Maxwell nodded, his mouth a grim line. "Yes."

"All right, Miss Delacourt, time to go," announced the head Runner. "There'll be a nice cozy cell at Newgate, just for you."

"No! Wait... I thought you were going to question me first. To let me explain."

Adam spun around to find the two younger, burlier Runners hauling a struggling Catherine to her feet while the senior officer and Lord Winthorpe looked on; the middle-aged Runner looked bored whereas the marquess's expression was one of disgust.

"Stop! She's innocent." Snatching up the brass elephant, Adam advanced across the room and thrust it in front of the marquess and the Runner in charge. "Look closely. This was the weapon used to strike Miss Delacourt. She's telling the truth."

Catherine stilled and the two junior Runners loosened their grip on her arms a little. But they didn't let her go.

Maxwell approached. "Gentlemen, please allow Miss Delacourt to take a seat again. I have a few more questions for her."

"I don't see the point," sniped Winthorpe, but nevertheless, the Runners allowed Catherine to reclaim the wingchair. "She might have used the statue to subdue Fortescue before she stabbed him. My servants caught her in the act for God's sake. Mr. Hurst here"—he nodded at the senior Runner—"has already taken their statements."

"And the injury to Miss Delacourt's head? How do you account for that?" snapped Adam. His patience was threatening to disintegrate.

"Perhaps Sir Louis fought back and she bumped it," suggested Hurst.

"Or perhaps someone—*such as the murderer*—struck her," Adam gritted out through clenched teeth.

Maxwell took the footstool in front of Catherine. "Miss Delacourt, before you were attacked, did you notice anything else? You had the impression the assailant was male. Why was that? Even the smallest detail might be significant."

"This is ridiculous," fumed Winthorpe before Catherine could respond. "I can't believe you are giving credence to anything this strumpet says."

Ignoring the irate marquess, Maxwell prompted Catherine again. "Did you see what he was wearing?"

"Yes. Black, well-shined evening shoes, white stockings, and black silk breeches. I caught a glimpse of his legs as he walked away. After he hit me."

Winthorpe snorted. "It could have been anyone then."

"And before he attacked you?" continued Maxwell. "Did you see or hear anything?"

"Well, all my attention was focused on Sir Louis. There was so much blood and he was in agony. He..." Catherine closed her eyes and swallowed. "He wasn't dead when I found him. In fact, he used his dying breath to try to warn me—"

"My apologies for interrupting, but what were his exact words. Do you remember?"

Catherine frowned in concentration. "It was difficult to hear him—as you can imagine, he had trouble speaking—but he told me to go. At first I thought he was just urging me to get help. But then he said there was danger. And he whispered something about making peace."

Maxwell's eyes narrowed and his gaze grew keener. "Making peace? Can you recall his *exact* words, Miss Delacourt?"

"Yes, I think so. He was very short of breath, but he definitely uttered the words 'make' and 'peace.'"

Maxwell shot to his feet. "Lord Winthorpe, where is Lord Makepeace? I saw him in the ballroom earlier on."

Shock jolted through Adam, rattling his bones. *Good God.* Albert, Baron Makepeace couldn't possibly have murdered Sir Louis.

But what if he had?

Lord Winthorpe gaped. "You're not seriously suggesting Makepeace did this? I've known the man for years. We were up at Oxford together. Besides, why the bloody hell would he?"

Adam and Maxwell traded glances. "We'd best mount a

search of the house and the grounds," said the Scots earl. "And call the coroner."

"No. I forbid it." Lord Winthorpe's eyes flashed with furious fire. "You will *not* create havoc and hold a coroner's court in the middle of *my* ball." He pointed at Catherine as his face turned an alarming shade of puce. "Enough of this ridiculous nonsense. My servants caught Miss Delacourt in the act. I'm more than satisfied she's the culprit." Addressing Hurst, he continued, "Take her away, right this minute. Use the French doors and slip out the side gate. Leave one of your Runners here to stand guard the rest of the night. The coroner can come in the morning to make his assessment."

Maxwell shot Winthorpe a contemptuous look. "You'll have the Foreign Secretary to answer to, then. And he'll be none too pleased if you've allowed Lord Makepeace to escape. Neither will Sir Louis's brother, Lord Rosemont. And for that matter, neither will justice."

Winthorpe's upper lip curled. "So be it. I'm willing to take the risk."

Catherine was shaking, her face as pale as milk as Hurst and another Runner seized her arms again. Her eyes, as they touched Adam's face, were wide with terror.

Before he could stop himself, Adam stepped forward. "I'll go with you."

Lord Winthorpe's sneer intensified. "If you do, Dalton, you *won't* be marrying my daughter. You're already skating on thin ice as it is. I'm willing to overlook the fact you've dallied with a mistress as most *ton* bucks are wont to do. I admit, I can see why you've dipped your wick in the woman. But your unsavory liaison must end, here and now."

Damn. Adam felt like he was teetering on the edge of a precipice. Catherine needed his help, of that there was no doubt. But for so many reasons—reasons that had nothing to do with desire or love, and everything to do with cursed familial duty—he couldn't break off his engagement to Lady Sybil. At this very moment, he was shackled as surely as Catherine was.

Somehow reining in his desire to protect her, he thrust his hand into his coat's breast pocket and pulled out a small roll of pound notes. "Here," he said roughly, offering the money to Hurst. "This is for the turnkeys. Make sure Miss Delacourt is looked after. And that means she gets a private cell at Newgate with adequate furnishings. She's not to be held in a communal area. And she's to keep every single item of clothing she's currently wearing. Including her jewelry. If I hear that any of it has been taken from her—or a single hair on her head has been harmed—you'll have me to answer to."

"And me as well. And Lord Castlereagh, the Foreign Secretary," added Maxwell grimly. "He'll be sure to have a word with Richard Ryder at the Home Office if this affair has been bungled and Britain's security has been put at risk. Or should I say, now that it has been firmly bungled with this idiocy."

The middle-aged Runner looked rattled for once as his ruddy countenance paled visibly. "Y-Yes, milord."

Adam caught Catherine's gaze and offered her what he hoped was a reassuring smile. "This will all be sorted out very soon. I give you my word."

Catherine's blue eyes gleamed brightly as they filled with tears. "Thank you, Lord Dalton," she whispered.

"It's the least I can do, Catherine." Ignoring Winthorpe's fulminating glare he added in a low voice, "Believe me, I wish I could do more."

She nodded then allowed the Runners to lead her toward the library's French doors. Without a backward glance, she was gone.

Hell. Adam wiped a hand down his face.

Maxwell gripped his shoulder. "She'll be all right. As soon

as I finish up here, and after I've seen Castlereagh, I'll check on her. With any luck, she'll be home before the sun has risen."

Adam nodded. "Christ, I hope so."

If anything happened to Catherine, he'd never forgive himself.

CHAPTER 3

Newgate Prison, London

Catherine shivered in her stained silk gown as a bull-necked, foul-breathed prison guard led her down long shadowy stone corridors and up narrow stairs, all reeking of filth and despair. The gag-inducing stench was an all too familiar reminder of long-ago privations and she had to fight against the urge to flee.

Thank God she would be installed in a private cell. At least, she prayed that was the case, otherwise Adam's pound notes—which the head turnkey had taken with covetous glee on her arrival—had been wasted.

Wails, shrieks, coarse insults, and the occasional volley of spit issued by the prison's inmates greeted Catherine as she tried to keep up with the guard's rapid pace. His large, grimy fingers dug into the tender flesh of her upper arm as he all but hauled her through an interminable nightmarish maze.

Things could be much, much worse, she reminded herself. If Adam *hadn't* provided the Runners with money to grease the palms of the prison staff... She shivered again.

The guard suddenly stopped and unlocked a heavy, iron-studded door. The key scraped in the lock and the hinges shrieked in protest as the door swung open revealing a small barren cell. It was empty of occupants—including rats, thank the Lord—but apart from a narrow pallet, a rickety wooden chair, and a steel pail, there was nothing else in the room.

Catherine frowned. This was all that Adam's coin had bought for her?

The guard thrust her inside but as he began to slam the door, she called out, "Wait."

The man's thick lips peeled back from his crooked teeth in a lascivious grin. "Yes, my sweet li'l ladybird. Wha' can I do you for? Or should I say, wha' can you do for me?" He gripped his crotch, adjusting his genitalia as he winked meaningfully at her.

Catherine swallowed. Damn the Runners to hell for stating on her arrival that she was a prostitute accused of murder. "The Earl of Dalton himself issued strict orders to the Bow Street Runners who escorted me here that I was to be provided with a private cell with *decent* amenities. And I hardly think *this* qualifies as decent." She narrowed her gaze. "Also, the Earl of Maxwell—he works for the Foreign Secretary, in case you didn't know—will be visiting me in a few hours. And he'll be none too pleased if he finds I've been mistreated."

The guard shrugged. "So you've fucked a few men in high places. Why don't you try somefink different, my darlin'? Something a l'il bit meatier and dirtier?" He stroked his groin again for unnecessary effect and smirked. "You take care o' me, an' I'll see my way to takin' care o' you."

Catherine lifted her chin, determined not to show any fear. "Don't be ridiculous. Here." She slipped a jeweled hairpin from her hopelessly disheveled locks and tossed it at the guard. "This should be sufficient to appease your appetite *and* cover the price of a blanket and a candle. I won't be left to freeze to death in the dark." She supposed she could have requested food and something to drink too, but the thought of ingesting anything right now—especially anything that this horrid guard might produce—turned her stomach. She wouldn't starve overnight.

The guard examined the pearl and amethyst studded pin before pocketing it. "I could warm you up," he said with a wink.

Even though her heart was racing at breakneck speed, Catherine kept her expression hard and her tone frosty. "I'd rather the blanket."

The man's mountainous shoulders heaved with an exaggerated sigh. "All right then, Miss High-and-Bloody-Mighty. Give me ten minutes." With that the door slammed shut, leaving Catherine alone with her terrified thoughts, her sorrow, and her pain.

A little ambient light from the corridor seeped beneath the door, allowing Catherine to reach the wooden chair without tripping or bumping into anything. She sat and wrapped her arms about herself in a futile effort to keep warm in the ice-cold chamber. She supposed the fact she was still queasy with a thumping headache wasn't helping matters. However, her physical discomfort paled into insignificance as a dark wave of despair and doubt engulfed her.

Earlier this evening, she'd been filled with anguish to learn the man she loved—the father of her child—was to marry another. But that set of circumstances paled into insignificance when compared to her current situation—her dear friend had been brutally murdered for unfathomable reasons, and she had been blamed. All she could do now was hope and pray that Adam and his friend, Lord Maxwell, could convince the Bow Street Runners to apprehend the real perpetrator, and thus clear her name. Otherwise, the future for her and her unborn babe did not look good. Not at all.

If she were found guilty and sentenced to death, Catherine could always plead for her life to be spared because she was with child. Even so, she couldn't stop her fingers straying to her neck. She could almost feel the hangman's noose slipping around it—the scratchy rope, the feel of it tightening, tightening, tightening about her throat. Of the gallows floor giving way and her body jerking in a macabre dance as her life slowly, painfully leached out of her.

An unbidden image of Sir Louis—slack-jawed, his eyes sightless, his shirt and waistcoat soaked with his life's blood—surfaced in her mind. She gagged violently.

Oh God.

Shuddering, throat convulsing, Catherine swallowed hard against a rising tide of panic and nausea and forced her thoughts in a different direction.

Adam. Think of Adam. She pressed her trembling hand against her still flat belly. Despite the fact she'd been accused of a heinous crime, Adam had been her unexpected champion tonight. Not only had he risked his relationship with his future father-in-law by publicly defending her, but his concern for her had been palpable. It made her wonder if Adam might care for her, even just a little—

No. Stop right there, Catherine Delacourt. Lord Dalton's heart holds no affection for you. His honorable streak has simply come to the fore. He's chosen Lady Sybil to be his bride. The sooner you accept the unpalatable truth, the better it will be for you.

He will never be yours.

Ever.

Although she'd been Adam's mistress for a whole year, in many ways, Catherine felt she didn't really know the man—not unusual for a woman in her position. For the most part, their time together had been spent engaging in bouts of mutually pleasurable bed sport.

No, it had been more than pleasurable. Their lovemaking had been astounding. For her, at least.

They'd certainly never talked about their feelings. Especially after Adam made it clear, quite early on, that he didn't believe in love. And Catherine had been loath to risk what she had with Adam by bringing up her utterly inconvenient tendre—which had rapidly turned into love—for the man.

Naturally, they'd also rarely discussed Adam's personal affairs. Any details she *had* learned, she'd gleaned from whispered *on-dits* that occasionally floated about Town or appeared in the scandal rags. One particular piece of gossip had caught her attention. If the rumors were to be believed, Adam had lost his father in tragic circumstances some years ago. Another woman had been involved—a *married* woman —and his father had died following a duel, bringing disgrace to the St. Clair family name and the Dalton title. It certainly explained why Adam was so wary of scandal.

And what could be more scandalous than marrying a courtesan?

Catherine almost smiled. Marrying a courtesan suspected of committing murder, of course.

By the time the guard returned with a candle and a scratchy, threadbare blanket, Catherine was quaking so much, her teeth chattered. It had been a very long time since she'd had to endure such intense physical discomfort and it seemed her body had grown soft.

Or perhaps the passage of time had simply dulled the edges of painful childhood memories—of the years she and her mother, Madeleine, had spent going without the most basic of creature comforts. Catherine sometimes wondered if the hardships her mother had endured, both in France and England, had weakened her body, and that was why she'd ultimately succumbed to an ague of the lungs at the age of only nine-and-thirty.

Well, Catherine could ill-afford to be picky about creature comforts tonight. When the guard thrust the blanket at her, she accepted it with alacrity. It might reek of body odor but at least it was dry. As she wrapped it around her shoulders, she prayed it wasn't riddled with fleas or lice. Although, all things considered, fleas and lice should really be the least of her concerns right now.

The guard placed a misshapen tallow candle stump on the flagstones near the end of the pallet bed and its oily guttering flame cast strange dancing shadows on the dank cell walls. When his greedy gaze slid over Catherine's ears and throat, she couldn't suppress a shiver. "If you'd be willin' to part wiv your pretty earrings or necklace, I'm sure I can dig up a mattress for you." He waggled his eyebrows. "And maybe another blanket we could share? It's colder than a bleedin' witch's tit in 'ere..."

Ugh. The revolting man was not only persistent, but his head was also filled with delusions. Catherine shook her head. "N-No, thank you. I shall b-be f-f-fine, j-just like this."

The guard gave a derisive snort. He clearly didn't think much of her stoic martyrdom or her refusal to part with any more jewelry. "So be it then, love. Sweet dreams."

It wasn't until Catherine heard the key scrape in the lock that she released a shaky sigh of relief.

Now all she had to do was survive until morning.

In the end, Catherine was so exhausted, she couldn't stay perched on the rickety chair. Curling up on the makeshift wooden pallet, she wrapped the blanket tightly about herself in a vain attempt to ward off the bone-penetrating cold. However, sleep eluded her; the shrieks and cries of other benighted souls and the odd scratching, scurrying sound of rats made her jumpy. And then of course, her mind continued to work feverishly, running through the horrific events of the evening and what would become of her and her baby. She doubted the candle would last until dawn, but if the darkness was kept at bay for a few short hours—even if her fears weren't —it was better than nothing.

When the feeble light of early morning began to creep through the bars of a tiny window set high in the wall, Catherine rose, her body stiff and numb with cold. After using the bucket in lieu of a chamber pot, she set to pacing the tiny cell in an effort to put some life back into her half-frozen limbs.

Lord Maxwell will come. Lord Maxwell will come. The chant played over and over in her head as she took twelve paces one way then twelve paces back. At one point she tried standing on the rickety wooden chair to look out the window, but the rough stone sill was above her eye level.

When Catherine at last heard someone at the door, she froze, clutching the blanket about her like a shield, heart crashing against her ribs. She prayed it was the kindly Lord Maxwell, not the odious prison guard from the night before— or worse, another of his ilk who might be even more opportunistic and lecherous.

Her spirits sank when a tall, cadaverous turnkey appeared on the threshold. However, the expression in the man's bloodshot eyes was one of boredom rather than interest as he grated out in a voice rustier than the hinges on the door, "Miss, you're to come wiv me."

"Where are we going? Is someone here to see me?" Catherine ventured as the man grasped her roughly by the arm, ferrying her down the corridor toward the stairs. She didn't want hope to flicker if she wasn't getting out of this godforsaken place.

"Aye."

"Who?"

"Didn't catch 'is name?'"

"Is it the Earl of Maxwell? He works for the Foreign Secretary, Lord Castlereagh."

The guard scowled when Catherine stumbled over an uneven flagstone. "Maybe. Maybe not. You'll soon see."

By the time they reached a hallway that was wider, quieter, and not as malodorous as the others, Catherine was short of breath and quivering with fear. They'd passed by a large open courtyard on the way—a public area—and the vile catcalls and malicious taunts of the other female inmates were still ringing in her ears.

Dear God, if Lord Maxwell couldn't intercede—if she were incarcerated here—she'd die, she just knew she would. And so would her poor babe.

After passing by a chamber which appeared to be a chapel, the guard halted before a wooden door. He delivered a fierce rap with his truncheon and when the door swung open to reveal some sort of sparsely furnished private office or study, Catherine didn't mind how bare it was. It wasn't a cell, and a fire crackled in the grate. More importantly, Lord Maxwell was standing by the hearth. Catherine was so relieved, she wondered if she might faint.

The attractive young earl's eyes were shadowed with fatigue and he was still wearing his evening clothes; he'd clearly been up all night. Nevertheless, he smiled gently as he offered a bow. "Miss Delacourt, how are you faring?"

She gave a short, mirthless laugh as she stepped into the room on shaky legs. "I will admit that I've been better. But I'm much heartened to see you here."

Lord Maxwell's eyes were kind. "I'm pleased to hear it. And I have no doubt you'll feel even better when you see that

Lord Dalton is here too." His attention skipped past her to the doorway.

What?

"Adam is here?" she whispered as she spun around.

Sure enough, Adam had been waiting in the shadow of the door. His gaze dragged over her, perhaps assessing her appearance to see if she was, indeed, all right. She knew she looked a mess, but she didn't care.

As she opened her mouth to speak, Lord Maxwell stepped forward. "I'll leave you both to it, shall I?"

As soon as the door shut, Adam strode toward her and gathered her into his arms, hugging her tightly. "God, Catherine. I've been worried sick about you." He then put her away from him and examined her face. His large warm hands ran up and down her arms. "Christ, your skin is like ice." He shrugged off his thick woolen greatcoat and draped it around her shoulders then continued, "Tell me truthfully. Were your treated well? Did anyone hurt you?"

She dredged up a smile as she hugged Adam's coat about her. It was warm from his body heat and smelled just like him and his delicious bergamot-scented cologne. "No one hurt me. I'm fine," she said. "Or relatively fine." In fact, her throat was dry and her heart hammered so hard and fast, she thought it might burst. Drawing in a tight breath, she managed to add, "Well, apart from being heartsick about Sir Louis. And worried about what's going to happen next. The suspense of not knowing is rather overwhelming. I-I did wonder if you, or Lord Maxwell, could tell me if there's any hope of the charges against me...being dropped."

"Of course. Both Maxwell and I should have said something straightaway." Adam held her gaze and upon seeing the smile in his eyes, the pressure in Catherine's chest began to ease. "I'm pleased to report there's very good news for you on that score. Lord Makepeace was apprehended leaving his club in St James's in the early hours of this morning. He was to be formally charged with not only the murder of Sir Louis Fortescue and the attack on your person, but treason as well."

Catherine gasped. "Treason?" What on earth had Sir Louis got himself mixed up in? But then, hadn't Lord Maxwell mentioned something about Britain's security being put at risk last night? At the time she'd barely regarded his comment as it hadn't made much sense to her. "Sir Louis told me that he had to meet someone about a business matter before we left Winthorpe House, but I had no idea he was involved in...espionage."

Adam's expression tightened. "As a matter of fact, the someone Sir Louis met with was Lord Maxwell himself. He passed a document to Sir Louis about a most urgent and highly sensitive matter. But it seems Lord Makepeace wanted that document too." Adam's brows descended into a deep scowl. "There is compelling evidence that Makepeace was a spy. I cannot go into too much detail, but it was clear to Lord Castlereagh at the Foreign Office that the baron has been stealing classified information by any means, fair or foul, and selling it to the French. For some time now. It appears Makepeace had been desperately short of funds and decided to betray his King and country for money. The man was a dangerous, soulless mercenary. A traitor."

Catherine's breath froze. "Wait—what do you mean, 'was'? You said Lord Makepeace was apprehended and was to be charged..."

"It seems fate has meted out a form of justice to the baron already," said Adam grimly. "As the Bow Street Runners walked him out of his club, there was a struggle and Makepeace managed to slip free. He..." Adam swallowed. "He bolted straight into oncoming traffic and the direct path of a hackney cab. He was killed immediately. So it seems, in a way, he's already been punished for his crimes."

"Good heavens." Catherine pressed a shaking hand to her forehead. "You were there at the club, weren't you? You saw it happen."

Adam nodded. "I was. And I can't say that I'm sorry. Part of me wonders if Makepeace deliberately ran in front of that hackney cab. Because he's dead, there won't be a trial in the House of Lords and his title won't be stripped from him. Perhaps he did it to save his family's legacy." Adam shrugged. "He has a son, Frederick, who I imagine will inherit the barony in due course."

"No doubt the family's legacy will be tainted, though. There will always be a cloud of infamy hovering over the Makepeace name."

Adam's gaze hardened. "No doubt." But then his expression softened. "But you, Catherine. You are very lucky you weren't killed by Makepeace as well."

"Yes," she said faintly. "Yes, I certainly am."

"And of course, all of this means that you are free to go. As I mentioned, the evidence against Makepeace is overwhelming. Not only was he in possession of the stolen document when he was arrested, there were blood splatters on his clothing as they attempted to apprehend him. One of the doormen at his club noted the stains as he helped the baron with his coat upon his arrival. Another guest witnessed Makepeace exiting Lord Winthorpe's library by the terrace last night, just as you'd recounted. There is no doubt whatsoever that he's the guilty party in Sir Louis's death."

Catherine bit her lip as a strange combination of grief for her friend and utter relief welled inside her.

Adam touch her shoulder. "You're safe, Catherine," he murmured. "When you're ready, Lord Maxwell shall see you home. I..." He sighed heavily and a shadow crossed his features. Sadness, and perhaps regret? "Neither Lord

Winthorpe nor my fiancée know I'm here. And Sybil doesn't know about us. Or what we had..."

What we had...

Oh, those words sliced straight through Catherine's heart. It was yet another indication that Adam was finished with her. That he was moving on to his new life. She swallowed as a lump of emotion constricted her throat. "I know, and..." she whispered.

Now. Now was the moment she should tell Adam about the baby—*his* baby. She had to. *Now or never.* But as she drew breath to say what needed to be said, there was a knock at the door and the prison guard opened it, admitting Lord Maxwell.

The Scots earl grimaced in apology. "I'm so sorry to interrupt, but I do really need to return to Whitehall and report to Lord Castlereagh. I have arranged a carriage for you, Miss Delacourt. It's waiting outside to take you home."

While Catherine was grateful for Lord Maxwell's assistance, she also had to blink away a rush of frustrated tears.

But, she reminded herself, *even if I tell Adam about this child, will it change anything at all at this point?*

Would he call off his engagement to Lady Sybil Gower? Confess he loved her, Catherine? Propose marriage to her instead?

Of course he wouldn't. It was far too late.

At last, Catherine knew in her own heart that this *was* over.

Pasting a falsely bright smile on her face, Catherine turned to Lord Maxwell. "I'm ready, my lord." Then she glanced at Adam and began to shrug off his coat, but he held up a hand.

"No, you keep it," he said gently. "It's freezing outside and it will help with..." His words trailed away as he gestured at her blood-stained gown, and Catherine inclined her head in understanding.

"Thank you. For everything," she whispered. "But most of all, for believing me. I wish you well, Adam."

Then she lifted her chin and turned resolutely away.

She did not look back.

Lord Maxwell escorted her out of Newgate into a chill and drear October morning. Even the domed cupola of St Paul's Cathedral looming nearby appeared cold and indifferent. As they walked along the road, Catherine hugged herself tightly. To ward off the bite of the frigid wind tearing around the corner of the Old Bailey and Newgate Street, she told herself. Not to cling to Adam's coat and the ghost of his warmth and his scent.

Not to stop herself falling apart.

Lord Maxwell handed her into a plain carriage waiting by Warwick Lane. Rumor had it the handsome earl was happily married to the Marquess of Rothsburgh's sister, Helena. *Lucky woman thought,* Catherine. *To have a such a chivalrous husband.*

His hand was on the door about to close it when Catherine rallied. "I need to thank you too, Lord Maxwell, for all that you've done for me. If it weren't for your intervention —" She broke off, too overcome to continue.

"No, it is you who should be thanked, Miss Delacourt," said the earl gently, his expression grave but also kind. "If it weren't for you, we wouldn't have known Lord Makepeace was responsible. You have done this country a great service, and Lord Castlereagh himself wishes to extend his personal thanks to you for your assistance and bravery. Indeed Sir Louis's brother, Lord Rosemont, also extends his heartfelt gratitude to you for your witness account, and for being with his brother at his passing. Lord Castlereagh, and I had the sad and difficult task of calling on him in the early hours to inform him of his brother's death."

Lord Rosemont. Catherine had met the elderly gentleman

in passing at the theater several years ago when she'd been in the company of Sir Louis. Despite his advanced years, the sharp gleam in the nobleman's eyes had reminded her of a wily fox.

"I see... I must confess, I'm quite relieved he believes I'm innocent. Unlike Lord Winthorpe." Catherine shuddered at the memory of the irate marquess's insults last night.

"Yes, Lord Winthorpe was quick to judge without knowing all the facts," said Lord Maxwell. "But you have nothing to fear. Not anymore. I wish you well, Miss Delacourt. My driver will see you safely home."

He closed the door and as the carriage moved off, Catherine at last succumbed to the tears she'd been holding at bay. Tears of overwhelming sorrow and sheer relief coursed down her cheeks. She was safe and free, but she'd lost so much. Not just Sir Louis, one of her best friends, but Adam, the man she was quite hopelessly in love with.

But survive she must, because of her child. Giving in to grief was not an option.

CHAPTER 4

W hen Catherine arrived at her Russell Square
townhouse over half an hour later—the streets had
been clogged with the usual early morning traffic snarls—she
wanted nothing more than to soak in a hot fragrant bath and
curl up in her warm, luxurious bed. But as she gathered her
soiled skirts in one hand and prepared to alight from Lord
Maxwell's carriage, a gentleman—not a liveried footman—
appeared in the open doorway.

A silver-haired well-dressed gentleman who looked vaguely
familiar. One gloved hand sat atop his black top hat to stop
the incessant gale stealing it, while the other held the door
for her.

"Lord...Rosemont?" Catherine blinked against another
blast of gritty wind.

"Yes, indeed." Sweeping his hat off his head, he tilted into
an elegant bow then held out his other hand to help her step
down. "Miss Delacourt, I know you have been through a
terrible ordeal, and of course I'm being shockingly presumptu-
ous, but might I have a word with you?" He gestured toward
her townhouse. "Inside, if you permit?"

"Yes, of course, my lord."

Her mind whirling with questions, Catherine let the earl escort her up the short flight of stairs to her townhouse's shiny black door. Mr. Chester, her only manservant, promptly answered at her knock, and with little more than a raised eyebrow, settled Lord Rosemont in the drawing room with a pot of tea and a plate of his wife's pastries. Mrs. Chester served as Catherine's housekeeper-cum-cook; a spectacular find, all in all, to have a dependable married couple manage her home, and without the judgment Catherine was sadly used to.

Her unexpected guest taken care of, Catherine repaired to her bedchamber to fix her appearance. She could hardly receive the earl when her clothes were stained in his brother's blood and she smelled like something that had been dragged through a refuse-strewn gutter.

A short time later after paying only brief attention to her toilette—she'd foregone the bath despite the vociferous protestations of Hetty, her lady's maid—Catherine set forth in a simple gown of white muslin silk and blue cashmere shawl. Curiosity warring with trepidation, she entered the drawing room. At least, Catherine supposed those were the emotions that made her stomach churn most uncomfortably. That and the fact she hadn't eaten anything for hours and hours.

Of course, she could also be suffering from a bout of morning sickness. It was a malady she'd started to succumb to of late. But she didn't have time to pay attention to it now.

Swallowing down a wave of nausea, Catherine curtsied to Lord Rosemont who'd risen from his fireside chair to greet her. "My lord. It was remiss of me not to say this earlier, but I'm so very sorry for your loss."

"Thank you, Miss Delacourt." Lord Rosemont's tone was grave, but compassion lit his dark gray eyes. "Perhaps we should sit..." He indicated the matching shepherdess chair opposite his.

"Yes, of course." Catherine sat, arranging her skirts carefully as she wondered how to ask the earl what he wanted with her.

But before she could formulate her question, he said, "I heard... Well, Lord Castlereagh and Lord Maxwell both informed me about your role in"—he waved a gnarled hand—"this dreadful business surrounding my brother. That you found him and tried to save him, but it was too late."

Catherine nodded. "Yes. I'm afraid so."

"And you also provided information to the authorities that was instrumental in catching the real culprit. Lord Makepeace."

"Yes..." Unsure of where this interview was going, Catherine frowned as she added, "I relayed what I could recall about your brother's assailant to Lord Maxwell and the Runners who were present at...at the scene. Which wasn't a great deal. But I'm glad it helped. Truly I am. As you probably know, Sir Louis and I have been friends for quite some years. It breaks my heart that he has been taken from this life so suddenly and in such an unjust and grievous manner. I will miss him. Very much."

"Indeed. As will I." Lord Rosemont paused as though weighing his words. "No doubt you are wondering the reason for my visit. And it's really quite simple. I wanted to thank you in person for your intervention, Miss Delacourt. You have shown great courage in the face of grave danger. You truly have a loyal and noble disposition. I can see why Louis valued your friendship even though you are..." Wincing, he studied his cup of tea as he trailed off.

"Even though I'm a courtesan?" Catherine supplied. Her cheeks grew hot with indignation and shame. It had been a long time since anyone had made her blush and she didn't like it. She especially didn't like the way Lord Rosemont appeared to simultaneously thank *and* insult her. It was...rude.

Her disgruntlement must have been clear as Lord Rosemont immediately looked contrite. "Please forgive me, Miss Delacourt. I shouldn't have tried to qualify my statement about your character. I misspoke. But, yes, I know you are a courtesan. One of London's most sought after, in fact. A woman who dazzles and fascinates. Lord Dalton—he is your protector, no?—has very good taste."

Catherine pursed her lips and poured herself a cup of tea. She didn't know if she should be flattered or angry at such a pronouncement. Fascinating, was she? Like a curio? A strange creature in a menagerie?

Lord Rosemont sat forward. His grizzled eyebrows arrowed into a deep frown. "I see I've upset you with my bluntness. I'm afraid it is one of my many faults. My sincerest apologies, Miss Delacourt. It was not my intention to distress you."

Catherine took a tentative sip of her tea then very carefully placed the cup on the saucer. Lord Rosemont seemed in earnest, so she offered a gracious incline of her head. "Your apology is accepted, my lord. Although I feel compelled to inform you that I am no longer Lord Dalton's companion. Indeed, I have recently retired from—" She was about to say "prostitution" but thought better of it. "Well, I've retired," she concluded.

"Oh. Really? Well then..." Lord Rosemont cocked a brow then sipped his tea. His gaze was entirely speculative as he examined her over the rim of his cup and Catherine had the uncharacteristic urge to blush again.

She suspected Lord Rosemont had been a rakehell in his younger days. Indeed, Sir Louis had always maintained his brother was quite the roué and Catherine was beginning to believe it. She prayed he wouldn't proposition her or ask her to become his mistress. Considering his brother had just been murdered, she had no wish to set him down. But she would, if she had to.

For want of something to do, she sipped her tea again and her stomach gave a violent lurch. *Oh no.* Catherine's hand shook as she deposited her cup on the saucer with an unceremonious clatter. She swallowed hard, but to no avail. She had to leave.

Now.

"Miss Delacourt, are you all right?"

"If you'll excuse me—" Even before Catherine had made it halfway across the drawing room, she knew she wasn't going to reach somewhere private. In desperation, she snatched up an empty peony-patterned vase from an occasional table and cast up the meager contents of her stomach.

When the violent paroxysms eased, she put down the vase, wiped a trembling hand across her mouth, then rested her pounding forehead against the yellow silk-papered wall. Her breath shuddered in and out as though she'd run a mile.

Mon Dieu. She'd just disgraced herself in front of a powerful peer of the realm. Shame and dizziness washed over her. She needed to apologize to Lord Rosemont then take her leave, but for the moment, all she could do was try to catch her breath and pray her knees wouldn't give out.

"Miss Delacourt?" Lord Rosemont was at her elbow. "You must sit down. Come."

"No, no." Catherine tried to wave him away but it seemed the man would not be put off.

After he settled her in the shepherdess chair, he poured her a glass of water from the pitcher that had arrived with the tea tray. "Shall I call for your maid? Or perhaps you'd like me to summon a physician...?"

Catherine accepted the water with a murmured thanks and took a sip to wash the dreadful taste from her mouth. "I am so sorry," she whispered, her attention fixed on one of the

Aubusson rug's crimson roses. "But no, that won't be necessary. To summon my maid or a physician."

"Are you certain?" Lord Rosemont was still hovering in front of her. Catherine could see the toes of his shiny black Hessian boots. "Lord Maxwell did tell me you'd also been attacked last night."

Grimacing, Catherine lifted her gaze to the earl's face. "I did, but it's not that. Being ill is perfectly normal for a woman in my con—" She bit her lip.

Sacrebleu. Had she just been about to tell Lord Rosemont that she was with child? Perhaps the blow to her head had addled her brain more than she wanted to admit.

Lord Rosemont reclaimed his seat and pinned her with an assessing look. "For a woman in your condition, Miss Delacourt? With child?"

Catherine sighed heavily. There was no point in denying it now. "Yes, I'm afraid so."

"I see." Lord Rosemont rubbed his chin with a gnarled finger as he continued to contemplate her. "Please pardon my bluntness, but is it my brother's child, Miss Delacourt?"

Catherine's eyebrows shot up as indignation flared again. "What? No! Of course not. Sir Louis has only ever been a friend to me."

Lord Rosemont's narrow shoulders lifted and fell with a weary sigh. "Pity."

Pity? Catherine blinked. "You're disappointed?"

"I'm seventy-one years old, Miss Delacourt, and I suspect not long for this world. I've never wed and therefore I've no son to inherit when I go. Over the years, I'd reconciled myself to the idea that my title would pass to Louis, but alas after last night, that is not to be. But if you were to bear his son..." Lord Rosemont cocked a brow.

Catherine placed a hand on her belly. "I'm confused, my lord. Even if this child were your brother's—and a boy—he will be born illegitimate and therefore ineligible to inherit your title."

Lord Rosemont sat back in his chair and his mouth twitched with a wry smile. "Not if you agreed to marry me and I claimed the child is mine."

Oh. Catherine swallowed and her fingers curled into the white muslin skirts of her gown. Oh, if only her child *could* possess such privilege and wealth. They wouldn't have to be ashamed of their name. Or their mother. "Be that as it may, the child is not Sir Louis's, my lord."

"Do you know who the father is?"

"Of course I do," Catherine flashed. "I'm not some common street doxy who's used by God knows who a dozen times a night."

Oh, dear.

She bit her lip. She shouldn't have spoken so rudely to the elderly earl. "I'm so sorry, my lord. Please forgive me. It's just...I've had a trying night as you can imagine. I'm not myself."

Lord Rosemont raised a hand. "It's quite all right, Miss Delacourt. It was tactless of me to ask. Call it curiosity. And perhaps self-interest."

"I don't take your meaning."

"Well..." The earl flicked a non-existent piece of lint off the cuff of his perfectly tailored coat sleeve. "If the child's sire happened to be another peer of upstanding character— perhaps someone like Lord Dalton—I think I'd still be tempted to make an arrangement with you."

"Arrangement? What sort of arrangement?"

Lord Rosemont's gaze settled on her again. "Miss Delacourt, I'm suggesting you become my wife."

What? Catherine shook her head. She'd never heard Sir Louis mention his older brother was losing his faculties. Because the earl's suggestion was insane. Ludicrous. "My lord, you cannot mean that. Such a match is impossible. What would Society say? There would be an enormous scandal. The censure of the *ton* would be unrelenting."

"It is entirely possible and I do mean it. And I'm too old to give a farthing about scandal or the opinion of others." Lord Rosemont's gaze drifted over Catherine's still flat belly. "It looks to me you are only *just* pregnant. If you don't mind me asking, how many months along are you?"

Catherine did mind, but nevertheless answered. "Two months. Three at the most."

Lord Rosemont's eyes narrowed. "And you're certain you're pregnant?"

Catherine couldn't suppress a small snort. "Yes, of course I am. And to confirm your earlier supposition, the father of my child is indeed Lord Dalton. Only..." She swallowed and lifted her chin. "Only he doesn't know. He's engaged to Lord Winthorpe's daughter, Lady Sybil."

"Ah, yes. I do believe I heard a rumor circulating about White's that he'd recently begun courting the gel."

Catherine nodded. It seemed everyone had known but her. But she'd never been privy to Adam's innermost thoughts, so it should hardly surprise her. Nevertheless, to hear Lord Rosemont casually mention he'd known about it, as though it were just a piece of inconsequential gossip, stung.

"I've upset you."

Catherine looked up from where she'd been fiddling with a loose silk thread on the arm of her shepherdess chair. "No, it's not anything you've said, my lord. It's..." She couldn't very well admit she loved Adam so she finished lamely, "It's of no consequence."

"You love him."

This time Catherine couldn't stop the brimming of her tears. She nodded. "Unfortunately, yes."

"Well, I can promise you any arrangement we will enter

into will be purely a marriage of convenience. As lovely as you are, Miss Delacourt, I'm too old for bed sport. I simply need an heir."

Catherine frowned. "If you don't mind *me* asking, don't you have other male relatives who would be eligible to inherit your title and estate?"

Lord Rosemont made a scoffing sound in his throat. "Only a distant second cousin by the name of Benedict. He's not such a bad fellow himself—he's a solicitor by trade and he married into money. But his ill-mannered, social-climbing wife, Lilith, and their profligate son, Gerald, would bring nothing but disgrace to the family name. Louis, God rest his soul, was a noble man, recognized for his service to King and country with a baronetcy. I'll not let the title go to just anyone."

"And I wouldn't bring disgrace upon your name? I'm a courtesan. A harlot. And I'm not even English. I'm French. The daughter of a courtesan. My inferior birth alone, let alone my nationality, should disqualify me as a prospective spousal candidate for someone like you."

Lord Rosemont's grave gray eyes were steady upon hers as he said, "Yet I see qualities in you that I greatly admire, Miss Delacourt. Not only are you beautiful, you appear to be noble, loyal, brave, and intelligent. Louis always spoke highly of you. And Lord Dalton is a man of integrity as well. I have every confidence your offspring would make a fine peer someday. Unlike my cousin, Benedict Fortescue." Lord Rosemont visibly shuddered. "The man has about as much personality as pounce powder and I'm certain his good-for-nothing son would send the estate to rack and ruin in the blink of an eye."

Catherine picked up her now cool tea and sipped it anyway. It seemed Lord Rosemont was indeed serious. Should she actually consider his outrageous proposal?

Her child would want for nothing. But she barely knew

Lord Rosemont. What would it be like to be married to such a man? Was he as kind and noble as his brother had been? She hardly knew.

She put down her tea and ventured another question. A crucial one. "There's no guarantee the child I'm carrying is a boy. What if I give birth to a girl?"

Lord Rosemont shrugged a shoulder. "She will bear my name. I will accept her as my own. But we'll cross that bridge when we come to it, shall we?"

Catherine studied the earl's face for a moment and couldn't detect any note of insincerity. He was offering her and her child a marvelous opportunity, yet still she hesitated.

There was so much to consider. After the night she'd just had, she really needed time to think the matter over. Examine all of the ramifications of taking Lord Rosemont up on his offer.

She drew a shaky breath in order to tell Lord Rosemont all this, but it seemed the earl had already guessed the direction of her thoughts.

"Miss Delacourt, I realize my proposition is wholly unexpected and highly unusual. And I suspect you will need a little time to mull things over. But rest assured, my proposal is entirely sincere. I desire a suitable heir and if entering into a marriage of convenience is the only way I will be able to gain one, then that is what I will do."

Catherine nodded. "Yes. I do need time to think over your offer. It is not unwelcome... It's just that I'm not sure I'd make anyone a suitable wife. I'm assuredly *not* a suitable countess."

Lord Rosemont waved a dismissive hand. "If old Charles James Fox could get away with marrying his mistress, a Miss Elizabeth Armistead, I don't see why I shouldn't wed a courtesan either." Rising from his seat, he approached and bowed over her hand. "Miss Delacourt, with your permission I will call on you tomorrow for your answer. If that is suitable for you…"

"Yes. Yes, of course." What else could she say?

After Lord Rosemont had taken his leave, Catherine retired to her room to take her much longed for bath. As she settled into the steaming lavender scented water, she closed her eyes and fell to contemplating what her future and her child's might look like.

She would be mad to accept Lord Rosemont's proposal. She would also be equally mad not to.

In any case, it was abundantly clear to her that she would never be Adam's countess.

A tear slid from beneath her closed eyelid. And then another.

What would Sir Louis have advised her to do?

It was almost as though she could hear him whispering in her ear as she drifted to sleep… *Do what's best for your baby— the child of an earl—and if it's a boy, why shouldn't he have the chance to gain a title? Despite Society's censure, seize this opportunity and give the babe every advantage that you can. A better childhood than you had. A better life then you could ever give him. Or her.*

Because in the end, that's all that will really matter.

CHAPTER 5

Briarwood Park, Hertfordshire
October 11ᵗʰ, 1816
Five years later...

"More tea, Lady Rosemont? I've brought a fresh pot from the kitchen."

Catherine glanced up from her day-old copy of *The Morning Chronicle* and smoothed her frown into a smile before she murmured, "Yes, thank you," in response to the footman's quietly spoken question.

Though she'd been a widow for over two years now, her name still appeared with alarming regularity in the social pages and gossip rags, whether she was in London or not. She really shouldn't read the rubbish the newspapers printed about her, but some days, she couldn't seem to help herself.

Indeed, since the very first day of her marriage to the Earl of Rosemont, there had been constant and salacious speculation about the nature of their union, and of course, her character. The headlines and accompanying articles all tended to run along similarly uncreative lines.

Had the seductive Lady R. really been a lightskirt and the illegitimate brat of a French émigré "actress" before she ensnared Lord R.? Was the notorious Lady R. faithful to her husband given her licentious past? What could Lord R. possibly see in his wife besides the blatantly obvious? Was the enigmatic Lady R. a murderess? After all, she'd been held in Newgate on suspicion of murder prior to her marriage.

And the worst rumor of all: was Lady R.'s young son, Louis, really Lord R.'s...or a by-blow? That particular story never failed to make Catherine see red. Anything that impugned her sweet little boy, she could not abide. At all.

At least Edward, her late husband, had appointed her as Louis's sole guardian. That had caused more than a few raised eyebrows because the mother of a young peer—even a woman with an impeccable background—was rarely afforded that sort of responsibility. Catherine suspected that Edward's cousin, Benedict Fortescue, his wife, Lilith, and their thirty-five-year-old son, Gerald, were especially disgruntled about that particular stipulation in Edward's will. But there was little they could do about it. And Catherine didn't really give a fig about any of their opinions.

Of course, since Edward had passed away, it had been widely purported that Catherine would inevitably return to Town on the prowl for another wealthy titled husband. Or at the very least, anyone in breeches who wasn't high enough in the instep to turn up his nose at her.

Ha, what did they know? Two years on, she barely traveled to London. There was nothing there for her except memories she'd rather forget. And she really *shouldn't* pay any attention to all the hateful gossip. As far as Catherine was concerned, just about all of Society could go to Hades. A quiet country life was more than satisfying. Indeed, since her marriage to Edward, she'd relished her time rusticating away at his ancestral estate, safely hidden from the judgmental eyes of the *ton*.

The country air was exactly what her four-year-old son, Louis Edward Adam Fortescue, her little Lord Rosemont, required.

Tossing the newspaper onto the polished cherrywood dining table, Catherine replenished her tea before drifting to the French doors of the morning room to look out at the garden. Her mouth lifted into a gentle smile. Under the watchful eye of his nursemaid Lizzy, and Jackson, one of the other footmen, Louis played with his new Cavalier spaniel puppy, Pippin. It was a cold, crisp morning but thankfully, not raining for once. When Louis chased Pippin around the horse chestnut then onto the open lawn heading toward the knot garden, a rare wash of morning sunshine glanced off his bouncing golden-blond curls. The yapping puppy circled back and dove for the tiny silver buckles on his shoes, and Louis squealed with glee.

Her son was such a lovely, gentle boy. Full of smiles and cuddles. And his big blue eyes reminded her so much of Adam's, her heart would sometimes ache with an odd combination of joy and bittersweet sadness. Of course, Edward had been immensely delighted when she'd delivered a squalling, robust baby boy into the world. He had his heir, and she had the gift of Adam's beautiful son.

Adam... Catherine bit down on her bottom lip. No, she must not think of Adam, otherwise her mood would grow as dark as the black bombazine widow's weeds she'd worn for an entire year. There was no point in pining for the lover who'd discarded her like a bothersome scandal sheet. He'd wed his debutante Lady Sybil and was as lost to her as Edward now was.

Another pang of misery squeezed Catherine's heart. While she hadn't cared for Edward in the way she cared for Adam, she missed him. His charming smile, his intelligent conversation, his wit. He'd been a kind and generous husband, and she'd grown genuinely fond of him over the course of their two-and-a-half-year marriage. He'd always treated her with the utmost respect. And he'd kept his word. He'd never visited her bedchamber to claim his conjugal rights. When she'd broached the topic on their wedding night—she'd been quite prepared to at least consummate their union—he'd merely smiled, kissed her forehead, then stated he was too long in the tooth for that sort of thing.

Although her husband had an appreciative eye for the opposite sex, Catherine had no reason to suspect he'd sought sexual gratification elsewhere. Not that she would have minded, but she truly believed he'd lost interest in physical pleasure. Sometimes she'd wondered if poor health had tempered that side of him, but Edward had never shown any overt signs of illness until a few months before his passing. A persistent wheezing cough and shortness of breath that wouldn't abate. He'd died peacefully in his sleep. But that hadn't stopped rumors spreading far and wide that she, Catherine, must have had something to do with her husband's demise. After all, wasn't it rumored she'd spent time in Newgate?

But she wouldn't dwell on all that ugliness today. The clouds had parted to reveal a newly washed blue sky and her son was laughing. And that was all that really mattered.

After Louis and his puppy disappeared into the knot garden with Lizzy and the footman, Catherine sighed and wandered back to the dining table to refresh her tea. With Edward gone, she couldn't deny she was lonely. While the local gentry tolerated her presence—insomuch as they never gave her the cut direct in church or in the village of Briarcombe—she'd never managed to make any close female friends in Briar-wood Park's vicinity. Indeed, her only real friend seemed to be Lord Maxwell's charming wife, Helena, who she saw whenever their visits to Town coincided.

Over the years, Catherine had managed to avoid any close

encounters with Adam and his countess, Sybil. Until this year at the start of the Season.

In early spring, Helena had coaxed her to London to refresh her wardrobe—after her year-long period of mourning followed by almost another year in the country, it very much needed refurbishing. Of course, it had been silly of Catherine to think she'd never cross paths with Adam again, so when she did—she'd spied him entering Hatchards across a crowded street—she had not been prepared for it at all. One glimpse of his aristocratically handsome profile, and her heart had all but stopped. Then she'd noticed Sybil by his side and the pain of seeing them together had been like a physical blow to Catherine's chest, rendering her completely breathless. After telling Helena she'd developed a megrim, she'd hailed a hackney cab straightaway and returned to Rosemont House on Park Lane. The very next day she'd quit London altogether.

She hadn't been to Town since and had no intention of visiting any time in the foreseeable future. No, the life of a quiet country widow would suit her and little Louis perfectly.

Reclaiming her seat at the table, Catherine sipped her tea and picked up *The Morning Chronicle* again. Despite the fact she knew she'd only be looking for trouble if she flicked through to the social pages, she did just that. She began to peruse the headlines...and then she promptly dropped her cup onto the table with a crash.

Tea spread across the page, staining it, but she barely noticed as she read...

The widowed Earl of Dalton has just arrived back in Town only six months after his wife, Sybil (née Lady Sybil Gower), tragically and quite unexpectedly passed away in April. He might be in half-mourning, but is he on the hunt for a new countess? He certainly needs a new mare in his stable to produce the requisite heir and spare. One hears that bets are already

*being laid at certain exclusive gentleman's clubs in the vicinity
of St James's...*

Catherine could scarcely believe it...

Sybil, Lady Dalton, was dead.

Adam is a widower.

How had she not known? How had she missed such significant news? Catherine didn't consider herself a morbid sort of person—she was not in the habit of scouring the obituaries—but she couldn't help but wonder what had happened to Sybil...

When she'd glimpsed the countess in March, she'd *seemed* well enough. The woman couldn't have been older than five-and-twenty. And she had died a month later?

Of course, Catherine had made the Maxwells promise *never* to mention Adam or his wife to her, ever, as it hurt too much to be reminded of all that she'd lost.

But still... This news was momentous. Catherine couldn't pretend it hadn't shaken her to her core.

Her hands trembling, she put down the paper. She hadn't liked Sybil but she'd never wished her ill. And poor Adam. He *must* have cared for his wife. He might have even loved her. Such a loss would surely be a blow. A tragedy indeed.

As one of the housemaids approached the table to attend to the mess of spilled tea, Catherine rose on legs as shaky as a newborn lamb's and crossed to the French doors again. Pushing one open, she stepped onto the flagged terrace and breathed in the crisp, damp morning air. It was a soothing balm to her shaken sense of equilibrium. She leaned over the marble balustrade to pluck the last of the year's roses—a dark red bloom—from a nearby bush. Brushing the velvet soft petals against her lips, she closed her eyes and inhaled. And that's when the budding thought she'd been trying to ignore popped into her head, fully formed.

Adam is no longer married and neither are you.

No, she mustn't think like that. Just because she and Adam were both free did not mean a thing. When he *did* decide it was time to marry again, he'd undoubtedly be on the lookout for another pristine debutante with the right sort of social connections and lineage. A woman who could give him the heir he'd need one day.

And that woman *wouldn't* be Catherine. It might have suited Edward to marry her, but in Adam's eyes, she would still only be a courtesan despite the fact she was now Lady Rosemont. He didn't want her as a wife years ago, and countess or not, he wouldn't want her as a wife now. Even though he cared for her a little when they'd been lovers, any tender feelings he'd harbored would have faded over the years. If he were inclined to seek out a mistress, surely he would look for someone new to assuage his carnal appetite. She would have as much appeal as stale bread or a cold cup of tea.

Catherine plucked a slightly bruised petal off the rose and after it fell from her fingers, she watched it drift across the lawn. She didn't want to become Adam's paramour again, either. If he didn't think she was good enough to be the next Countess of Dalton, she didn't want him. No, if she ever wed again, it would be to a man who loved her entirely and didn't give a jot about her scandalous past.

She deserved so much more.

All in all, it was best not to think about Lord Dalton any longer.

Catherine descended the short flight of stairs to the gravel path and headed in the direction Louis had gone. She was sure he'd led his nurse toward the Chinese pavilion and the goldfish pond on the other side of the knot garden. No doubt he'd ask Lizzy or Jackson to push him on the swing which hung from the nearby ancient willow tree.

She was just wending her way through the intricately

arranged flowerbeds and low hedges of the knot garden when she heard a woman's scream.

Lizzy?

Oh, God. What had happened?

With her heart catapulting into the vicinity of her throat, Catherine picked up her skirts and ran faster than she'd ever run in her life.

When she emerged from the towering box hedge on the other side of the garden, it was to discover Jackson striding toward her with little Louis lying limp in his arms.

Oh, no. Dear God, no.

Catherine almost tripped over her gown as she hastened toward the footman. Lizzy, following close behind with Louis's puppy clutched to her chest, gave an almighty wail as soon as she saw her mistress. "Oh, my lady," she cried, tears streaming down her face. "I'm so sorry. There's been a terrible accident."

"What happened?" Catherine gasped as she stumbled to a halt beside them. Along with a scrape and a bruise blooming near his temple, Louis's face was as white as a sheet. But when she touched his neck beneath the frilled collar of his fine cotton shirt, a pulse fluttered beneath her trembling fingers. She could see the rise and fall of his little chest.

Oh, thank heavens.

The footman's face was as pale as milk. "M-My lady. The swing—the rope just snapped. And his lordship fell and hit his head."

Catherine's heart tumbled in turn to the ground. It must have been quite a fall for him to have been knocked unconscious. "I don't understand. He's only a little boy. He weighs nothing. How could the rope have broken?"

Jackson shook his head. "I don't know, my lady. Perhaps it rotted through... There's been a lot of rain of late."

Catherine nodded. Regardless of the reason for the accident, they needed to get Louis up to the house. And then she'd get the butler, Kingsley, to send for the physician who lived just outside of Briarcombe.

It wasn't until Jackson lay Louis down upon his bed in the nursery that the boy stirred. His eyes fluttered open, and he gave a tiny whimper. "Mama?"

"I'm here, my darling." Catherine sat beside him on the sky-blue silk counterpane and took his tiny hand in hers. "Mama's here."

His bottom lip wobbled and tears shimmered in his impossibly big blue eyes. "Mama, my head hurts."

"I know, my sweet, brave boy," she said gently, brushing a stray blond curl from his brow. "The swing broke and you bumped your forehead. Dr. Byrne will be here soon."

A small crease appeared between Louis's brows. "Where's Pippin? Is he all right?"

"He's perfectly fine. He's fast asleep at the foot of your bed."

Louis's mouth lifted into a tremulous smile. But as he tried to lift his head to see the puppy for himself, he let out a small cry of pain and the tears that had been welling slipped onto his pale cheeks.

Catherine's heart contracted with fear. "I think it's best if you lie still." Turning to a whey-faced, red-eyed Lizzy who hovered at the end of the bed, she said, "Can you fetch a damp washcloth for his lordship's brow perhaps? And a little warm milk from the kitchen."

The girl had been beside herself all the way back to the house, and Catherine had been obliged to threaten her with banishment from the nursery unless she managed to regain a semblance of composure. Given Lizzy looked as though she would burst into tears again at any moment, it seemed like a good idea to keep her busy.

The nurse curtsied and with a subdued, "Yes, my lady," hurried from the room.

It wasn't until Dr. Byrne had been and gone—he'd pronounced that the young Lord Rosemont merely had a bump and bruise, and was otherwise hale and hearty—that Catherine at last allowed herself to fully subside into the arms of relief.

Louis had fallen into a light sleep. As she settled in a plump bedside armchair with a cup of tea, she thanked God for the thousandth time that her little boy would be all right. Dr. Byrne had also assured her that the concussion appeared to be mild, but if Louis displayed any new symptoms such as a severe headache, blurred vision, vomiting, or heaven forbid, became insensible, she should send for him straightaway.

She was just pouring herself another fortifying cup of tea when there was a gentle knock at the door. Lizzy, who'd been sitting by the nursery mending a ripped frill on one of Louis's cuffs, leaped to her feet and hastened across the room.

It was Jackson, the footman. Catherine beckoned him over so he wouldn't disturb her son's slumber.

He bowed and murmured. "My lady, I'm so sorry to disturb you, but Mr. Kingsley wanted you to know you have visitors."

Visitors? Unable to hide her annoyance, Catherine's brows snapped together. "Who?"

"Mr. Benedict Fortescue, his wife, and their son, Mr. Gerald Fortescue, my lady. Kingsley has already shown them to the drawing room."

Urghh. They were the last people Catherine wanted to see right now. Benedict, despite the fact Edward had always maintained his cousin wasn't a bad sort of chap, seemed a trifle fawning rather than well-meaning in Catherine's eyes. But perhaps that was because his wife, Lilith, had such a sly, superior manner. And

Gerald, he was the worst of the trio. Catherine found the man to be slimier than pond scum. She would be forever grateful that Edward had not made Benedict one of Louis's guardians.

The last time she's seen Benedict, Lilith, and Gerald had been in late April; they'd stopped by to see "little Lord Rosemont" to wish him a happy fourth birthday. Benedict had given Louis a set of toy tin soldiers, a book entitled *The Life and Perambulations of a Mouse*, and a bag of barley sugar sweets, while Lilith and Gerald had looked on with false smiles. *This* visit was certainly unexpected. And unwelcome, given the circumstances.

But what could she do? She supposed it would be better if she made short shrift of them herself.

With a weary sigh she put down her cup, gave instructions to Lizzy to summon her if Louis awoke during her absence or there was any change in his condition, then ventured forth to greet her odious visitors. She couldn't bring herself to think of them as guests.

As soon as she entered the drawing room, Benedict tilted his spare form into a stiff bow, Gerald cast her a smarmy smile, whereas Lilith simply stared down her sharp beak of a nose at Catherine with her usual expression of distaste which bordered on insolence. For a woman who spoke with a thick-as-treacle "plummy" accent and whose background was decidedly "lower gentry"—her father had been a mill owner from Yorkshire—how she had the gall to affect such a haughty demeanor, Catherine did not know.

Indeed, her high-and-mighty attitude always made Catherine itch to do something wild and unladylike in retaliation, like dumping the contents of the grate over her overly coiffured head. Or picking up the nearby Wedgwood vase, removing the roses, and tossing the water in her sullen face.

That would at least give the woman a reason to ooze disapproval.

Pushing aside her fantastical but highly satisfying musings, Catherine made an effort to use a civil tone even if her greeting was unceremoniously blunt. "You wanted to see me?"

"Yes..." Perhaps rattled by her frosty reception, Benedict swallowed nervously and cleared his throat before continuing with a small smile which was clearly an attempt to ingratiate himself. "Lilith, Gerald, and I were in the area...visiting acquaintances near St Albans. Well, we thought it would be remiss *not* to pay our respects to you and my little cousin considering we were in the vicinity. Before we return to London."

"I see. Most admirable that you should think of us. But now is really a most inopportune time." Catherine gestured toward the door, her meaning clear: there would be no offer of hospitality this afternoon. Not even a cup of tea.

"Oh?" Benedict's smile slipped a fraction. "Oh. I hope everything is all right"—his gaze darted to his prune-faced wife and then to his smugly smiling son before returning to Catherine— "with you and his lordship."

"Yes," agreed Gerald in a tone of voice that was somehow smooth yet irritating at the same time. "We wanted to swing by. I hope nothing untoward has befallen you, my lady. Or young Louis, for that matter. Oh, pardon my slip of the tongue..." His smile broadened as he raffishly tossed a wing of dark brown hair out of his eyes. "I mean, his lordship."

Catherine frowned. Gerald's choice of words—"swing" and "befallen" and "slip"—instantly set alarm bells ringing in her head. There was something about Benedict's manner and the looks he'd traded with Lilith and Gerald which made the back of her nape prickle with suspicion. Or perhaps it was the way in which Lilith Fortescue studied Catherine far too closely. The gleam in her eyes wasn't just disdainful. It had turned keen. Predatory, like a rat or a weasel.

The Fortescues must have heard about Louis's fall. Catherine was absolutely certain of it.

Of course, bad news always traveled fast and there was probably talk in the village by now about young Lord Rosemont's accident. It was entirely possible they'd heard something if they'd stopped at Briarcombe's small coaching inn.

If that were the case, it would explain their unexpected visit. They obviously wished to hear first-hand how Louis fared.

"I am well," she replied through tight lips. "Whereas my son is sleeping at the moment. He had a...a bit of a fall, earlier today. Aside from some minor bruising and a bump, my physician has declared he's quite fine."

Lilith, eyes wide, put a bony hand to her throat. "Goodness gracious," she declared. "How shocking, And quite appalling. How could you have let such a thing happen? You're his mother. *And* guardian. You should take better care of your son. But then considering your background"—her gaze turned scornful as it raked over Catherine—"I can't say I'm surprised."

Gerald made a clucking sound. "Now, now, dearest Mama, one shouldn't believe all the gossip one reads in the papers. And I'm sure little Louis's accident isn't entirely Lady Rosemont's fault." His false smile didn't waver as he added, "Thank goodness he only bumped his head."

Catherine could bear Lilith's insults about her past but her temper flared at the insinuation that she wasn't looking after her son properly.

And Gerald's comment ignited a spark of suspicion. Her gaze narrowed on the man. "I didn't mention the precise nature of Louis's injury," she said curtly. "How did you know?"

Benedict Fortescue, whose cheeks had turned a deep red hue as though embarrassed, jumped into the fray. "Yes. Quite right. Quite right. You didn't, my lady." He spread his hands in a placatory gesture. "There was talk in the village when we stopped to take luncheon at the inn."

"Well, as you have already dined, I won't ask you to stay." Catherine opened the drawing room door and spoke to the footman who stood outside in the gallery. "The Fortescues are leaving. Please escort them to their carriage." Turning back to her gaping visitors she said, "I'm sure you won't mind if I don't see you off. Given the circumstances, you'll appreciate I have more pressing matters to attend to right now."

And with that, she quit the room before she *was* tempted to hurl more than dirty water or ashes at the deplorable trio.

Catherine's chagrin and unease dissipated when she returned to the nursery and found that Louis was awake and complaining that he was hungry. After he'd eaten a late luncheon—a coddled egg with buttery toast—he spent most of the afternoon playing quietly before the nursery fire with Lizzy, Catherine, and Pippin. It seemed Dr. Byrne's pronouncement that Louis would be all right was indeed quite true. Catherine was nothing but relieved.

However, Catherine's peace of mind was shattered anew when Kingsley knocked delicately on the nursery door as twilight was descending, and quietly announced the grounds-man, Sanders, had some disturbing news.

Even though Louis was napping, Catherine stepped outside the nursery to listen to the young man's report. She didn't want her son to overhear anything that might frighten him if he woke.

Apparently, due to all the wet weather, one of the swing's ropes had rotted through. Of course, Sanders regularly checked on the swing's condition because he knew his young lordship loved to play on it, weather permitting. Last time he'd made an inspection—but a week ago—there had been nothing wrong with either of the ropes. When Catherine asked him how the rope's condition could have deteriorated so quickly, Sanders shuffled his feet, turned red in the face, and suggested there might have been a chance the rope *had* been tampered with. That perhaps something like a saw had been used to partly sever the rope's fibers so it wouldn't be apparent that anything was amiss on casual inspection. But as Louis had played on the swing that morning, the rope had frayed and unraveled until it had given way completely.

If Sanders spoke the truth, it meant that someone had *intended* to injure Catherine's little boy. Or worse …

Catherine's chest tightened with fear. *But who? Who would want to hurt her sweet baby? Why, he'd only just begun wearing breeches a few months ago.*

Too unsettled to sit on her return to the nursery, Catherine crossed to the window to look out at the darkening grounds. It had begun to rain again and a shiver slid over her.

This hadn't been the first "mishap" that had threatened Louis's safety. Or her own, for that matter. Indeed, there'd been several accidents that had occurred over the last ten months—near misses Catherine had dismissed as bad luck as nothing overly untoward had happened.

But what if she'd been mistaken? What if something more sinister was afoot?

What if this series of accidents were not accidents at all?

The first incident had occurred just after Twelfth Night, right here at Briarwood Park. With Jackson's assistance, she'd planned to take Louis sledding on the estate's frozen lake. Jackson had assured her the ice was a safe thickness, but as soon as Catherine had stepped onto the lake's surface, the ice had proved to be fragile and it cracked like an eggshell. Needless to say, there'd been no ice-sledding after that. Sanders later reported he'd discovered a rusty icepick in the nearby reed beds, but he hadn't seen any evidence of actual physical tampering with the ice.

The second near miss had been in March. On her return to Hertfordshire with Louis—right after she had glimpsed Adam with his wife and she'd decided to quit London—they'd been involved in a minor carriage accident. A wheel axel on the coach had inexplicably broken. While the carriage had ended up in a muddy ditch, it hadn't tipped over and thankfully no one had been hurt. Well, bar a few bruises and rattled nerves. But now, with hindsight, it played on Catherine's mind that her supposedly well-maintained conveyance had suffered a mechanical failure which could have resulted in catastrophic consequences.

And then in the summer—or what passed for this year's summer for it had been cold and dismal for months on end—there'd been another "mishap" that could have ended in disaster. Louis had begun riding lessons on a pony, and the buckle securing the girth strap on his tiny saddle had somehow come undone. The groom had caught his young master before Louis had fallen to the ground, but again, it was a decidedly odd and disconcerting event...

Catherine didn't like to think she and Louis were ill-starred, but she would own to feeling as though a dark ominous cloud had begun to follow both of them around. As her son's guardian, it was incumbent upon her to make sure that not only was the young Earl of Rosemont's substantial inheritance well-managed, but that *he* was always kept safe. But what if someone *did* intend to hurt him?

Just the idea that someone wished Louis harm curdled Catherine's insides.

With a heavy sigh heavy, she drew the curtains then moved to the fireside to stir the flames back to life. Maybe she was just starting at shadows. Maybe all these unfortunate incidents *were* just cases of bad luck.

But then her thoughts returned to the Fortescues. Benedict had claimed they'd simply stopped by Briarwood Park because they'd been visiting friends in the area. But was that truly the case? What if...what if there were another reason to account for their presence here? Ordinarily, Catherine would admonish herself for being so fanciful, but the swing *could* have been tampered with...

If Louis had fallen the wrong way...

Catherine put down the poker and pressed her hands to her roiling stomach.

It was disturbing in the extreme to think someone would go out of his, or her, way to commit such a malicious act. Even though Benedict Fortescue had married into money—by all accounts, Lilith had inherited a decent fortune from her mill-owning father—he still had a strong motive to harm Louis. He would inherit an earldom and another enormous fortune, after all. And Lilith would become the new Lady Rosemont. In time, Gerald would be the next earl...

Considering they were also in Hertfordshire—and familiar with the estate—it wasn't beyond the realms of possibility that any one of them, or even all three of them could have had a hand in orchestrating Louis's swing accident.

But to go so far as to attempt to kill a child... Surely not...

Something Lilith had said, suddenly drifted through Catherine's mind: *How could you have let such a thing happen? You're his mother.* And *guardian.*

Yes, Catherine was Louis's guardian. And it was *very* clear that particular fact irked the Fortescues no end. But rather than hurt Louis, could it be that they wished to challenge the status quo? If Benedict and Lilith went to the Court of Chancery and accused Catherine of being an unfit mother, and the Court sided with them... She *had* been a courtesan. Her name was always in the newspapers for the wrong reasons...

Catherine suddenly felt as though all the air had been knocked from her lungs. If the Court of Chancery took Louis away from her, if his guardianship was given to the Fortescues, they would control the Rosemont estate and fortune... She clutched at the mantelpiece as anger and horror and foreboding rolled through her in a great wave.

She would not lose Louis. She would not.

Tomorrow, if Louis were well enough, she would travel to London and hire an inquiry agent to look into Benedict, Lilith, and Gerald's affairs. And keep a watchful eye on them. If anything untoward occurred, they would know her wrath.

In the meantime, she would not let her son out of her sight. There was already a large contingent of servants here at Briarwood Park, and in London at Rosemont House on Park Lane. Servants Edward had hired and who he'd trusted for a good many years. No further harm would befall her son. She wouldn't let it.

Louis whimpered in his sleep and Catherine carefully curled up on the bed beside him. His plump cheeks were slightly flushed but not unnaturally so, his breathing deep and even.

She carefully smoothed one of his tousled curls away from his cherub-like mouth then laid her head on the downy pillow. Lizzy was presently taking dinner in the servants' hall, and she always slept on a pallet bed in a far corner of the nursery. Even though the nurse would awake and attend to her charge if he needed anything, Catherine would also sleep here tonight.

As she watched Louis, she couldn't help but wonder what Adam would make of everything that had happened today. And indeed, over the last ten months.

Would he care? She liked to think he would. But then, he still didn't know he had a son.

Should I tell him? Would he even want to know?

His union with Sybil hadn't produced any children. Catherine imagined that one day, perhaps even very soon if that bluntly worded article in *The Morning Chronicle* were to be believed—Adam would be obliged to remarry to continue the family line. The laws of inheritance were such that Louis would never be the Earl of Dalton's heir apparent.

But that didn't mean Adam *wouldn't* want to ensure his child was safe, even if he could never publicly claim Louis as his own.

Too tired and dispirited to sort through her tumbling thoughts any longer, Catherine succumbed to the urge to close her eyes. She prayed she *was* starting at shadows. That maybe Sanders had been wrong about the rope and Louis's fall was purely accidental. That perhaps the ice on the lake hadn't been tampered with. Or the carriage's wheel. Or Louis's saddle...

And that there was nothing behind Lilith's comment that had insinuated Catherine was a lax mother...

One thing was certain: Catherine would do anything at all to keep her child—and Adam's—from harm. Anything.

CHAPTER 6

Latimer House, Mayfair
October 18ᵗʰ, 1816

The hubbub in the ballroom of Latimer House was at such a fever pitch that Helena, the Countess of Maxwell, had to lean very close to Catherine to make herself heard. "My dear Lady Rosemont," she murmured in the conspiratorial fashion of a schoolgirl as she touched Catherine's gloved forearm. "I'm so glad you came tonight. Phillip is too."

Catherine offered her friend a genuine smile. "So am I."

The day after she'd arrived at Rosemont House, a gilt-edged invitation to the Maxwell's ball had been hand-delivered by Helena herself. Of course, Catherine had initially baulked at the idea of leaving Louis alone. Not only that, but she was sure to be stared at and gossiped about. But when Helena insisted no one on the guest list would give Catherine the cut direct—or they would have her and Phillip to answer to—Catherine had at last acceded.

Helena could be *very* persuasive. And Catherine couldn't disagree with her logic. Even though the widowed Lady Rosemont's "reentrance" into Society was bound to create a stir, spending a single night dancing, sipping champagne, and admiring handsome men might take her mind off her worries...at least for a little while. Phillip was already looking into finding an inquiry agent for her, and Rosemont House was guarded from top to bottom with burly footmen.

Surely one night on the Town was permitted.

Helena wound her arm through Catherine's to promenade around the edges of the crowded ballroom. "I'm so pleased you're wearing one of your new gowns, by the way. You look gorgeous in blue, and I'm utterly *determined* that you will have a good time," she declared, her dark eyes twinkling with mischief. "Remember, you're only nine-and-twenty, not a crotchety old dowager countess."

Catherine sighed. "Yes, I do forget that sometimes."

"Well, it's a good thing you have me to remind you. And to point out potential suitors if you are tempted to have a little fun..." Devilry sparked in Helena's eyes as she leaned closer to Catherine and murmured, "I saw earlier on that the mysterious and dashing Lord Markham had caught your eye..."

Catherine laughed. Apparently the earl had only recently returned to London and the gossip was that he was a retired spy for the Crown. "Yes, he's certainly both of those things." It had felt good to flirt a little with someone as handsome as Lord Markham, even if it didn't mean anything or wouldn't lead anywhere. Despite the fact she was lonely, she wasn't in the market for another husband. Or a lover. "But I think he only has eyes for Georgiana, the widowed Duchess of Darby tonight."

They'd paused by the doorway to the card room where the duchess was presently playing piquet with the handsome earl.

"I think you might be right," agreed Helena. "It would be lovely if Georgie would give him a chance. He'll have his work cut out for him though, wooing our Ice Duchess. Thank goodness he's a brave man."

They watched the handsome couple for a moment longer before Helena added with a sigh, "You know, speaking of eligible men, I had rather hoped a gentleman I am forbidden to name might put in an appearance tonight. Oh, look." She nodded toward the arched doorway leading to the billiards room. "There he is now. He must have snuck in when I wasn't looking, the wicked man."

What? Catherine clutched Helena's arm as panic gripped her. "I'm not ready to see him again and you assured me he wouldn't be here," she hissed. "That he'd declined the invitation because it's only been six months since Sybil passed. You knew I wouldn't come if he...if he..."

Heedless of the fact she was crushing her gown of shot blue silk, Catherine pressed a hand against her stomach where it seemed a whirlwind of butterflies had suddenly taken up residence. While no one had blatantly snubbed her during the evening, the knowing stares, smirks, and whispers she'd endured on her arrival tonight—even the orchestra had stopped playing—had been torture enough. But the thought of encountering the man who still owned her heart, even after all this time, was far, far worse.

Helena shrugged a shoulder. "He must have changed his mind. Either that or Phillip persuaded him to come. You know what men can be like. How long has it been since you and Adam parted ways, again?"

Catherine sent her traitorous friend a heated glare. "You know very well it's been five years. And counting."

Helena toyed with the rubies about her neck. "Good heavens. Has it really been that long?"

"Yes." Catherine slid her arm from Helena's. "I'm sorry, but I must go. Louis is probably fretting anyway. I don't like to leave him for too long."

"No. You mustn't go." Helena touched her shoulder, a concerned frown creasing her brow. "And don't use Louis as an excuse. He will be fine. Of course, I'm assuming there hasn't been another odd accident..."

Catherine shook her head and sighed. "No, thank goodness. Nothing since we quit Briarwood Park. Believe me, I would have told you if anything else untoward had happened," she added. "I cannot wait until I have an inquiry agent to look into things."

Helena nodded. "Yes, Phillip will find someone of the highest caliber for you. Now, if you'd like to retreat to the ladies' retiring room for a short while, or down another champagne or two to shore up your defenses, I shall come with you—"

"Helena, how lovely to see you and... And Lady Rosemont."

Oh, God. Adam was beside Helena and all at once the air had been sucked out of the ballroom. Catherine's breath caught as her gaze locked with the Earl of Dalton's. His piercing blue eyes searched hers, and for a moment everyone and everything else faded away. It was just her and Adam, and a yawning chasm of things left unsaid between them.

Shaken to her core, she opened her mouth to speak but not a sound emerged. Thank goodness Helena jumped in.

"Adam, why so formal?" her shameless friend admonished. "You mean Catherine, don't you?"

"Forgive me." Adam bowed. The black superfine of his evening coat stretched over his broad shoulders with the movement, accentuating his athletic physique and making Catherine's head spin with longing. "It's been such a long time since we last met and I wasn't sure how such familiarity would be received."

"I... It's quite fine. Honestly. Lord knows, I'm not a stickler for ceremony. I don't mind how you address me." Catherine's face was on fire as vivid memories of the past flooded back. Afternoons and nights and mornings spent in bed with Adam, and the very familiar terms of endearment he'd used. *Minx, wicked wench, sweetheart. Ma belle. Ma chérie.*

And once, only once, *my love.*

Of course, he hadn't meant that last one. After all, he'd whispered it in the throes of passion when he'd been buried deep inside her. He probably had no idea he'd uttered such a thing.

But Catherine remembered everything. Then again, perhaps Adam was recalling some of those moments and his pet names for her too as his wide mouth tilted into a roguish smile. The blue of his eyes darkened. "As long as you call me Adam, I shall call you Catherine."

Her throat tightened and she had to swallow before she could speak. "Very well. Adam."

Adam's eyes roamed over her face. Lingered on her mouth before skimming the bare flesh of her décolletage.

Catherine's pulse bolted like a rabbit released from a snare, careening out of control. Her breasts rose and fell as her breathing quickened and Adam's smile widened. *Curse him.* He was toying with her and it wasn't fair. Not when she felt so overwhelmed and vulnerable. Not like herself at all, certainly not like the sophisticated, confident woman she'd once been.

It was Helena who broke the spell. "Excellent," she said, touching Catherine's arm. "Now that you two are happily reacquainted, I shall make myself scarce. I do believe Phillip is looking for me. If you'll excuse me..."

Before Catherine could think of anything to stop her

friend's retreat, Helena slipped into the throng of guests in the ballroom and disappeared. *Curse her too and her meddlesome matchmaking!*

"Catherine. You look well." Adam moved closer.

When Catherine drew in a much-needed breath, the almost forgotten scent of his pleasantly spicy cologne invaded her senses. Made her head swim all over again. It appeared the desire she thought she'd stamped out long ago had only been lying dormant, waiting to spring to life again.

"As do you." She took a step backward to create some distance between them but found herself bumping into the marble column flanking the arched doorway behind her. "I didn't know you would be here tonight."

"Do you mind?"

How to answer such a question? Catherine focused on the sapphire pin nestled in the artful folds of Adam's cravat. It was hard to look him the eye. She didn't want him to see how much he'd affected her after all these years. She drew a bracing breath and whispered, "I'm not sure. I'm...I'm thrown. It's been such a long time since we..."

"Yes, too long." Drawing closer, Adam reached out and with the back of his bare fingers, skated a whisper-soft touch across the exposed flesh between her sleeve and the top of her satin glove. "Perhaps we could move somewhere a bit quieter. To talk."

"Talk?" she repeated like a moonstruck ninny. Trying to ignore the potent desire still swirling through her blood, Catherine raised her gaze to Adam's face. She really didn't think intercourse of the verbal kind was all he had in mind, considering the heat in his eyes and his smoldering smile. But it would give her the chance to tell him what she should have done five years ago.

"Yes." His voice stroked over her like a dark caress. "I've missed you, Catherine."

Then why did you cast me aside like an old scandal rag? She pressed her teeth firmly into her lip to stop herself hurling the accusation at him. Past hurts she had thought dead and buried flared to life once more.

"I know that frown. You're angry with me."

She inhaled a shaky breath. "No. I'm confused. Well, perhaps I'm a little angry. As I said, it's been a long time and things have changed. Things have happened..."

A crease appeared between his brows. "Is there someone else?"

She almost laughed. "No. But I would like to talk. Would you give me a few minutes?"

A wry smile tugged at the corner of Adam's mouth. "I haven't frightened you off, have I?"

"No. But I would like to freshen up. Shall we meet in the small parlor beside the music room upstairs, in, say, ten minutes? It's not far from the ladies' retiring room. Do you know it?"

This time, Adam's smile was charm personified. "I'm sure I'll find it."

"Good." Without sparing him another glance, Catherine slid away. She truly did want to speak with Adam. And while it was probably unwise to meet him in such a private location, she couldn't possibly tell him about Louis in a crowded ballroom where others might overhear.

It was their secret alone.

No stranger to Latimer House, Adam found the parlor easily enough. It was a small, intimate room, and he could see why Catherine had suggested it. Gold-hued fabrics, gilt legged furniture, and polished walnut panels gleamed in the glow from the fire and several branches of candles. It was the perfect setting for a tryst.

Crossing the Persian rug, he drew the heavy amber curtains closed before taking up a position by the fire. What he wouldn't do for a glass of something strong like cognac, or even better, whisky right now, to help temper the desire heating his blood along with an uncharacteristic bout of nerves. Both made his heart beat hard and fast like the thundering drums of a military tattoo.

Catherine had no idea how much he'd missed her over the past five years. Not just her incomparable skills as a lover, but her company—her wit and intelligence. The way she made him smile. The year they'd spent together as protector and courtesan had been the best of his life.

And then he'd given it all away to marry Sybil, the young woman his mother had convinced him would make a perfect wife.

How wrong his mother had been. He shouldn't think ill of the dead, but being married to the socially poised yet vapid Sybil had been at best, tolerable. Perhaps it was unkind of him to think so, but she reminded him of the Ming porcelain vase sitting on the mantel where his forearm now rested—beautiful to look at yet empty inside. A passionless vessel who cared more about her equally vacuous friends and the contents of her armoire, jewelry box, and the latest gossip than him. Her death had been so unexpected Adam had barely been able to believe it at the time—a case of typhlitis or a "diseased appendix vermiformis," the physician had reported. He'd never wished her harm, yet all the same, he couldn't help but feel a sense of relief that he was now free.

Several years into their marriage, he'd even begun to rethink his position on securing the services of another mistress. It was something he'd *never* wanted to do—the idea of going outside his marriage for sexual gratification seemed ignoble and grubby and he knew he'd be plagued by guilt if he did so—but his wife had not exactly welcomed his presence in her bed. Sybil had always assured Adam that she was happy to do her "duty," in the hope that one day she'd be "in the family way." She *did* want children. However, she'd never been an enthusiastic bed partner and Adam found his conjugal visits to be nothing but disheartening, perhaps even demoralising given that Sybil repeatedly rebuffed any of his attempts to show her the true pleasures of lovemaking. Indeed, Adam had almost forgotten what those pleasures were himself and over time, he'd begun to visit his wife's bed less and less. He hadn't wanted to lie with a woman who very clearly did not take much pleasure in lying with him. In his mind, bed sport should be more than perfunctory or a means to an end.

After Sybil had passed, Adam waited several months before he visited an upper-class brothel in St James's, but while he'd easily slaked his lust, he'd never been truly sated. Those experiences didn't compare to those he'd shared with Catherine.

Catherine. She fired his blood like no other. The question was, would she want to take up with him again? She was now Lady Rosemont, a wealthy widowed countess. A courtesan no more. He burned to know if she was as lonely and unsatisfied as he. Did she wish to take a lover? According to Helena and Maxwell, she'd remained steadfastly chaste since that old roué Rosemont had died.

Adam blew out a heavy sigh and poked at the logs with the fire iron, watching the flames dance and the sparks fly up the chimney. He supposed he was about to find out what Catherine truly wanted.

As if his mere thoughts had summoned her, she appeared in the doorway. His pulse leaped higher than the fire's flames and he almost felt ashamed when his cock stirred. Watching her every movement, he drank in the sight of her, the way her gown of dusky blue silk slid over her slender curves as she stepped into the room then pushed the oak door closed with a soft snick.

Damn. She didn't turn the lock. But he could always do that later if needs be. One thing he wouldn't do was rush her, even though lust was presently hammering through his veins, straight to his groin.

Fine tendrils of Catherine's pale blonde hair brushed her flushed cheeks, her blue-gray eyes darkening as her gaze drifted over his body from head to toe. Was it just wishful thinking that made him imagine she yearned to be with him too?

He needed to say something to break the burgeoning silence, but all at once he was tongue-tied like a callow youth about to ask a debutante if he may kiss her for the very first time.

It was Catherine who spoke first. "I still can't thank you enough for helping me...that night at Winthorpe House," she began in her lyrically husky voice, a voice which did nothing but inflame his desire. Stepping farther into the room, she continued, "If...if it weren't for you, I..." She halted, stumbling over her words. Shaking her head, she placed a hand against her stomach as though to quell a surge of emotion and blinked away tears. "You and Lord Maxwell saved me. And for that, I will always be eternally grateful."

"Believe me, I wish I could have done more." It wasn't a lie. Adam still cursed himself for not being the one to pull the strings to free her. To whisk her away from the hellhole that was Newgate Prison. That had been Maxwell's doing. And the Foreign Secretary's.

"It's all right." She offered a small smile. "I never expected you to be my knight in shining armor. I know you were in a...difficult position, shall we say?"

Adam huffed out a sigh as he recalled Lord Winthorpe's

dark, glowering stares when he'd defended Catherine's innocence. "That's one way of putting it."

"But as the saying goes, all's well that ends well. And here we are." Catherine crossed the rug and claimed one side of an ivory damask settee. "Come, sit with me," she said, patting the empty seat beside her.

He sat carefully. Close, but not too close, his thigh a few inches from hers. Within reach but not obviously so. He sensed a brittleness in Catherine. Her smile seemed forced rather than genuine. He would need to proceed with caution if he were to win her over.

Her next words startled him. "Do you miss her? Your wife?" she asked softly, but then she continued on before he could respond, "I must admit, I was rather shocked when I heard about her passing. I only read about it just recently. *The Morning Chronicle* mentioned something..."

"Ah, yes, that piece that said I might be on the prowl for another wife." Adam snorted and shook his head. It was true he did need an heir one day, but he wasn't ready to rush into marriage again. Not unless he could find a woman who would at least welcome him, not just tolerate him in bed. He certainly wasn't looking for a love match. In his opinion, love turned men into irrational idiots. "It's all gossip and groundless speculation."

Catherine nodded. "I thought so. About the wife-hunting bit, anyway. All the same, she was very young, your Lady Dalton. Too young to have passed away. Helena mentioned it was typhlitis that claimed her. Heavens." Catherine pressed her elegant fingers to her full lips in a gesture of self-recrimination. "Here I am, blathering on, and I haven't even offered my condolences. And that is unforgivably remiss of me. I'm sorry for your loss, Adam. Truly I am."

"I have been remiss not to offer my sincerest condolences to you, too."

To say Adam had been surprised to learn Catherine had married Lord Rosemont within a week of her release from Newgate would be an understatement. While any rumors of Catherine's involvement in the terrible affair at Winthorpe House had been quickly surpassed by the scandal of Lord Makepeace's arrest for Sir Louis's murder—and sudden death while in the process of being apprehended—her subsequent marriage to Rosemont had certainly made for another sensational *on-dit*. One which had never truly dissipated. She was still known as the "Courtesan Countess" in some circles, a blatant term of disrespect which galled Adam no end.

Putting aside his chagrin on Catherine's behalf, he continued, "To answer your initial question, about whether I miss Sybil, I must confess that while her passing saddened me, I..." He trailed off and wiped a hand down his face as he struggled to find the right words to describe his relationship with his late wife. "Look, I know it may sound dreadful, but my marriage to Sybil was a duty more than anything else. Neither Sybil nor I ever developed any real affection for each other. Our families had always had close ties and it was a union our parents—my mother Drusilla, and Lord and Lady Winthorpe—expected. As you know, I was fast approaching the age of eight-and-twenty and Sybil had just made her debut. I'd decided long ago that a man in my position should marry for convenience rather than for love, so it seemed best to just get on with it. For better or for worse, so to speak."

Catherine's gaze dropped from his and she began to toy with the gold silk tassel on one of the cushions. "My marriage to Edward was one of convenience as well. I grew quite fond of him, actually. He was a kind man, considering the circumstances. Or perhaps I should say, *my* circumstances."

Ouch. Adam flinched. Was she intimating he hadn't been kind? To her or to Sybil because he'd married a young woman he hadn't loved? He'd tried to do the right thing by Sybil, but when all was said and done, he was certain his wife hadn't given a flying fig about him. She may have even welcomed the notion of him taking a mistress if it meant far fewer visits to her bedchamber. "Of course, I cared for Sybil's wellbeing," he said carefully. The need to plead his case suddenly seemed of paramount importance. "I want you to understand, I didn't wish to end the arrangement I had with you, Catherine. But for many reasons I felt obligated to wed, and it wouldn't have been fair to Sybil if I'd continued to share a bed with you. I *wanted* to be a faithful husband. And I'm supremely sorry I didn't tell you all this at the time I parted ways with you. To end things so abruptly was both shabby and cowardly."

"I will admit, I was rather taken aback when you broke things off without much of an explanation. And when I learned of your betrothal that night at Winthorpe House..."

A crease had appeared between Catherine's finely drawn brows and she was fiddling with the cushion again. Avoiding his gaze. It was apparent he'd hurt her. At the time he'd ended things, it hadn't occurred to him that she might have developed a *tendre* for him. She'd seemed so sophisticated. So self-contained.

She hadn't seemed particularly enamored of her past protectors—a middle-aged baron and then a rakish viscount. Well, as far as Adam knew. Talking with Catherine about her past paramours had never been high on his agenda when he'd been with her.

But *had* it been different with him? *Had* she cared for him a little?

Surely not. Catherine—his fiercely proud, passionate lover —had never seemed like the sentimental type.

All of a sudden Adam was possessed with the urge to smooth her frown away with gentle kisses. To bring her smile back and rekindle the fire in her lovely blue-gray eyes. Drawing a deep breath, he placed his hand over hers to still her restless fingers. "Catherine, I also want you to know that while I thought Lady Sybil Gower would make a suitable Society wife, it soon became abundantly clear we weren't that suited at all. In fact, our relationship became quite strained."

At last Catherine lifted her gaze to meet his again. "I had no idea you'd been so unhappy."

Adam shrugged. "Aristocratic marriages often turn out that way. Indeed, my parents were a case in point. But"—he grazed his thumb over the delicate flesh of Catherine's wrist—"I don't think either of us came here to talk about our former spouses, did we?"

Her slender shoulders rose and fell with a sigh. "No..."

Reaching out, he gently caressed Catherine's cheek with the back of his fingers. "I truly meant it when I said I've missed you. More than I can say." He dropped his gaze to her mouth. A deliberate ploy to stir her. To tease her. But the sight of her luscious lips, slightly parted as though in invitation, the heat of her body and the scent of her floral perfume, all sharpened his own arousal. Five years suddenly seemed like an eternity. He had to taste her, and soon, or he'd go mad.

"I've missed you too." Her murmur was a velvet whisper, smooth yet husky with an emotion he hoped was desire. "There's something I need to tell—"

"Shhh." Adam captured her chin then leaned in closer and let his breath brush across her lips. "We've talked enough for now, don't you think, *ma belle*?"

Catherine curled her fingers into the lapels of his evening jacket. "Adam," she sighed, her breath as sweet as he remembered. "*Mon chéri*."

And what was left of his control completely disintegrated.

Lashing her pliant body against his, he claimed her delectable mouth. It was a hungry kiss. Hard. Demanding. A crush of lips. A wild tangle of tongues. Plunging his fingers into the elaborate arrangement of curls at the back of her head, Adam pushed Catherine down onto the settee. Her legs parted to cradle his hips and her hands slid over his shoulders then down his back, exploring his body with frantic movements.

Pulling away to drag in a much-needed breath, he buried his face in her neck, licking and sucking, feasting on the fragrant satiny flesh in the sensitive hollow below her ear, along her collarbone, and then lower to the upper swells of her bosom.

Christ, why had he waited so long to seek her out? He'd been such a fool to deny himself such exquisite pleasure. Catherine was made for him. Her ragged moans and soft pants were music to his ears. His blood sang. His cock throbbed.

He needed more from her. With rough, clumsy tugs, he pulled down her bodice, stays, and chemise, exposing one of her firm round breasts. The strawberry pink nipple was tightly puckered as though in invitation, and he flicked his tongue against it before drawing it between his lips to suckle.

Catherine's fingers threaded through his hair, gripping his head. Her body arched against him as though urging him on. He slipped a hand beneath the hem of her rucked-up gown but as he slid it up the silken skin of her bare upper thigh, she stiffened.

"Adam," she gasped. "You go too far. We must stop."

What? Stop? His hand froze and he lifted his head. *Bloody hell. The door.* She was right. With reluctance, Adam pushed himself up. Then frowned when Catherine did so as well, dragging her undergarments and bodice back into place. Not only did she look disheveled, her expression was troubled. Had he misunderstood? She really *did* want to stop, but perhaps it wasn't for the reason he'd imagined.

Guilt and confusion began to dampen his raging lust. "What's wrong? I'm sorry if I misread—"

"No, you didn't. I wanted to kiss you too. But as for

anything else..." Catherine pushed a loosened curl away from the corner of her mouth. Her lips, as red and tempting as ripe raspberries, were still slick from his kisses and he had to stifle a groan. "I'm not ready for this. No..." She shook her head. "That's not what I mean." Her gaze was steady as she regarded him. "What I should say is, I'm not available."

"Not available?" he repeated like a simpleton, then frowned. "I don't understand. Have you...have you taken a lover? Are you involved with someone else?"

"No... There's no one else." She sighed and her eyelashes flickered downward, shielding her expression. Her hands were now clasped primly in her lap. "I'm not being clear. While I desire you, Adam—I always have—being your lover, it isn't enough. Not anymore." Her eyes met his again. He'd never seen such a determined expression on her face before. "At least not for me. I want you to understand, I won't just tumble into bed with you and pick up where we left off. I don't wish to become your mistress again. Or indeed any man's."

"I..." Adam ran a hand down his face. Of course, that's exactly what he wanted: Catherine in his bed once more. Filling his days and nights with ecstasy. "I don't know what to say." Another shocking thought occurred to him. One that made his heart plunge. "You... you want...marriage?" he whispered. "You want me to marry you?"

Catherine lifted her chin. "Yes."

"But..." He shook his head. Pushed up from the seat and laced his fingers behind his neck as he paced the Persian rug. What Catherine asked for was impossible. Impossible, for so many reasons.

Yes, he'd missed her. Yes, he wanted her and she clearly wanted him too. And they were both free to pursue their mutual passion.

But marry Catherine? She might be a countess, but *everyone* knew what she'd been before the Earl of Rosemont wed her. At best, the *ton* labeled her a former "actress." At worst: a murdering, manipulative, grasping whore.

He shouldn't care—in his eyes, Catherine was remarkable in every way. She was the one woman who captivated his interest like no other. However, it wasn't just his own needs he was obliged to consider. There were his family's needs—his mother and his two younger sisters. Viola and Cordelia both expected to wed within the ranks of the *ton* in the next few years. If he wedded Catherine, they would *never* forgive him. His mother especially. Polite society would turn its back on all of them as it had threatened to do years ago when his foolish father had brought humiliation—and tragedy—to their door.

That almost forgotten scandal...what his father had done for the love of another woman without care or consideration for his family, it shackled Adam. The yoke of responsibility was tight indeed.

Turning to face Catherine, Adam's throat constricted as he all but choked out the hateful words. "You ask too much of me. I can't."

I can't.

Catherine gripped the edge of the settee as pain lanced through her. Of course he couldn't—no, *wouldn't*—marry her. She'd been a fool to think otherwise. She might bear the title of "countess," but she was not of his world.

She wasn't good enough and never would be.

She might have been a whore, but she wouldn't become Adam's mistress again, no matter how much she wanted to be with him. Inevitably, he would find another young woman from his class—someone with untainted lineage and a pristine reputation—and he would wed her. And yet again, she, Catherine—the Courtesan Countess—would be discarded.

She wouldn't be able to bear it. Not a second time.

"Catherine, say something."

Even though her heart was threatening to crack, she rose to her feet and met Adam's confused gaze. "There's nothing more to say. I want a husband who will care for me, and you want a mistress." She shrugged a shoulder. "It seems we are at an *impasse* with no way forward."

Of course, she could still tell him about Louis. But what purpose would that serve now? She doubted it would make any difference to how Adam felt about her. Perhaps it would make things just that little bit worse. If Adam wanted to see Louis periodically, it would only prolong her agony. She would have to marshal her defenses every time she saw him. Despite his rejection of her, she was sure she would always want him. Eventually, when Adam did take another lover or a wife and didn't look at her with keen interest in his eyes anymore, when he began to think of her and Louis as a burden, it would be like dying a death of a thousand small cuts.

No. It was better to sever ties with Adam now. Completely.

She'd been an idiot to meet with him like this.

Swallowing past a boulder of barely suppressed anguish in her throat, she whispered, "Goodbye, Adam. I hope you find whatever it is you are looking for in a woman. And I'm sorry you couldn't find that in me."

Her hand was on the brass door handle when he called after her, his voice low and rough. "Don't leave like this, Catherine. We've only just been reunited. Won't you reconsider?"

She glanced back at him and took in his devastatingly handsome face—all clean, strong, aristocratic lines. It was the face she dreamed of in the middle of the night.

In that moment, she fancied he looked almost as bereft as

she felt. But she shouldn't remark on that; he might have some tender feelings for her beyond lust, but he clearly didn't *love* her. She wouldn't change her mind. "No, Adam. I won't. You said before that I ask too much of you. But I rather think the opposite is true. You ask too much of *me*."

And with that, she closed the door on him.

CHAPTER 7

Somehow, Catherine managed to maintain an air of composure while she'd waited long minutes for her carriage to be brought round at Latimer House. But after she'd climbed into the cab's dark interior, the tears flowed freely. Helena and Phillip had been otherwise engaged—apparently their young daughter had taken ill and a physician had been summoned—so she hadn't been able to bid her hosts adieu. Of course, she was sorry little Phillipa was unwell, but part of her was grateful she'd been spared Helena's gentle prodding about how things had gone with Adam.

Thank God Adam hadn't pursued her. She was certain she would have come apart at the seams if he'd approached her in public again. At least she'd retained her dignity—and perhaps avoided feeding the scandalmongers—if nothing else.

Although now that she was home, Catherine found she couldn't settle. Her mind was in turmoil. Thoughts about Adam—how much she loved and wanted him but could never have him—wouldn't leave her alone and she did something she hadn't done for such a long, long time...

She went to her dressing room and retrieved Adam's old

greatcoat. The one he'd given to her when he'd visited her in Newgate. She'd never been able to bring herself to get rid of it. It felt like she always had part of him with her, and from time to time, she'd put it on and pretend it *was* actually him enfolding her in his arms and holding her tight. She knew it wasn't healthy to indulge in such a useless fantasy, but in weak moments, she couldn't seem to help herself.

Even though the garment had been laundered, she always fancied she could still detect Adam's body heat and his masculine scent—hints of the bergamot cologne he'd favored and something that was just "Adam". She thought she could smell his cologne now as she slipped the coat over her evening finery. The silk lining slid coolly against her skin while the heavy wool enveloped her like a comforting heavy blanket. Then she visited the nursery and curled up in the arms of the plush chair beside Louis's bed. With Adam's coat wrapped about her, Catherine's vision misted as she watched over their son. Louis lay on his back, one arm flung out toward Pippin on the other side of the bed, the other across his narrow chest. Cheeks flushed from sleep, his breath intermittently stirred one of the fine golden curls lying beside his slightly parted lips.

A peculiar pang—a potent blend of love and remorse as sharp as any blade—penetrated Catherine's heart.

When she'd been a courtesan, she'd known full well how to protect herself against pregnancy. And indeed, she had done so successfully until she'd met Adam... And then she'd been so swept away, too caught up in the moment—too much in love—to take care. She'd let down her guard in more ways than one. But she would never, ever regret that she'd had Louis.

Although, it pained her no end he would never know his real father. All she could do was be the best mother she possibly could.

She must have dozed off for the next thing she knew, Pippin was yapping madly and Lizzy was shaking her awake.

"My lady!"

Catherine's eyes flew open. All at once she was struck by a paroxysm of violent coughing. Her lungs couldn't seem to drag in enough air and the dimly lit room was full of a thick, suffocating miasma.

Smoke! Oh, God, there was a fire!

Ignoring the terror rampaging through her veins, she swiftly hauled a coughing Louis into her arms. "Lizzy, grab Pippin. We need to get out."

Where was the fire coming from? There was enough light coming from the low burning fire in the fireplace and a lamp to ascertain the source of the smoke wasn't in the nursery. Her gaze darted to the door. It stood ajar and smoke appeared to be billowing in from the hall. But there weren't any flames licking at the doorway. Nor was there an unearthly, red-hot glow. Dare she make a run for it?

They were three floors up. Escaping through the window was impossible.

Clutching Louis against her, she threw up a silent prayer to heaven and dashed toward the door. Lizzy with a yapping Pippin in her arms followed close behind.

"This way, my lady!"

Thank God. It was Jackson. Through the cloud of thick smoke, Catherine could just discern the footman beckoning at the far end of the hall.

Ignoring the burning in her lungs and the stinging in her eyes, she tore toward him. He met her halfway, taking Louis from her arms. "There's less smoke below," he gasped in between fits of coughing as they rushed helter-skelter down the stairs. "But we'd best go out to the street."

"What of the other staff?" They were on the ground floor now, heading for the vestibule, the air growing considerably clearer.

"Kingsley and Mrs. White roused them." Jackson ushered

Catherine and Lizzy out of the door onto the footpath. "They're on their way out. Look."

Catherine whirled around and sure enough, the indomitable Kingsley, along with the housekeeper, were shooing the maids—some of them wailing—out into the cold, wet night. It was raining but Catherine counted that as a blessing. She'd rather be soaked to the skin than burned to a crisp.

"Lady Rosemont." Kingsley was at her side. Even though he was clothed in a nightshirt, banyan, and askew nightcap, he still commanded attention. "I've marshaled some of the other footmen to start a bucket brigade. I wasn't sure how long it would take for the insurance office to rally their own fire brigade and deploy a water pump. But it looks like there's more smoke than anything else."

"Yes, thank heavens." Louis was crying for her so Catherine took him from Jackson's arms. He clung to her, his little face damp with rain and tears pressed into her neck. "I wonder how it started. The smoke was particularly thick just outside the nursery. But I couldn't see any flames."

Kingsley shook his head. "I've no idea, my lady. God willing, the house will be all right if we've caught the fire early enough. It appears to be all bark and no bite."

"Yes." There was no ominous fiery glow behind any of the windows, no flames devouring the roof or the walls. It appeared that Rosemont House wasn't in any immediate danger of burning to the ground, especially as the rain began to intensify. Indeed, it was growing heavier by the moment and even though Adam's greatcoat helped to shield Louis to some extent, Catherine wanted to take him somewhere warm and dry. The problem was, such was her notoriety, none of her neighbors would offer them shelter.

A small crowd was gathering in Park Lane and she couldn't help but notice the furtive glances directed her way. There was one person in particular who caught her attention

—a man in a greatcoat with the collar turned up, standing just beyond a pool of light cast by a nearby gas lamp. Even though she couldn't see the stranger's face clearly through the veil of rain and dark shadows, she swore she could feel his pointed stare. It seemed to crawl over her, like some sort of malevolent presence. A frisson of fear slid down her spine and she looked away, chiding herself for being so fanciful.

Louis coughed and shifted restlessly in her arms. She could feel him shivering. "Mama, I'm cold."

"I know, my darling. We'll go somewhere nice and warm soon." Catherine adjusted Adam's coat again to better shelter her son, but his little legs were still exposed to the icy rain. She was loath to turn up on Helena and Phillip's doorstep. With a ball still underway and a sick child on their hands, they had enough to contend with.

She certainly wasn't going to foist herself upon Adam. He probably hadn't even returned home to his Grosvenor Square residence yet.

The only real option available was to open up her Russell Square townhouse. Thank goodness she'd had the sense to retain a skeleton staff. Her former housekeeper Mrs. Chester, and her husband, had maintained the property since her marriage to Lord Rosemont.

After explaining her plan to Kingsley, he nodded in agreement. "Rest assured, I'll take care of everything here, my lady. And with your permission, I'll send some of the other staff on to Russell Square"—he gestured toward a knot of shivering maids clad only in sodden nightgowns and shawls—"after you've had time to settle his lordship."

"Of course." Mrs. Chester and the capable Mrs. White would have the townhouse and staff sorted out in no time at all. A hackney coach was hailed, and after Catherine clambered inside with Louis, Lizzy, a shivering Pippin, and Jackson, they were on their way.

She was relieved Louis's coughing and shivering began to ease as the hackney rolled along the dark, wet London streets. He slid from her lap and drew a very bedraggled Pippin into his arms. "Mama, I'm scared."

"My poor boy. It has been rather frightening, hasn't it? But everything will be all right. I promise you." She smoothed a dripping lock of hair away from his cheek. "We're going to my old house. It's not far away. And very soon you'll be tucked up safely in a nice warm bed. I'll even get Lizzy to make you some hot chocolate as a special treat if you like."

Louis nodded then rubbed his eyes—no doubt they were stinging, too. "I don't like fires. Or smoke."

"Neither do I." At only four years of age, it always surprised Catherine how self-contained and observant her son was. "But we're lucky because it doesn't seem to be a very big fire. And hopefully the rain will help put it out."

"Good." Louis leaned against her and fiddled with Pippin's ears. "I wonder how it started."

The comment chilled Catherine to the very bone because it was the question which was uppermost in her mind too. "I'm sure it was just an accident. Perhaps a candle or lamp fell over. That's why we're always careful with our candles, aren't we?"

"Yes." Louis yawned and Catherine's heart nearly broke in two as he began to suck his thumb.

It had been months since he'd succumbed to the habit. She cast Lizzy a warning glance when she looked as though she were about to rebuke her charge. She wouldn't let the nurse admonish her son for such a minor transgression. Especially not tonight.

～

Less than an hour later, as Catherine's old bedchamber and the adjacent guest room were being made up for her and Louis, one of Rosemont House's footmen arrived at Russell Square with the good news that the smoldering fire had been confined to the third floor. In fact, it had been extinguished soon after Catherine had departed in the hackney cab. Despite the extensive smoke damage to the house, Kingsley had opted to stay on with another pair of footmen to ensure everything was locked up tight against opportunistic thieves.

After Louis was safely settled and fast asleep in a guest bedchamber—along with Lizzy and Pippin—Catherine finally retired to her own room next door. It was well after three in the morning, and she was drooping with exhaustion. As she slid into her old four-poster bed, her son's remark about how the fire had started loomed like a menacing specter in her mind. She was *sure* it hadn't been an accident. When she'd made her way to the nursery, the third-floor hall had been dark. She'd taken a candle to light her way but had snuffed it out when she'd claimed the armchair beside Louis's bed.

Had someone been waiting until the household was asleep before they'd struck? Had that shadow-shrouded man who'd been staring at her been involved somehow? Or was he just an oddly curious passerby and Catherine's imagination had cast him as a villain who wished her, and perhaps even Louis, ill?

It was deeply unsettling not to know the identity of the stranger or what his presence had meant. Maybe nothing at all.

Catherine's instincts told her that his presence *did* mean something though.

Despite the fact she was tucked up beneath fine sheets and a thick goose-down quilt, icy tremors of fear snaked across Catherine's skin. Sleep seemed impossible, and indeed, it was as all sorts of disturbing questions without answers tumbled around and around in her mind like a whirlpool.

When the cold gray light of dawn began to filter into her bedchamber, Catherine finally gave up on tossing and turning, and rang for a bath. She might not be able to dispel her troubled thoughts, but at least she could wash the lingering smell of smoke off her body and out of her hair.

As she waited for the tub to be filled, she quietly slipped into the bedchamber next door to reassure herself that everything was all right with Louis. He was still fast asleep and Lizzy reported he hadn't woken at all, so that was a relief of sorts.

Catherine had just finished attending to her toilette when her lady's maid, Hetty, brought in a breakfast tray. Nestled between the pot of tea, hot crumpets, honey, and jam was a folded piece of parchment with her name, *Lady Rosemont*, scrawled across it.

"What's this?" she asked, plucking the paper from the tray as the maid began to lay her breakfast out upon the small walnut table by the fire. The sheet was grimy and damp, and the ink used to write her name had run a little. It was too early in the day for the post to arrive and besides, hardly anyone aside from her staff knew she was here. Unless Kingsley had sent her another message about how things fared at Rosemont House.

But why hadn't he come here to speak with her directly now the danger had passed?

"I don't rightly know, my lady," replied Hetty. "The footman mentioned a street urchin delivered it to the house a short time ago."

"I see." Taking a seat at the table, Catherine cracked the plain wax seal and opened up the letter. Pure horror blasted through her as she took in the words.

You filthy whore. Both you and your dirty little bastard brat should've burned. This won't stop until I get what I want.

Oh, God. Catherine flung the paper away from her as though it had scorched her fingers. A wave of bitter bile burned her throat and for a moment she thought she might faint as dark spots danced before her eyes.

Someone did indeed want to hurt Louis. And her as well.

And that someone had followed them here.

Perhaps that person was waiting outside right now. Watching. Waiting to launch another attack.

Yet again she recalled the man she'd espied near the lamppost on Park Lane last night.

Could it have been Benedict or Gerald Fortescue...? Or maybe someone who'd been hired by the Fortescues to stalk her and Louis...or do something worse?

A stranger who'd been paid to set fires? To set traps and stage accidents? If Catherine counted each "mishap" including the fire last night, there'd been five in the past ten months.

Five. That was too many incidents to dismiss as a run of bad luck.

But...if the Fortescues wanted to paint her as an unfit mother so they could challenge her right to Louis's guardianship, why go to such *extreme* lengths to prove their point? They could just as easily attest that the "Courtesan Countess" was an immoral sort of woman and the Court of Chancery would undoubtedly listen.

And why send a vile, threatening note?

And what did—*This won't stop until I get what I want*—actually mean?

How could Catherine possibly know what this horrid person wanted from her? Did he or she want to hurt her? To hurt Louis? Or was it something else? Something she knew nothing about? None of it made sense.

"My lady, are you all right?"

Hetty's voice seemed to come from far away and

Catherine clung to the edge of the table to anchor her consciousness to the here and now. She couldn't afford to collapse in a heap.

She needed to be strong, for Louis's sake.

"Hetty, could you please bring me a glass of sherry? A large one? Mrs. Chester is sure to have some stashed somewhere in the kitchen."

Hetty's brow knitted into a deep frown but she curtsied and answered mildly, "Of course, my lady."

As she waited for the maid to return, Catherine poured herself a cup of tea with shaking hands, then retrieved the vile message from where it had fallen on the hearthrug. Malevolence oozed from every word as she reread it.

Filthy whore.

Dirty little bastard brat.

Searing tears of anger burned her eyes. She gripped the page so tightly, the parchment crumpled.

How dare *anyone* say that about her baby boy?

The Rubicon had been crossed.

She could no longer pretend any of these "accidents" weren't malicious or premeditated. Hiring an inquiry agent wasn't going to be enough to keep Louis safe.

There was no doubt in Catherine's mind about what she had to do next.

She needed help, and she knew exactly who she must approach to get it.

CHAPTER 8

Dalton House, Grosvenor Square

It was not a good day, by any means.

A ray of pale, watery sunlight shone through the morning room window and glanced off the silver coffee pot on the breakfast table, making Adam wince.

Aside from the fact he had a raging headache—he'd foolishly downed more than half a bottle of cognac last night after Catherine had roundly rejected his proposition—he was also nursing a bad case of bruised pride along with a sizable dose of sexual frustration. To top it all off, his mother and sisters had unexpectedly turned up on his doorstep while he'd been at the Maxwell's ball.

He enjoyed the company of his sisters, but he was not in the mood to deal with his mother's exacting standards today. Indeed, he'd love nothing more than to pack her off to the dower house, but seventeen-year-old Viola and sixteen-year-old Cordelia needed her, especially as they were due to be presented at court in the next year or two before formally entering the marriage mart.

After pushing his plate of kidneys, bacon, and congealing eggs away, Adam poured himself another cup of black coffee then slid a glance in his mother's direction. She sat at the other end of the breakfast table perusing the day's broadsheets with a gimlet eye through her gilt-edged quizzing glass. Viola and Cordelia were still abed—apparently they were greatly fatigued by the six-hour journey from Adam's country estate, St Clair Abbey, near Oxford—and weren't likely to emerge from their rooms for another few hours.

At least his mother hadn't nagged him that he was still in an informal state of "undress". He'd simply thrown on trousers, a cambric shirt, and a blue silk banyan when his valet had announced his mother wished to take breakfast with him. "Mother dearest" had made a rather pointed remark about the fact he hadn't shaved when he'd bent to kiss her cheek in greeting. But dash it all, if she expected him to show up in the morning room at the ungodly hour of eight o'clock, she was just going to have to put up with his less than civilized appearance.

He was about to read one of the papers—*The Times* was within easy reach—when his butler, Parker, appeared in the doorway looking rather contrite. "My lord. You have a visitor."

Adam blew out a sigh and tossed the newspaper aside. "Who is it?"

His mother lowered her quizzing glass and arched an imperious eyebrow. "It's far too early for morning calls," she said dryly. "Whoever it is, he or she is incredibly rude. Or socially inept. Or both. I'd suggest you turn them away, Adam."

Ignoring his mother, Adam waved the butler over. The man proffered a silver tray upon which lay a rich, cream-colored calling card with elegant gold lettering.

"To answer your question, it is the Countess of Rosemont, my lord," Parker said as Adam picked up the card. "She apologizes for visiting at such an unconventional hour, but she insists the matter is most urgent."

What? Curiosity and hope flared. Had Catherine changed her mind about becoming his mistress?

His mother shot him a suspicious look. "Why on earth would *that* woman call on you, Adam?" Before he could answer, she turned her sharp gaze on the butler. "And I can't believe you let a creature like *her* leave a card, Parker. People will talk if they notice her arrival. Tell her to go. At once."

Adam pushed out of his seat and threw down his napkin. "That's enough, Mother," he said in a tone that brooked no argument before addressing a flushed-faced Parker. The man was clearly embarrassed, though whether by the apparently inexcusable discourtesy of Catherine or the expected rudeness of his mother, he was not sure. "Where is Lady Rosemont?"

"I've installed her in the drawing room, my lord. I hope that's acceptable."

"It is indeed."

"Adam! You can't meet her dressed like that," called his mother as he headed toward the door. "I know she has a reputation for being indecent, but really, you shouldn't stoop to her lev—"

"She said it was urgent," Adam returned without breaking stride. "I'm sure she won't mind." He was tempted to add the lady had seen him countless times before in an even more salacious state of undress, just to see the look of horror on his mother's face, but he didn't wish to malign Catherine.

A smile tugged at the corner of his mouth as he crossed the hall. Hopefully, if things went well, it wouldn't be long before Lady Rosemont was in a salacious state of undress too. Then they could explore all manner of indecent things together.

However, as soon as Adam entered the drawing room and took one look at Catherine's drawn face and agitated state as she paced the hearthrug, he knew something was horribly amiss. All thoughts of doing anything salacious or indecent fled.

"Catherine, what's wrong?" His alarm flared even higher when he noticed one of her hands was pressed to her belly and the other to her forehead as though she were in great distress. Closing the door firmly behind him, he added gently, "What can I do for you?"

She stopped pacing, but when she spoke, her words tumbled out in a great breathless rush. "Thank you for seeing me at such short notice. I told your butler it was urgent and I'm glad he believed me."

"Yes, he did." He'd never seen Catherine so undone. It was as if she were unraveling before him. Not only was her hair tumbling down about her shoulders as though she'd paid scant attention to her appearance, but as he drew closer, he observed her eyes were red and her eyelids puffy as though she'd been weeping. Her voice, when she'd spoken, had been huskier than usual. "Can I get you anything? Tea...or brandy?"

"Yes, please. Brandy would be perfect."

Her fingers trembled as she took the crystal tumbler from him and took a large sip. "Thank you. I needed that."

"I can see." Adam gestured toward the damask uphol-stered sofa by the fire. "Would you care to sit down?"

She nodded. "Yes. Yes, that would be a good idea." She placed her glass on the nearby polished oak table where her reticule already sat, then smoothed her scarlet velvet skirts as she took the seat beside him. "I really don't know where to begin."

"Clearly something happened last night after we parted ways. Or this morning?"

"Yes." Catherine dropped her gaze to her lap where her tightly clasped hands lay. "The problem is, there's been more than one troublesome incident over the past ten months, but I didn't realize until this very morning that the danger was very real. Too real, in fact. But it's not just my own safety that I'm worried about. Actually... " Catherine raised her eyes to his face again. "I also fear for the life of my...my son."

"Your son." Adam frowned. "You're telling me your son is in some kind of danger? How could that be? He's so very young, isn't he?"

"Yes, Louis is but four. It hasn't been reported in the papers yet but early this morning, not long after midnight, there was a fire at Rosemont House. A fire that appears to have been deliberately lit. Just outside Louis's nursery."

"Dear God, Catherine, I'm appalled. Is your son all right? Are *you* all right?"

"Apart from being a bit shaken, he's quite fine. On the other hand, I am—" She gave a brittle laugh that belied the haunted look in her blue-gray eyes. "I'm terrified actually. Because..." Her expression changed again. Determination and perhaps a sliver of anger hardened her gaze and her voice as she continued, "Because I know it wasn't an accident. It was a deliberate act of arson."

Adam was torn between the urge to gather Catherine into his arms and the impulse to grind whoever was responsible for making her so afraid into a pulp. A muscle began to tick in his jaw. "Tell me exactly what happened."

He listened carefully to Catherine's account of how she, her son, and Rosemont House's staff had managed to escape a fire which had apparently begun near the nursery on the third floor. "And how does Rosemont House fare this morning?" he asked. "Does it still stand?"

Catherine nodded. "Yes, thank heavens. It turns out it was a smoldering fire. One that didn't really take hold. Before I came here, an investigating officer from Phoenix Insurance informed me that it appeared as though a lit clay pipe had been left on one of the wingchairs in the hallway. As the pipe burned through the fabric upholstery, a significant amount of smoke was generated, but thankfully the chair didn't go completely up in flames. My staff managed to douse the smoldering embers before anything else caught alight, even before Phoenix's fire brigade arrived with their water pump."

"You're very lucky then."

"It would seem so."

Adam frowned. "I must ask this question: how do you know it *wasn't* an accident? Could it be that one of the male members on your staff left a pipe on the chair? Your butler, or one of the footmen? 'Tis an easy, innocent mistake."

Catherine shook her head. "None of them smoke tobacco, nor even take snuff for that matter. Not only that, but it appears the servants' entrance at the back of the house was broken into. The lock had been forced and the wood around the door jamb is splintered. And then there's this..." She reached for her reticule and pulled out a folded and slightly crumpled sheet of paper. "I clearly couldn't stay at Rosemont House for what remained of the night, so I opened up the house at...at Russell Square," she said, handing him the page. "Even though hardly anyone knew where I'd gone, this note was delivered to my door by a street urchin early this morning."

As Adam unfolded the note, a string of vile words leapt out at him.

You filthy whore. Both you and your dirty little bastard brat should've burned. This won't stop until I get what I want.

The urge to pummel the abominable person who'd done this to Catherine was back, stronger than ever. Adam placed the sheet of paper very carefully on the table and then curled his hands into fists on his thighs as wild, impotent fury roiled about inside him like a raging sea. "This is unconscionable, Catherine. Whoever wrote this is despicable. I take it you have no idea what this person wants?"

"No... I have no idea at all. That's probably what frustrates and frightens me the most. It implies this campaign of terror will continue for some time. I don't even know what they want. Does this person mean they want me dead? Or God forbid, my little Louis dead? Or is it something else entirely?" With trembling fingers, she stuffed the note away in her reticule again then added, "This isn't the first time my son's life has been put in danger either. Someone tampered with the ice before we went sledding on the pond at Briarwood Park in January. It cracked when I set foot on it, but according to the groundsman, it shouldn't have. An icepick was found nearby —and that's only the start."

Catherine went on to describe a series of minor but potentially fatal "near-misses" including the most recent directed at Louis—a swing accident. "The rope could have been sawn through. I have sometimes wondered if Edward's cousin, Benedict—he's next in line for the Earldom of Rosemont— might have designs on the title. Or his wife Lilith, or even their adult son, Gerald. Or maybe they just wish to take Louis's guardianship away from me. They visited Briarwood Park the same day Louis fell from his swing so they were in the area, and made noises questioning my competency as a mother. But I have no proof they're behind anything untoward that has happened. Just suspicions." Catherine shook her head. "I just don't know what to think. Or what to do anymore."

Adam's mind was reeling. He forced himself to breathe evenly and slowly. "To say I'm shocked would be an understatement. Who would do such reprehensible, malicious things? And to such a little boy? You said he was but four?"

To his surprise, Catherine's cheeks pinkened as she

regarded him. She was not a woman who blushed easily. "Almost four-and-a-half, actually."

Four-and-a-half? Adam frowned as confusion clamored with a niggling suspicion that he was missing something, an important detail he'd overlooked. He did a quick calculation in his head. "But that's not possible," he murmured. Then he recalled the words of the note. It had asserted young Louis was a bastard. There'd been rumors old Rosemont was too old to beget a child so his son must be a by-blow. Adam had always dismissed them because...well, because it had suited him to dismiss them.

His jaw clenched hard enough to crush gravel. *Perhaps I shouldn't have.*

"Catherine, what are you trying to tell me?" Adam asked, his tone harsher than he'd intended. "If your son is four-and-a-half years old, that means he was conceived before you wed Lord Rosemont."

"Yes..." Catherine's blush deepened, but she didn't look away. "He was conceived two months before I married Edward. In late July or early August. When you and I were... When I was still your mistress."

Good God! Adam pushed out of his seat and stalked across the room. Catherine had been exclusively his—indeed, he was so certain she'd been faithful to him during their year together, he'd stake his life on it. So that could only mean one thing.

"Who is Louis's father, Catherine?" he grated out as a great wave of conflicting emotions battered him—shock, exasperation, reservation, and underneath it all, burgeoning expectation. "His true father. Tell me."

Rising to her feet, Catherine faced him. Her gaze didn't waver. "You are, Adam. You are Louis's father."

"Christ. Sweet Jesus Christ." Adam dragged a hand down his face.

He was a father. All this time he'd had a son, and he hadn't known.

And Catherine had kept the knowledge from him.

He forced the words out through clenched teeth. "Why didn't you tell me? If it weren't for the fact that you had to come to me to ask for help, were you *ever* going to tell me?"

Catherine flinched but then lifted her chin as she answered. "I wanted to. Honestly I did. I actually attended the ball at Winthorpe House so I could tell you that very night. But then I heard you were engaged to Sybil. And then of course, Sir Louis was murdered. I was attacked, then I was accused of committing that terrible crime and dragged away to Newgate." Catherine shook her head. "The timing was all wrong. And I didn't want to make a fuss."

"Still, you should have told me."

Fierce anger flashed in Catherine's eyes. "When, Adam? When Sybil came out to the terrace and mentioned her father was about to announce your betrothal? After I was hauled out of Lord Winthorpe's stationary cupboard, injured and terrified and heartbroken that Sir Louis had just been brutally murdered and I was being blamed? When you came to see me at Newgate the next day? What difference would it have made? On each occasion, you made it abundantly clear that your arrangement with me was over. You seemed determined to wed your lovely young debutante no matter what. One thing I'm absolutely certain about is that you wouldn't have made an offer for *my* hand."

The tick was back in Adam's jaw. God damn it all to hell. She was right.

"But I thank God that Lord Rosemont proposed," continued Catherine, the light in her eyes softening a little. "At least Louis wasn't born into this world with the label of bastard."

"But someone suspects that he is." Adam frowned. "Do

you have any idea who might have sent that note? Apart from your late husband's cousin or his kin?"

"Not really. But there's been speculation about Louis's parentage since he was born, so in actual fact, it could have been anyone. Indeed, I'm surprised you hadn't suspected Edward wasn't Louis's father."

Adam shook his head. "I'm sorry, but I didn't—" He bit his tongue. He'd been about to say he hadn't given Catherine much thought after she'd been released from Newgate. But that would have been a lie. He'd thought about her too much. "To be perfectly honest, I do recall being quite astonished to hear old Rosemont had proposed to you. And I wondered why he had. Considering you'd been accused of his brother's murder."

Catherine's mouth flattened. "And the fact I was a whore?"

"Don't call yourself that, Catherine. I certainly don't think of you in that way."

She waved a dismissive hand. "Whether you label me a whore or something less crude sounding like 'mistress' or 'courtesan', it doesn't change the truth of the matter. I once sold my body to you, and to two other wealthy, titled men just like you before that. It's why you wouldn't have married me then. And why you won't even contemplate it now."

Catherine crossed the hearthrug and took up a defensive stance on the other side of the fireplace. Disdain and hurt were etched into every line of her countenance. Indeed, her blue-gray eyes were as cold and turbulent as a winter sea as they settled on his face. "But wonder no more about Edward's motive for marrying me. On the morning I was released from Newgate, he sought me out at Russell Square to thank me for helping to identify the real murderer, Lord Makepeace. But during our interview, I became ill and he correctly deduced I was with child. He confessed he didn't wish the earldom to go to his cousin Benedict Fortescue or Benedict's son, Gerald—he'd always counted on the fact Sir Louis would inherit—and so he offered me his hand in marriage. As odd as it sounds, he didn't seem to care the next earl wouldn't be the fruit of his own loins. He simply didn't want Benedict to inherit. Actually"—Catherine's mouth lifted into a small wry smile—"Edward was most pleased to hear you were the father. Apparently your bloodline was good enough."

Aside from having a reputation as a rake, it was common knowledge that the Earl of Rosemont had a ruthless streak. Catherine's account confirmed that in spades.

Aloud, Adam simply said, "I'm sincerely glad for your sake, and for young Louis's, that it all worked out then."

"Well, it did... Until now. Because now it appears that someone is trying to kill my son. At the very least, the Fortescues might try to take Louis from me. And I have no idea what to do to keep him safe. Apart from Phillip and Helena, I don't know who to trust, and I certainly don't want to drag them into this awful mess. It's far too dangerous." The wild, haunted look was back in Catherine's eyes as she continued, "I'm sorry. Now I'm dragging you into it too. And the more I think on it, there's probably nothing you can do to help. Other than to..." Catherine faltered then shook her head, her gaze falling away from his. "Never mind. I ask too much. It was wrong of me to come here. I should go."

In a flash she crossed to the table, retrieved her reticule, and all but ran for the door, her skirts of scarlet velvet flaring then swirling about her legs.

But Adam wasn't finished with her, not by a long shot. She couldn't fire such a devastating cannonball—the existence of his son and the fact some monster wished that innocent child dead—into the midst of his life, then simply walk away.

"Catherine." Adam followed and captured her wrist. "Wait."

"Please let me go," she implored, swinging back to face him. Her eyes were bright with tears. "I don't want to leave Louis for too long. I just... I had a sleepless night and I panicked when I opened the note. Louis and I, we'll be all right. I'm not without means. I'll simply secure the services of a good lawyer if the Fortescues go to the Court of Chancery and attempt to take Louis away from me. And I'll hire an inquiry agent to watch them. Someone Phillip recommends. And a few more footmen." She attempted to smile, her lips quivering with the movement. "Young, strapping specimens. And perhaps a fierce guard dog or two."

"No." Adam released Catherine's wrist but he positioned himself so he was between her and the door. "You can't go. I have a son—a son who needs me. You said there's nothing I can do, but I don't believe that, not for a minute. I have to protect him. Whether he bears my name or not. My blood runs through his veins."

Catherine swallowed. Her voice when it emerged was little more than a husky whisper. "Yes. It does."

"And not just Louis. *You* shall have my protection too, Catherine."

"But how? How will you protect us?" she demanded, her eyes frantically searching his.

"Both of you will live under my roof—"

"I told you last night, Adam. I won't become your mistress again."

She made to push past him, but Adam grasped her by the shoulders and spun her round so she was pressed against the door. "That's not what I mean, Catherine, and you know it."

Catherine's eyes darted fire. "I have no idea what you mean. Speak plainly, Adam. Or let me go." Her hands pushed at him but he wasn't going to budge. "I don't have time for games."

"This is no game." Adam's chest heaved as drew a

steadying breath. What did Society's censure matter when a little boy's life—his son's life—hung in the balance? "I'll marry you, Catherine. I'll be the father Louis needs. Your protector, and his, in truth before the world. I'll go to the Court of Chancery and request that I be made his guardian too. The Lord Chancellor won't deny me."

"Don't jest." Though anger laced Catherine's voice, her bottom lip trembled. "Don't you dare."

"I'm not jesting. I've never been more serious about anything in my life."

Catherine shook her head. "You don't have to marry me," she whispered. "I know you don't want to. I can see it in your eyes. It's the reason you called off our arrangement all those years ago, why you rejected me last night—nothing has changed. Your duty to your own family is of paramount importance to you. You cannot deny it. Your mother and sisters, they'll resent me for all of the scandal I bring to your door. And in time, you'll resent me too. There must be another way."

Adam firmed his gaze and his voice. "There isn't. It's the only way and it's the right thing to do. I do indeed have a duty. But now it's to Louis."

Catherine closed her eyes and a tear escaped onto her cheek. "Yes. Yes, you do."

"So we are agreed?"

She nodded and sagged against the door, her resistance ebbing away. "Yes."

"Good." Adam frowned. Why did she appear so dejected? Based on their encounter last night, she'd clearly stated that she wanted marriage, not another affair. But perhaps she'd changed her mind. Regardless, he needed to focus on doing what was best for his son. Any examination of their complex feelings could wait. "I'll arrange a special license today," he continued, "and we'll wed within a day or two. By the way, where is Louis at the moment?"

"At Russell Square. I wanted to bring him, but I didn't know how this meeting would go. I...I must get back to him."

"I understand. I'll need five minutes."

Catherine frowned. "Five minutes for what?"

"To get ready. I'm coming with you, obviously. I want to meet my son."

CHAPTER 9

"I'm coming with you, obviously. I want to meet my son."

Catherine drew a deep breath. "Of course," she said, forcing down her impatience to quit Dalton House. It was only natural Adam would wish to see Louis. "I'll wait here."

Adam nodded. "Excellent. Ring if you need anything." Halting at the door, he turned back and cast her an apologetic grimace. "Just so you know, my mother, Drusilla, and my sisters Viola and Cordelia are here. They arrived last night. But I don't expect that you'll cross paths with any of them, especially my sisters. The pair are still ensconced in their rooms. I promise I won't be long." And with that, he was gone.

Catherine stared at the smoothly polished oak panels of the door as it fell shut with a soft snick. Naturally, she'd never met the Dowager Countess of Dalton or Adam's younger sisters and she rather hoped that she wouldn't today. Indeed, now was not an opportune time for such an encounter. An encounter that was bound to be...difficult.

No, she had other, more important things to worry about. Beneath the ever present, smothering anxiety that something terrible would happen to Louis while she was away, a fluttering, fledgling emotion, not unlike anticipation, suddenly swelled in Catherine's breast. At long last, Adam would meet his son. Louis would know his real father.

And she would have the husband she'd dreamed of for so long.

But he's not really yours, Catherine, is he?

All at once, crushing disappointment descended upon her, the same leaden weight which had fallen upon her heart when Adam had so matter-of-factly proposed. If one could call what he'd said a proposal. He'd simply asked her if she agreed with his plan to wed—ostensibly for Louis's sake—and she'd acquiesced because logic dictated she had no other choice. There'd been no declarations of love. No mention of how he'd always wanted to make her his wife. Of the joy he felt when he thought about spending the rest of his days with her. He hadn't even kissed her.

Yes, Adam was going to marry her. But not because he loved her.

He was doing his duty. Nothing more.

The idea hurt more than Catherine cared to admit.

Returning to her seat, she reclaimed her glass of brandy. Her hand was shaking so much as she took a sip, the crystal stem slipped between her fingers and she almost spilled it all over the plush Persian carpet. When she'd come here, her only thought had been to secure Adam's help in protecting Louis. She hadn't really thought through what that might really mean.

One thing was certain: Adam's family would not be happy with his choice of bride.

But she couldn't think on that now. Not when every fiber of her being was urging her to return to her son's side posthaste. Whoever had set fire to Rosemont House had followed her and Louis to Russell Square. That person or persons unknown might be plotting something else just as deadly.

Mon Dieu. What if next time they actually succeeded?

The gilt mantel clock struck the half hour and Catherine put down her glass. Adam was taking too long. She needed to go.

Before she'd even crossed the room, the door swung open to reveal a tall, slender woman of middle age. Her graying hair was perfectly styled, her gown of striped lavender-gray silk and lace was of an expensive cut, and her fichu was fastened with an elaborate pearl and silver brooch. Catherine instinctively knew exactly who the lady was even though they'd never met...

Drusilla St Clair, the Dowager Countess of Dalton.

"Lady Dalton," Catherine said stiffly. She suspected that if she hadn't been so worried about Louis, she might have felt a trifle nervous. In fact, it was impatience and annoyance that prickled beneath the surface of her plastered-on smile. "I wasn't expecting to see you this morning."

The dowager countess's pale gray eyes glittered with malice as she regarded Catherine. "Nor I you, *Lady* Rosemont," she said in a tone so frosty, it could have turned water to ice. "I thought you'd already departed."

Catherine bit her tongue, determined not to rise to the woman's bait. She had better things to do than to waste her time trading barbs. "Not quite. But don't worry. I was just leaving."

"Good." Lady Dalton stepped aside to let Catherine pass. But as she did so, the dowager countess added, in a voice dripping with disdain, "You know, I'm surprised my son actually agreed to meet with a creature like you. If I'd had my way, I wouldn't have permitted the staff to even let you through the front door. The sooner you return to whatever gutter it is you crawled out of, the better."

Catherine stopped and turned to face Adam's mother. She

couldn't afford to ignore such a slight, not when she was about to become the new Lady Dalton in the next day or two. If there were to be a power struggle within the household, it was best she made it clear who outranked who. It was a simple matter of survival.

Arching a brow, she replied as coolly as she could, "Not that it's any of your business, but it would appear your son thinks differently. As far as I'm concerned, it's only his opinion that matters."

Lady Dalton's glare turned from ice-cold to scorching within the blink of an eye. "Shall I ask the footman to summon a hackney for you then? To take you back to wherever it is you ply your sullied wares? The docks, perhaps? Or some back alley in Covent Garden or the rookeries of St Giles?"

"No need. I've successfully plied my *sullied wares* right here in your son's drawing room, Lady Dalton. Perhaps you'd best ask your staff to clean the damask cushions on the sofa." Catherine tapped her chin in apparent thought. "Oh yes, and the Persian rug. Or better yet"—she made a sweeping gesture with one hand—"why not have them burned? Heaven knows if the stains will ever come out."

Catherine experienced a brief flash of satisfaction as Lady Dalton's face blanched, her jaw dropping in a gasp of horror. Then with a proud lift of her chin, Catherine turned on her heel and walked away. She'd much rather wait for Adam on the street—where she apparently belonged—than spend another moment in that vile woman's company.

The only problem appeared to be that the vile woman was about to become her mother-in-law.

Catherine shuddered as she took her gloves and bonnet from the footman in the vestibule. As if she didn't have enough to contend with. At least Adam would be by her side.

She liked to think he would protect her from his mother's vitriol, but when all was said and done, would he?

She really had no idea. About anything. Events were moving at such a rapid pace, her head was spinning.

Focus on what you need to do, keeping Louis safe, she told herself as she swiftly tied the black satin ribbons of her capote bonnet beneath her chin. *Nothing else matters. Nothing at all.*

Not your heart which yearns for Adam's love. Nor your fears that he will begin to despise you because you've truly ruined his family's good name.

Only Louis matters.

Yes, Louis.

Good Lord—Catherine roughly tugged on her black calf-skin gloves—how was she to tell her baby boy he was about to gain a new father? How would he react?

And how would Adam?

"I'm sorry I took so long." Adam was suddenly at her side, accepting his own hat and gloves from the footman. He leaned close and murmured, "My valet insisted I couldn't leave the house until I'd shaved. Aside from that, I'd rather not frighten young Louis with my unkept appearance."

"I'm sure you wouldn't," said Catherine gently.

"Oh, and then I also felt obliged to bid my mother farewell." Adam released a heavy sigh as he shrugged on his greatcoat. "She's in a frightful mood this morning, even for her. I'll count it as a blessing that you didn't run into her."

Catherine's cheeks heated guiltily and she focused on doing up the buttons on her gloves. She *should* say something about her fraught encounter with Lady Dalton, but as she struggled to find the right words to explain their horrid, waspish exchange, Adam took her arm and escorted her outside to where the hackney she'd hired earlier still waited.

The short journey to Russell Square passed in uncomfortable silence, the blanket of awkward tension inside the cab so thick and heavy, Catherine wanted nothing more than to throw it aside, but she had no idea how. Instead she slid occasional, surreptitious glances Adam's way, but was at a loss to know what to say.

What was going on inside her reluctant fiancé's head? He clearly wanted to make a good first impression, so that was a positive sign, wasn't it?

The Adam she used to know had been passionate, kindhearted, and affable behind closed doors, even if he often presented a cool, aristocratic veneer to the rest of the world. But she also suspected he possessed a will of iron and a steely spirit. He was governed by a strong need to do the "right thing", no matter the consequences, hence his desire to marry her and be the father Louis needed. But everything he'd hitherto known—the ordered world he'd lived in—had just been thrown into complete disarray. It were as though she had just waltzed in and upended his chessboard or torn up his maps, destroying his carefully laid-out plans for his family and himself.

Did he resent her right now for doing such a thing? Was that part of the reason for this awkwardness between them? Why he keep flexing and unflexing his gloved fingers on his trouser clad thighs? Why a muscle flickered in his lean jaw?

He wouldn't even look at her. His attention was firmly fixed on the passing view of crowded London streets beneath a lowering, pewter-gray sky.

No doubt he was nervous about meeting his son. And then of course, there was a good chance he was preoccupied with thoughts about the coming days. All the new plans he would need to put in place to accommodate her and Louis and their exacting circumstances. The explanations he'd need to give his mother and sisters. Their horrified reactions to finding out the notorious "Courtesan Countess" and her child would be part of the family.

Good God, what sort of catastrophe had she unwittingly set in motion?

Catherine supposed she would soon find out.

When Adam stepped into the elegant vestibule of Catherine's townhouse, he was struck with the oddest feeling—a sensation akin to tumbling into a long-forgotten dream or waking up in a place that was both familiar yet alien. Memories of hedonistic, abundantly happy times came flooding back and he suddenly wondered why he'd been such a fool to say goodbye to Catherine. To stay away all these years.

But he didn't have time to dwell on the past right now. He needed to focus on the coming interview with his son, Louis Edward Adam Fortescue, the Earl of Rosemont.

Christ.

Nervous anticipation coiled through his body, tightening his gut as Adam paced the thick Turkish carpet in a small parlor at the front of the house. The furniture in the main drawing room and study were still shrouded in dust sheets and "not fit to be seen" according to the housekeeper who had ushered him into the room with the promise of a pot of tea. Not that he wanted tea right now. Despite the fact that his forehead still throbbed with a dull pain, a shot or two of brandy would be most welcome to quell his uneasiness. To help him come to terms with the fact he had a son. A four-and-a-half-year-old son.

With all the gossip flying about, he should have realized long ago that Catherine's child was his, and not Rosemont's.

Good God, what a self-absorbed dunderhead he'd been. And that name...

Louis Edward *Adam*.

Above the ponderous ticking of the longcase clock in the

entry hall, and the spit and crackle of the freshly lit fire in the parlor's grate, Adam could just discern the excited yaps of a dog and the unmistakable squeals of a child. Apparently young Louis was playing in the back walled garden under the watchful eye of his nurse and a pair of footmen. Quite understandably, Catherine wished to speak to Louis before any introductions were made. He could well understand why she wanted to prepare the boy for the news that his mother was to marry someone who was a complete stranger to him. A stranger who would become his new father.

Pausing by the window, he examined the street and the empty park beyond with its forlorn looking trees and damp drifts of spent brown leaves piling up along the wrought iron fence line and around the base of the Duke of Bedford's statue.

The traffic was light and Adam couldn't see anything untoward. No one appeared to be watching the house from the street or the park's environs, at least. Nevertheless, an uneasy shiver washed over him. Of course, that didn't mean someone *wasn't* watching Catherine and Louis for a chance to strike again. There were many townhouses in Russell Square and thus many places to conduct surveillance from if one were so inclined. He gripped the window ledge with such force, his knuckles cracked. One thing was certain, he would do everything that he could to protect Catherine and the boy.

His boy.

At the soft creak of the door he turned, half-expecting to see one of the servants with a tea tray, but it was Catherine.

She gave him a tentative smile as she pushed an errant blonde curl away from her cheek. "Louis is still playing outside," she said in a voice laced with uncharacteristic shyness. "I thought it might be easier to meet him in a less formal setting. If you don't mind. I will warn you, he's a bit mucky from running about with his dog, Pippin. And the gardens are in a frightful state after all the rain we've had. But considering the events of last night, I didn't want Louis to feel ill-at-ease by dressing him up in his best Sunday clothes."

"Of course I don't mind. I think that's an excellent idea." Drawing a deep breath, Adam crossed the room and gave her a reassuring smile in return. "I want him to feel comfortable in my presence, after all."

"Thank you. For your understanding." Again, a look of uncertainty crossed Catherine's features as she took his proffered arm. "I don't know how you're feeling, but I've never been quite so nervous about anything in my life."

Adam squeezed her hand as he escorted her down the hall toward the back of the house and the French doors leading to the terrace. "I will confess that I feel the same way. This is new for me too."

As soon as they stepped onto the flagged terrace and Adam caught sight of the little blond-haired boy gamboling through the overgrown, sodden garden with a lively spaniel puppy at his heels, his breath caught in his chest and an odd lump lodged in his throat.

Louis Fortescue, Lord Rosemont, was a bright ray of sunshine despite the streaks of mud and grass stains on his breeches and stockings.

Clearing his throat, Adam murmured, "He's been breeched already."

"Yes," replied Catherine with pride in her voice. "On his fourth birthday. The twenty-fourth of April."

Adam squeezed her hand which was still tucked into the crook of his arm. "I shan't forget it."

He felt Catherine's gaze touch his face. "I believe you."

The nurse, who'd obviously noted their arrival, had begun to ferry Louis along the gravel path toward the terrace. As the young woman ushered him up the stairs, Catherine stepped away from Adam and held her hand out to her son. "Louis, darling, here's the gentleman I wanted you to meet. Lord Dalton."

The boy regarded him with solemn blue eyes—blue eyes Adam recognized. "How do you do, my lord?" he said before perfectly executing a small courtly bow. "I'm happy to make your acquaintance. Mama says you are an earl, just like me. And that you will soon be wed."

Impressed by Louis's clear speech and quietly confident manner, Adam bowed in return. "Indeed I am, Lord Rosemont. And yes, I am going to marry your mother." He caught Catherine's gaze as he added, "I'm greatly looking forward to our wedding day."

"I am most pleased to hear it, sir." The boy nibbled on his bottom lip for a moment, suddenly unsure before glancing up at Catherine. She smiled reassuringly and gave his narrow shoulder a gentle squeeze.

"And do you remember what you wanted to say next?" she prompted softly.

The young Earl of Rosemont's face brightened. "Oh, yes. Lord Dalton, you may call me Louis. Just as Mama does."

Even though Adam wanted to crouch down to talk to his son at the same eye level, he resisted the urge. The boy was making such an effort to behave in a gentlemanly manner, he felt he should respond in kind. "I should like that, Louis. Very much. And what should you like to call me after your Mama and I are wed?"

Louis traded glances with Catherine again before his blue eyes—as blue as Adam's—returned to his face. "May I call you Papa?"

Adam swallowed as an unexpected surge of emotion tightened his throat. "Of course," he said with an incline of his head. Had Catherine noticed that his voice had grown husky? "In fact, I would love that."

Louis beckoned Catherine closer, and when she leaned

down he whispered loudly, "Mama, he is not so very old. And he looks like the prince in *Cinderella*. Do you think he has a glass slipper in his pocket?"

Catherine bit her lip. She was clearly trying to suppress a smile. "No, he is not so very old. And while I suspect he hasn't any slippers, glass or otherwise on his person, I would venture to add"—she glanced up through her eyelashes at Adam—"just like the prince in *Cinderella*, he is very handsome."

Adam couldn't resist flashing a deliberately rakish grin her way at the compliment. When they'd been lovers, Catherine had often praised his countenance and physique, but he'd never been entirely sure if she'd been sincere. After all, he'd been paying for her "services". But for some reason, he truly believed she meant what she'd just said. And he liked that feeling. That she was genuinely attracted to him.

Straightening, Catherine kept her eyes locked with his. "Perhaps we could go inside for tea and cake. In the front parlor."

Louis clapped and Adam smiled at his youthful exuberance. "That sounds like a capital idea," the boy said.

How wonderful to feel so joyous at the mention of something as simple as cake. Had he been this carefree when he was a child? Adam rather doubted it given his mother had always been—and still was—such a stickler for propriety.

To his surprise, Louis stepped forward and took his hand. "I'll show you the way to the parlor, Lord Dalton." As he enthusiastically tugged him toward the French doors, Adam happily followed, touched by the little boy's eagerness and warmth.

My son.

As Adam watched Louis devour a piece of cinnamon and apple cake with relish, he realized he was grinning like a ninny. Catherine's gaze met his over the top of the boy's golden head —Louis was currently installed between them on a crimson silk sofa—and his smile softened. "You've done a splendid job raising him, Catherine."

A becoming blush suffused her cheeks. "Thank you. But I really can't take all the credit. It's not hard to parent a child who clearly takes after his equally wonderful father."

Now it was Adam who felt his face heat—a flush of pleasure at her unexpected compliment, and something else entirely. A selfish, burning need to kiss her. To make her his again, this beautiful, fierce, passionate woman. But now wasn't the right time or place to give in to his desires. They would be married soon enough.

Which reminded him. He had much to do. A visit to Latimer House to see Maxwell was in order to organize an inquiry agent. Then he would seek an audience with the Archbishop of Canterbury at Doctor's Common to obtain a special license. And then there was the conversation he must have with his mother and sisters...

Adam put down his tea. "I'm afraid the time has come for me to go. But perhaps we could all visit Gunter's Tea Shop for more cake after your Mama and I have wed. So in a day or two. And if the weather permits, we'll also take a ride in my new landau in Hyde Park." He reached out and gently ruffled Louis's blond locks. "Would you like that?"

Louis nodded eagerly. "Yes, sir. Indeed I would."

"Good." Adam smiled. "Then it's all settled."

Catherine accompanied him to the front door. "Thank you for everything you are doing. You've been marvelous with Louis. He's usually quite shy around strangers, but I think he likes you."

"I'm relieved." Adam moved closer to Catherine so the footman hovering nearby wouldn't overhear. "I can't quite explain it, but it seems my heart already holds a warm affection for him, an affection which I suspect will only grow stronger over the coming days. I would love nothing more than to stay longer, but I must make some arrangements. For our wedding. And for your safety, and Louis's. My vow to protect both you and our son is sincere."

Catherine nodded. "I don't doubt it. I know you are a man of your word." Another shy glance. Or was it a look of apprehension? "So we shall see you tomorrow?"

"Of course." Adam pulled on his gloves, wondering where the sexually confident woman he used to know had gone. He'd never seen such a subdued version of Catherine before. But perhaps he was misreading her, and it was simply the case that the terrible events of last night were taking their toll. No doubt she was fatigued, frightened, and fretting about the future. "I would ask you and Louis to stay at Dalton House tonight," he added softly, "however, it might invite too much comment." Which was an understatement. It would create a furor.

Catherine's gaze dropped from his, her long and surprisingly dark lashes shielding her blue-gray eyes. "I understand. Your family will need time to...to adjust."

The thought of how his family would react to the news of their nuptials clearly troubled her. Standing so close to Catherine, he could almost feel the tension radiating from her body. The urge to offer comfort and reassurance was suddenly strong. "But with your permission," he continued, laying a gentle hand on her arm, "I'd like to spend the night here. If you can spare one of the guest bedchambers. I'd rest easier knowing I was close at hand if you needed me."

Catherine's gaze met his again. For one long moment, she searched his eyes, then murmured, "I'd like that. And would you like to dine here as well? That is, if you finish your business in time."

"How could I refuse? I should be back before seven."

"Wonderful." This time, Adam was pleased to see her smile reached her eyes. "I look forward to it."

As he quit the townhouse and descended the stairs to the street, his own smile faded.

He had a fine son. He was going to marry Catherine, a woman he'd long desired.

His mother and sisters would be upset, of that there was no doubt. But all that paled into insignificance when compared to the fact someone in the world meant a little boy —his own flesh and blood—and his mother harm.

Whoever the cur was, he would pay.

CHAPTER 10

Adam was late.

"More wine, my lady?"

Sitting alone in the small, intimate dining room with no one but a footman for company, Catherine sighed then placed her silverware carefully on her now empty dinner plate. "No, thank you, Jackson."

The claret was very good, as the roast beef with mustard sauce and buttered vegetables had been. Catherine had forgotten what an accomplished cook Mrs. Chester was. But she wanted to keep a clear head. For a number of reasons.

First and foremost, she didn't want to be anything less than sober if something untoward happened during the night. Her apprehension had eased somewhat when Adam had sent four of Dalton House's youngest and most strapping footmen to guard all the doors and the gate to the walled garden. Nevertheless, if another fire started or someone tried to break in via a window, she wanted to be alert, not addled by alcohol.

And then of course, she didn't want to be in a tipsy state when Adam did eventually return.

If he returned…

They had much to talk about and impatience gnawed at her. He'd been gone for hours. The only word he'd sent to Russell Square had been about the footmen. Obviously, there might be any number of reasons why Adam had been delayed. He might have had difficulty securing an audience with the Archbishop of Canterbury. Lord Maxwell might have been otherwise engaged and so perhaps he'd had to wait to speak with him about securing the services of a skilled inquiry agent.

Or maybe he'd simply changed his mind about spending the night here.

Or about everything.

Adam was risking so much for her and Louis: his reputation, his relationship with his family, and now even his own safety. It was only natural that he might have had second thoughts.

Lord knows, she did. How would their marriage work? She loved him, but for all his care and consideration, he had never declared his love for her. Carrying out a duty—no matter how noble the cause—didn't equate to love.

Apprehension laced with other emotions knotted Catherine's stomach. She loathed feeling so insecure and uncertain and despondent about the future. Drinking another glass of wine suddenly didn't seem like such an awful idea. She'd only had one, after all. "Actually, maybe just a little more, Jackson," she said, pushing her glass toward the edge of the mahogany dining table. "Then that will be all for this evening."

"Yes, my lady."

Her glass refilled, Catherine retired to the adjacent drawing room. The Rosemont House maids had cleared the dustsheets during the course of the afternoon, and now the comforting scents of beeswax polish, fresh-cut flowers, and wood smoke filled the room.

Claiming her favorite chair by the fireside, Catherine settled against the yellow silk cushions and sipped her wine.

Tomorrow she would visit Rosemont House herself to assess the smoke and water damage firsthand. In the early afternoon, a gentleman from the Phoenix Insurance company had called at Russell Square to discuss the fire and what would need to be done to restore the Park Lane residence. Nearly all of the third-floor furnishings along the gallery, the nursery, and adjacent rooms needed replacing. Louis would need new clothes, and so would she until everything could be laundered. And if any of the servants' belongings had been damaged, they would need to be compensated as well. Clearly, it would take some weeks to set things to rights.

At least she was lucky enough to have somewhere else to stay. But would it be here, or at Dalton House?

Or somewhere else entirely like Adam's country estate in Oxfordshire, St Clair Abbey?

It was torture, not knowing what was going to happen.

The mantel clock marked the time and Catherine yawned. A quarter past nine. Where *was* Adam?

Then a terrifying thought struck her like a lightning bolt from above.

What if something had happened to Adam? Because of her? If someone had been watching the Russell Square townhouse, had they noted Adam's visit? What if... What if that someone thought the Earl of Dalton might prove to be an obstacle and must be removed? What if Adam had been waylaid on the way here?

That would explain why he hadn't sent a message explaining why he would be late.

Catherine's stomach lurched at the thought that right at this very moment, Adam might be lying injured and alone somewhere. Or worse. *Oh, sweet heaven.* She couldn't live with herself if anything happened to the man she loved.

Casting aside her wine, Catherine leapt to her feet. Should she send for the Runners? No. That seemed too drastic. She would send a note to Lord Maxwell. Surely he would have had an idea of Adam's plans for the evening if he'd visited Latimer House earlier in the day.

Catherine paced the Aubusson rug and tried not to let panic engulf her. Logic told her she was probably overreacting. Adam had just been delayed. He had a great deal to organize, he'd said so himself.

But try as she might, the image of the sinister stranger who'd been lurking in the shadows outside Rosemont House kept intruding into her mind. Him, and the words of the noxious note she'd been sent that morning.

Filthy whore.

Dirty little bastard brat.

She couldn't sit still and wait any longer. She needed to do something.

Crossing to a small mahogany table where her writing slope was set up, Catherine took a seat and pulled out a fresh piece of parchment, quill, and ink.

Dear Phillip, she began.

I know the hour is late, but please—

A quiet knock at the door made Catherine jump. Ink splattered across the page.

Was it Adam at last? "Come in," she called, but her heart sank when Kingsley stepped into the room.

"My apologies for disturbing you, my lady, but it appears there's a message for you."

"Is it from Lord Dalton?" During the afternoon, Catherine had informed her staff that she and Lord Dalton were newly engaged and that he was expected for dinner.

"I'm not sure, my lady," replied Kingsley as he approached. His grizzled brows had descended into a deep frown. "Actually, I'm more than a tad concerned it's rather like the message I heard you received this morning. I hope I'm mistaken but..."

When Catherine saw her name written in a messy script across a folded sheet of paper of inferior quality, her heart began to hammer so wildly she could hear the blood pounding in her ears. She couldn't disguise the trembling of her fingers as she took the page from her butler. "I don't think you are. Who delivered this?"

"I don't rightly know, ma'am. One of the new footmen, Fitz, said it had been pushed under the front door."

"I see." Catherine knew she had to crack the wax seal and open the note, but right at this moment, she couldn't bring herself to do it. "And you're certain there's been no word from Lord Dalton?"

Kingsley shook his head. "I'm afraid not, my lady."

Catherine nodded then stared at the note in her hands. Whoever was doing this—making her life hell—deserved to burn for eternity in that fiery pit.

A surge of searing anger shot through her veins and gave her the confidence to slice open the wax seal with her letter opener. When she parted the folded page, she really wished she hadn't.

Your fancy man and all the footmen in the world won't stop me, you fucking bitch. I'm coming for you. You and your dirty by-blow. And I will make your life a misery until you give back what you stole.

Stole? Stole what exactly?

She'd never stolen anything from anyone.

Unless... Unless this message was from one of the Fortescues. Louis *had* inherited an earldom that he wasn't actually entitled to. Not really.

Catherine's hands shook as she placed the note on her writing slope. Indeed, her whole body quaked as ice-cold fear rushed through her, replacing the vengeful fury she'd felt only moments before.

"Are you all right, my lady?"

Catherine looked up to find Kingsley watching her with concerned eyes. "N-No. No, I'm not all right," she said. Good Lord, even her voice trembled. "You were right, Kingsley. It is another threat."

Kingsley's mouth tightened. "Words cannot express how shocked I am, my lady. Shall I ask the staff to check all the doors and windows immediately? I'll also question the night footman again."

"Yes. That would be wonderful. And please check on my son. Then I want Jackson to deliver a message to Lord Maxwell at Latimer House. If you could summon him here to be at the ready? It's most urgent."

Kingsley bowed. "Yes, of course, my lady."

After setting the abusive, hostile missive aside, Catherine picked up her quill and resumed her message to Phillip. She was just signing her name at the bottom of the swiftly thrown together note when the door snicked open again. "I'll only be a moment, Jackson—"

"It's not Jackson."

"Adam!" Catherine flew across the room and threw her arms about his neck before he'd even had a chance to close the door. "Oh, God. I was so worried you wouldn't come. That something terrible had happened to delay you." For a moment she clung to him, breathing in his scent, relishing the feel of his strong arms about her, his hands caressing her back, soothing her. Pulling in a deep breath, she drew back. "But that's not the worst of it. Another horrid note arrived a short time ago. Just like the one from this morning."

"I know." Even as Adam touched her cheek, fire sparked in his blue eyes. "Your butler informed me when I came in. I'm livid. May I see it?"

"Yes." Catherine nodded toward the table where the note lay. "It's over there. Beside my writing slope."

A muscle worked in Adam's lean jaw as he perused the letter. "This is beyond the pale," he grated out as his gaze met hers. "And again, there's that demand... *I will make your life a misery until you give back what you stole.*"

"I wish I knew what that meant, but truly, I don't," said Catherine. There was a catch in her voice. "What have I stolen? The right for Benedict Fortescue to inherit an earldom? I really have no idea what's going on."

"Neither do I. But we'll get to the bottom of it, I promise you." The expression in Adam's eyes softened. "I'm so very sorry I was late, Catherine. That you had to deal with this on your own. But everything took much longer to organize than I'd anticipated, and the time just flew. I should have sent word so you wouldn't worry."

Catherine drew closer. She wanted to take Adam's hand. To press his palm to her cheek, but she wasn't certain how such an overt display of tenderness would be received. Desire and affection were entirely different things and she'd already shown too much of her yearning heart by throwing herself at Adam as soon as he'd walked into the room. So she simply said, "I understand. I suppose, given everything that's happened, my imagination is getting the better of me. Was Phillip able to recommend an inquiry agent?"

"Yes. A fellow by the name of Walsh. I'm going to speak with him tomorrow morning. I hope you don't mind, but he's going to call here at nine o'clock. I think it would help if you spoke with him as well. Especially in light of this." Adam placed the note back on the table. "Whoever is doing this— threatening you and Louis—is both a coward and a low cur."

"I agree. And of course I'll speak with the inquiry agent. I'll do anything to help catch the culprit responsible for these attacks."

Adam's attention returned to the writing slope. Then he frowned. "You really were worried about me," he said, picking up her note to Phillip.

The note in which she'd poured all her worries.

Catherine felt her cheeks grow hot. "Yes. I...I don't want anything to happen to you, especially considering I'm the one who's just turned your life upside down. Yesterday you only wanted a mistress. And now you'll be saddled with a wife and child who are bringing nothing but trouble into your life— "

"Stop." Adam pressed a finger to her lips. "You are not to utter another word along those lines. Or even think it. I wouldn't have offered to marry you if I didn't truly believe it was the right thing to do. And I promise, as your husband and as Louis's father, I'll do whatever it takes to make this madness stop. I don't want anything to happen to you, or to Louis, either."

Adam seemed like he was about to say something else, but at that very moment, Kingsley arrived to report the house was secure and his lordship was sleeping soundly in the makeshift nursery upstairs.

After Catherine thanked him, the butler addressed Adam. "Lord Dalton, is there anything you require? I apologize for not asking on your arrival."

"That's quite all right," replied Adam. "Taking caring of your mistress's and his young lordship's safety is paramount, after all."

"Adam, you missed dinner," remarked Catherine. "Would you like anything now? Mrs. Chester can put together a tray."

He shook his head. "Helena provided a substantial late luncheon," he said, placing a hand over the navy satin waistcoat which hugged his trim but muscular torso. "I fear I shan't need to eat for a week."

Kingsley bowed. "Very good, my lord." Turning to

Catherine, he continued, "The guest room has been made ready as you requested, my lady."

To the man's credit, he hadn't batted an eyelid at the idea that her fiancé was staying the night. Catherine was grateful for his open-mindedness. "Thank you, Kingsley," she said, "for all you've done. That will be all for now."

"Yes, my lady."

After her butler had closed the door, Catherine drew a fortifying breath. There was one more subject she needed to broach with Adam before she retired for the evening. "In all the fuss created by the arrival of that horrible note, I haven't yet asked whether you were able to speak with the Archbishop of Canterbury."

"God, yes. Sorry." Adam patted his breast pocket. "I have the special license right here. We can wed tomorrow if you like. Or the following day. Perhaps at St. George's in Hanover Square. Or here, or even at Maxwell House. Phillip and Helena are more than happy to act as witnesses." His expression grew grave. "For my own peace of mind though, I would rather it was tomorrow. But it's really up to you."

Catherine's heart did an odd somersault. At long last, she would become Lady Dalton. Adam's wife. Such a momentous thing still didn't seem real.

The circumstances were certainly far from ideal.

It is the right thing to do, Adam had said. At this very moment, Catherine wanted to curse his damnable sense of duty. Her heart yearned for him to acknowledge he possessed feelings for her beyond lust and a modicum of affection.

How ironic. She was about to wed the man she loved. But he didn't love her. If he did, surely he would have told her by now.

His consistent avoidance of those three little words—*I love you*—spoke volumes.

Tamping down the disappointment suddenly welling

inside her chest, Catherine somehow pasted a smile on her face. "I don't mind where the ceremony is held. But I agree we should marry tomorrow. Perhaps in the late afternoon? You have arranged to meet the inquiry agent in the morning. And due to the fire, there are urgent matters I need to attend to at Rosemont House."

"Tomorrow afternoon it is." Holding her gaze, Adam lifted her hand and glanced a whisper-soft kiss across her fingers.

Despite her misgivings and fears, Catherine shivered at the contact of his lips upon her skin. A warm wave of desire washed through her and her cheeks grew hot.

The guest room was directly across the hall from her bedchamber, and she'd already dismissed her lady's maid, Hetty, for the evening.

Would Adam really stay in his room all night? His deep desire for her had been evident the night before at Latimer House. When he'd been pressed against her, plying her with intoxicating kisses, he hadn't been able to hide his arousal.

She certainly couldn't deny her own desire. She'd been celibate for five long years, and the ache of unfulfilled lust was almost too much to bear. Her pulse racing, her mouth dry, Catherine swallowed. "If there's nothing else to discuss," she murmured in a noticeably husky voice, "I suppose I should check on Louis and then retire for the night. If you don't wish to retire just yet, well, I know you'll be able to find your room. It's the one directly opposite mine."

A flash of uncertainty crossed Adam's face. "Would... would it be all right if I accompanied you upstairs? To see Louis?"

Surprise sparked inside Catherine, followed by a rush of unexpected happiness. "Why yes," she said, her smile genuine this time. "Of course you can. He'll be asleep though."

Adam frowned. "I hope my intrusion won't wake him."

"Don't be silly. It's not an intrusion. He's your son." Threading her fingers through Adam's, she led him upstairs to the makeshift nursery but then paused outside the door. "Even though Louis sleeps soundly, just let me warn his nurse that you are coming in. Her pallet is in the adjoining dressing room. After everything that's happened lately, she might be alarmed at the unexpected sight of a man entering her young charge's room."

Adam nodded. "I certainly don't want to scare anyone."

Catherine squeezed his hand before letting it go. "You won't."

In less than a minute she returned to usher Adam inside. "Louis's dog Pippin sleeps at the foot of his bed. Don't worry," she whispered, quietly closing the door behind him, "as he's already met you, he won't bark or bite. Although he might attempt a sly lick or two."

"Well, I won't hold that against him," murmured Adam, curling his fingers around hers, drawing her against his side. "I've been known to indulge in a bit of sly licking when the occasion calls for it."

Cheeky man. Catherine's lips quivered with mirth. Now this was the Adam she knew and loved—the playful, wicked rake, not the serious nobleman who was all buttoned up and constricted by responsibility. Looking up through her lashes, she cast him a coquettish smile. "I haven't forgotten."

Adam's breath was a warm caress against her ear as he leaned in and whispered, "Neither have I."

Oh my. Catherine's heart began to beat double-time. Thank goodness they were in Louis's room right now or she might be tempted to take things beyond flirting. She suspected Adam might too. Firmly pushing all thoughts of lovemaking aside, she murmured, "Come," then gently tugged him toward the curtained four-poster bed. "Let's say goodnight to our boy."

Drawing back the pale blue and gold damask drapery, she revealed the bed and its small occupant. Louis was curled up on his side, cheeks flushed in sleep, one little fist pressed against his chin. Pippin lifted his head, blinked twice and yawned, then snuggled back into the disheveled covers near the footboard.

Catherine stole a glance at Adam.

The expression in his eyes was soft as he gazed upon his son. "I still can't quite believe I'm a father. Yet I know... No, that's not right." Adam shook his head then placed his fist upon his chest. "I can *feel* that he's mine. In here. As though there were an empty space—a hollow—inside me that has suddenly been filled." His mouth lifted in a wry smile as his eyes met Catherine's again. "That probably sounds odd to you. I can't explain it any other way."

"It's not odd at all and it warms my heart to hear you say it. For so long, I've been worried about how you would react to the news that Louis is yours. I should have known you would welcome him with open arms."

Adam frowned. "I won't lie...not everyone in my family will be quite so...accepting."

"I know that. But your opinion is the only one that counts. We'll weather the storm together. And keep Louis safe." Dear Lord, Catherine hoped with all her heart that would prove true.

"Yes." Adam reached for her hand again and squeezed it. "We will."

Bending down, Catherine adjusted the covers then placed a gentle kiss on Louis's forehead. After she drew the bed's curtains closed, she then led Adam from the room.

Her bedchamber was next door. Adam's opposite.

The corridor was dimly lit by a lamp on an occasional table in a nearby alcove. In the muted light, she read uncertainty in Adam's face. It was a mood which matched her own.

Adam's fingers stayed intertwined with hers as she paused in the middle of the hall. There wasn't a servant to be seen. The townhouse and the square outside were still and quiet. Indeed, the very night was hushed and expectant as though holding its breath, just as she was.

"I suppose I should bid you goodnight once more. It's been a very long day."

"Yes... Yes, it has, Lady Rosemont." Adam lifted her hand to his lips and bestowed a gentlemanly kiss. "But I'm very much looking forward to tomorrow when you will become my wife, and the world shall know you as Catherine, Lady Dalton."

Did he speak the truth? Did he truly look forward to their union? Catherine had no idea. She wanted to ask him what would happen after they were wed. Where would they stay? Here or at Dalton House, or at St Clair Abbey? Would his mother and sisters still be in residence? Had he already told them what was going to happen? And how had they reacted to the news?

The questions tumbled about in her mind, demanding attention, but now didn't seem like the right time to ask any of them. Not when her hand still lay in Adam's and he was running his thumb back and forth, back and forth along her knuckles. The teasing graze sent a shiver across her skin and up her arm. Made her pulse quicken.

"I'm looking forward to becoming your wife too," she managed to say, her voice no more than a breathless murmur. "Very much."

Should she invite Adam into her room? She couldn't deny she wanted him. *Ached* for him. But even though she'd never been shy about initiating sexual encounters in the past, she hesitated now. It might be illogical, but she *needed* him to show her that he wanted her, too. That he didn't resent her because he felt obligated to marry her.

Sliding her hand from his, she moved away, and to her secret delight Adam followed. He placed an arm along the doorframe and leaned in close behind her, his body pressed to her back as her fingers closed around the brass door handle.

His lips skimmed along the curve of her ear. "I want you to know that even though we went our separate ways, I never stopped thinking about you, Catherine." A gentle tug on her earlobe with his teeth. "Just as I never stopped wanting you."

Catherine's chest tightened with longing. "Neither did I. But perhaps we should wait until tomorrow night..." She knew she wasn't being fair by playing games, testing him to see whether he would press his suit. But it felt oh, so lovely to be pursued like this.

Adam's fingers brushed along her nape, raising gooseflesh, making her tremble. His warm breath stirred the flyaway curls at her temple. "Yes...we should," he murmured, but he didn't move away.

His hand which rested on the door by Catherine's head curled into a fist. Even through his clothes, she felt his muscles tense. The press of his hardening manhood against the soft swell of her buttocks.

Last night she'd denied herself, and Adam, the pleasure they both hungered for. She couldn't do it again. She wasn't strong enough. Not when they were about to be wed.

Not when she loved him.

He might not love her in return, but at least she could satisfy her body's incessant craving. And his.

Decision made, Catherine unlatched the door. When she looked over her shoulder, the fire and candlelight escaping from the room illuminated Adam's handsome face. His blue eyes burned with such intensity, Catherine's breath caught. "I've changed my mind," she whispered. "There's no real reason to wait."

When Adam groaned, "Thank God," her heart leapt.

As soon as they crossed the threshold he reached for her, then pushed her up against the now closed door. Panting, his hands at her throat, his thumbs roughly caressed her jaw before prizing her lips apart. And then his mouth crashed down upon hers. It was a hot, mindless, ravaging kiss. A kiss that felt like an act of possession, and Catherine welcomed everything about it. The velvet thrust of Adam's tongue. The sting of his teeth as he nipped and sucked on her lower lip. The way his light night beard abraded her skin. The tight grip of his fist in her hair and how he forced his leg between hers so that she had no choice but to straddle him. There would be no tenderness in this coupling. It would be fast and furious. Catherine didn't want it any other way.

She returned every one of Adam's frenzied, abandoned kisses with a wildness that matched his. Moaning, she clutched at Adam's wide shoulders and rode his strong thigh in an attempt to assuage the unrelenting throb of desire in her sex. Perhaps sensing her desperation, Adam yanked up her skirts and petticoats and lifted her leg, exposing her drenched folds. As she wrapped her leg about his hip, he slid a hand between their bodies and found her clitoris. His fingertips expertly teased the swollen nub, making her gasp and pant, and she shamelessly rolled her hips like a concubine dancing for her master. When Adam thrust two fingers between her nether lips and entered her, pumping furiously, her desire flared brighter and hotter, her desperation to come-off threatening to consume her.

"Take me, Adam," she pleaded, fumbling at the fall front of his trousers. "Please, I have to have you inside me. Now."

"God yes." Within moments, Adam had freed his cock. Wrapping her fingers about the thick, rock-hard shaft, Catherine helped him to guide the weeping head to her slick entrance. And then with one unerring, powerful thrust of his hips, he buried his entire length deep inside her body.

Oh, sweet Lord. Catherine bit down on Adam's shoulder to stop a cry escaping. She was pinned against the oak door by a hard wall of muscle, crammed full of rigid, pulsating cock, and everything about it felt so, so good. Wantonly good. Her memories of Adam's sexual prowess just didn't compare to the actual, overwhelming reality of him. The agony was so exquisite, it bordered on ecstasy, especially when Adam began to pump in and out of her, pounding frantically. Ruthlessly.

Catherine's head began to spin. She had no time to catch her breath, no time to adjust to Adam's enormous size or the breakneck pace he set. All she could do was close her eyes and wrap her arms about him as he drove her closer and closer to the edge. The door rattled in its frame each time Adam hammered into her, her rhythmic gasps and Adam's groans loud in the night. But she didn't care if anyone heard. Not when blissful oblivion was fast approaching—

"Oh, fuck. Oh, God. I'm so sorry... I can't... I have to—" Adam's whole body tensed and then he shuddered and jerked violently, engulfed by his own release. He sagged against her, his cock pulsing inside her, his ragged breath hot against her neck, and Catherine tried not to feel disappointed she hadn't achieved climax too.

Even though her blood began to cool, her body vibrated with tension and the throbbing ache of unfulfilled desire. She stroked his heaving back and ran her fingers through his thick hair, enjoying these intimate moments when she could pretend that his heart was truly hers too.

That it wasn't just fucking.

"My darling Catherine." Adam raised his head and captured her face with gentle fingers so she couldn't look away from his searching gaze. "You didn't come, did you?"

"No." Catherine made herself smile. "But it's all right. I've missed you so much that just being with you, even like this, is more than enough for me."

"Well, it's not enough for me." Adam's voice was laced with gruffness as he withdrew from her body and pushed his spent manhood back into his trousers. He retrieved a silk handkerchief from his coat pocket and offered it to her. "You deserve so much more than a quick, rough fuck up against a door."

Catherine rejected the handkerchief with a wave of her hand and crossed the room, heading for the washstand which stood beside a cherrywood screen featuring peony-patterned silk. "What, have you already forgotten that I quite enjoy a quick, rough fuck?" she quipped, trying to make light of the situation as she poured water from a fine china jug into a basin.

"But you didn't enjoy it this time." Adam followed her then wiped his hands on the washcloth she offered. "Not completely. And it's all my fault." He sighed and tossed the cloth beside the basin. "I'm sorry for being such a self-absorbed ass," he said gently, covering one of her hands with his. "I...I was overcome with the need to have you and I lost control. It's just been so long. Of course, that's no excuse, but that's all I have."

"You don't need to apologize. I understand. I was over-whelmed with want, too. Over five years is a long time to wait to have sexual inter—" Catherine bit her lip to stop herself saying anymore, but it was too late.

"Wait..." The frown creasing Adam's brow deepened. "It's been over five years since you last...? Are you... Are you seriously telling me that you and Rosemont never actually...? When was the last time you had sexual congress before this occasion, Catherine? Was...was it with me? Just before we... before *I* ended things?"

Catherine swirled a cake of jasmine-scented soap in the water. She didn't want to answer, but there didn't seem any point in lying when the cat was out of the bag. "I'm afraid it was," she said quietly as she submerged another clean washcloth in the delicately scented, soapy water. "I've been celibate ever since we parted ways. Edward and I, we never consummated our union. Even though he never admitted it, I always suspected ill health prevented him from..." She shrugged a shoulder. "Well, you know."

"Christ, Catherine. And I just took you like that? Without care, like a raging, rutting beast?" Adam ran a shaking hand through his already tousled hair. "Please don't tell me I hurt you? Because if I did—"

"No, of course you didn't." Catherine wrung out the cloth then slipped behind the screen to wash herself. "Truly, I would have told you to stop if I hadn't wanted you to take me like that."

Silence. Catherine imagined Adam was quietly fuming. Not only was his male pride piqued, he was rattled. The idea of physically harming a woman was clearly anathema to him. Though he may not know it, it only made her love him all the more.

When she emerged from the screen a minute later, Adam's brow was furrowed...and he was holding his old greatcoat. The one Catherine had worn last night because she'd been feeling foolishly sentimental. It had been draped over the arm of a chair by the fire; Hetty had evidently forgotten to put it away.

Damn and blast and merde.

Glancing up, Adam's gaze met hers across the room. "You still have my old coat."

Double merde. He'd recognized it. Catherine's cheeks heated but she affected a nonchalant shrug. "I-I grabbed it last night when I was fleeing Rosemont House. It was raining and...it seemed like a practical garment to wear. To keep Louis warm."

"I see..." Seemingly satisfied with her flimsier than a chemise explanation, Adam tossed the coat back onto the chair. In a few strides, he was at her side and catching her about the waist, drawing her close. "Let me take you to bed. My performance before was abysmal and I want to make it up to you ." He brushed a kiss across her cheek. "We have all night."

Catherine shook her head and touched his face. "You can, but not now. Tomorrow. Even though Louis sleeps well—and I know he's exhausted—if he needs me in the night, I don't want anyone to discover us in bed together. It may sound hypocritical considering what we just did—and what I used to do for a living—but maintaining at least an appearance of propriety is important to me, for his sake."

Adam's sigh matched his disgruntled expression. "Very well, Catherine. But"—he trapped her gaze—"there'll be no naysaying me on our wedding night. Prepare to be pleasured like you never have before. Do I make myself clear?"

Speechless with longing, all Catherine could do was nod.

"Good." Adam slipped a hand behind her head and then dropped a kiss on her forehead. "Goodnight, *ma belle*. I hope you're able to get some sleep. And if you need anything at all in the night, do not hesitate to call on me. I'm here for you."

And with that, he quit the room.

I'm here for you...

Catherine released a disconsolate sigh as she began to loosen the fastenings of her gown. *Yes, you're here, Adam, because you feel obligated to take care of me and Louis.*

Not because you love me.

For now though, it would have to be enough.

CHAPTER 11

53 Russell Square, London
20th October, 1816

Fire in Park Lane Residence, Mayfair!

*In the early hours of yesterday morning, there was a
near disaster at Rosemont House on Park Lane—the
residence of the Earl of Rosemont—when a fire broke
out on the third floor. However, by all accounts, the
conflagration was successfully extinguished within less
than an hour, thanks to the brave actions of the Phoenix
Insurance Company's fire brigade. A representative of
the Insurance Company would not comment on how the
fire started at the exclusive Mayfair address, but it is
believed investigations are continuing. No injuries have
been reported, but according to witnesses at the scene,
the very young Lord Rosemont and his widowed mother
(the erstwhile Covent Garden actress, née Catherine
Delacourt) were driven onto the street along with the
townhouse's other occupants...*

C atherine cast the broadsheet onto the table with a scowl and picked up her cooling cup of tea. She'd been half-expecting there to be a story about the fire in at least one of London's newspapers this morning. But it irked her no end that they'd mentioned Louis by name, then slighted her in the very same sentence. It wasn't fair on her little boy. No, not at all.

What would the papers say about her tomorrow when the *ton* learned she'd wed Adam St Clair, the Earl of Dalton? That his second wife was a most unsuitable choice for a countess. *His* name would be smeared with muck this time. And that of his mother and two sisters.

Catherine shivered and replenished her Spode china cup with fresh tea from the pot. Better not to think about that furor for now. She could only deal with one crisis at a time.

Picking up her cup, she wandered over to the morning room window and studied the view below. The day was cold, blustery, and rainy. Dark, bruise-like clouds hovered over the square and rainy squalls bullied the fallen leaves, chasing them down the street and across the sodden park in the middle of Russell Square.

She thanked the Lord above that no more sinister notes had been delivered during the night. As far as she could see, there were no strange men lurking outside, watching her townhouse.

According to the gilt mantel clock it was only eight o'clock, but Catherine had risen, dressed, and breakfasted early because the new inquiry agent Adam had hired would be arriving at nine. Louis was still fast asleep, and she was just beginning to wonder if Adam was too when the morning room door snicked open and he entered.

And just like he always did, he took her breath away.

"Good morning, Catherine," he offered as he approached.

His smile was warm with appreciation as his blue gaze swept over her. "You look very well."

"Thank you," she replied, pleased she'd taken trouble with her appearance this morning. Her day gown of periwinkle blue velvet enhanced the color of her eyes. Or so she liked to think. "So do you." From the top of his artfully ruffled light-brown locks to the tips of his shiny black Hessians, Adam was the epitome of masculine sartorial elegance.

"Would you like to take breakfast?" she continued. "I can ring for fresh tea or coffee. And Mrs. Chester is happy to cook whatever you would like. She assures me she still remembers your favorite dishes. I know you always liked something substantial after...well. You know."

Adam's smile widened to a grin as he took up a position on the other side of the window. "Thank you. But I've already crossed paths with your butler this morning and breakfast is on its way."

"Wonderful." Catherine was suddenly assailed with a wave of self-consciousness as Adam continued to study her face. Her cheeks grew warm, and she turned her attention to the rainy aspect outside.

How odd that she'd begun to behave like a silly young girl around him. She didn't like feeling so vulnerable. She certainly didn't want him to work out that she was deeply, irrevocably in love with him. It would be too humiliating and painful, considering he didn't feel the same way. If anything, he might pity her, and she rather thought there could be nothing worse than that.

"Did you sleep well?" he asked softly.

"Well enough," she lied. She'd tossed and turned for hours in fact, listening for strange sounds in the night while also weighing up the fors and againsts of stealing into Adam's bed. "It helps having you here. It means a great deal to me." That much was true.

He nodded. "Thank you. But there really is no place I'd rather be."

Catherine really hoped *that* pronouncement wasn't a lie. "Have you... Have you decided where we shall wed today?" she asked, hating that she sounded so hesitant.

"Yes. At Dalton House." Adam's expression was grave as he added, "After our meeting with the inquiry agent, I'll return there to make sure everything is ready for you and Louis."

Which really meant he was returning to make sure his mother and sisters had vacated the premises before his socially unacceptable bride arrived with her by-blow of a child.

Catherine nodded. "That sounds perfect." She made herself smile, praying that it didn't look too forced. "And I take it we will spend the night there?"

"Yes... Catherine." Adam drew closer. He lightly captured her elbow. "I've been thinking about what you disclosed last night. That you've been celibate since we parted ways. I never imagined that... Well, it still bothers me immensely that I was so demanding and thoughtless. So rough and inconsiderate."

"I won't break, Adam." Her smile slipped a fraction. While she was touched by his concern, she was also oddly disgruntled. "And it's really not your fault. After all, it's only natural that you would assume that someone like me—a former courtesan—would continue to have sexual congress. That I wouldn't abstain."

A deep frown furrowed his brow. "I really wish you would stop bringing that up, Catherine. I don't like it when—"

"When I keep reminding you that I was a harlot?" Catherine stiffened. "I hate to say it, Adam, but I'm not the only one who will bring it up. Society will never let me forget it." She gestured toward the discarded newspaper on the table. "*The Morning Chronicle*, which contains an article about the fire at Rosemont House, also decided to report I was once an actress. And of course, everyone knows the term is little more than a euphemism for prostitute. I doubt your family will let you forget it either. The stain associated with my name will spread to yours and all those you care about. And it can never be washed away. Are you truly ready for that?"

Adam's jaw tightened as though he were about to do battle. "Yes. I am."

She sighed then. "I hope so, Adam. The last thing I want is for you to—"

Resent me. The words died on her lips when the door burst open, and Louis came racing in with Pippin at his heels.

"Mama," he cried and gave her an exuberant hug about the legs. Lizzy, following in his wake, blushed as red as a beet when she saw Adam was in the room. No doubt she suspected that her mistress and the Earl of Dalton had indulged in a spot of pre-marital sexual congress during the night. Which of course, they had.

Although the good opinion—or not—of her son's nurserymaid mattered little to Catherine at this point in time. Not when there were so many other critical issues to deal with.

If only the opinion of Adam's family and the rest of Society didn't matter either.

The oak longcase clock in the library of Dalton House was chiming eleven o'clock when Adam decided to pour himself a glass of cognac. He rather feared he was becoming too reliant on alcohol to get him through the day. But these were unusually turbulent times and God help him, he needed something to help gird his loins. To help weather the almighty storm that would erupt when he told his mother that she needed to quit Dalton House within the next few hours because his new bride and her son were moving in.

My son, Adam reminded himself. One day he would tell his mother the truth about Louis. But not today. She would have enough to come to terms with, and that went for Cordelia and Viola as well. No doubt there'd be tears and histrionics.

Christ. Adam poured another measure of cognac into the crystal tumbler then downed the whole lot in one large swallow. If he weren't due to get married at three o'clock this afternoon, he'd probably drink the whole fucking decanter. His mouth twisted with an ironic smile. Then again, if he *weren't* getting married, he wouldn't need to.

Bloody hell. His life was about to become exceedingly complicated. He just prayed that the inquiry agent he and Catherine had met with that morning—a chap named Walsh —could uncover something remotely useful about these attacks aimed at little Louis and Catherine. The most obvious suspects—the ones who stood to gain the most if anything truly terrible befell Louis—were Benedict and Lilith Fortescue and ultimately, their son, Gerald. But Catherine didn't have any direct evidence implicating them in the series of "accidents" that had occurred since the New Year.

But after the fire at Rosemont House and the two notes threatening both Catherine and Louis, at least there were a few more leads to chase up. Adam had directed the inquiry agent to watch the Fortescues like a hawk over the coming weeks and days. Mr. Walsh had also asked Catherine if she could think of anyone else at all who might wish her or Louis ill, but no other suspects had sprung to mind.

It was all so damnably frustrating. So much so, Adam felt that his insides were tied into a thousand knots. Although, as he sipped a third nip of the strong alcohol, the tension inside him seemed to be loosening a fraction.

His thoughts returned to last night—to his encounter with Catherine in her bedroom. He still deeply regretted that he had not acquitted himself well. The fact he'd failed to give her the pleasure she so deserved twisted his guts with mortification. He'd been such an insensitive brute. And to think she hadn't had sex with anyone else at all for five long years...

He really didn't know what to make of that. Or the fact she'd kept his old greatcoat all this time. The one he'd given her in Newgate Prison. When she'd been his mistress, he'd given her so many material things of great value. A townhouse. Jewels. He'd also given her—unbeknownst to him of course—the most precious gift of all, a son. Yet she'd hung onto that old coat too... It might mean something significant, or nothing at all...

Adam sipped his drink. Perhaps she'd just forgotten to throw it away. Or it had become mixed up with some of her late husband's clothes...

When there came a knock at the library door, Adam found himself stiffening.

"Come in." He rose from his chair behind the oak desk that was once his father's and tried not to grimace when his mother and sisters entered.

"Parker relayed your message that you wanted to see us," his mother began, and her thin brows snapped together when she saw the cut crystal decanter and his tumbler of cognac on the desk's leather blotter. "Far be it from me to tell you what to do, Adam, but I really don't think you're setting a good example for your sisters."

Adam tilted into a bow. "My apologies, Cordelia, Viola"—his fair-haired sisters inclined their heads in acknowledgment before he added—"Mother... But I hope you can forgive me because I'm celebrating." That was a lie of course, but it seemed as good an excuse as any to give. And it had the added benefit of directing this conversation straight toward the contentious subject he needed to broach.

His mother arched a brow. "Celebrating what, may I ask?"

Adam gestured toward the arrangement of chairs at the fireside. "Why don't we all take a seat?" he suggested.

His mother gave a haughty sniff. "Very well. But it rather sounds like you are about to deliver bad news, Adam, not good."

Adam couldn't shield his grimace. *You will certainly think so, Mama dearest.*

He waited until his sisters and mother had chosen seats and then he flipped out his coattails and claimed the brown leather wingback chair—it too had once belonged to his father.

When his mother had finished smoothing her purple silk skirts to her satisfaction, she pinned him with a suspicious, narrow-eyed stare. "I'm not sure if I should be excited or petrified," she said.

Horrified probably. And livid. Adam only just suppressed the urge to utter the words aloud. Guilt pinched as he took in Cordelia and Viola's hesitant expressions. Unlike their mother, they were sweet, good-natured girls, always ready to please. Adam had long suspected it was simply to keep the peace. Indeed, he too tended to accede to the dowager countess's wishes. She could be a veritable tyrant if she didn't get her own way. For the most part, it made life easier just to give in.

Not for the first time, Adam wondered if that's why his father had ultimately strayed. It would be difficult to preserve an abiding affection for such a demanding, prickly pear of a woman once the first flush of romantic love had faded. Indeed, it was hard for Adam to imagine that his parents had ever had a romantic attachment.

Viola, recently turned seventeen, offered him a nervous smile. "I agree with, Mama. You are being far too cryptic for my liking, Adam," she said. Her fine brows dipped into a worried frown. "Has this got something to do with my debut next year? I had hoped we might discuss it soon. Plans will need to be made."

"Yes," agreed the dowager countess. "Viola will need a whole new wardrobe. And Cordelia and I will too."

Clearing his throat, Adam marshaled his courage to say what needed to be said. "In a way it does, Viola. Actually"—he caught his other sister's eye too—"my news will no doubt affect your Season the following year as well, Cordelia."

Cordelia's light blue eyes grew round with worry. "Oh... Oh, I don't know if I like the sound of that, dear brother."

"Yes, neither do I." His mother's tone was cool. "Please get to the point, Adam. I don't have all day."

Adam forced himself to draw a calming breath even as apprehension gripped his lungs. Meeting his mother's gaze directly, he spoke in as calm a voice as he could manage. "This afternoon I am marrying Catherine Fortescue, Lady Rosemont."

The dowager countess froze as though she'd been struck while his sisters gasped.

"What did you just say?" His mother's words seemed to be forced through stiff, bloodless lips. Her gray eyes were colder than arctic ice.

"Lady Rosemont?" Viola's voice was equal parts hushed and horrified. "Do you mean the...the countess who everyone says was an actress, but she was really a—" His sister turned as red as the silk upholstered settee upon which she sat. "I can't say it," she whispered.

Cordelia frowned at Viola then at Adam. "Can't say what? I don't understand. What's wrong with Lady Rosemont?"

"*Everything* is wrong with Lady Rosemont." His mother's voice quivered with fury and her cheekbones were flagged with high color as she shot to her feet. "I forbid it, Adam. I forbid it."

Adam rose too. "That won't do you any good, Mother. I won't be swayed."

"But, Adam," began Viola in that same shocked tone, "what will people say?" Her bottom lip wobbled ominously. "Who will want to marry me if my sister-in-law used to be a...a ladybird? I'll be mocked, shunned. Locked out of every ballroom and drawing room in Town and indeed, probably throughout the entire country! You wouldn't!"

"A ladybird?" gasped Cordelia. "You mean a har—"

"Enough," snapped their mother. Turning to aim her heated glare at Adam, she continued, "How dare you do such a thing to this family? It will socially ruin us. It's taken years and years to recover from the scandal your selfish father plunged us into—" She broke off and drew a shuddering breath. "I won't let you drag our family's good name through the mud all over again."

"Mother, I know this will be difficult," Adam said and crossed his arms, bracing for the storm of tears and tantrums gathering around him.

"Why would you do this? To me? To us?" demanded Viola, leaping to her feet. Her eyes glittered with angry tears.

"Yes, why Adam?" repeated Cordelia.

He knew they would ask this question and there was no easy answer to give that they would readily accept. So he simply said, "It's a complicated matter."

"Complicated?" His mother's cutting tone could have sliced flesh from bone. "What's so very complicated about you wanting to bed—"

"Enough, Mother," growled Adam.

"I mean, why can't you just hire a dox—"

"I said enough." The angry lash of Adam's voice made his sisters jump.

His mother blanched and took a step backward. "There's

no need to shout, Adam," the dowager countess said with a sniff and an obstinate hitch of her chin.

Adam attempted to moderate his tone. "And there's no need to insult the woman who will be my wife."

His mother clasped her hands in front of her slender waist. It was a gesture that was somehow both prim and defiant at the same time. "You're really set upon this insane course, aren't you?"

Adam ignored her question. "The ceremony will take place here at three o'clock. The minister from St. George's will officiate and Lord and Lady Maxwell have offered to act as witnesses. Afterward, there will be a small wedding breakfast. You are all"—he caught the gazes of his sisters and then his mother in turn—"very welcome to attend."

"Don't be ridiculous," snapped the dowager countess. "I won't be a party to this...nonsense. This vile union."

"I'm sorry you feel that way. I take it that all of you will be quitting Dalton House then?"

His mother's mouth flattened. "You've given us no choice. We cannot live beneath the same roof with a woman like... Wait." Her eyes narrowed. "Doesn't the Courtesan Countess have a young son? Is that woman's baseborn child coming here too?"

Adam bristled at the slight to his son. "I'll ask you not to impugn the name of my fiancée's child, Mother. And he was born *within* wedlock. But yes, Louis, Lord Rosemont, is but four years old, so of course he will live here."

His mother shuddered with apparent revulsion. "You're destroying this family, Adam. I will *never* forgive you for this."

"Me either," said Viola with a mutinous thrust of her chin. "I can't believe you would be so cruel and selfish, Adam. My life will be ruined because of you."

"Come, girls." Brisk steps carried the dowager countess across the library floor to the door, and Viola and Cordelia obediently followed. "We must pack and leave at once." She caught Adam's eye. "I trust that you won't turn us out of St Clair Abbey just yet? It will take some weeks to have the dower house opened and made fit to live in. It's almost as derelict as the old abbey ruins themselves."

"I'm not turning any of you out, Mother," returned Adam, exhaustion weighting his words. "And while the dower house has been neglected for some time, it is *not* a crumbling ruin. But you can refurbish it as you see fit. As I keep saying, you are all welcome to stay."

The dowager countess's lip curled. "I always feared you would turn out just like your reckless, foolish, self-centered father, Adam. And it seems I was right."

When the door slammed shut behind his mother and sisters, Adam threw himself back into his chair and closed his eyes. Gripped the bridge of his nose.

Christ. He hated it when his mother spoke uncomfortable truths. For years—ever since he'd met Catherine—he'd struggled to be the exact opposite of what his father had been. To be a better man. To choose his family and not Catherine, the woman he wanted beyond all reason. But circumstances outside of Adam's control meant that he'd been forced to take Catherine's side. They shared a son.

Louis. A precious, innocent little boy.

Adam might be more than a little bit like his father—just like he'd always feared—but he was truly caught on the horns of a dilemma. Right now, doing the "right thing" by Catherine and Louis meant doing the "wrong thing" in the eyes of polite society.

Well, polite society could go hang.

Adam might be a fool, but at least he was an honorable one. He would do all he could to protect Catherine and their son. He just prayed that it would be enough.

CHAPTER 12

Dalton House, Grosvenor Square
Later that afternoon...

"You look beautiful, my dear, there's no need to be nervous," declared Helena, Lady Maxwell as she fiddled with the sit of Catherine's puffed sleeves. Her brown eyes were warm as she met Catherine's gaze in the gilt-framed looking-glass in her new bedchamber at Dalton House. "If Adam doesn't swoon the minute you walk into the room, there must be something wrong with him. Indeed, I would even go so far as to say he's either losing his sight or going mad."

Catherine laughed. "You always make me feel so much better, Helena."

She *did* feel quite elegant. Not only was her blonde hair arranged into a stylish pile of curls studded with seed pearls, but she'd donned a relatively new silk gown for the occasion. Helena's Bond Street modiste had described the becoming dusky blue shade as "lavender-in-the-mist" when Catherine had chosen the fabric at the beginning of the year—on the very same day she'd glimpsed Adam and Sybil entering Hatchards, in fact. She barely suppressed a shiver at the thought that poor Sybil had passed away not long after that.

Would her own life be cut short too? And her darling Louis's? Dear heaven above, as Adam's new wife, she prayed they would be safe. Now more than ever she was convinced she'd done the right thing in seeking Adam's help.

Helena gave her arm a gentle squeeze. "Where did you go just then, my friend?"

"Oh..." Catherine's cheeks took on a rosy hue. "I was... I was thinking about how grateful I am to Adam. He's doing so much for Louis and me." Like risking his relationship with his mother and younger sisters. Catherine hadn't failed to notice that the dowager countess and her daughters had vacated the townhouse. No doubt Adam had had a difficult morning.

"*He* is the lucky one, Catherine," Helena said with a soft smile.

Catherine turned around and embraced her friend. "I can't thank you enough for being here today. You and Phillip. You've always been so kind to me." Drawing back a little, she added huskily, "To think that you are willing to put up with all of the scandal associated with my name means a lot. More than I can say in fact."

Helena waved a dismissive hand. "Pfft. Phillip and I are no strangers to scandal ourselves. Why, my brother James, the Marquess of Rothsburgh, is cloaked in scandal given the notoriety of his first wife, Isabelle. There's certainly been no end to the gossip surrounding his lovely new wife, Elizabeth. So don't you fret about our reputation. I don't give a flying fig about being the subject of the *ton's* latest *on-dits*. I know my true friends."

Catherine had to clear her throat to speak. "Thank you, Helena. From the bottom of my heart. Your reassurance and support are valued indeed."

Helena's smile was watery too as she said, "It's the least I can do. Now..." She moved across the plush Aubusson carpet and picked up two glasses of champagne from a nearby satinwood occasional table. "Let's have a celebratory tipple. Because I'm absolutely certain Adam and Phillip are drinking cognac as we speak."

～

By half-past three, they were wed.

Catherine could hardly believe she was the new Countess of Dalton. She could *almost* pretend that Adam cared for her the way she wanted him to when they were pronounced man and wife, and he kissed her with lingering tenderness in front of the Anglican minister from St. George's, the Maxwells, Louis, his nurse, and several members of Dalton House's extensive retinue of servants.

Adam's cook had provided a lavish wedding breakfast. How she'd managed to whip up extravagant dishes such as lobster with artichokes and butter sauce, roast partridge, and a rich, brandy-soused wedding cake at such short notice, Catherine had no idea.

The merrymaking continued with the Maxwells until they departed at nine o'clock. Indeed Louis, who'd been allowed to join them all in the dining room in honor of the auspicious occasion, had fallen asleep at Adam's feet beneath the enormous mahogany table with Pippin in his arms. Not even their rowdy, postprandial game of vingt-et-un had woken him up.

Lizzy, who had ensconced herself in a corner of the dining room, was all disapproving frowns and pouts until Adam ducked beneath the table to retrieve Louis and carry him up to bed. Then, to Catherine's wry amusement, the nursemaid followed her new lord and master just like Pippin, up to the third floor where Louis's new nursery lay.

Lizzy was only four-and-twenty, and Catherine suspected the young woman had begun to harbor a *tendre* for the handsome Earl of Dalton, given how she blushed every time he so much as looked her way. Catherine didn't feel threatened though. Adam might not love her, but he possessed so much honor, she suspected he'd rather blind himself than give more than a passing glance to a female servant in his employ.

Even so, she accompanied Adam and Lizzy to the nursery as well. She wanted to tuck her little boy into bed and ensure he was settled before she retired for the night with her new husband.

Goodness. Catherine's heart was doing odd little flip-flops just like an affection-starved wallflower at the thought she would soon be all alone with Adam. After she'd dropped a kiss on Louis's forehead, then watched Adam do the same, his words from the night before tripped through her mind.

Prepare to be pleasured like you never have before.

When Adam straightened and turned to look at her, Catherine's breath quickened. His gaze was as hot as a smoldering fire, all deep blue flames and burning intent. He reached for her hand, his fingers entwining with hers and there was no doubt in her mind that he would deliver on his promise.

Adam wanted her. For better or for worse—and even if it was just for a little while—at least she could take joy and comfort in that.

Adam's pulse was racing faster than a runaway horse as he took Catherine by the hand and led her from Louis's nursery into the barely lit hallway, and then down the oak staircase to their suite of rooms on the floor below.

She didn't say a word and neither did he. But he sensed her

excitement. Her breathless anticipation. When he'd caught her gaze in Louis's room, her pupils had dilated into deep dark pools of liquid longing, and he'd sworn he'd seen the flutter of her own pulse in her throat.

Since he'd kissed Catherine this afternoon—indeed, since he'd failed to satisfy her last night—he'd been champing at the bit to have her all to himself.

The physical relationship he'd shared with Sybil had been tepid at best. Not once had they been overwhelmed with the burning need to be together. They'd never rushed headlong down staircases and along dark corridors like this, the very air around them crackling with sparks.

Indeed, whenever he'd been with Catherine in the past, Adam had only ever experienced thought-robbing, breath-stealing, heart-stopping pleasure. Of course, as her protector, he'd paid Catherine well. The arrangement had suited them both, and they'd been eminently compatible in bed. He'd truly been confounded last night when Catherine had disclosed she'd been celibate for so long. For a woman with an undeniably passionate nature it was, in a word, surprising.

Unless she simply pretended to enjoy bed sport all those years ago.

After all, he'd failed to make her come last night—and she'd admitted that plainly. What if that had happened countless times in the past? As he'd just reminded himself, he *had* paid her for her services. She was a courtesan, ergo there was always the inherent expectation that she would be ready and willing and an enthusiastic partner whenever he called upon her. And she *had* once been a Covent Garden actress. But Catherine didn't seem like a woman who played games. He'd always believed her to be unreservedly honest and forthright.

In any event, Adam was determined to find out if his memories were more than romanticized fantasies. It was more than a matter of reassuring himself he was a gifted lover to assuage his male pride. It was a matter of...of what? Of honor? No, that didn't seem like quite the right word either.

As they approached Catherine's bedchamber on the second floor, Adam stopped himself from thinking any further on it. He didn't want to think anymore. He wanted to give himself over to the pursuit of mindless pleasure. To feel alive again. Replete. And more than anything, he wanted Catherine to feel that way too.

"I've already dismissed my lady's maid for the night," Catherine murmured as Adam closed the door to her bedchamber then locked it.

"Excellent." Turning to face her, Adam took a moment to drink in her exquisite loveliness.

Standing by the white marble fireplace, the flickering firelight and glow of the room's candles highlighted strands of pale gold in her thick, flaxen hair. While she didn't align to the *ton's* rigid expectations of feminine beauty, her features were nothing less than arresting. At least, Adam had always thought so. Because she possessed a heart-shaped face, her jaw was perhaps a little too long, her chin a little too pointed. Her mouth was also a little too wide. But there was something about her large, blue-gray eyes with their knowing glint, her high cheekbones, and a certain feline cast to her smile that Adam found enthralling. Even the way she held her slender body—the tilt of her head, the slope of her shoulders, even the proud jut of her firm round breasts—was elegant. Indeed, she possessed the bearing of a queen. Or a mysterious sensual goddess.

At this very moment, Adam sensed she was both eager and nervous. Just like he was. Even though lust pounded through his veins, urging him to claim her, his heart hammered wildly against his ribs as though he were about have a woman for the very first time.

"Would you like a drink?" he asked. He'd drunk champagne and claret with dinner, but suddenly felt the need to imbibe something stronger to temper the fire inside him. He wanted to make love to his wife at an unhurried, leisurely pace tonight. Draw out her pleasure. He wouldn't stray from his resolve to thoroughly satisfy her.

Catherine's mouth curved into that enigmatic smile of hers that he found so appealing. "That would be lovely. I'll pour, shall I?"

It was an old habit of hers, to serve him like this, and Adam let her even though he'd done the offering. Something inside his chest unfurled. A delicious warmth and a loosening of the tension in his body. It had been such a long time since he'd felt this way.

Catherine crossed to a small satinwood sideboard nestled between the fireplace and the window where a tray of crystal decanters and glasses sat. "What would you like?" she asked over her shoulder. "Brandy or port? I recall you never liked sherry all that much. Not unless it was Amontillado sherry."

"Brandy, I think." Adam moved to the fireside, removed his jacket and waistcoat, and then sprawled upon a settee, content to watch Catherine as she carefully dispensed two measures of the amber-hued liquor into tumblers. His eyes drifted over the elegant line of her neck and spine, imagining the satiny, ivory skin beneath, and his cock twitched.

He couldn't wait to let down her hair and lay her body bare. Slowly. Taking his time. Caressing and kissing every luscious inch of her. When Catherine joined him on the settee, he was tempted to drop his drink on the floor and taste her instead.

They sat for several minutes in companionable silence, sipping their brandy and watching the flames dance in the grate. When he lay his arm across the gilt back of the settee, Catherine leaned back against him and Adam inhaled deeply, breathing her in. Her delicious, floral musky scent reminded him of dark red roses and some other essence he guessed was quintessentially "Catherine." How many times had he dreamed of this, simply being with her in this way?

But his feeling of contentment didn't last for long. Not when Catherine adjusted her position and the side of her breast brushed his chest, her slender thigh pressed firmly against his. Blood surged, heading straight to his loins in a great searing rush.

"I want to thank you, for everything you've done—and that you are doing—for Louis and me," she murmured, her eyes meeting his. "I know this isn't easy for you."

He brushed an errant lock of hair away from her cheek, tucking it behind her ear, then let his fingers trail down the delicate sinews of her neck to rest upon her shoulder. "You've had a difficult time of late. But I'm here to make things easier for *you*. Actually"—he took her tumbler and put his drink and hers down upon a nearby table—"I'm here to make things better for you. Tonight I want to chase away all of the dark shadows and help you forget your troubles. The townhouse is secure with a guard posted at every door. You and Louis are completely safe." He traced the tip of his index finger along one of her fine collarbones. "I just want you to be here with me. To enjoy these quiet hours we have together. I want to spoil you, *ma belle*..." His gaze locked with hers. "Will you let me?"

She nodded and whispered, "Yes of course, my dearest Adam. I would like nothing more." Her mouth twitched with a smile. "And now you're my husband, you do have conjugal rights, after all."

She reached for his cravat and began to tug it loose, but he stopped her. "Not yet," he said in a low, velvet voice that he hoped would inflame her desire. "You don't have to do anything tonight. My conjugal rights don't matter a jot. This is all about you, Catherine"—he gently bracketed her face

with his hands as though she were a rare, precious bloom—
"and your pleasure. Not mine."

And then he lowered his head and kissed her. Her plush,
silken lips were pliant beneath his as he brushed kiss after
teasing kiss across her mouth. Her hands wound around his
neck and when he deepened their connection, sliding his
tongue between her lips into the hot, delicious recess beyond,
she moaned and tangled her fingers in his hair.

Christ, she tasted good. Like brandy, and tart summer
berries, and sun-warmed honey. The feel of her slick tongue
stroking against his, tasting him back with such fervent abandon, fired his lust all the more. His balls began to throb, but
Adam ignored the discomfort. He would come in his breeches
before he gave into his own thunderous need.

He speared a hand into the mass of artfully arranged curls
at the back of her head, dislodging and scattering pearl-
studded pins everywhere. Suddenly possessed with the
pressing need to taste her skin, he slid his mouth along her
delicate jaw then set to work on her neck, sucking and
nibbling, nipping and licking all the sweet, sensitive hollows he
knew would make her moan with delight. He skated his other
hand to her breast, brushing his thumb back and forth over
the silk of her bodice, taunting the nipple beneath into a hard,
straining peak.

"Adam... Oh, sweet Lord..." she breathed. "What you do
to me..."

God, he prayed she really was coming undone. That this
wasn't a well-rehearsed act. But he wouldn't be satisfied until
she was quaking and panting and begging him for mercy.
Raising his head, Adam murmured in a voice that was far
from steady, "Turn around. I want to undress you. It feels like
forever since I've seen you naked."

Without hesitation, she did as he asked. His hands were
shaking as he gently pushed his fingers into her hair, feeling for

any remaining pins, freeing the rest of her pale golden tresses until they tumbled about her shoulders. Then he unfastened the pearl buttons securing the back of her silk gown and pushed the fabric off her shoulders and down her arms, his fingers skimming a whisper-soft caress over her flesh, raising goosebumps.

Catherine's breath caught as he raised his hands and drew her back against his chest while simultaneously cupping her breasts. *Damn her stays and chemise. They needed to go.*

"Stand up, *ma belle*," he whispered against the shell of her ear, and she did so immediately. Her gown slid to the floor, puddling at her feet, and he gritted his teeth, pushing away the urge to rip the rest of her garments off.

Slowly, slowly, he reminded himself as he rose to his feet behind her, then gently tugged at all the tapes and cords and ribbons until not a stitch remained except for her stockings, silk slippers, and a pair of diamond and amethyst earrings he'd once gifted her. He'd noticed them the moment she'd approached him in the drawing room to become his wife.

His hands found her breasts again. The smooth creamy mounds filled his palms and when he plucked at the tightly furled, rosy nipples, Catherine gasped and squirmed. Her luscious arse pressed against his pulsating groin and once again he had to rein in the desire to take her right then and there.

Turning her head, Catherine looked up at him through her lashes. "What now, Adam?" she asked in a husky voice. "You know I'll do anything you ask of me."

Adam swallowed. He knew this to be true. Decadent, erotic, delicious memories filled his head and if his cock hadn't been standing to attention before, it certainly did so now, and in a spectacular fashion. The fall front of his breeches was fully tented. If he hadn't vowed to put her needs above his own, he'd ask her to drop to her knees and use her mouth on him.

Lust roughened his voice as he commanded, "Lie before the fire."

Her mouth lifted in a coquettish smile. "Very well."

She kicked off her slippers then sauntered across the hearth rug, her delicious hips and peach of a derriere swaying. Her movements slow and sinuous as a cat's, she lay down on her side, facing away from him, her head propped on one hand, her legs slightly curled.

Sweet Jesus, she was magnificent. Aphrodite brought to life.

Adam untied his cravat, tugged off his boots and hose, then threw off his shirt. He couldn't resist the idea of Catherine touching at least some of his bare flesh too. But he left his breeches on. The temptation to enter her and pound himself mindlessly into sweet oblivion would be too strong otherwise.

Perhaps wondering why he was taking so long to join her, Catherine glanced back over her shoulder as he approached. And then she pressed her perfect teeth into the soft, full pillow of her bottom lip.

Fuck. Adam fell to his knees on the rug. "Roll onto your back," he urged. "I want to use my mouth on you. And I won't be satisfied until you come around my tongue."

Oh, dear Lord above.

How could she resist such a deliciously wicked request? Excitement like she'd never known swirled through Catherine, making her dizzy. Her gaze still connected to Adam's, she did as he asked and lowered herself onto the plush rug. Her breasts rose and fell with the increased pace of her breathing and desire pulsed low in her belly. She was wet and swollen and oh, so ready.

He wouldn't make her wait long, would he?

Adam loomed over her, staring into her eyes for one long moment. The firelight illuminated the strong planes of one side of his proudly handsome face. "Do you know how beautiful you are, *ma belle*?" he whispered hoarsely.

"I feel beautiful when I'm with you," she returned. When Adam said things like that, with blue fire in his eyes, she could *almost* believe that he loved her. That what they were about to do wasn't just some base, meaningless act.

That it meant something.

"Good," he whispered. And then he dipped his head and claimed her mouth in a brief but passionate kiss.

"Put your arms above your head," he rasped and when Catherine complied, he caught her about the wrists with one hand. Then he set to work pleasuring her breasts, tormenting her aching nipples with wicked flicks and swirls of his tongue, and decadent, toe-curling sucks.

When she was arching and writhing and begging him for release, he let go of her hands and began a slow, torturous assault involving licks and long, lingering kisses everywhere except where she truly needed him. Across her ribs, in the crooks of her arms and knees, the arches of her feet and ankles after he peeled off her stockings. Over her belly and the dip of her waist, and then, finally, the quivering flesh of her inner thighs. Close, but not close enough.

"You're a cruel, cruel, man, Adam St Clair," Catherine panted as he spread her legs wide and placed a hot, open-mouth kiss in the sensitive hollow beside one hip bone.

She felt his lips curve against her skin as he smiled. "The more I tease you, the greater your cataclysm will be in the end," he murmured before planting a kiss by her opposite hip.

"If I don't expire with longing first," she said, arching her back to encourage him to move lower.

He looked up, his gaze meeting hers along the length of

her body. "Are you asking me to pleasure your hot wet cunny, Catherine? To use my fingers and tongue and lips on you until you scream?"

"God yes, Adam," she whimpered. "Please, I can't wait—"

Her capacity to speak all but fled as Adam nestled between her legs and slid his fingers along the drenched furrow of her sex. Gently parting her nether lips, he then licked along each side before capturing her clitoris between his lips. And then he drew on her with such perfect, exquisite suction, Catherine bucked and clutched at his head, fingers curling in his hair.

Oh, sweet heaven above. If he kept doing that she would come in a matter of sec—

Adam slid one, then two long fingers inside her quim and began to thrust. He released her pulsing clitoris and instead used his tongue on her, setting up an alternating dance of rapid yet devastatingly precise flutters and flicks and whorls that soon had her panting and twisting beneath him.

It had been so, so long since she'd experienced such a decadent, wonderfully salacious act, she knew that in no time at all, a breath-stealing orgasm would overwhelm her. Her insides were coiling tighter and tighter. It was agony but pure ecstasy at the same time. If Adam would just...

He suddenly threw her off balance by withdrawing his fingers and thrusting his twisting tongue deep inside her, plunging in and out in the manner of a cock. On and on he went, his wicked forays driving her inexorably higher. Her inner passage rippled, her body quaked on the brink, and when he finally rubbed her clitoris with his thumb in precise, tiny circles, she fell.

Pure pleasure burst behind her eyes like heavenly fireworks and wave after wave of pulsating bliss assailed her body. If she cried out, she had no awareness of it. She was adrift in a wondrous sea, floating and replete.

She would have been content to remain in that sublime

state, but Adam began to kiss her pulsing clitoris again. The sensation was so acute, it was almost too much to bear. Exquisite yet so intense, she shied away from the contact with a roll of her hips. Surely he couldn't intend to—

But Adam placed a firm hand on her belly and held her still. "I want you to come again," he growled, his warm breath gusting against her most intimate flesh. "I demand it."

She opened her eyes and pushed herself up onto her elbows. "I can't. Have mercy, Adam."

"You can and you will, Catherine. Just like me, you've been waiting for this for more than five long years, haven't you?"

"Yes. God damn you, yes." She couldn't contain her rising anger. It was as though Adam had opened up some deep well of emotion inside her and everything was rushing out.

The good and the bad. The passion and the pain. All the bright joy and her stark fear that he would never be able to give her more than this. It was all too much and she was suddenly terrified that he might guess the truth—that she was shamefully in love with her husband.

Adam's breath caught. Was it resentment or the aftermath of devastating pleasure that made Catherine's voice shake? Her eyes flash? Or was it some other emotion which made them shimmer?

For one absolutely awful moment, he thought he might have reduced her to tears. But then she inhaled a shaky breath and sank onto the rug. Her eyes closed again. She lifted a hand and her fingers drifted through his tousled hair, an infinitely tender gesture. "Do what you will, Adam," she whispered huskily. "I love everything you do to me."

Confusion warred with lust. He'd upset Catherine when

that was the last thing he'd wanted to do. One thing was certain: she'd definitely achieved orgasm. He'd felt her come around his tongue and he'd been so aroused and exultant, he'd almost lost control himself.

He crawled up her body and captured her jaw with gentle fingers. Kissed her with deliberate languor until she was sighing into his mouth and tangling her tongue with his.

"I'm sorry if I pushed you too far," he murmured, drawing back a little so he could see her eyes. "I just can't seem to get enough of you. You make me..." He swallowed, struggling to find the right words. "My desire for you is so great, so all-consuming, I lose control." He gave a small grin in an attempt to lighten the moment. "But I'll endeavor to temper my enthusiasm. For now."

To his relief, she smiled and pushed his hair from his brow. "I understand, Adam. I feel the same way. And the pleasure you just gave me, it was so astounding, I simply needed a moment to recover. Th-That's all."

He bent his head and after gently tugging off her earring, nipped and nuzzled at her earlobe. "Are you ready for more yet...?"

She gave his back a playful swat. "You insatiable rogue. What do you have in mind?"

"Whatever you want to do this time. Well"—he nudged her body with his hips—"as long as it involves me burying myself deep inside you in some way. I don't think I can hold this almighty cockstand in check for much longer."

She laughed then. "Yes, I can feel it. You're as stiff as a stone pillar. And we wouldn't want that impressive hardness to go to waste, now would we?"

"I'm so glad you agree. Now, tell me how you want this." He pushed his painfully constrained length against her belly again.

She raked her fingernails lightly down his chest, making

his nipples contract as a shiver of anticipation rippled over his skin. "Hmmm." Her mouth twitched with a smile. "So many ideas spring to mind. But I think I want you to take me from behind."

Behind? That was his favorite position, not Catherine's. At least, if his memory served him correctly. But he wasn't willing to argue with her, not when he was primed to explode at any moment.

As he tore open the fall of his breeches, releasing his weeping cock, Catherine rose to her hands and knees, her delicious derriere facing him. Tossing her wild, cascading mane of blonde hair to one side, she turned her head and looked back over her shoulder. "Hurry, Adam. I need you."

That makes two of us, he thought as he reached for her lusciously curved hips. "Are you ready, sweetheart?"

When she whispered a soft "yes," he gripped himself with one shaking hand, then slid his length between her folds, coating himself with her slick dew. She gasped as the swollen head of his cock came into contact with her clitoris. If he wasn't possessed by the ravening need to be inside her straightaway, he might have spent a little more time teasing her. But the lust inside him was like a gathering tempest, the tension inside him too great to dally.

He had to have her. *Now.* He found her entrance and surged forward, sheathing his entire throbbing length to the very balls on one smooth glide. Then he promptly swore beneath his breath when she contracted around him, sucking at him greedily. Jesus Christ, she felt so damn good. Like a hot slick satin glove, squeezing him tightly like she never wanted to let him go.

As he set up a sure and steady pace, he started to sweat and his heart crashed against his ribs. Catherine met him stroke for stroke, even when he began to pump harder and faster. Harsh, rhythmic pants escaped him and Catherine's answering, breathy gasps were like the sweetest music to his ears. A perfect harmony.

His orgasm was fast approaching. He could feel it gathering strength, a blazing inferno that was curling around his spine, licking at his ballocks, making him quake. The exquisite heat and tension were building, building...

But he wanted Catherine to find heaven with him too. He wanted to feel her body spasming around his again. Hear her cry his name in ecstasy.

Call it masculine pride, call it stubborn determination, call it embarrassment and guilt for failing Catherine last night, Adam would damn himself to hell if he failed to bring her to orgasm with his cock tonight of all nights. Their wedding night.

Not breaking his frantic tempo even for an instant, Adam leaned forward and slid a hand to her sex. Fretted her hard-as-a-pearl clitoris. Beside himself with acute need, he all but grunted into her ear, "Come... Come with me."

"Oh, God... Adam..." Her hands gave way and she fell to her forearms.

But he was relentless, and kept pounding and pounding while ruthlessly rubbing her tiny nub of pleasure faster and faster.

"Come, Catherine... You must... I won't... I won't stop until you—"

And at that moment, Catherine released a harsh sob. "Oh, please... Oh, yes, Adam. Yes..." Her back arched, her hips pushing back against him, her inner sheath contracting so tightly, stars exploded behind his eyes.

Fuck. Adam couldn't hold back. The fraying remnants of his control snapped. With an almighty roar of triumph, he came too. He bucked then collapsed over Catherine, clutching her ribs as his body jerked and shuddered, spending his seed inside her in a series of hot, volcanic spurts.

Good Lord, his release seemed to go on forever. The ripples of sheer pleasure rolling over him and through him were indescribable. He prayed Catherine's climax was just as magnificent too.

At length, when he could summon the will to move, he levered himself off Catherine's prostrate form. Bending down, he then gathered her into his arms and rose to his feet.

"Thank you, Adam," she murmured. Her hands wrapped around his neck and she smiled up into his face as he carried her to the wide tester bed. "Your skills as a lover are unsurpassed and they're just as wonderful as I recall." Her expression softened and she placed a hand against his jaw. "You make me feel so very special."

"I could say the same about you, *ma belle*," he returned as he lay her gently upon the counterpane of dusky rose silk. He slid alongside her and drew her close. "We're well-matched, don't you think?"

She sighed sleepily and snuggled into him. "Yes. Yes, I do."

Adam dropped a kiss on her forehead and buried his face in her hair. Yet again he realized how much he'd missed this. This closeness. This warmth. The simple contentment of just being with Catherine.

Whatever happened in the coming days—for surely there was more trouble ahead—at least he would have this.

CHAPTER 13

Hyde Park, London
21ˢᵗ October, 1816

"Mama, can I feed the ducks now?" asked Louis. He was bouncing up and down in the seat of Adam's landau, staring at the Serpentine with bright eyes.

"Of course you can, darling," replied Catherine. She glanced up at the leaden-gray sky then caught Lizzy's eye. The nursemaid was sitting beside her young charge on the opposite side of the open carriage. "You might want to take an umbrella with you," she suggested. "It looks like rain again."

At that moment, a chill breeze with a damp edge ruffled the Serpentine's waters and caught at Louis's blond curls. "I don't mind the rain, Mama," he declared. "And neither does Pippin." On hearing his name, the spaniel gave his young master's hand a lick and Louis giggled.

"I agree with your Mama," said Adam. "While rain doesn't bother me either, umbrellas are very a good idea all the same. We don't want to get wet and then catch a cold." He gave Catherine's gloved hand a quick squeeze. "I'll have the driver dig a few umbrellas out before he puts up the landau's hood."

Catherine nodded and returned his smile. So far, it had been a lovely day. Though it had been pouring when she'd woken in Adam's arms, the rain had abated by mid-morning. During a late, leisurely breakfast taken with Louis in Dalton House's well-appointed morning room, Adam had proposed that weather permitting, he'd like to take make good on his offer to take Louis to Gunter's Tea Shop in Berkeley Square, followed by a jaunt in Hyde Park. Of course, Catherine hadn't been able to say no to the idea when she'd watched Louis's whole face light up at the suggestion.

Although it had only been two days since Louis first met Adam, it was clear that the boy was quite taken with his new Papa already. Not only did Louis look to him for direction, he seemed to hang on Adam's every word. It warmed Catherine's heart immeasurably.

Everything would have been quite perfect if she hadn't been plagued with the constant urge to keep looking over her shoulder. Indeed, Catherine felt as jumpy as a hind during hunting season as Adam helped her to alight from the landau and escorted her toward a willow tree by the lake.

Because it was mid-afternoon, the park was relatively quiet and there didn't appear to be any sinister men lurking about, watching them. Not that Catherine could see anyway as she scanned the surrounding copses and open stretches of park-land. All the passersby, whether on foot or on horseback or in carriages, seemed perfectly ordinary too. Earlier at Gunter's, Catherine had done the very same thing, studying the faces of everyone in the tearoom while Louis had feasted on a bowl of berry sorbet and vanilla ice cream.

Of course having Adam by her side, helping her to watch over Louis, was immensely reassuring. So too was the burly carriage driver, her own footman Jackson, and Fitz, another strapping young footman from Dalton House who'd accompanied them on their excursion.

"He'll be fine," Adam murmured as they watched Louis with Pippin at his heels race down to the water's edge ahead of them. Lizzy and Jackson followed in hot pursuit. "You can't hide how nervous you are, my lady-wife. Not from me."

From beneath the brim of her leghorn bonnet, Catherine looked up at him and smiled. "You know me so well," she said. But that was a lie. Adam might be able to tell she was as worried as an anxious mother hen watching over her chick when there might be a fox nosing about, he also didn't seem to realize she was hiding so much more from him.

Like the irrefutable yet inconvenient fact that I love you...

Even though Adam had stayed with her all night, holding her in his arms, not for a minute could she afford to entertain the thought that it really meant anything. After all, he'd often stayed the whole night with her when she'd been his mistress. He'd even *told* her, all those years ago, that he didn't believe in love. He'd been *very* clear about that.

And then of course, he'd cast her aside to marry another.

Adam had taken her twice more—once during the middle of the night and again when they'd woken—and each time she'd found heaven. This morning's bout of bed sport had actually felt like lovemaking—the way he'd kissed and touched her with such deliberate tenderness, tears had filled her eyes. But she hadn't let him see. She'd decided it was much safer if she faced away from him or kept her eyes closed when raw emotion threatened to overwhelm her. It was far easier to pretend she wasn't affected by him if she never looked him in the eye or better yet, simply played the part of a coquettish mistress as she'd once done.

Yes, she did not doubt for a moment that she was the sort of woman he would eschew—a mawkish fool who'd fallen in love—if he knew. Even more lowering—no, terrifying if she were perfectly honest with herself—was the thought that in time, he would begin to despise her, given he was now trapped in a socially disastrous marriage with her. She didn't think she would survive the pain if he rejected her a second time.

The pain. Yes, she needed to hold onto the memory of that pain. Indeed, she swore there was still a scar on her heart from the damage Adam had inflicted all those years ago. That pain, that barely knitted wound, was something she could press to remind herself that she needed to take care. Always.

All in all, it was best to tell herself this was just a marriage of convenience. That was what Adam expected, so that was what he would get. Somehow, she would learn how to harden her battered, all too vulnerable heart.

She must be "Catherine the Courtesan Countess," not a woman in love.

"Mama! Papa! Come and help," called Louis happily over his shoulder.

Catherine pushed aside her troubled musings and plastered a carefree smile on her face. "Of course."

As soon as they reached Louis's side, he eagerly thrust crumbling dry crusts of bread into their hands to share with the ducks and swans swarming at the water's edge. As Adam sank to his haunches and put his arm about Louis's shoulders, Catherine thought her heart would burst.

So much for remaining unmoved, she chided herself. But watching Adam form a bond with his own son was an altogether different kettle of fish. One would have to be entirely heartless *not* to be affected in some way.

It seemed the more time she and Louis spent with Adam, the more enmeshed they would become in his life. And of course she wanted that for Louis. More than anything. To develop a close relationship with his father even if her own relationship with Adam deteriorated.

Without conscious thought, one of her hands drifted to

her belly. If Adam got her with child again and she gave him the heir he'd long desired, at least she could be happy that she'd been able to do that for him. Perhaps that would make up for the fact that she wasn't, and would never be, a socially acceptable wife.

Just as the bread ran out, the first raindrops began to fall. Catherine picked up Louis and Adam shared his umbrella with them both.

"Mama, where's Pippin?" Louis asked, a worried frown creasing his brow.

Catherine glanced around them—along the grassy bank, beneath the nearby willow tree, and the surrounding stretch of lawn—but she couldn't see any sign of the spaniel. Even though panic fluttered in her chest, she endeavored to use a calm tone of voice. "I'm sure he's somewhere close by, darling."

Adam gave Louis's arm a small squeeze. "Jackson, Lizzy, and I will go and look for him," he said with a reassuring smile. "He's probably run off to chase a squirrel."

Louis nodded with enthusiasm. "Yes, he likes to do that."

Adam caught Catherine's gaze as he handed her the umbrella. "You and Louis should hop in the landau. Fitz and Hobbs"—he nodded toward the attendant footman and carriage driver—"will look after you until I get back. I won't be long."

Catherine offered him a smile. "Thank you."

The rain was growing heavier by the moment as Catherine carried Louis back to the landau. Lizzy had an umbrella but no doubt Adam and Jackson would be soaked to the skin by the time they returned. Fitz assisted Catherine into the landau and she sat beneath the carriage's raised canopy with Louis in her lap.

"I'm scared, Mama," Louis whispered. His bottom lip

wobbled. "Pippin isn't like me. He doesn't like the rain. Where is he?"

Catherine smoothed a curl away from his pale cheek. "I'm sure your Papa will find him soon, my darling. He can't have gone far."

Louis nodded then turned to regard the rainy aspect. Then he squealed and pointed. "There he is. Look. With that man."

Catherine's attention swung in the same direction. She gasped. Through the veil of scudding rain, she could see a tall man about fifty yards away, standing by a cluster of towering fir trees. And tucked beneath one arm was Pippin.

Ice-cold foreboding slid down Catherine's spine as she took in the stranger's appearance. He wore a long black coat with the collar turned up at the neck. Though his features were obscured by the brim of his hat and the shade cast by the umbrella he carried, there was something oddly familiar about him. The way he remained stock still, staring toward the landau, despite the fact Pippin was squirming to get free.

The hairs on Catherine's neck rose. It was the man she'd seen outside in Park Lane after the fire at Rosemont House. She was absolutely certain.

She opened her mouth to summon Fitz but then the man bent down and released Pippin and the spaniel bounded off, heading straight for the landau.

"Pippin," cried Louis. He tried to get down from her lap but Catherine wouldn't let him.

"Stay here," she began but in the next instant, a sodden Pippin was leaping into the carriage and jumping all over Louis. The dog's excited yaps and Louis's squeals filled the air around them.

"Fitz?" Catherine called over the rain drumming on the landau's roof and the joyous hubbub of a boy and his dog reunited. "Fitz, there's a man—"

At that moment, the stranger raised his large, gloved hand as though bidding her farewell, then he disappeared into the crowded fir copse. The trees swallowed him whole, leaving no trace at all.

The young footman appeared at the side of the landau. "Yes, my lady?" His brow creased with concern when he took in how rattled she was. As soon as Catherine explained what had happened and her suspicions, the young man bolted off toward the stand of trees.

Her heart hammering against her ribs, her whole body shivering, Catherine sank back into the seat. *Dear Lord*. She prayed Fitz would catch up to the man. She had to know who he was. Whether he was just a Good Samaritan returning a stray dog to its owner or instead, a malevolent stranger who watched her and Louis from the shadows and sent them nasty, threatening messages for some reason she was yet to fathom.

"Catherine." Adam's large frame suddenly filled the doorway of the landau. "I can see Pippin's ba—" His words and his smile died on his lips when he took in Catherine's expression. "What's wrong? What's happened?"

Catherine drew a shaky breath to reply but Louis piped up. "The man from Gunter's found Pippin," he said, climbing up beside her. The spaniel shook himself, splattering them all with water, then jumped onto the seat too.

"The man from Gunter's?" Catherine frowned in confusion and caught Adam's gaze. "There was a man—dressed all in black—by that copse of firs over there. He had Pippin but he let him go. Fitz has given chase because there was something about him that reminded me of the stranger I saw in Park Lane, the night Rosemont House was set on fire."

Adam's brow arrowed into a deep frown as he climbed into the landau and sat on the opposite seat. "Louis, the man who had Pippin, did you really see him in Gunter's today?"

Louis nodded eagerly. "Yes, Papa."

Another frisson of deep unease swept over Catherine. "I didn't notice anyone like that when we were there."

Louis pouted. "He *was* there, Mama. When you and Papa were choosing ices. And he gave me this. I was going to share them with you later."

He reached into his pocket and pulled out several sticky sweets wrapped in a crumpled piece of paper. Scrawled upon the sheet in heavy black ink were the following words:

I know what you did, bitch... I'm watching and waiting...

Oh, God. A strange clamoring sound filled Catherine's ears and she struggled to catch her breath.

Adam took the note and the sweets—they looked like innocuous lumps of barley sugar. Then he looked up at Catherine. There were lines of tension bracketing his mouth as he said, "Lizzy and Jackson should be back any minute. They were with Louis the whole time in Gunter's. Perhaps they can provide a good description of this cur... I mean this man."

But when Adam questioned them, neither Lizzy nor Jackson could recall anyone approaching their young master. At one stage, Jackson had taken Pippin outside, but it had only been for a minute or two. Lizzy reported that the only time she hadn't been paying complete attention to her surroundings was when she'd been refastening the buckle on one of Louis's shoes.

Louis's little face crumpled. "Did I do something wrong?"

"No, of course not, darling." Catherine gathered Louis into a hug. "It's just that we don't know this man. And it's never a good idea to take things from strangers."

"All right, Mama."

Over the top of Louis's head, Adam caught Catherine's eye. "With any luck, Fitz will have caught up with him. In the meantime, I'll have a word with Hobbs. He would have had a good view of the copse from the driver's seat. He's been in my family's employ for years and has spent endless hours waiting in London streets outside of clubs and townhouses. If this man is a member of the *ton*, Hobbs will know him."

As Adam exited the landau, Lizzy and Jackson returned. Lizzy gave a delighted cry and entered the carriage in a flurry of damp wool when she saw Pippin was back safe and sound.

When Adam joined them a minute later, his expression was nothing but grim.

"What is it?" Catherine asked over the excited coos of Lizzy.

"Hobbs isn't certain because of the distance involved, but he thought the man looked familiar." Adam said in a low voice laced with steel. "But I must say, I'm not relieved in the slightest by the knowledge."

Oh... Catherine swallowed to moisten her dry mouth. "Well, don't keep me in suspense any longer, Adam. Who is it then?" She *had* to know.

The answer, when it came, made her heart stutter and almost stop.

"Lord Makepeace," he said, his blue eyes as hard and cold as an arctic glacier. "The new Lord Makepeace. Frederick...the son of Albert."

"Do you know him? What he looks like?"

Adam's jaw tightened. "Yes. He used to put in an appearance at White's and other clubs around St James's on the odd occasion. I haven't seen him for a good while, though. Because of the rumors about his father, he was never welcomed with open arms. Most gentlemen tended to give him the cut direct."

Catherine drew a shaky breath. "I wonder if he blames me for his ostracism. If...if he heard that I had something to do with his father's arrest—if he feels I'm in some way responsible for Albert Makepeace's death—it might explain why I've suddenly begun to receive threats. My sudden return to Society's fold could have been some sort of trigger for his ire." Then she huffed out a frustrated sigh. "That doesn't explain all the other accidents that happened over the last ten months though. Unless they *were* just accidents... I hardly know anymore."

Adam's brow creased with deep frown. "The fire at Rosemont House seemed like a deliberate act of sabotage. The threat you received the next day certainly confirmed it. In any event, I do think you're right to be suspicious about Makepeace's motive. Especially if he's fallen on hard times. But don't worry." Sliding a gentle hand behind her nape, Adam tilted her head forward and brushed his lips across her temple. "I will take care of him."

Adam's touch might be tender, but there was nothing but steel behind his words. Catherine had no doubt that he spoke the truth.

CHAPTER 14

St Andrews Hill, Blackfriars, London
Later that night...

A chill, creeping fog curled around Adam and obscured his view of St Andrew's Hill when he and Maxwell exited a hackney coach onto the narrow street. The Thames was but a short walk away and the smell of dank river water permeated the air. As Adam took stock of their surroundings for a moment, he buttoned his greatcoat to stop the damp cold penetrating through to his very bones.

"God, I hate cockfighting," muttered Maxwell as they strode up the slope toward a soft golden glow suffusing the gray, roiling miasma. "It's enough to make a man cast up his accounts."

Given the cacophony of raucous laughter, excited voices, and cheers echoing down the street, Adam assumed it was emanating from their destination, the Cockpit Tavern. Since the Royal Cockpit on Birdcage Walk in St James's had closed down, enthusiasts of the notorious "sport" apparently flocked to a number of other public houses around London that held cockfights, including this establishment in Blackfriars.

"However, I trust Walsh's information is correct and that Makepeace is here tonight," the Scots Earl continued. "He's one of the best inquiry agents I know of, and Lord Markham wouldn't have recommended him if he couldn't deliver the goods."

"I trust him, too," remarked Adam. "And I agree with you about cockfighting. I'm happy to watch a round of boxing or wrestling, but blood sport involving defenseless animals..." He shuddered, but not from the cold. "I don't understand the appeal, not at all. But must needs when the devil drives, as they say."

After the unnerving incident at Hyde Park, Adam had summoned Walsh to Dalton House in the late afternoon. Within the space of a few short hours, the man had managed to find out where Frederick, Lord Makepeace, intended to spend the evening.

Apparently Makepeace's staff hadn't been paid in a while so Walsh was able to extract a good deal of information from one of the baron's male servants for a handful of coins.

"It makes sense that Makepeace would hold a grudge against Catherine given her witness account led to his father's arrest all those years ago," said Maxwell. "But what I still don't understand is, why is he threatening her now? And why threaten and actually harm her young son? An innocent child?"

Adam hadn't yet disclosed to Maxwell or his wife, Helena, that Louis was actually *his* son. And now didn't seem quite the right time to broach such a subject. "I suspect Makepeace is a soulless bastard like his father," said Adam. "As to why he's waited so long to enact his sick revenge...perhaps it's related to the fact he has a rampant gambling habit. That was certainly a useful nugget of intelligence that his manservant divulged to

Walsh earlier this evening. Being in dire financial straits might have caused Makepeace to become unhinged in his desire for revenge. He's lashing out at Catherine because he wants to blame someone else, rather than acknowledge his father's heinous wrongdoings or take responsibility for his own failings."

"Yes, a lack of blunt can make a man do desperate things," agreed Maxwell as they drew to a halt outside the public house's narrow door.

The taproom was packed and several men loitered in the street. Maxwell's breath puffed out in a frigid cloud as he added, "At the Foreign Office it was suspected that Albert Makepeace had lost large sums at the gaming table and had decided to sell secrets to the French to replenish his estate's dwindling coffers. It would seem the problem runs in the family."

"Mmm. I don't know why I didn't think of Albert Makepeace's son sooner," said Adam grimly. Guilt sliced through his gut at the memory of Catherine's pale, distraught face as she'd listened to Louis describe the man who'd brazenly approached him in Gunter's. It was clearly Frederick, Lord Makepeace. Thank God the blackguard hadn't hurt Pippin. He'd obviously followed them to Hyde Park then seized the spaniel to invoke fear. And to emphasize his note's sinister message—*I'm watching, bitch*. The man could evidently get close to Catherine and her son at any time.

But to do what? Physically harm them? That wouldn't alleviate Makepeace's financial problems. The man clearly *was* unhinged. But Adam would do everything in his power to ensure this man's personal *vendetta* ended tonight.

"You know…" Maxwell frowned. "The notes you told me about—the ones sent to Catherine demanding she return something that's been stolen…"

Adam's interest was piqued. "Yes?"

"When we went through Albert Makepeace's personal papers, immediately after his botched arrest and subsequent death," said Maxwell, "we of course confirmed that he'd been selling secrets to the French. One of the most damning pieces of evidence against him was an encrypted letter which suggested he would receive payment in the form of a stolen French Crown jewel—the magnificent Tavernier Blue or the French Blue diamond to be exact—if he successfully procured the information that Sir Louis Fortescue was carrying the night he was murdered."

"What?" Adam had heard of the famed flawless blue diamond. Rumor had it that it had been stolen from the Royal Storehouse almost twenty-five years ago during the Reign of Terror—along with nearly all of the French Crown Jewels. "That jewel is beyond priceless. I thought it had been lost."

"It's true it's been missing for years. The most recent rumor I'd heard was that it had been smuggled across the Channel and into London, and that it had been split into two pieces," said Maxwell. "At any rate, no such jewel was found in Makepeace's possessions on the night he was arrested. But if Fredrick knew about the possibility of his father's payment... and Catherine was there when Sir Louis was murdered. And no doubt Frederick's aware that she's French by birth..." His friend shrugged. "Maybe he thinks Catherine has something to do with the payment his father never received. Perhaps he thinks Catherine owes him something because she got in the way and somehow foiled his father's crime... I know, my theory does seem far-fetched. As I said, the letter that talked about the payment was encrypted so I doubt Frederick could have read it. Indeed, the cipher was deuced hard to crack."

"What, because it took you more than half-an-hour?" jested Adam.

Maxwell grinned. "Something like that."

"At this point, I'd be willing to entertain just about any

idea or follow any lead, just to bring this whole God damned thing to end," muttered Adam. He turned his attention back to the Cockpit.

"It's going to be difficult routing Makepeace out in such a crowd," observed Maxwell, looking in the grimy lower windows of the public house. He delved into his Garrick coat, pulled out a silver pocket watch, and flipped it open. "It's almost midnight. I'm happy to wait out here for him if you are."

Adam's fingers and toes were already numb but he didn't care. "That sounds like an eminently sensible idea. With any luck, he'll run out of money to place wagers sooner rather than later." The thought of watching men placing bets on cockerels and then cheering them on as the birds tore each other to pieces was obscene. Like Maxwell, it was enough to make Adam's stomach turn.

Maxwell stamped his feet. "Damn. I should've brought a flask of whisk—"

At that moment there was a great, swelling roar that spilled out from the public house onto the street. Angry shouts and jeers filled the night air, there was a scuffle at the front door, and a man was ejected onto the cobbled pavement.

He stumbled a few paces before righting himself. "Fuck you," he shouted at the pair of burly doormen who stood on guard at the entrance.

The taller one grunted and flexed his knuckles. "Now, now, guv. Title or no', if you're not goin' to play nice, you're not welcome. An' it might 'elp if you paid yer bleedin chit—" He broke off as another tall, dark-haired gentleman placed a hand on his arm and murmured something in the doorman's ear. And then money—the glint of gold strongly suggested guineas—changed hands.

Interesting... Adam focused his attention on the benevolent stranger with deep pockets but most of his face, aside from his sharply hewn jaw, was in shadow.

While all this was taking place, the ousted "gentleman" was muttering another string of curses beneath his breath as he swayed on his feet. He teetered a few steps to the right—he was clearly three sheets to the wind—and a wash of light from the tavern's window glanced across his brow.

A white-hot burst of anger seared through Adam's blood when he recognized who it was.

Frederick, Lord Makepeace.

Maxwell must have seen murder in Adam's gaze as he gripped his shoulder. "Steady on, my friend. Don't do anything you'll regret," he murmured. "There are too many eyes and ears about. And Makepeace might have an ally here too." He jutted his chin toward the stranger who hovered in the doorway of the tavern, still watching. "Let's not start a brawl out here. Not unless we have to."

Adam's fingers clenched into fists so tight, his knuckles cracked as he strove to harness his fury. Maxwell was right, of course, but that didn't mean he could stand by and do nothing at all. Makepeace had to be told in no uncertain terms that he needed to stay away from Catherine and Louis, or else there'd be a heavy price to pay.

Yes, Adam was more than willing to spill a bit of the baron's blood to get his point across whether Makepeace had an "ally" hovering in the background or not. Although, when Adam glanced back at the entrance to the tavern, the stranger had disappeared from view...

Makepeace suddenly lurched past a nearby laneway, bumping into a rough brick wall. The man was a mess. If he slipped over and cracked his head open, Adam would not lament the cur's demise.

With Maxwell at his side, Adam followed the drunken baron a short distance down the street.

"All right, all right, you ham-fishted bruishers," mumbled Makepeace, clutching onto a lamppost. "No need to follow me. You've made your point... I'm leaving..." But then he looked up. "Do I know you?" he said, squinting at Adam's face. Then he tapped his nose. He missed the first time. "Yes, I do. You're the bloody Dalton of Earl. Earl of Dal...Dalton." He teetered alarmingly back on his heels but then somehow righted himself. "What d'you want?"

"You fucking well know who I am," growled Adam. "What the hell is wrong with you?"

Up this close, it was evident Lord Makepeace was in a bad way. The lamplight revealed his cravat was askew, he was sporting a good deal of stubble on his jaw, and there were dark bruise-like smudges beneath his hooded eyes. A fog of unpleasant odors clung to his person—cheap alcohol and sweat—and Adam wondered if the baron could no longer afford to employ a valet.

This man who *must* be stalking Catherine—turning her life into a waking nightmare—was quite pathetic, all things considered. But that didn't lessen Adam's anger. In fact, it only made it worse.

Using the lamppost as a support, Makepeace drew himself up to his full, not inconsiderable height. "Whatsh wrong with me, you ask?" His lip curled in a derisive sneer before he emitted a bitter laugh. "Oh, nothing at all. My life is all wine and roses. Sunshine and smiles. Cocks and cock sucking." He pulled at the hem of his stained and rumpled waistcoat and puffed out his chest. "I'm Lord Makepeace. *The* Lord Makepeace. The toasht of the *ton*. The son of a traitor. Haven't y'heard? Everyone loves me, they love me they do, and I'm welcome everywhere. Except for ballrooms, drawing rooms, Almack's, White's, Brooks's, Baboodles...Kaboodles... Boodles's, I mean... Most places really. Exshept for this one." He hiccupped and waved drunkenly at the pub. "They all adore me here, can't you tell? Especially the ha'penny whores who'll take you into that nearby back alley for a bit of that cock shucking I just mentioned." He winked. "You'd know all about that wouldn't you, dear chap?" He reached out and clapped Adam's back. "Considering what you've just married. I'd wager y'new slut of a wife could suck the very marrow out—"

He got no further because something inside Adam snapped. He raised his fist, there was a wince-inducing crunch, and Makepeace was sprawled on the pavement. The felled baron raised himself onto an elbow then spat a mouthful of blood into the gutter.

"I'd call you out right now and put a bullet between your eyes at dawn for that slur alone, except for the fact you're not worth the effort," growled Adam, flexing his hand. Inside his gloves, his knuckles stung—he was certain he'd split the skin—but it didn't matter. Taking a step forward, he loomed over Makepeace and the man visibly shrank. "But know this. If you ever come near my wife or my son again, I will gut you like a fish and throw you into the Thames."

Makepeace grimaced as he wiped a shaking hand across his split lip. "Oh, I think your message is loud and clear." His gestured clumsily at something behind Adam. "And jusht about everyone in the *Cockpit* heard it too."

Fucking, bloody, blazing hell. Adam glanced over his shoulder and swore aloud. A crowd had gathered on the pavement outside the pub. He'd created a spectacle—a scandal—which was the last thing he'd wanted to do.

His mother had certainly been right. He was going to ruin the St Clair name.

Makepeace sat up and laughed. "So, I'd say that if my body is found floating in the Thames, everyone will know who to point the finger at."

Adam bent down. "What makes you think anyone would

ever find your body, you pitiful dog?" he gritted out in a low, gravel-laced tone. "If you have any modicum of decency, or sense, you'll stay away. You won't send any more vile threats or make cryptic yet asinine demands. You won't stalk my family. You'll skulk back into the shadows where you belong."

Makepeace grunted as he clambered to his feet and gripped the lamppost again. "Whatsha mean, vile threats?'" he slurred. "What demands?"

"Oh, you're going to play the innocent party now, are you? Deny that you've been sending hate-filled messages to my wife? Or that you've been following her and my son around?" Adam had to clench his fists to stop himself lunging for the baron again. That didn't stop him leaning closer to the swine as he said in a quietly menacing tone, "She *saw* you in Park Lane the night of the fire at Rosemont House. And in Gunter's, and Hyde Park this afternoon. So did my staff."

"What utter ballocks," declared Makepeace. "I live in Mayfair, for Chrissake. So what if I enjoy drinking a coffee or eating an ice now and again at Gunter's? And maybe I like to ramble about Hyde Park on the odd occasion. Most of the bloody *ton* do! There'sh no law against it. You can't prove a God damned thing."

"Mark my words, I'll be watching you, Makepeace," snarled Adam. "If you ever come near my wife again, or my son, it will be the last thing you ever do."

With that, Adam turned on his booted heel and strode away down St Andrew's Hill lest he lose complete control and batter Makepeace to within an inch of his life. Even Maxwell wouldn't be able to hold him back.

Hopefully his warning would be sufficient. But if it wasn't and the baron continued to torment Catherine and Louis for whatever perverse reason he had, Adam would be hard pressed not to do exactly as he'd threatened: to call him out and end him with a bullet to the brain.

CHAPTER 15

When Adam arrived home at Dalton House, anger was still pounding through his veins like a military tattoo. He was on fire. Gripped by blood lust. Even though he'd been wearing gloves when he'd planted a facer on bloody Makepeace, his knuckles were bruised and slightly split. He should probably repair to his bedchamber and bathe and bandage his hand, but he was too wound up to retire for the night.

He headed for the library instead. Once he'd shed his coat and loosened his cravat, he poured himself a cognac. He'd just downed the fiery alcohol in two gulps when the door clicked open and Catherine entered. She was in her night attire, her blonde hair unbound, a blue silk wrapper clutched about her chest. As she padded across the floor toward him in satiny slippers, the pale white gauziness of her night rail floated about her bare ankles.

"You're up late, *ma belle*," he said softly. According to the mantel clock, it was half-past one.

"I know…" She leaned her hip against the sideboard where the silver drinks tray and all the crystal decanters sat. "I couldn't sleep. I was..." Her gaze lifted to his face and a faint line appeared between her elegant brows. "I was worried about you."

Adam was touched. Reaching out, he pulled her into the circle of his arms and dropped a kiss on her forehead. "I know how to look after myself. And Maxwell was with me."

"Even so..." Her frown deepening, Catherine dropped her gaze and absently pleated the trailing fabric of his cravat. "Did you find Makepeace?"

"Yes." He stilled her restless fingers with his own. "He wouldn't admit his role in any of the recent goings on. Of course, I didn't expect him to. But I rather think the cur will think twice about coming anywhere near you or Louis again." Adam also filled her in on Maxwell's theory that maybe Makepeace might mistakenly think that Catherine was in possession of the famed French Blue diamond.

"What? Merely because I'm French?" She made a scoffing sound. "If Lord Makepeace thinks I had anything to do with the espionage plot his father and Sir Louis were involved in— or the payment Albert Makepeace was promised and never received—he must be stark raving mad."

"I know," agreed Adam grimly. "Maxwell did say it was a far-fetched idea. And I agree it doesn't really make sense, at least on the surface. But whoever is stalking you and sending threats must be at least a little unhinged. Who knows what they might believe?"

"Yes, I suppose you're right," said Catherine with a sigh. She nodded at his cognac glass. "May I have one?"

"Of course." As Adam poured her a sizable nip he added, "One thing that *is* abundantly clear after tonight is that Makepeace isn't doing very well. Not only was he ousted from a tavern in a rather unsavory part of town, but he was foxed to the eyeballs and his clothes were worse for wear. There also appeared to be another man with him who paid his chit."

Adam explained how the stranger had passed a handful of guineas to one of the Cockpit's disgruntled doormen.

Catherine arched a brow as she accepted her drink. "Oh?" She took a delicate sip of her cognac. "Now *that* sounds rather interesting."

"I couldn't see this fellow's face properly, and who he is might be neither here nor there. But all the same, I'll ask the inquiry agent to investigate Makepeace's associates further." Adam replenished his own drink and took a swig. "Although, the more I think on it, the odder that whole particular incident seems. If this apparently benevolent gentleman is Makepeace's friend, why didn't he step in when Maxell and I approached the baron in the street? But he didn't. After he paid off the doorman, he disappeared."

"That *is* odd," agreed Catherine. "But you should trust your instincts."

"That's why I also think we should repair to St Clair Abbey as soon as possible," said Adam heavily. "I don't know what is going on with Makepeace, but I know you and Louis will be safer on my estate in Oxfordshire." He gave rueful smile. "There are fewer dark alleys for nefarious types to lurk about in. Less opportunities to deliver threatening notes. Strangers visiting the nearby village of Upper Godstow will be noticed."

"You may be right." Catherine's brow furrowed in thought as she ran a fingertip around the rim of her glass. "If Makepeace was responsible for sending me those awful messages and starting the fire at Rosemont House, he'll be less likely to take action when I'm in the country... Although, Louis's swing accident did happen at Briarwood Park. And the ice incident. Although they *could* have been accidents, pure and simple..." She sighed heavily and drank a little more of her cognac. "My thoughts seem to be going round and round in circles."

"It's only natural that you're worried and uncertain. Hopefully we'll have more answers, very soon," said Adam gently. "It might help you to know that I've started the legal process to become one of Louis's guardians. I met with my lawyer before we went on our jaunt to Gunter's and Hyde Park, so the paperwork will be filed tomorrow—I mean later today"—he nodded at the mantel clock—"with the Court of Chancery. We'll repair to the Abbey the day after that. Will that suit you?"

Catherine gave a nod. "It does... Although..." She winced. "Aren't your mother and sisters there?"

"Yes... But they'll adapt and survive because they don't have a choice. At some point my mother will need to get used to you and my son being in my life. And she can always move into the dower house on the estate whenever she so chooses."

Catherine sighed and put down her cognac. "I imagine that will just be one more thing she resents about me."

"The situation is what it is, Catherine. My mother has always been difficult. An arrogant prickly pear. I have hope for my sisters, Viola and Cordelia, though. They have far sweeter dispositions."

As Adam tossed back the rest of his drink, Catherine gasped. "Adam. Your hand." She clasped it lightly and examined his damaged knuckles. "What on earth did you do to Lord Makepeace?"

Adam shrugged a shoulder. "I only threw one punch. It was a decent one, if I do say so myself. I rather think Makepeace might be sporting a loosened tooth or two, and a frightfully bruised and swollen jaw come morning. It's no less than he deserves. If Maxwell hadn't been there to talk some sense into me, Makepeace would have lost more than a tooth."

Catherine gently pressed her lips to his hand. "Thank you for looking out for me and Louis," she whispered. Her eyes suddenly glimmered with tears. "I'm so very grateful. I've been alone for so long. Trying to be brave for so long… It feels rather lovely to know I have a champion."

Adam's heart clenched with a pang of bittersweet emotion. The awful truth was, for five long years, he *hadn't* been Catherine's champion. He'd let her walk out of Newgate Prison, and his life, and he hadn't seen her again until the night of the Maxwell's ball. The other terrible truth was, even if he'd known she was with child back then, he wasn't sure he would have done anything differently.

He'd been a horse's arse and he'd failed her in every possible way.

But he wouldn't now.

"Oh, *ma belle*," he murmured huskily and cupped her cheek. He rubbed the pad of his thumb over the crest of her high cheekbone. "Don't cry. I'm here for you. I promise you that you can depend on me. I'll look after you and our son until there's no longer breath in my body."

Catherine met his gaze. Her blue-gray eyes no longer glimmered but glowed with a soft warm light. "I believe you, Adam." She turned her head a little and kissed his palm. "You're a good man."

Adam's chest rose as he drew a deep breath. "Your words humble me, Catherine. I try. I could do better. I could—"

Love you? Those two small yet momentous words hovered on the tip of Adam's tongue, but he let them die away.

Is that what he was beginning to feel for Catherine? This wellspring of devotion flooding his chest…was it love? This need to guard her, to fell men in the street for her, even raze the whole of London to the ground for her if he had to… Were these feelings and powerful urges provoked by something deeper than just affection or even desire? While his physical craving for Catherine was—and always would be—undeniable, the emotion rushing through him *was* more than mere lust.

Adam swallowed. Catherine was studying him intently. Waiting for him to finish what he'd begun to say. But he couldn't, because he was suddenly gripped by confusion and indecision and frustration. He wasn't sure what being "in love" really felt like. He had no way to judge or measure. And underneath all of that, was fear. His father had been possessed by a peculiar madness years ago. He'd fallen hopelessly in love with another man's wife and his reckless behavior and the subsequent scandal had brought shame crashing down upon the family.

Adam didn't want to be like that. He wouldn't be governed by wild emotions he couldn't control.

But maybe he was... Maybe it was too late already...

Maybe it wasn't just duty that had prompted him to marry Catherine...

Christ and all his saints. Adam's chest tightened. His heart stuttered.

But then the fear inside him began to subside as he focused on his wife's beautiful face. She was looking up at him through her lashes, her mouth curved in a siren's smile. Her fingers began to undo the silver buttons of his waistcoat and he could at least own that he was completely in her thrall.

Yes, he was enthralled. That was all. He released a shaky breath.

"You could do what, Adam?" Catherine repeated softly, pushing his waistcoat off his shoulders and then down his arms until it fell to the floor. "Make love to me? Make me forget about everything but you? Is that what you were going to say?"

Her whisper was a velvet-soft invitation that slipped through all Adam's defenses and stilled his turbulent thoughts. Stroked along his nerves and curled through his body, setting him alight, driving him to take action.

"God yes." His mouth crashed down on Catherine's and

his tongue thrust into her deeply, plundering and savoring her lush, honeyed warmth.

This was what he wanted. This, right now, was enough.

Catherine yielded completely to his every demand. Her tongue tangled with his and her fingers twisted into his hair. Her wrapper fell to the floor and she pushed her breasts against him. Through the thin diaphanous lawn of her night rail he could feel the tips of her nipples, as hard as pearls, pressing into his chest. It made him ache to taste her there. To fondle and tease and devour until Catherine was mindlessly writhing with want.

Tearing his mouth from Catherine's, Adam began to feast on the fragrant flesh of her neck. He licked and nibbled and kissed his way along her collarbone while his frantic fingers tugged the ribbon securing the bodice of her night rail undone. Yanking down the fabric, he exposed the satiny pale mounds of her breasts with their impudently puckered pink points to his hungry gaze.

He seized the lush plump flesh with both hands before burying his face between them, inhaling her intoxicating scent. As he set about tormenting Catherine's nipples with his fingers and tongue, she clutched at his shoulders and a sweet moan fell from her lips.

But he wasn't satisfied. Not yet. Not by a mile.

Although it seemed Catherine had other ideas.

She wriggled out of his hold then swept off her night rail and tossed it on the floor. She toed off her slippers next and then tossed her pale blond hair over one shoulder. Her eyes met his, a spark of challenge—and perhaps excitement—glimmering in their smoky blue depths. She was entirely and unabashedly naked, and as she bit her lip, her attention slid to Adam's groin where the long hard ridge of his erection was plain to see. If he wasn't spellbound before, he certainly was now.

"I want to pleasure you with my mouth," she murmured huskily. "Go over to your desk and lean against it."

Adam immediately acquiesced. He couldn't resist. It had been forever since he'd experienced this particular act.

Sybil had found even the most sedate forms of bed sport distasteful, and Adam had never engaged another mistress. His visit to the high-end bawdy house in St James's—when he was a widower—had been impersonal and brief and had involved the use of a French letter.

Yes, it had been five years since Catherine had gone down on him, and he was *not* going to say no.

Hot lust racing through his veins, Adam leaned back, his palms flat on the smooth mahogany surface, his arms braced for the erotic onslaught that was to come. His wonderfully wanton wife knelt before him and freed his pulsing member from the confines of his buckskin breeches. His whole body seemed to twitch and shiver in agonized anticipation as she grasped his shaft, and then, her eyes locked with his, she edged her lips closer to his tip. As he watched her, she quite deliberately swirled her pretty pink tongue around the swollen crown of his cock, pulling a choked groan from his throat.

Fuck, she was a temptress. A saucy goddess. The sweetest tease. She laved his shaft until it was slick. Fondled his ballocks with her clever fingers. When she greedily lapped up the bead of moisture that seeped from the slit in his cock, Adam's hips bucked and he groaned again. And then, when he thought he might actually have to beg her to end his torment, to take pity on his desperate state of feverish arousal, her wonderfully wicked mouth engulfed him. His cock rode her tongue, thrusting deeply before she hollowed her cheeks and mercilessly sucked his throbbing length.

Blood blazing hell, she was good at this. Better than good. She was outstanding.

Adam gripped the table and pumped his hips in time with

the rhythmic plunge and retreat of Catherine's hot sweet mouth. His legs were shaking, his balls tightening. Incoherent groans and filthy words of praise fell from his lips. He didn't know what he said as any semblance of rational thought was all but obliterated from his mind.

All he could do was hold on for this wild ride that he knew was about to swiftly come to a tumultuous, spectacular end. One of his hands snaked into the tumbling mass of Catherine's silken hair, gripping her head as he hurtled toward climax. And then all at once, a wave of hot blinding bliss tore through him like a lightning bolt and Adam at last gave into the overwhelming urge to come. As a torrent of his seed poured forth, Catherine swallowed everything without hesitation.

The fact that she would do this just for him—this decadent erotic act—was not lost on Adam. He also couldn't deny how humbled and touched he was. Something deep inside him made him want to give Catherine just as much pleasure too. The world might be spinning out of control for both of them, but here, tonight, they could find both ecstasy and solace in each other's arms.

Satisfaction humming through his veins, Adam gathered himself together and urged Catherine to rise. His hand still in her hair, he brought her lips to his and kissed her soundly. "You wicked minx, you interrupted what I was about to do beforehand," he growled as they drew apart. "And you thoroughly unmanned me. For that you should be punished. In kind."

She arched a fine brow. "Well, I, for one, was nothing but impressed with your display of masculine prowess before you fully surrendered. As for your suggestion of punishment..." Catherine's eyes sparkled with saucy mischief. "You could always spank me first, my lord."

Adam gave a low growl. "While part of me wouldn't mind

turning your delectable arse pink with the palm of my hand, I'm also dying to use my mouth on your pretty pussy. To have the taste of you on my tongue."

"I'll do whatever you want," she murmured, her lashes fluttering down, shielding the expression in her eyes. "I'm your wife and yours to command."

He lifted her chin and captured her gaze. "You know that we will only ever do what you want, don't you, Catherine? That it's you who holds all the power. That you make the rules." He pulled her hard against him. "You've ensorcelled me, body and soul, my beautiful wench of a wife. Everything I do, I do for you."

Her teeth snagged her plump lower lip. "I know," she whispered. But there was something in her eyes. A fleeting shadow in their depths that made Adam wonder if she actually did believe him.

But then the moment passed. Her mouth tilted into a feline smile and she all but purred as she slid her hands up his chest and laced her fingers around his neck. "So, I'm ready to take my punishment. Where would you like me to be? How do you want me?"

"On the sofa by the fire." Grasping her slender torso, Adam lifted her and she immediately wrapped her legs around him. Within a few strides, he'd crossed to the fireside and he gently lay her on the scarlet silk damask. "Lean back and spread those luscious thighs of yours," he continued, dropping to his knees on the hearthrug. "I want to see every little bit of you."

She immediately did as he'd requested, draping one leg over the stuffed arm of the sofa. Her arms stretched up behind her head as though she was surrendering herself to him—as though displaying herself for him to admire. Her other foot slid to the floor and she posed so prettily for him, Adam sat back on his heels and took a moment to drink in the breath-stealing view.

Over the years they'd been apart, how many times had he fantasized about having Catherine like this again? Deliciously naked with desire in her eyes? Ready and wet and wanting and all his?

Adam reached out and slid his palms up Catherine's slender calves to her thighs. She shivered and parted her legs a little more. The sight of her sex, glistening and pink and swollen and so damn inviting made his cock instantly hard again. Once he'd brought Catherine to climax with his mouth, he'd plunge into her and make her come a second time.

He dipped his head and nuzzled one inner thigh, then the other.

His night beard gently scraped across her silken flesh while his fingers flirted with the feathery blonde curls covering her mound. But he didn't touch the hardened pearl at the apex of her sex and it wasn't long before he'd wrung a frustrated whimper from Catherine. Her fingers speared into his hair. Clutching. Tugging. Urging.

"Cruel man, stop taunting me with promises of what's to come." Her voice was threaded with desperation as she lifted her hips. "You know what I want. What I need."

Adam raised his head and caught her desire-glazed gaze. "I do. And I can guarantee you that I want to give it to you more." He skimmed a fingertip along one side of her dew-slick nether lips, but again, he deliberately avoided where she craved him the most. "I know that I'm teasing you, but it will only heighten your pleasure. Rest assured, I won't be satisfied until I feel you come all over my tongue." He slid his finger down the other side of her sex. "Do you understand? Do you trust me to make this good for you?"

"Yes, my lord," Catherine whispered. She sucked in a

sharp breath and shivered when Adam at last lightly grazed his thumb over the plump hood just above her clitoris.

But that was only the beginning.

He spread her delicate folds even wider with his thumbs. The musky scent of her arousal only served to intensify his own ravening need. His own hunger.

His mouth watering, his body burning, Adam at last lowered his head and feasted. His tongue explored every bit of Catherine's sweet sex. Lapped and tasted and relished. Swirled and savored.

And Catherine seemed to love everything. She arched into him, grinding her sex against his mouth. Gripped his head and moaned and whimpered and whispered how wonderful he made her feel. How she loved the feel of his wicked tongue.

"What about my wicked fingers?" he growled, lifting his face just long enough to insert his index and middle fingers inside her tight, slick channel. While he suckled her clitoris, he curled his fingers and stroked deeply, over and over again, and her answering gasps and shudders were all the confirmation he needed that she was enjoying his erotic ministrations.

If he'd rendered her speechless, he was doing well.

He could feel her edging closer to orgasm when her silken inner walls began to clasp his fingers tightly. He increased the pace of his thrusts. Rapidly flicked her clitoris with precise but delicate flutters of his tongue. It was enough to push Catherine into the arms of pleasure. Her whole body arched, she gasped, and let out a bliss-drenched cry. Adam's fingers were suddenly bathed in a fresh rush of moisture, then she subsided back onto the sofa with a soft murmur of content-ment, her limbs quivering.

"When I regain full consciousness, just be warned I'm going to kiss you," she whispered huskily. Her eyes were closed but she was smiling.

Adam rose up and loomed over her lissome, elegantly sprawled body. "What if I want a kiss now?"

She gave a small laugh. "You're insatiable."

"When it comes to you, my beautiful wife, always." Adam kissed Catherine tenderly and she wrapped her arms about him, drawing him down on top of her.

When the kiss ended, she pouted and a line appeared between her brows. "Why are you still half-dressed?" She ran her hands up and down his cambric shirtsleeves. "Especially when I can feel your bare, hard-as-iron cock pressing into my belly?" She wriggled a little to emphasize her point.

Adam laughed then stood. "Do you want me to strip, *ma belle?*"

"Yes, please," she said, her eyes aglow. "It will give me enough time to recover before I bend over the sofa and you have your wicked way with me from behind."

"Are you sure?" Adam asked as he pulled off his shirt then cast it on the floor. On their wedding night he'd taken her that way. "You can ride me if you'd prefer. It used to be *your* favorite position if I recall..."

"I'm sure." Catherine smiled her coquette's smile as she pushed to her feet. She then sauntered to the end of the sofa and bent over the padded arm so seductively, Adam realized he wasn't going to naysay her. What man could?

He was so impatient to be inside her, he didn't bother to remove his breeches or boots. Instead he moved behind her, freed his aching cockstand, and growled, "Brace yourself, wife."

She glanced back over her shoulder at him. "I'm ready," she returned as she rocked back toward him, deliberately brushing her slickness against him.

Adam hissed, half in pleasure, half in agony. "Tease," he groaned. Gripping her luscious arse with one hand, he dragged his already weeping cock through the moisture welling at her entrance...and then he pushed inside her tight wet heat until he was deeper than he thought possible.

Holy hell... Adam gritted his teeth and froze, fighting for control. He didn't want to spend too soon—he really did want Catherine to orgasm a second time—but the impulse to take her hard and fast was also irresistible.

Part of him didn't want to mindlessly rut like a beast ruled by base urges alone. Which was exactly what he'd done when he'd poured himself into Catherine after they'd reunited. When he'd failed to satisfy her.

No, he was better than that. He wanted Catherine to experience just as much untold pleasure as he was going to. He wanted this to be as spectacular as their wedding night.

He wanted... He didn't just want Catherine to feel desired, but also cherished. He wanted her to know that her needs were just as important—if not more important—than his own.

He wanted her to feel like he was making love to his wife, even if no words of love had been exchanged. That they weren't simply screwing as a man screwed his mistress.

Somehow harnessing his runaway lust, Adam set up a slow steady rhythm stroking deeply and then retreating, prolonging the excruciating yet exquisite friction. Gliding in and out of Catherine, stoking the fire bit by bit, drawing out the pleasure. He wanted to revel in the intimacy of each moment. The closeness they shared...

God how he'd missed this. All the little things about Catherine. Not just the tight lush clasp of her feminine muscles but other minuscule yet precious details. The freckle on her left shoulder. The elegant line of her neck and the satiny smoothness of her curves beneath his palms. The sweet dimples at the base of her spine and the perfectly luscious globes of her derriere. The way her pale gold hair spilled about her shoulders. The music of her breathy pants and moans as she moved perfectly in concert with him.

The heady taste of her still on his lips and tongue.

Having Catherine like this was bliss. More than ever, Adam was convinced they were made for each other. That they belonged together. That marrying her—while a seemingly mad and foolish act in the eyes of Society—was the best decision he'd ever made.

But coming was inevitable. As much as Adam wanted to stay buried inside Catherine's delicious wet heat forever, worshipping her body, he couldn't.

He increased the tempo of his thrusts. Ignoring the sweat dripping from his body, the sawing of his breath and the hammering of his heart, he pumped his cock harder and faster, driving Catherine inexorably toward heaven.

He felt the exact moment that she peaked. She cried out as she convulsed and shuddered and squeezed him so tightly, Adam had no choice but to follow her into ecstasy. Pleasure surged in a great hot wave and he pistoned into Catherine frantically for another moment or two before he emitted a harsh groan and then collapsed, exhausted but satisfied, on top of her.

"Well, I'd say you've outdone yourself again, husband," murmured Catherine. "That was a spectacular performance." She was resting on her forearms on the sofa, turning her face toward him, offering Adam a kiss.

He clasped the back of her head and claimed her mouth. "I agree," he whispered.

It wasn't until they'd both retired to his ducal bedchamber, and Catherine was lying asleep in his arms, that Adam realized something was bothering him about Catherine's pronouncement at the end of their bout of lovemaking. She'd said his "performance" was spectacular.

Performance.

The old concern flickered back into his mind. Could it be...was it possible that *Catherine* was performing? Was she simply playing the courtesan in the bedroom? She couldn't hide her orgasms. He could *feel* her body tremor and quake. He knew he could satisfy her physically. He also knew she was an eager participant in all that they did.

But...but was that enough, for him or for her? The idea that Catherine might be playing a part—that she was not being her true self—suddenly troubled him.

Aside from the fact Adam was protecting her—and without question, their son—did she feel anything for him at all? Well, apart from a genuine fondness for his company and boundless physical attraction?

The bigger question was: would it matter to him if his wife never felt anything for him beyond that?

This *was*, for all intents and purposes, a marriage of convenience... But what if it *could* be more than that?

What if he could let go of his emotions and let himself fall in love with his wife? And what if Catherine could love him too?

Would they be happy forever like the couple in a fairy tale or a romantic novel? Or would their love fade over time? Would their marriage become just a hollow, brittle shell of a thing, just like the one he'd had with Sybil? Or a bitter disastrous tragic failure, just like his parents' marriage?

Adam pressed a kiss against Catherine's temple. She murmured in her sleep and snuggled against his side. The problem was, he was a jaded soul. He'd never believed marriage could end in a happily-ever-after. At least, not for him.

For so long—years and years in fact—he'd been governed by the need to be an upright nobleman. To not be ruled by irrational emotion. To not repeat the terrible mistakes of his father. So he'd endeavored to make everyone else in his life happy—Sybil and his mother and his sisters—but never himself.

But it wasn't enough. It would never be enough...not without love.

What a painful, profound, and earthshaking epiphany.

Adam sighed and hugged Catherine a little bit tighter. Maybe when this terrible campaign being waged against Catherine and Louis was all over, he might let himself pursue the happy future he'd secretly always wanted with this beautiful, generous-hearted woman in his arms...

Maybe then and only then, he'd let himself fall in love.

If only Catherine could love him too.

CHAPTER 16

The day after Adam applied for joint guardianship of Louis, they all quit London. Catherine was nothing but relieved as the Earl of Dalton's convoy of carriages rolled out of the capital, heading for lovely Oxfordshire. Catherine, Louis, Pippin, and Louis's nursemaid, Lizzy, traveled with Adam whilst another pair of carriages conveyed Adam's valet, Catherine's lady's maid Hetty, and the ever-faithful footman Jackson along with umpteen trunks of their belongings.

Although Adam wasn't sure how long it would take for the Court of Chancery's Lord Chancellor to make a ruling, he was hopeful it wouldn't be more than a week or two. To Catherine's way of thinking, it couldn't happen soon enough. Then and only then would she be able to rest easy in the knowledge that the Fortescues would not be able to take her son from her by claiming she was an unfit mother. Not when Louis was under the care of the well-regarded Earl of Dalton.

Of course, Catherine worried that her husband might *not* be well-regarded any longer considering who he'd just married, but Adam reassured her that he had enough friends in high places that her past would not signify in the Court of

Chancery's decision-making process. He was an earl with wealth and influence. The Fortescues were at the very best, well-monied landed gentry, and if Benedict launched a counterclaim, it would likely be viewed as self-serving because he was next in line for the Earldom of Rosemont. The only thing Catherine could do was trust that the Lord Chancellor would agree with Adam's line of reasoning.

The journey took the best part of a day—the usual six-hour trek took a good deal longer with a little boy and a dog who required regular comfort stops—but the weather held and they were not hampered by rain. When Adam's carriage at last negotiated the road leading down to St Clair Abbey—the elegant Baroque-style manor house was nestled in a vale surrounded by gently rolling wooded parkland—it was late afternoon. The setting sun, peeking out from behind a low bank of clouds, softly illuminated the building's golden stone walls and Catherine couldn't hide her delight. In the distance, she also caught a glimpse of the familiar River Thames.

"Your home is beautiful, Adam," she breathed. "Although —and I hope you don't mind me saying so—it doesn't look much like an abbey. In fact, it reminds me a little of Blenheim Palace."

Adam, sitting beside her, squeezed her hand and smiled, his blue eyes alight with pleasure at her praise. "I was rather hoping you'd like it," he said. "And no, it doesn't look overly much like a church. After the Dissolution of the Monasteries and the original abbey went into decline, my great-great grandfather used its stones to build this new edifice. Well, along with stones from a local quarry at Headington, because the new St Clair Abbey is considerably larger. All that remains of the old church is a crumbling wall and two rather dilapidated towers. With all the wet weather we've had this year, the site has deteriorated even further. In fact, my groundsman tells me that the window arches are almost ready to fall. It's best to avoid getting too close to the ruins, picturesque though they are."

"I'd like to see them some time," said Catherine with a smile. "From a distance, of course. How far away are they?"

"Not far at all. Less than half a mile from the house in fact. On the eastern edge of the grounds on the banks of the Thames. The dower house is nearby." Adam pointed at a small wood in the distance. "Beyond those trees on that low rise."

Turning his attention to his son who'd been sitting beside his nursemaid and Pippin, he then said, "What do you think, Louis? Do you like the look of your new home?"

Louis slid off the bench seat and climbed onto his father's lap. "I like it," he said after a moment. "Is there a swing in the gardens? I like swings. But only if they have strong ropes."

Adam ruffled his son's golden hair. "No, there isn't. But I will have one built for you. There's a nice big sturdy oak tree that will be perfect for such an addition. And I will personally make sure the ropes are the strongest ropes in England."

"Good," said Louis. "I should like that very much."

"I also think you'll enjoy meeting the pony in my stable. There's one waiting just for you."

Louis' eyes lit up. "There is?"

"Yes, his name is Bramble and I'll take you for riding lessons if you'd like." Adam caught Catherine's eye. "With your Mama's approval of course."

Catherine inclined her head. "Of course." She was touched Adam would be spending so much time with Louis. He'd missed out on so much precious time already.

"My sisters learned to ride on Bramble's sire," Adam continued. "Bramble is a Shetland pony and very gentle."

Catherine smiled. "I trust your judgment."

Adam answering smile was warm. "Thank you, *ma belle*." Then a shadow crossed his countenance. "I just hope my family can accept the change in status quo."

Catherine swallowed a sigh. "I suppose we shall soon see."

Adam's next words indicated he'd detected her deep reservations but sought to reassure her. "Until the dower house is ready, I'll imagine my mother and sisters will occupy the rooms in the southern wing of the house. That has been my mother's custom for some time, at any rate. Our apartments are located in the north wing, so I suspect you will see little of her. I'll make it's clear that you are the new lady of the manor and all staff are to defer to you for direction in managing the household."

"Thank you," said Catherine. "I appreciate your support. Very much."

"You'll have it always, *ma belle*," he returned in a low voice and Catherine's heart flip-flopped in her chest. Of course, she wanted his support, but she also wanted more than that...

Maybe here, living with him on his quiet country estate, away from all the dark deeds and chaos, perhaps his love would grow...

Within five minutes, Adam's carriage had passed through the Abbey's grand iron gates and was drawing to a stop on the gravel forecourt in front of the house's main wing. A long line of servants assembled before the front stairs as Catherine and Louis were helped from the carriage. Noticeably absent from the welcome party was the Dowager Lady Dalton, Lady Cordelia, and Lady Viola. Catherine couldn't say she was sorry. At least she wouldn't have to affect a falsely polite demeanor when greeting her new mother-in-law. She had no idea how her young sisters-in-law would receive her, but she would worry about that later.

Adam presented her to the staff as his new wife, Catherine, Lady Dalton. Louis was introduced as his stepson, the Earl of Rosemont. Catherine learned that the silver-haired butler went by the name of Quigley and the estate steward was a Scot named Mr. Kerr. Both gentlemen bowed with due deference.

The middle-aged housekeeper, Mrs. Beckett, also had an outwardly pleasant manner. She curtsied to Catherine and politely offered to meet with her to discuss the running of the household whenever it suited her.

So far, so good, thought Catherine as she and Louis were ushered through the front doors of St Clair Abbey into a magnificent entry hall that was a study in gold and sparkling glass. Adam's bootsteps echoed as he escorted her and Louis across the marble floor—a black and white checkerboard—toward the huge, divided staircase of white marble. An ornate glass cupola arched overhead and beautiful gilt-framed artwork—a mixture of portraits and landscapes and scenes from classical mythology—lined the scarlet flocked wallpaper above the picture rails. The balustrades and wall sconces were also gilt as were the legs of side tables and plush upholstered occasional chairs. Small alcoves at regular intervals housed marble busts and classical statues. There were so many soaring arched windows that afforded views of the gorgeous grounds outside, Catherine almost didn't know where to look.

"I had no idea St Clair Abbey was so lovely or so opulent," she murmured as they began to scale the staircase—toward the north wing, no doubt. Mrs. Beckett and Quigley trailed behind along with Hetty and Lizzy. "There's so much to admire. I'm sure I'll get a sore neck from staring at all the artwork."

Adam grinned. "I'm glad you like it." He glanced down at Louis who was holding his hand. "What do you think, my son?"

"It's big," he said as he stared up at the paintings. "I hope I won't get lost."

"You won't," said Catherine. "You'll always have me or your father or Lizzy or Jackson with you."

"Or my new grandmama and my new aunts?" said Louis

with a hopeful note in his sweetly piping voice. "Aunty Violet and Aunty Cordial? Will I get to meet them soon?"

Catherine gave an inward grimace. Louis had clearly paid attention to some of the discussions she and Adam had shared during the long carriage ride; one of the topics had been how to manage such an introduction.

Pausing on the landing, Catherine leaned down to meet her son's eyes. "Aunty Viola and Aunty Cordelia," she gently prompted. "And yes, I imagine you will...soon..." Upon straightening, she exchanged a look with Adam. "All going well..."

Adam canted his head. There was a hesitant expression in his eyes. It mirrored her own uncertainty and apprehension. "All going well..."

Catherine took Louis's other hand as they resumed their ascent. "Let us get you settled in your new bedchamber first." Adam had sent word ahead that they would all be arriving today so a room for Louis had been set up in the same wing as the earl's main suite. The original nursery was located on the floor above, but given the new environment and the uncertainty surrounding Catherine and Louis's safety, Adam agreed it would be best if their son slept close by.

Once Louis was happily playing in his room with Lizzy and Pippin—a huge array of toys, including a sturdy rocking horse that used to be Adam's, had been brought down from the old nursery—Adam showed Catherine to the countess's apartments.

"The furnishings were chosen by my mother, but you are free to redecorate," said Adam. "I want you to feel at home."

Catherine reached up and kissed his cheek. "Thank you. The rooms are already lovely." And she meant it. Drusilla, the Dowager Lady Dalton, might not ever accept Catherine as her daughter-in-law, but Catherine couldn't deny they woman had good taste. The spacious sitting room and bedroom beyond contained elegant pieces of gilt and satinwood furniture. The sumptuous fabric of the curtains, upholstery and bedding—satins and velvets and silks in muted shades of soft gray and lavender and lilac—complemented the plush Aubusson rugs and their delicate floral motifs. The apartments really were exceptional—almost fit for a duchess, or even a queen.

"My suite is through there." Adam gestured at a white wooden door with a gilt handle, just to the left of the white marble fireplace. "It will always be unlocked and you may join me in my bed whenever you want."

Catherine looked up through her eyelashes at him. "The invitation is mutual, my lord," she murmured. Heat flared in Adam's blue eyes, but then a glimmer of uncertainty flickered across his features.

Catherine's heart immediately plummeted. "Have I said something wrong?" she whispered. Was Adam's desire for her already fading? They'd been married less than a week...

"No. No, of course not, *ma belle*." Adam cast her such a winning smile, Catherine wondered if she'd imagined his moment of hesitancy. Unless he was just tired—he'd been keeping late hours. Or perhaps he was simply worried about living with a wife and mother-in-law who were bound to clash.

"You know how much I want you, don't you?" he added. "Don't ever doubt that. Ever."

Catherine stared into his eyes, searching them for any hint of a hidden meaning. That maybe he felt more for her than desire. But she couldn't tell. "I won't," she returned softly. "I... I want you too."

Adam clasped her face and his thumb caressed her cheek. "More than anything, I want you to be happy here." He kissed her gently, and when he drew back he added, "Why don't you spend some time freshening up after the journey, and I'll see what my mother and sisters are up to? Dinner is usually served around seven in the dining room downstairs. But due to our late arrival I'll have the kitchen staff delay it until eight. I'll send word so that you know for sure. I imagine you'll also want to make sure Louis is settled for the night."

Catherine smiled back. "That all sounds perfect."

As a pair of footmen, directed by Mrs. Beckett and Hetty, began to bring Catherine's trunks upstairs, Adam bid Catherine farewell and retreated down the hall, heading for the opposite wing of the house. His long strides were purposeful, but his wide shoulders looked tense beneath the well-cut lines of his coat. No doubt he was preparing himself to do battle with his family.

You and Louis are his family now, Catherine reminded herself sternly as she crossed to one of the sitting room windows and stared out at the immaculate gardens. *You are Lady Dalton and this is your domain. You belong here.*

Maybe if she kept telling herself that, she'd begin to believe it.

Adam found his mother and sisters ensconced by the fire in one of the larger parlors in the south wing of St Clair Abbey. It looked as though the room had been turned into a makeshift drawing room. Through a connecting doorway, he could see an adjacent chamber now sported a small round dining table for four.

Right then, he thought. *The battlelines have been drawn. Territories have been marked.* While he'd undoubtedly lobbed a grenade into his sisters' grand plans for their debuts in a year or two, he couldn't undo what had been done. Hopefully, in time, he could negotiate and establish a long-lasting peace accord.

"Adam..." The Dowager Lady Dalton looked up from her needlework but didn't put it aside as Adam stepped into the parlor. "Mrs. Beckett sent word you had arrived."

"Yes. My wife and stepson are here too. They're settling into the north wing as we speak."

His mother's lips thinned. "Yes... I heard that, too."

"I hope all of you will make them feel welcome." Adam caught his sisters' gazes in turn. They were also engaged in some sort of needlework. "Louis is particularly looking forward to meeting his aunts. And of course"—his attention turned back to his mother—"his new grandmama." There was no point in beating about the bush. He wasn't going to hide Catherine and Louis away like he was ashamed of them. Sooner or later, they were all going to have to learn to live together.

Cordelia and Viola offered him weak smiles before their gazes darted to their mother for direction. They were obviously going to follow her lead.

"I cannot make promises, my son," replied the dowager countess, "but I shall try my best to be civil. Young Lord Rosemont obviously isn't to blame for his mother's...predilections. I shall endeavor to meet him on the morrow."

Cordelia's and Viola's smiles relaxed a little. "We should like that too, dear brother," said Viola. She sounded sincere and Cordelia was nodding her agreement.

"Excellent," said Adam. "I'm sure Catherine will be most happy to hear that. And Mother Dear," he added in a sterner tone, "you shouldn't believe everything you read in the gossip columns. Catherine's reputation has been spotless for some time now. And I care for her. Very much. I'd be grateful if you could at least give my wife a chance to show you that she is of good character and possesses a kind heart. She's also very accomplished and a clever conversationalist. The girls"—he glanced at Viola and Cordelia—"could practice their French with her. She was born in Paris."

"No doubt your wife could also provide expert tuition in how to use one's feminine wiles to ensnare a man." Drusilla's eyes gleamed. "But the less said about that the better, don't you think, my son?"

Adam felt his cheeks heat even as he narrowed his gaze in warning. "Catherine *is* my wife, and the mistress of this home, and I suggest you afford her with the respect that's her due. You will not insult her. You will not undermine her status here. You will not spread rumors about her past to anyone in the neighborhood. You will not speak ill of her in front of any of the servants, including Mrs. Beckett or Quigley. Do I make myself clear?"

His mother's expression hardened. Nevertheless, she inclined her head. "Perfectly."

Adam gave a curt nod. "Good. To demonstrate you and my sisters are extending an olive branch, I should like to see you join Catherine and me for dinner in the main dining room at eight o'clock. I've already asked Quigley to have a word with the cook and Mrs. Beckett. From tomorrow, Catherine will be meeting with the housekeeper to make the decisions about menus and other matters pertaining to household management. Just like Sybil used to do."

"Of course." His mother lifted her chin a little. "Just so you know, I've already inspected the dower house and have begun to make plans with Mr. Kerr about what needs to be done. Unfortunately it's in such a state of disrepair, it may take some months to make it habitable. There's rising damp and dry rot in some of the window frames. And everything needs repainting both inside and out. And that's just to begin with."

"I understand," said Adam. "Take all the time you need. Despite what you believe, I'm not entirely selfish and heartless.

I do not wish you to feel that I am forcing you to live in inferior accommodation."

During his marriage to Sybil, his mother and sisters had continued to reside within St Clair Abbey. For the most part, they'd all seemed to get on. Although, Adam suspected that his mother had long lamented that the union hadn't produced any children. He did wonder if Louis might be able to help bridge the gap between his mother and Catherine. Especially if his mother suspected Louis might actually be his son.

Perhaps her delay in vacating her Abbey apartments might be an indication that she was at least a *little* curious about Louis...

If his mother asked him, he would be honest about the little boy's parentage. And he would tell Catherine to do the same. There was no point in keeping secrets.

There'd been too many secrets in this family already.

CHAPTER 17

A few hours later, after Louis was settled in his room and fast asleep—he was so exhausted, he'd almost nodded off during his dinner in the makeshift nursery—Catherine had returned to her own suite to prepare herself for the evening ahead.

"How do I look?" she asked as Hetty made the finishing touches to her elegant coiffure. The lady's maid had gone to extra effort this evening—Catherine wanted to look her best at dinner should Drusilla put in an appearance—and her hair had been styled into a lovely Grecian arrangement. Braids had been looped and coiled on top of her head while an abundance of curls cascaded down toward her shoulders. Hetty had also woven tiny seed pearls throughout the arrangement.

Hetty opened her mouth to reply but got no further as Adam's deep voice drifted into Catherine's new dressing room. "You look divine, my lady. Like a goddess."

Catherine's heart tripping, she turned on the padded seat at her dressing table and smiled at her husband. He looked equally divine in formal evening attire. He clearly wanted to put his best foot forward when dining with his mother, too.

"Thank you, my lord," she replied. Then she caught Hetty's eye. "That will be all for this evening. I'm sure you're exhausted from all the traveling. Why don't you retire to your new quarters and have an early night?"

The maid bobbed a quick curtsy. "Of course, my lady." As she quit the room, Catherine couldn't help but notice the admiring glance she cast the Earl of Dalton's way as she passed him by.

Catherine couldn't say that she blamed her. Adam *was* breathtakingly handsome in his midnight-blue evening coat that fit him like a glove. The dark blue, almost black fabric was the perfect foil for his hair; it brought out the strands of dark gold and caramel in the thick light-brown waves. His blue eyes even seemed a shade brighter. Or perhaps it was a gleam of masculine appreciation as his gaze raked over her figure. It was the sort of look that never failed to make Catherine's pulse pick up speed and her mind think of all the wicked things they could do together.

But there would be ample time for bed sport later.

"I have something for you," said Adam as he approached. His eyes met hers in the mirror.

"Oh?" Catherine arched a brow and she smiled.

"Yes..." Adam reached into his jacket and pulled a slender box covered in dark blue velvet from one of the inner pockets. "It's a little something from the Dalton family jewelry collection. I never presented you with a gift on our wedding day. It was remiss of me."

Catherine's hands fluttered to her throat and her vision blurred with tears as she accepted the box with trembling fingers. She was touched beyond measure. "My goodness. You don't really need to give me anything, Adam. I have all I need."

"Yes, I do. You've been through so much of late. I wanted to do something that would make you smile." Adam nodded at the box. "Are you going to open it?" Then he added, "And just so you know, neither Sybil nor my mother have ever worn it. Just in case you were wondering."

"That *is* good to know." Catherine placed the slender case on the dressing table and unfastened the clasp. When she lifted the lid, she couldn't suppress a gasp of delight. Nestled upon a bed of white satin lay an exquisite sapphire and diamond necklace.

"It's not the French Blue diamond," said Adam, "but I hope you'll like it all the same. It reminds me of your eyes."

"I-I love it," declared Catherine. She sought Adam's gaze in the mirror. "And it's more precious to me than any French Crown Jewel could ever be, because...because you gave it to me..." And then a bright pink blush bloomed in her cheeks when she realized she was looking at her husband with open adoration in her eyes.

She immediately dropped her gaze. She'd been so overwhelmed she'd let her guard down. She'd let Adam catch a glimpse of how she really felt about him...and she was suddenly all at sea. Floundering in confusion and embarrassment.

She didn't want things to be awkward between them. She didn't want him to feel obligated to her. To have to pretend that he cared for her. It was far easier to hide her true emotions.

So she tucked her feelings away and slipped into her familiar role of seductress. She reached out and stroked the enormous, deep blue sapphire in the center of the necklace. Caressed the line of sparkling diamonds surrounding the magnificent gemstone with her fingertip.

As she looked up through her lashes at Adam, she said, "I can't wait to wear this and this alone for you."

As she'd hoped, heat flared in her husband's eyes. Maybe he'd ascribe her own blush to a rush of desire and nothing more.

"After dinner, I'll strip you naked but for this," he said huskily as he reached for the necklace and draped it around her neck.

"I hope that's a promise."

After he fastened the clasp, he leaned down and grazed his lips along her ear. "It is." He bent lower and placed a hot, open-mouthed kiss on her neck. "And to think that just two nights ago you told me that *I* was insatiable..."

Catherine shivered. In the mirror she could see the bare tops of her breasts rising and falling above the blue silk of her gown as her breathing quickened. "Perhaps we should repair downstairs for dinner posthaste so we can at least appease one type of hunger," she whispered.

"Yes...I think that would be eminently sensible, my lady."

By the time they reached the drawing room for a prandial drink, Catherine was nervous and fidgety.

And Adam noticed. "Everything will be all right, *ma belle.* You've braved far worse things than my mother's company. But perhaps we should have a fortifying Amontillado sherry or two." He beckoned one of the young men over who was bearing a tray of small crystal glasses filled with amber-hued liquid.

Catherine laughed as she took a glass and sipped. "I think that's a good idea. And I suppose you're right," she added after the footman had retreated to a safe distance. "I have faced far worse. It's just that when I met your mother at Dalton House—the morning you offered to marry me—she and I had...words." She winced. "I might have gone a bit too far by intimating we'd sullied the sofa and carpet in your drawing room."

Adam tipped his head back and released a full throaty chuckle. "Oh, that would have raised her hackles no end."

"I know. And I shouldn't have deliberately provoked her. But I was in no mood for her condescension that day."

Adam squeezed her hand. "Don't let her intimidate you. You are my wife. I chose you."

"But did you?" The words slipped out before Catherine knew what she was saying. "I mean, I forced your hand. Only the night before you'd told me you couldn't marry me because of your duty to your family. A family that is clearly upset by our marriage."

"I know. I was...I was wrong."

"No... No, I think you meant what you said. It was only after I told you about Louis and all of the untoward happenings and the threatening note that you changed your mind. You chose Louis."

"I chose both of you."

"I wish I could believe that. I wish..." Catherine bit her lip... "I'm sorry. I've created friction between us when we really should be presenting a united front in front of your mother and sisters."

"Catherine," said Adam, his voice low. "*You* are my family now. You and Louis. My duty—my allegiance is to you."

There was that word again. *Duty.* How she hated that word. She wished it didn't exist. She wanted to crumple it up and throw it on the floor and stomp on it. Or better yet, throw it in the fire and watch it burn.

Somehow Catherine swallowed her frustration. "That's not really true though, is it, Adam?" she said in a tone she hoped sounded measured rather than brittle and liable to crack. Her gaze skipped to the footman, but he stood some distance away, his expression as impassive as the ancestral portraits hanging at regular intervals about the walls of the elegantly furnished drawing room. If he could hear any of this exchange, she had to trust it wouldn't be repeated. "You might profess your devotion to me and to Louis, but I know you still want your sisters to have successful debuts and make good marriages one day. It's only natural that you would. Rightly so. They are blameless in all of this...this complicated quagmire we're in." She sighed. "Perhaps when my messy situation is sorted out, I should just retire to Briarwood Park with Louis again. I estimate it's less than a five-hour journey from here. You could visit us regularly. If I kept my distance, there'd perhaps be less friction and less gossip about your family."

"What utter ballocks," said Adam heatedly. "You're staying here, where you belong, by my side. I paid a visit to my mother earlier and she said that she'd be civil. I think that was her way of saying she would give you a chance. Maybe you need to give her a chance too. Not just for me, but for Louis. She *is* his grandmother."

"Does she know that he actually is your son?" murmured Catherine.

"No..." Adam raked a hand through his thick hair, ruffling the artful tousles into spikes. "But I will tell her at some point. In the next few days. If she asks you directly about Louis's parentage, I would be honest. My mother hates being lied to and doesn't suffer fools."

Catherine nodded. "Who knows, it might even help if she knows the truth. I—" She got no further as the dowager countess and two pretty young blonde women—Catherine assumed they were Adam's sisters—arrived.

Adam affected the introductions. Drusilla greeted Catherine with an inclination of her head and a tight smile and both Lady Viola and Lady Cordelia observed the expected proprieties as well. They dipped into graceful curtsies and murmured perfectly polite "how-do-you-dos".

As mundane pleasantries were exchanged about the journey from London and the weather, Lady Viola studied Catherine keenly—Catherine understood that she was seventeen and the older of the pair—while Lady Cordelia seemed bashful and perhaps even a little awe-struck. No doubt both girls had heard the rumors about Catherine's past. She didn't blame them for gawping at her as though she were some sort of exotic curio one might find in the British Museum or a rare wild creature which had escaped from the Tower of London Menagerie. It wasn't every day that gently bred young ladies dined with a courtesan. Especially one who'd been rumored to have spent time in Newgate Prison for murder.

Former courtesan, Catherine reminded herself. *And your incarceration was a mistake.*

When dinner was announced, Catherine found herself gawping when Drusilla suggested that Adam escort his new wife into the dining room and that they should all sit *en famille* at one end of the long table.

As Adam took Catherine's arm and they crossed the drawing room, she whispered, "I hope this is a sign that your mother's attitude toward me *is* softening. But another part of me simply wonders if she's just trying to avoid sitting next to me."

Adam's mouth quirked in a wry smile. "The cynical part of me would tend to agree. But she and my sisters *are* here. It's more than I expected, to be honest."

"I'll be keeping an eye on what your mother does with her cutlery though. I'd rather not be speared with a sharp implement."

Her husband patted her hand. "I'll make sure the carving knife and fork are kept well away from her. And if I see her about to hurl the gravy or butter boat at you, I'll tell you to duck."

Catherine laughed, relieved the tension between them had dissipated. "Ever the hero."

"I try, my lady. I try."

Adam sat at the head of the table with Catherine to his right. Drusilla claimed the seat to Adam's left, and Cordelia sat beside her. Viola took the chair beside Catherine. The dinner service then commenced.

During the first course—an excellent cream of mushroom soup—Catherine made polite conversation about how fascinated she was by the Abbey's history, how lovely the house was, and how much she admired the dowager countess's taste in furnishings. She hoped she could reassure the woman she wasn't here to upset the apple cart and change everything about the place all at once.

Drusilla nodded and made bland remarks, but any smile she attempted never quite reached her eyes. When the dowager countess mentioned that Sybil had had excellent taste—apparently Adam's first wife had helped Drusilla to redecorate all of the main bedrooms, the morning room, and the drawing room—Adam shot his mother a pointed look.

"I can assure you that Catherine has excellent taste too, dear Mother," he said. "After all, she married me."

"Yes. Quite," the dowager countess said in a tone so clipped, it could probably deadhead roses.

"I...I heard that you might redecorate the dower house," said Catherine. Of course, she immediately regretted her choice of topic. Drusilla's demeanor turned frosty.

"Yes, no doubt you'd rather see the back of me sooner rather than later, *Lady* Dalton," the woman said with a haughty sniff, "but these things take time. The dower house is in a terrible state." She cast her son an affronted look. "You really *should* inspect it, Adam. You wouldn't even stable your precious horses in there."

"Rest assured, I'll take a look tomorrow, Mother," he replied smoothly. "As I've said before, no one will make you live in a hovel."

"Yes...I didn't mean to suggest that you should move out straightaway, if at all," said Catherine hurriedly. "If you would all rather stay on here at the Abbey"—she caught the gazes of Adam's sisters too— "especially since winter is just around the corner, I'm sure we can find a way to make things work amicably."

The dowager countess raised an imperious brow. "I rather think the issue is a little more complicated than that, Lady Dalton. It's not simply a case of everyone making an effort to be amicable. It's about what is right and proper and what is tolerable and acceptable."

Apparently I'm none of those things. Right or proper or tolerable or acceptable. Catherine had to bite her tongue to stop the bitter retort escaping. Instead, she pushed away her soup bowl and picked up her wine. At least Adam kept an excellent cellar.

When the second course arrived—a smooth-as-butter smoked trout paté—Adam caught up on all the local news from the nearby village of Little Godstow and the estate's tenants. Catherine listened with interest, and asked the occasional question, but felt a little at sixes and sevens. It was difficult not to feel excluded, given she had no idea who any of the local families or farmers or business owners were.

During the third course—roast lamb and vegetables with a choice of mint sauce or rich gravy—Catherine began to toy with her food. Her appetite had fled and she began to wonder whether she could claim she was fatigued and cry off dessert—but then talk turned to the estate's stables.

Apparently Adam had recently acquired a new Thoroughbred stallion from Tattersall's horse auctioneers in London. "I'm keen to take him out first thing in the morning," he said. "To put him through his paces."

The dowager countess sliced into her lamb. "Do you ride, Lady Dalton?" she asked in a deceptively mild tone.

"No," Catherine returned. "I don't. I grew up in Paris and my mother and I emigrated to London when I was nine years old. I'm afraid I was never afforded the opportunity when I was young. And by the time I wed..." She shrugged a shoulder. "I had Louis and there never seemed to be a good time to learn." She cast a smile at Adam. "I might even venture to say that after all this time, I might even be a little afraid."

"Oh, perhaps Viola and Cordelia might join you if you need company, Adam," the dowager suggested with a smile. Then she fixed her attention on Catherine. "My girls are both accomplished equestriennes. They've been riding for years."

Hmmm. Catherine really wasn't in the mood for this sort of petty one-upmanship. She pressed her lips together and stabbed one of her Brussel sprouts with her fork instead. Maybe Adam should take *her* cutlery away.

Thank goodness Adam attempted to steer the conversation in a slightly different direction. "I've been thinking about taking little Louis to the stables to meet Bramble tomorrow. Just before lunch," he said as he reached out and placed his hand on Catherine's arm—a signal that perhaps he was aware she was struggling to rein in her temper. "My dear lady-wife, you've mentioned before that our son had begun riding lessons at Briarwood Park during the summer. Or what passed for summer this year."

Catherine put down her fork and knife. "Yes. He did. I know he's very keen to continue despite the fact—" She broke off. She'd best not mention the broken saddle incident because that might lead to all sorts of inconvenient questions, and perhaps even erroneous assumptions that she was a "bad mother." Aware that everyone was looking at her, she finished her remark. "Despite the fact he hasn't met Bramble yet."

"Oh, Bramble is a lovely little pony," declared Cordelia brightly. "He's so very gentle. I'm sure Lord Rosemont will adore him. Won't he, Viola?"

Lady Viola looked a fraction more circumspect as she replied in a pleasantly neutral tone, "Yes. Quite." Perhaps she was aware that across the table, her mother had gone very still. Catherine had certainly noticed.

"Adam, we'll visit the stables with you and Lady Dalton

and Lord Rosemont tomorrow. If you don't mind, of course," said Cordelia. "I'll filch an apple from the kitchen for Bramble."

"I'm sure my son...our son," Catherine amended as she caught Adam's eye, "would love that. He's very eager to meet you all. I'm also certain he won't mind if you call him Louis. He's only four years old, after all."

"Perhaps we could *all* meet Louis tomorrow, Adam," said Drusilla lightly. "You could come to my makeshift drawing room to take tea... Or we could visit your makeshift nursery before you head to the stables. Heavens"—she emitted a small laugh—"I hope I don't put my foot in it and suggest your marriage is makeshift."

"It's not," said Adam, his brow descending into a ferocious frown. "Why would you even suggest such a rude and outrageous thing, Mother? I suggest you apologize to my wife immediately. Or you'll find you'll be moving into the dower house sooner rather than later."

"You're quite right, Adam," conceded the dowager countess. "I don't know what came over me." She picked up her napkin, dabbed the corners of her mouth, put the linen down again, then fixed her cool gray gaze on Catherine. "My lady, may I offer my sincerest apology for misspeaking? I wish you and my son many happy years together. You and your son are most welcome here at St Clair Abbey. I hope you can forgive me for being insufferably rude."

Ha! Catherine didn't believe a word of Drusilla's "makeshift" apology. And she was suddenly so very tired of playing games. She *would* stand up for herself. She wouldn't back down from calling the dowager countess out. If she did, the woman would try to walk all over her forevermore. "I understand how difficult change can be, Lady Dalton. However, I don't believe for a minute that you 'misspoke.' I think your verbal barb was very much to the point and nothing but calculated. But for the sake of maintaining some sort of 'amicability' I do forgive you. And tomorrow, when you do meet my son, I would ask that you be kind to him. He is only a little boy. And a sweet-natured one at that. Now—" Catherine put aside her own napkin and rose—"I shall bid you all good night. I find I'm rather weary from the long day of travel."

As she'd risen, Adam, ever the gentleman, rose to his feet too. "Shall I escort you upstairs, *ma belle?*" he asked softly. Concern lit his eyes.

But Catherine shook her head. "No, you stay and finish your dinner. I'm sure your cook has prepared a wonderful dessert."

She quit the room without a backward glance. Before the odious Dowager Countess of Dalton could see the frustrated, angry tears brimming in her eyes.

It seemed that winning Adam's mother over was going to take a great deal of time and patience. And tonight, Catherine was not in the mood for it.

At least the woman hadn't tried to stick her with anything sharp and pointy or throw anything other than an occasional insult.

Catherine would count that as a win.

Adam followed his wife. How could he not, after an altercation like that?

He was on her side and always would be. And he had to let her know.

"Catherine," he began as he entered her sitting room then stopped. Though the open doorway to her bedchamber, he could hear the soft sound of weeping.

Christ. The sound tugged at him in the most peculiar way.

It made his own heart ache and made him want to throttle his damn mother for being such a judgmental cow.

He paused on the threshold of his wife's bedroom and found her sitting on the edge of her bed, her head in her hands. "I'm sorry for intruding," he began, "but I couldn't stay at the table. Not when I knew you must be upset."

Catherine looked up and dashed the tears from her cheeks with trembling fingers. "I'm sorry too," she said in a choked voice. "I didn't want to snap and create discord. I...I certainly didn't want the evening to end that way...but you know me." She offered him a watery smile. "I'm my own worst enemy sometimes. I need to learn to bite my tongue."

"Don't be sorry." Adam crossed the room and sat beside her. "Not at all. I love your indomitable spirit and how you won't let anyone intimidate you." He slid his arm about her shoulders and when she leaned against him, his chest was flooded with a rush of bittersweet emotion. "Look, if you want us all to decamp to Briarwood Park, just say the word, *ma belle*."

"No... We've only just arrived. If this marriage is to work, your mother and I do need to find a way to coexist. Of course, I'm not expecting that to happen straightaway. And I am prepared to put in the effort. I only hope your mother can meet me halfway."

Adam nodded. "I hope so too." This was difficult for all of them. His mother had her own scars that she hid beneath a veneer of upright superiority. It was the mask she'd begun to wear after her own husband had publicly humiliated her a decade ago.

Perhaps if he told Catherine about his parents' story, she might begin to understand why his mother was the way she was. "I've never really spoken to you about this before, but the reason my mother is so persnickety when it comes to

238

protecting the family name is because of what my father did ten years ago."

A look of sympathy crossed Catherine's face. "I'm aware there was some sort of scandal that hurt your family... I don't know the precise details though. And I'm sure a lot of the whispers are untrue." The corner of her mouth lifted in a wry smile. "Lord knows, my reputation has been badly damaged by gossip over the years."

"Yes...it has. And unfairly so." Adam reached for her hand and gave it a squeeze. His heart ached for the pain she'd suffered at the hands of scandalmongers too. When he spoke again, he couldn't hide the grim, almost scathing note in his voice. "I'm afraid my father—his name was Stephen—deserved to be socially condemned though. You see, he had an affair with another man's wife. He was, in a word, besotted. Madly infatuated. I was completing my final year at Oxford when it all began, so I didn't witness my mother's heartbreak firsthand. But my father wasn't discreet. Everyone who was anyone in London Society knew about it. And when the other woman's husband, a fiery Scots viscount by the name of Lanark found out, he threw down the gauntlet. Called my idiot of a father out."

"I...I heard that your father accepted the challenge."

"Yes, he did." The impotent anger Adam felt for his father —violent emotions he usually kept locked up tight and buried deep in his heart—suddenly rose up and rolled through him like thunder and he had to inhale a calming breath to continue. "The terms of the duel were to fight until first blood rather than to the death. I think it was more a matter of honor for Lanark than anything else. Lord Lanark came out of the duel unscathed, but my father took a bullet to the thigh. The surgeon patched him up but as infection set in..."

"Oh no..." Catherine squeezed Adam's hand. "I suspect the purulence spread?"

"Yes..." Grief and bitterness welled up to replace Adam's anger. "My father died a fortnight later, in agony, a broken man. I was at his bedside when he passed away. It was then I realized what a monumental fool he'd been. My mother never forgave him for ruining what they had. I can't say I blame her."

"What of Lord Lanark?" asked Catherine. "Was he not held accountable for your father's death? Dueling is illegal, is it not?"

Adam shrugged. "My father wasn't killed on the 'field of honor', so to speak. Of course, everyone knew it was the bullet wound that ultimately killed him. But there didn't seem to be any sort of will to charge or prosecute Lord Lanark. I was angry at my father and didn't want to prolong the scandal by dragging the viscount in front of the House of Lords. And my mother, as I mentioned, was too humiliated to make any noises about it all. Perhaps she even thought her husband got his just deserts for betraying her in such a public manner. If Lanark *had* been tried in the House of Lords, he may or may not have been found guilty by his peers. My father had certainly openly cuckolded the man. There would have been a great deal of sympathy for Lanark."

"And what became of Lady Lanark?"

"The viscount divorced her a year later—it seems to be a far easier process to divorce one's spouse in Scotland than here—and she faded into obscurity. It seems there was untold damage on both sides. The notoriety of our family name has faded a little over time, but still, some people in Society remember. My mother has friends, but I know she still secretly feels shamed."

Catherine kissed the edge of his jaw. "I can certainly understand why your mother, and you, Adam, were loath to expose your family to further scandal. I'm so sorry for embroiling you in another one."

"No," said Adam gruffly. "Don't say another word." Damn Society and its censure. *He* was the one who'd employed Catherine as his mistress years ago. *He* was the one who had paid her for her company and to share his bed when it suited him. Yet *she* was treated with disdain. She was the one his mother looked down upon, not him.

These different rules that governed the lives of men and women, they weren't fair, and they grated upon Adam no end.

He turned his body to face Catherine and met her troubled gaze before brushing a lock of her lovely hair behind her ear. "I won't have you feeling guilty. You've done nothing wrong. I married you to protect our son. I won't ever regret my choice."

He skimmed his hand that had been resting upon her shoulder, down her back to her waist. Was it his imagination or did Catherine suddenly stiffen beneath his touch?

Had he said something wrong?

He searched Catherine's face. Noticed the shadows in her eyes. "You said you were tired. I can retire to my room. Let you get some sleep..."

But Catherine shook her head. "No... No, I want you, Adam," she whispered. Her eyelashes fluttered down as she focused on his mouth. "I always want you." Her lips curved in a seductive smile as she slid a hand beneath his evening coat. "Besides, you promised you'd strip me naked so I'd only be wearing this for you." She touched the necklace at her throat. "Wouldn't you like to see me like that? Bare but for your jewels?"

Adam's blood turned to molten fire in his veins. His cock grew harder than a steel ramrod. "Hell yes," he growled.

Even so, as he began to remove Catherine's clothing, kissing and caressing her satiny flesh as it was revealed bit by delicious bit to his gaze and hands and mouth, a little piece of his mind wondered again if his wife was playing a part.

But like Catherine he was also tired, and he was also plagued by worries. A good deal of him didn't want to think about anything troubling anymore. At least not tonight. He simply wanted to lose himself in Catherine.

Being with her, making love to her, never failed to soothe his soul. She made him feel right. She made him feel whole. She made him forget he was the Earl of Dalton and all that responsibility which came with it.

When Catherine was entirely, gloriously naked bar for her sapphire and diamond necklace, Adam kissed her everywhere before burying his face between her thighs. He feasted until she was writhing and moaning his name. He stripped too, casting off every stitch of his clothing, loving the way she watched him with unabashed desire in her eyes. How she shamelessly stroked herself while she waited for him to join her on the bed again.

When she rolled onto her side, facing away from him, he nipped at her earlobe and growled, "While I love taking you from behind, I don't want that tonight. I want you to ride me. I know how much you love it. And I want to watch your face as you take your pleasure. I want to see you come."

Catherine stilled. Then she laughed softly. "I might not be able to ride a horse but yes, I'm willing to ride you any time, my lord."

As Adam leaned back against the plump pillows and oak headboard of her bed, she rose up then straddled him. Grasping his hard as iron cock, she expertly lowered her body, taking him inside herself in a long slow slide, clasping him so tightly with her hot wet sex that Adam fought the over-whelming urge to come immediately.

His fingers flexed against her hips as she began to move. The feel of her body rising and falling against his, the sight of her caressing her own luscious breasts, plucking and pinching her own nipples, was the most erotic damn thing Adam had ever witnessed. All the while the diamond and sapphire necklace sparkled and winked at him. Reminded him that Catherine was even more precious to him than the most priceless of jewels.

It was a slow, lingering coupling. A sensual undulating dance. At first.

To increase the closeness of their bodies, to intensify the torturous but delicious friction, Adam pushed himself upright and wrapped his arms about Catherine's lithe body. She pressed her breasts into his face and he latched onto a nipple, suckling hard. Her fingernails scored his shoulders as she whimpered and rocked faster, grinding against him.

"Yes. Use me. Fuck me. Ride me. Find your pleasure," Adam urged, his voice rough and raw and desperate. He gripped Catherine's hips and frantically pumped his cock up into her, harder and faster.

When her orgasm struck, he felt her spasm around him. She gasped and cried out. Her hands clutched at his head, gripping hard, and his face became buried in her breasts. It was too much, and he bucked and shuddered and groaned as an almighty climax roared through him.

Afterward, as Catherine lay sleepy and sated in his arms, Adam realized that she'd never once looked him in the eye while he'd been inside her. Her eyes had been closed or she'd distracted him with her breasts. She'd never once caught his gaze...

Did she ever really look deeply into his eyes when they made love?

It might mean nothing that she avoided that sort of intimate connection...or maybe it *did* mean something. Something wholly significant. Something he'd not wanted to admit to himself. Did it make their coming together easier for her if she didn't have to pretend to feel any sort of deeper emotion for him? That what they shared was simply sexual?

Adam frowned up at the canopy of Catherine's four-poster bed. The thought that she might keep part of herself separate and hidden from him was beginning to bother him more every single day.

But the truth was, he was too afraid to talk to her about the issue. Just the thought of doing so made his throat tighten and his heart lurch uncomfortably in his chest. Because if he *did* broach the subject, then he might have to admit how he felt about Catherine...and coward that he was, he wasn't ready to properly examine, let alone own his feelings.

But we've only just wed, he reminded himself as he closed his eyes and pressed his lips to Catherine's temple. *And we have a lot to contend with.*

He'd wanted her back in his arms for such a long time and now that she was here, he could at least be thankful for that.

CHAPTER 18

"**M**ama!"

Catherine smiled as Louis flung himself at her and hugged her tightly about the legs, squashing the skirts of her blue woolen walking gown. Pippin bounced around Catherine too, yapping happily.

"Lord Rosemont," cried Lizzy, hurrying across the nursery carpet toward her over-exuberant charge. "You mustn't knock your Mama over. Goodness, she was here just a few hours ago while you ate breakfast. What has gotten into you today, my young man?"

Catherine laughed as she smoothed her son's tousled hair. "It's all right, Lizzy. I expect it's just the excitement of being in a new place." She knelt down beside Louis. "Have you heard that your Papa is going to take you riding very soon? At noon." Adam had filled her in on his plans for the day after he'd returned from his own morning ride and they'd break-fasted together in her rooms. He was currently sequestered in his private study with the steward, Mr. Kerr, attending to a multitude of estate matters. Not just the refurbishment of the dower house, but what to do about the precarious state of the old abbey ruins. Apparently they were on the verge of collapsing entirely.

"Yes! I know!" Louis was bouncing up and down on his toes, mimicking Pippin. "On Bramble. He told me to get ready."

"Oh, he did? How wonderful." Catherine's heart warmed to hear that her husband had made time to stop by the nursery to see their son. After the way last night's "family" dinner ended, Catherine had no idea if the Dowager Lady Dalton and Adam's sisters had reconsidered their plans to visit the nursery today. Or the stables. She supposed she would find out in due course.

"Yes, Lord Dalton came by about an hour ago to say hullo to his lordship," said Lizzy. "And as you can see, he is now dressed for riding."

"I am," declared Louis, "See, Mama? I even have my breeches and boots on, just like Papa." He pouted. "They are only half-boots though. Not top boots or those ones with tassels like Papa wears. What are they called?"

Catherine smiled. "Hussar boots or hessians. And you will wear bigger boots in good time. Top boots, hessian boots, Wellington boots. You will never want for boots, my dear boy. Papa will take you to Hoby's the bootmaker in London when you are old enough."

Louis grasped the lapels of his little coat, just like a gentleman. It was such a grown-up mannerism, Catherine's heart clenched. "Can I ride the rocking horse before we go, Mama?" he asked, his eyes bright with excitement. "I'd like to practice."

"Of course." Louis took her hand and led her over to the white wooden mount. It sat on a corner of the plush rug, right by a large window As Catherine lifted her son onto the red child-sized saddle, she asked, "Have you named your horse?"

"Snowflake," he said solemnly as he took up the tiny pretend reins of red leather. "Because he's white."

"I think that's a wonderful name." Catherine took a step back as Louis began to rock sedately back and forth. A pale ray of late autumn sunshine broke through the clouds and caressed her son's golden locks. He looked like the sweetest cherub, with his slightly chubby rosy cheeks and big blue eyes. Catherine decide that when it was time to have his likeness captured in a portrait, she might dress him in the same blue velvet riding coat and white shirt with its lace trimmed collar. Of course, Pippin would have to be in the painting too—

All of a sudden, there was a decidedly feminine gasp from the other side of the room. Pippin gave a warning yap and Lizzy dropped into a low curtsy. Naturally, Catherine's attention swung to the nursery doorway to see what all the fuss was about, and while she didn't gasp herself, she certainly felt a jolt of surprise.

It seemed the dowager countess had deigned to visit Louis' "makeshift" nursery after all. She stood on the threshold, hand at her throat as she stared at Louis. Her gray eyes were wide and her mouth had dropped open. Just behind her, Catherine could see Lady Viola and Lady Cordelia who were also blinking in surprise past their mother.

"Lady Dalton, is everything all right?" asked Catherine.

"I-I..." Drusilla's gaze was riveted on Louis. "Your son," she murmured, taking a few steps into the room. Her brow had furrowed into a puzzled frown. "Lord Rosemont... He looks just like my Adam did at that age. I feel like I've somehow stepped back in time..."

"Mama, you're right," declared Lady Viola. She and her sister had followed the Dowager Lady Dalton into the room. "He looks exactly like Adam in that portrait in your parlor."

Catherine couldn't say she was all that surprised by the dowager countess's admission, though she was bemused by the woman's reaction. It was not what she'd expected given the dowager's usual stuffy, even hostile demeanor. At least, whenever she interacted with Catherine.

By this stage, Louis had stopped rocking and was staring solemnly at the newcomers. "Mama," he whispered, reaching a hand out toward Catherine. "Who's that?"

Catherine took his hand while she slid her other arm about his small shoulders to reassure him. "Remember yesterday when I mentioned you might meet your Papa's sisters and your new grandmama?"

Louis nodded. "Yes."

"Well, here they are. I will help you down so you may be introduced properly."

She lifted her son down from the rocking horse and gently ushered him toward the dowager countess and the two young women, who were all still openly gawping.

"This is the Dowager Lady Dalton," said Catherine, indicating Drusilla, "and this is Lady Viola and Lady Cordelia."

"I'm very pleased to meet you all," said Louis gravely then he executed gentlemanly bows to each woman in turn.

Drusilla inclined her head graciously while Lady Viola and Lady Cordelia both bobbed curtsies.

"Mama, isn't he the sweetest?" crowed Cordelia, turning to her mother.

"I must say, I'm very impressed by your manners, Lord Rosemont," said Viola.

Louis smiled shyly. "Thank you, Lady Viola," he said. Then he wrapped his small fingers around Catherine's hand. "My Mama taught me how a gentleman must address a lady. Good manners are important."

Catherine bent toward Louis's ear. "Would it be all right if your grandmother and aunts called you Louis rather than Lord Rosemont? I didn't think you'd mind."

Louis nodded. "Yes please. I should like that."

"Oh, and you must call us Aunt Cordelia and Aunt

Viola," said Cordelia. She bent down too. "I hear you are going to go riding on Bramble very soon, Louis. I have an apple in my pocket for him. He loves apples and you may feed it to him if you like. Well, if your Mama thinks that's all right." The young woman looked up at Catherine and smiled.

Catherine's heart was flooded with an overwhelming sense of pride. And relief. "I do," she said warmly. Then she glanced at the clock. It was almost a quarter to twelve. She hoped Adam would arrive soon. It was such a shame he hadn't been here to witness the introductions between Louis and the rest of his family. But she would tell him all about them later and how swimmingly they'd gone.

"Mama," Louis whispered, tugging on her hand. "What should I call the Dowder Lady Dalton?"

Catherine glanced at Drusilla and nearly fell over when the dowager countess's mouth curved into an indulgent smile. "He may call me, Grandmama. Would you like that, Louis?"

Louis nodded eagerly. "Yes, please. I've never had a grand-mama before."

The dowager countess's gray gaze grew soft and warm. "Well, you do now, my dear boy."

"What's all this then? Is there a party in the nursery but I haven't been invited?"

Adam.

He strode into the room and when Louis rushed over to him, Adam swept him up into his arms. "How's my lad?" he asked, his blue eyes shining with good humor.

No, it's more than humor, thought Catherine. There was also genuine affection in Adam's gaze as he regarded his son.

"He's winding us all around his little finger," returned the older Lady Dalton with mock disapproval. But there was twinkle in her eyes and a hint of a smile about her mouth. "Which very much reminds me of someone else I know, my son." She gave Adam a pointed look.

In return, he cocked a brow. "I have absolutely no idea what you are talking about, Mother." To Catherine he said, "I'm sorry I've been so busy this morning. I was trying to get a few things done before Louis's lesson."

"It's quite all right," she replied. "And I understand perfectly. I know how much work is involved. I've managed Briarwood Park on my own for two years." Of course, Adam knew that, but it didn't hurt to mention it in his mother's hearing.

"So you have, my lady. And very well." Adam gave Catherine a smile which spoke of his admiration and triggered a little throb of pleasure in her chest. "Right"—Adam turned his attention back to Louis—"are you ready to go riding, my boy?"

Louis grinned. "Yes, Papa. Aunty Cordelia even has an apple for Bramble."

"Lucky Bramble," said Adam. "Off we go."

As Adam and Louis quit the nursery with Cordelia and Viola following in their wake, Catherine began to follow too... but then the dowager placed a hand on Catherine's arm, staying her.

"Lady Dalton," the older woman said quietly in a voice that Lizzy the nursemaid wouldn't be able to overhear, "before you go, I just wanted to ask... I just wanted to know..." She gave a little huff of annoyance. "Look at me beating around the bush. I should just come out and say it..." She looked Catherine straight in the eye. "Little Louis. He's Adam's son, isn't he? Not your late husband's."

There was no point in lying. Catherine drew a fortifying breath. "Yes, Adam is his father, my lady. There's no doubt."

"You married the late Lord Rosemont to give your child a name."

"Yes...I had to. Adam was betrothed to Lady Sybil and I wanted to make sure our son wouldn't bear the shame of being called a bastard. Lord Rosemont knew. No one was duped."

Drusilla nodded. "You were...very shrewd. It was a most sensible thing to do."

"Thank you."

The dowager countess's gaze hardened. "Of course, this doesn't change my overall opinion of you or what I think of your marriage...but I am grateful Adam will be able to be part of Louis's life. And I'm grateful that Louis will be a part of ours."

Catherine nodded. "I appreciate how difficult it is for you, and for your daughters, now that Adam and I are wed. But I'm not sorry my little boy will get to spend his life with his real father."

"And you will get to spend your life with the man you love."

"What?" Catherine felt a telltale blush scorch her cheeks. "What do you mean?"

Drusilla made a scoffing sound. "Don't pretend it's not true. I see that adoring light in your eyes and the softness of your smile whenever you look at my son." A bitter expression flitted across her face. "It was the way I used to look at my husband before he made a choice to ruin everything... Does Adam know how you feel?"

Catherine swallowed. "I...I'm not sure. He might have guessed. I haven't told him though. I don't want him to feel uncomfortable when he's with me."

"Well, you should. Men can be complete dunderheads when it comes to recognizing their own feelings let alone anyone else's." Drusilla turned to leave but paused in the doorway. "You should get Adam to teach you to ride, too. For someone with your indefatigable spirit, I'm sure you'll be galloping around the estate like an Amazon in no time at all." And with that, the dowager countess quit the room leaving

Catherine with a sense that somehow the scales had tipped in her favor for once.

She and the Drusilla might never be friends, but at least she no longer had an out-and-out enemy to contend with.

She had enough of those already.

CHAPTER 19

A relatively calm week went by at St Clair Abbey, and Catherine was nothing but grateful for the respite from fear and chaos and horrible sense of impending doom.

A little voice at the back of her mind sometimes nagged her that it was simply the calm before the storm. She supposed she was so accustomed to bad things happening, to being on edge and watchful and wary—for waiting for the sword of Damocles to fall—that it was only natural for her not to relax entirely. Until the culprit who'd sent her threatening letters and started the fire at Rosemont House was found, until she knew whether or not the accidents that had befallen her and Louis were really accidents or deliberate acts of sabotage, until she knew that Adam had been awarded joint guardianship of Louis so the Fortescues were no longer a potential threat...she could not let down her guard completely.

Louis settled easily into his new routine at the Abbey. He had two energetic young aunts who seemed to dote on him and were quite happy to keep him amused. Aside from joining his grandmama and aunts for afternoon tea in the dowager countess's apartments on several occasions, Viola and Cordelia regularly entertained Louis in the music room, teaching him simple songs to play on the pianoforte. Hide and seek had become a popular pastime too; St Clair Abbey was so huge, there was no end of places to hide. Weather permitting, Adam took Louis for riding lessons on Bramble and in the early evening, father and son spent time together in the "new" nursery. Adam had even admitted to Catherine that reading Louis a bedtime story had become a favorite part of his own day. All the admission did was make Catherine love Adam even more.

Still she hesitated admitting in turn how she felt. On their first night at St Clair Abbey, Adam had mentioned once again that he'd married her to protect Louis. That it was his duty. She couldn't seem to get past that recurring remark. Every time she was on the verge of revealing that she loved him, something in her held her back.

She supposed it was hard to change old habits. While she was brave about so many other things, it seemed she wasn't brave enough to confess her feelings. Just in case Adam baulked and began to put a wall up between them. To distance himself from her because he felt uncomfortable being the recipient of her adoration when those same feelings weren't reciprocated.

While she enjoyed "making love" with Adam, she was a little relieved when her courses began two days after their arrival at the Abbey. It meant she didn't have to hide her emotions when she and Adam were being intimate—the time she was most likely to accidentally confess her love.

Of course as the week progressed, she offered to satisfy Adam in other ways outside of intercourse, but ever the gentleman he'd declined, telling her that he wouldn't enjoy himself if she wasn't fully able to participate in the sorts of lovemaking activities that *she* particularly enjoyed.

Part of her also wondered if Adam might also be a little disappointed that she wasn't with child. But then, they'd only been together a handful of weeks. It had taken her a whole year of vigorous lovemaking to fall pregnant with Louis. There was plenty of time to provide Adam with the heir he would need one day. But still, she was five years older now...

Well, there was nothing she could do about that other than have faith that she was still fertile and to keep trying. Not that that was an onerous wifely duty by any means. She just had to continue to hold her tongue and not let an awkward "I love you" slip out while she was in the throes of mindless passion.

While her nights had been rather subdued, Catherine found she had enough to keep her busy during the day. Apart from spending lots of lovely time with Louis, she liaised with Mrs. Beckett, the housekeeper, about household matters and got to know the other staff. She was also surprised, and pleased, when Drusilla took her on an extensive guided tour about the Abbey one rainy afternoon.

The dowager countess seemed quite happy to impart all she knew about the great house's history. Indeed, Catherine was fascinated to learn about Adam's ancestors as she was shown through the Abbey's enormous portrait gallery—one Lady Dalton had been a lady-in-waiting to Queen Anne and one second son, who'd fancied himself as a bit of a swashbuckler, had run off to fight Barbary Coast corsairs. And of course, Catherine couldn't help but admire the portrait of her own handsome husband. Noticeably, and perhaps understandably absent, was a painting of Adam's late father. There didn't seem to be a portrait of Sybil either.

Catherine wasn't sure what to make of that.

Along the way, the dowager countess also pointed out some of the house's interesting architectural quirks—things like secret jib doors and several priest holes and hidden passageways—which Catherine found most intriguing. The tour had concluded with a brief look into the St Clair family crypt—the stone and marble vault adjoined the Abbey's small private chapel.

While her mother-in-law was still a little standoffish at times, Catherine appreciated that at least the woman was making an effort to be agreeable. She was also canny enough to realize that it was all because of Louis, not because Drusilla had any real liking or affinity for her new daughter-in-law.

In any event, Catherine was grateful for any small crumbs of sociability the dowager countess sprinkled her way. Following the Abbey tour, as Catherine had shared a late luncheon with Drusilla in her rooms, the dowager countess had invited Catherine to inspect the dower house with her in the next week or so. Naturally, Catherine knew what the woman's ulterior motive was: she clearly wanted Catherine to see what an awful state the dower house was in so she could continue to reside in the main house. But as far as Catherine was concerned, if the Dowager Lady Dalton continued to let Catherine run the household as she saw fit, continued to be amiable rather than outwardly hostile, and maintained her warmth with Louis, Catherine had no issue with the woman and Adam's sisters staying on.

The day after Catherine's courses ended, Adam summoned her to his private study just before midday. A courier from London had arrived with messages of rather significant import. Mr. Walsh, the inquiry agent Adam had appointed, would apparently be visiting the Abbey during the course of the afternoon to report on his investigation to date. Perhaps even more importantly, Adam's lawyer had sent word about the Court of Chancery's ruling.

As soon as Catherine entered Adam's study, her husband swept her into his arms. "Such wonderful news, my beautiful wife," he declared, his face alight with happiness. "The Lord Chancellor has appointed me as Louis's second guardian. You must worry no more about the Fortescues trying to take him from you."

"Oh, thank God." As a heady feeling of relief washed through Catherine, her eyes filled with tears. "I can't thank you enough. To know that you are Louis's guardian in truth —" She broke off, too overwhelmed to continue.

"Oh, my darling wife"—Adam captured her chin and tilted her face so she couldn't look away—"you don't need to thank me. It was the right thing to do. For Louis. For you. And yes, for me. You'll never know how happy I am being able to spend my days with him. He's a wonderful boy. I never thought I could feel such a deep and abiding love for anyone at all. I would do anything for Louis."

"I know exactly how you feel," murmured Catherine. "Being a parent is an immense responsibility but the most precious and rewarding thing in the world. I just wish..." Her words trailed away.

Adam frowned. "Yes..."

"I wish you could have met Louis sooner. I wish things could have been different."

I wish you could love me. I wish you'd chosen me over Sybil.

Adam's expression grew infinitely soft and sad at the same time. He brushed a thumb along her cheek, smoothing away an errant tear that had slipped out. "So do I, *ma belle*. So do I. But at least we have now. And we have tomorrow and the next day, and all the days after that to grow together as a family."

Catherine tucked away her regrets about what might have been and what might never be. Adam made perfect sense. Being altogether, safe and sound, was a blessing in and of itself.

She reached up and kissed her husband, and he kissed her back with such ruthless but thorough tenderness, Catherine's head was soon spinning. She was just going to suggest that they lock the door to Adam's study and take things further when there were three sharp raps on the door.

"Damn it," cursed Adam beneath his breath when he broke the kiss. "Whoever it is had better have a good reason for the interruption."

"Perhaps it's Mr. Walsh from London," said Catherine, checking that her hair wasn't too mussed up.

"Yes, perhaps," agreed Adam with a sigh. "If it is him, I can't be too miffed. Especially if has some useful intelligence." He straightened his waistcoat, pulled at his cuffs, then crossed the room and claimed the seat behind his desk. Catherine settled herself upon a nearby window seat.

Adam called, "Enter," and sure enough, it was Quigley announcing Mr. Walsh.

Adam welcomed the brown-haired, bearded inquiry agent, and after the man had greeted Catherine with a bow, Adam invited him to take a seat and to share his latest news on the investigation.

Mr. Walsh, once installed in a comfortable chair in front of Adam's desk, pulled a small notebook with a brown leather cover from his breast pocket and thumbed through the pages until he got to a particular entry. "Right, my lord," he said in a gruff voice that reminded Catherine of carriage wheels crunching on gravel, "Perhaps I should start with Lord Makepeace..."

"Yes, I would be most eager to hear what you've managed to dig up about the baron and his activities of late," said Adam. "I've been hoping he's gone to ground ever since our... conversation outside the Cockpit Tavern."

The inquiry agent cleared his throat. "Yes and no, my lord. Even though Lord Makepeace is still in considerable financial strife, every now and again, he seems to be the recipient of small windfalls. I can't seem to work out where the money is coming from, though. By all accounts—and from what I've seen—he's quite addicted to high stakes play in the most disreputable of gaming hells about London. He loses more than he wins. He has creditors chasing him on and off, but all are tight-lipped about their dealings with Makepeace."

"Have you managed to find out anything about that fellow I spotted in the Cockpit Tavern? The one who appeared to settle the baron's chit?" asked Adam.

Mr. Walsh shook his head. "No, my lord. The staff at the Cockpit could not recall the man—or so they claimed—and Makepeace has not been back to the establishment. When I've followed him around other gaming hells, I haven't spotted the dark-haired gentleman you described to me or noticed anyone in particular accompanying him. Makepeace, for all intents and purposes, appears to be quite the loner."

Adam drummed his fingers on the leather blotter. "Hmmm. Maybe my assumption that Makepeace had some sort of benefactor was incorrect then. Maybe the man I saw paid the doorman off for some other reason that was entirely unrelated."

"Perhaps, my lord," said Mr. Walsh. "I wish I'd been able to discover more." He frowned at his notes and then glanced at Catherine. "My lady, what I'm about to divulge might be a tad...unsettling. It concerns both your residences in Park Lane *and* Russell Square."

Catherine sat up straighter. "I can assure you that I'm no withering violet who carries hartshorn in her reticule, Mr. Walsh."

She traded a glance with Adam and he gave her an approving nod. "Yes. Mr. Walsh, my wife is one of the strongest characters I know. There's no need for smelling salts or beating about the bush. Just tell us what you've learned."

"Right." Mr. Walsh drew a breath. "It looks like someone has been back to both houses in recent days and has rummaged through each place at night. It's like they've been looking for something. The searches have been subtle though and hard to miss. But the skeleton staff at Rosemont House reported that the door to the kitchen had been found unlocked early one morning. One of the maids who'd been cleaning thought that some of the drawers in your rooms, my lady, had been left slightly ajar and that some of the contents had been riffled through. She hadn't said anything to your butler at first because she'd assumed it had something to do with comings and goings of the tradesmen fixing up the house after the fire damage. It's a similar story at your Russell Square house. A rear door was found unlocked, but your manservant, Mr. Chester, believed he'd just been absent-minded. Your housekeeper, Mrs. Chester, did wonder if someone had been through various drawers downstairs and in the bedchambers. But nothing was missing or seemed overtly wrong, so she assumed her imagination was playing tricks on her and she dismissed the incident. All perfectly innocent, until taken as a whole."

A chill turned Catherine's blood to ice. She might not be the fainting kind, but right at this minute, she did feel a trifle ill. To hear someone had broken into both her London homes and had been through her personal items felt like the worst sort of invasion of her privacy. It felt wrong. Sinister.

She traded looks with Adam. Her disquiet must have shown on her face because a muscle twitched in his lean jaw and the light in his eyes grew hard. "I must say, I'm not happy to hear about this," he said to the inquiry agent. "It's also clear I need to increase the security on each of my wife's properties. And Dalton House too. Staff must now report any sort of odd occurrence, no matter how small, to me straightaway. Through you, Mr. Walsh. Or through Lord Maxwell. I'll send word to him after we conclude our meeting."

"Of course, my lord," said the inquiry agent.

"I wonder if it's Frederick Makepeace—or someone he's

hired—looking for that cursed French diamond his father was promised," said Catherine. "The threatening notes indicated I'm supposedly in possession of *something* this person wants."

"Perhaps..." Adam's mouth had flattened into a grim line. "I also think we should check if anyone has broken into Briarwood Park and has gone through your things," he added darkly and Catherine agreed. "If you've the time I'll send you there, Mr. Walsh, before you return to London."

The inquiry agent inclined his head in assent. Then he flipped to the next page in his notebook. "As to what the Fortescue family has been up to..." He regarded both Catherine and Adam in turn. "The son, Gerald, is a bit like Lord Makepeace in some respects. He tends to favor high stakes play in London's gaming hells. While the family does have a decent fortune courtesy of Lilith Fortescue's family's wool cloth manufacturing interests, there has been a downturn in the business this year because of all the wet weather we've had. It's apparently affected production. I haven't heard that the family is in any particular financial trouble, but I'll keep my ear to the ground."

"Hmmm," said Adam. "I'd also be interested to find out if they have any sort of reaction to the news that I am now one of Lord Rosemont's testamentary guardians."

"Does the Court of Chancery have to inform them of the change in status quo?" asked Catherine. "Benedict is merely Louis's first cousin once removed, not a trustee the estate after all."

"No, the Court doesn't have to tell them anything. So they wouldn't necessarily know," said Adam. "Unless they go nosing about because Benedict and Gerald feel like they have a vested interest in Louis's future and the future of the earldom. No doubt they've learned that you and I are now wed, so they'd be keeping an eye on me. A lawyer or solicitor working for the Fortescues could make discreet inquiries about the

Court of Chancery's latest cases and rulings." He shrugged. "I suppose we shall soon find out if they know and if they are unhappy about it."

"I suppose all I can do is just pray that they will accept that the earldom is Louis's and that they will never play a role in his life." Catherine hugged herself, trying to ward off a looming sense of dread. Or was it a tiny sliver of guilt? By blood, Benedict *should* be the current Earl of Rosemont.

But Catherine couldn't be held responsible for the choice Edward Fortescue made years ago. It was his choice to wed her, his choice to give another man's child his name. Legally, there was nothing that could be done to change the situation.

But the truth of the matter was, Benedict *had* been swindled out of a title and fortune, and Lilith did seem like the sort of person who would bear a grudge. Gerald seemed like the sort who might act on that grudge...

Mr. Walsh cleared his throat. "I have a few more pieces of intelligence in relation to the Fortescues that you *might* find interesting." He caught Catherine's eye. "Your husband told me that the last time you saw the Fortescues was at Briarwood Park. That they'd visited you unexpectedly on the very same day that your son, Lord Rosemont, had a swing accident. That they claimed they'd been visiting friends in nearby St Albans."

"Yes," said Catherine. "That is correct."

"Well, it appears they might very well have lied," said Mr. Walsh. "As far as I can make out, it seems the Fortescues do not know anyone at all in St Albans or anywhere about aside from you, my lady. The dates when mishaps occurred at Briarwood Park—the frozen lake near-miss, the broken saddle incident, and the swing accident—also coincide with dates that someone by the name of Fortescue stayed at the Great Red Lion Inn. Two rooms were paid for on the most recent occasion. But only one bedroom was hired out the two previous times. All the stays were for two nights."

Oh... The chill was back, snaking its way down Catherine's spine, making her shiver. A sick feeling settled in the pit of her stomach. She was suddenly flooded with the sense that malevolent forces were at work and she could do nothing to stop them.

Adam cocked an eyebrow. "I'm impressed by your detective work, Mr. Walsh, as St Albans has quite a few inns and taverns. And while the information you've unearthed is interesting indeed, it's also rather...ominous." He locked eyes with Catherine. "I'll make sure there's increased monitoring of their movements. This cannot be a coincidence. It's something we definitely cannot ignore."

The inquiry agent concurred before adding, "My lord, I have a few more men at my disposable who could surveil the comings and goings of the Fortescues around the clock. As far as I'm aware, they're all currently in London."

"Yes, make it so, Mr. Walsh," said Adam grimly. "I'll direct my man of business in London to pay you the additional fees required."

"Thank you, my lord," replied the inquiry agent as he shut his notebook and tucked it back into his coat. "I shall travel to Briarwood Park directly after I leave here to see if there has been any sort of incident involving a suspicious entry—an unlocked door or window, a tampered with lock—or any reports of a minor disturbance inside the house. Then I'll journey back here to relay my findings before returning to London. I should be back in a day or two."

Catherine dashed off quick notes to Briarwood Park's steward and housekeeper—Kingsley was still in London—to let them know who Mr. Walsh was and that all staff should answer his questions, then the inquiry agent took his leave.

As the door closed behind him, Adam pushed out of his

chair and gathered Catherine into his arms. "Everything will be all right. I can see how worried you are, but I promise you and Louis are safe here with me," he said gravely, almost fiercely. "If Makepeace is responsible for these break-ins and threats, we will catch him. If the Fortescues are seeking to harm you and Louis, they will be stopped. And they *will* be punished to the full extent of the law. Every single one of them."

"I believe you," Catherine said. She wrapped her arms about Adam's lean muscular torso and leaned her cheek against his chest. When she felt him drop a kiss upon her temple, she felt a bittersweet pang in her heart. Adam cared for her, she knew that. As always, she just wished he felt...more.

The nearby window afforded her with a view of the Abbey grounds and the dreary afternoon. It had begun raining, quite heavily, while Mr. Walsh had been talking with both her and Adam.

Adam stroked her back. "I had been planning on taking you for your first ever riding lesson this afternoon," he said softly, "if you were amenable of course and not otherwise engaged. And not indisposed...in a physical sense." His chest rose and fell on a small sigh. "But now it's pouring."

Catherine smiled. It seemed Adam was on a fishing expedition; he wished to know if her courses were finished. She was also touched he'd planned on taking time out of his busy schedule to be her riding instructor, rather than palming the task off to someone else like a groom. "Yes, it's such a shame," she murmured, "considering I'm not indisposed at all and have no particular plans. A good distraction would be most welcome..." She slid a hand beneath his silk waistcoat and flexed her fingertips against his cambric-clad torso. "What on earth shall we do instead?"

Adam's fingers found the buttons at the back of her gown's bodice. "How do you feel about mounting something else this afternoon? That window seat looks like it should be put to the test."

Catherine laughed softly. "I don't care who does the mounting, or where it occurs, as long as it happens, my lord." She boldly cupped his stiffening member through the fall of his trousers. "There's no doubt that you're already up to the task."

Adam groaned and captured her mouth in a possessive kiss. "Oh, it's going to happen, my lady," he returned gruffly, pushing her down onto the seat and following her. "Right here and right now. Prepare to be distracted like you never have before."

It might be dark and dismal outside, with all kinds of awful and sinister things lurking in the shadows, but here in her husband's private study, Catherine could push all that away.

She needed this respite. She needed Adam.

Together, they could visit heaven, at least for a little while...

CHAPTER 20

"My brother Longtail led the way; I followed. Softdown came next; but Brighteyes would not be prevailed upon to venture..." Adam's voice trailed away as he felt Catherine's hand upon his shoulder.

"Look, our boy is sound asleep," she murmured beside his ear.

Adam smiled and closed Louis's favorite nighttime tale, *The Life and Perambulations of a Mouse*. "So he is. I think I've barely read two pages tonight."

He carefully put the small volume upon on the bedside table beside Louis's half-drunk glass of warm milk, then snuffed out the candle. As he regarded his sleeping son a moment longer—his tousled blond curls and the way his delicate lashes fanned against his flushed, chubby cheeks—his chest was flooded with a sweet tender warmth. A feeling which could only be love.

Yes, he'd only met Louis a handful of weeks ago, but he could readily acknowledge that he loved his son with a strength that astonished him. Lurking beneath a layer of softer emotion was a fierce protectiveness. Adam knew that he would move heaven and earth, do anything to keep his boy safe. And woe betide *anyone* who hurt him.

He suddenly had a new appreciation of why Catherine had come to him for help. How brave she'd been to seek him out, risking his censure for keeping such a huge secret from him—that she'd borne him a child. Naturally, a little part of Adam was jealous that Louis bore the surname of Fortescue and another man's title. But he did understand why Catherine had done what she'd done to give Louis the best life she could.

His son might never be the next Earl of Dalton, but at least he would know his father. And Louis would want for nothing. Ever.

Leaning forward, he placed a kiss on Louis's brow, ruffled the fur of Pippin who was curled up at Louis's feet, then rose.

"Shall we go down to dinner, my lady?" Adam asked softly. According to the mantel clock, it was a quarter to eight. Just like reading his son a story, sharing an *aperitif* with his wife had become one of Adam's customs since returning to St Clair Abbey. This routine was one of the best parts of his day.

Catherine nodded. "Yes... Only..." She frowned. "I might just have a word with Lizzy. Louis fell asleep so quickly tonight, I'm worried he might be coming down with a cold." She gently felt his forehead then added, "He doesn't feel feverish, so it's probably just me fretting unnecessarily."

Adam kissed her temple. "You have a lot on your mind. But if it makes you feel better, we can ask Lizzy to check on him periodically and let us know straightaway if he seems unwell. Now"—he took Catherine's arm—"I don't know about you, but I need a drink. There's a particular Amontillado I'd like you to try. It's quite old and from Cordova. I had Quigley dig it out from the cellar late this afternoon and I'd value your opinion."

When they reached the drawing room, Catherine's footman, Jackson—now attired in new Dalton livery—served them glasses of the Spanish wine.

Catherine was just giving her opinion on the sherry when Adam's mother and sisters arrived in a flurry of "good evenings" and bright smiles.

Adam was thrilled that his usually aloof mother and often self-absorbed sisters not only doted on Louis but were all warming to Catherine, too. Given how frosty his mother had been at the start, he was nothing but grateful. No doubt meeting her grandson had something to do with her change of heart. Catherine had told him that his mother had guessed Louis was actually his child because of the remarkable resemblance between father and son. His mother had obviously decided that she must make the best of the new situation and treat her daughter-in-law civilly to cultivate any sort of meaningful relationship with her grandson.

His mother might be exacting in her demands and a haughty prig at times, but she wasn't foolish. No one could deny that she didn't love her children. And now, it seemed, her grandson.

After his mother took a glass of sherry from the silver tray proffered by Jackson, she frowned at the drawing room windows. "It's a miserable cold and wet evening yet the curtains have not be drawn," she pronounced stiffly. "You, young man." She frowned at Jackson. "Please close them, at once. None of us wish to catch our death." Beneath her breath she muttered to Catherine, "Really, we must have a word with Mrs. Beckett. The staff should know better."

Jackson bowed. "Of course, my lady." He put down the sherry tray upon a side table then crossed to one of the wide, mullion-paned windows on the opposite side of the room. His reflection in the glass showed him frowning into the night before he began to tug at one of the thick velvet drapes. The fabric seemed to be snagged on something.

Something about the young man's expression—his frown—made Adam's nape prickle. Had the footman seen something odd outside? Adam had posted additional staff on all the Abbey's doors and there were extra guards stationed at the main gate. But in light of Mr. Walsh's news, he could not help but be on edge.

He took a step away from Catherine toward the footman. "Is everything all right, Jack—"

He got no further as chaos erupted. A windowpane shattered, screams filled the air, and suddenly Adam's left side felt like it was on fire.

Fuck. Someone had open fired on the drawing room. At him!

Adam instinctively dropped to the floor, pulling Catherine with him. "Get down," he barked out at his mother and sisters. "Everyone get down." To Jackson he cried, "For Christ's sake, try to draw those bloody curtains closed. We're all sitting ducks in here."

Holy blazing hell. Adam couldn't believe he'd taken a shot. How else could he explain the searing pain in the vicinity of his left flank? It burned like the very devil. But he'd take that as a good sign. He was still alert and even though his heart was crashing against his ribs, he was still breathing. He could still move all his limbs.

And now he was *fucking* mad. The blistering anger in his veins would keep him going, no matter what.

Catherine, kneeling on the carpet beside him, gasped and blanched when she saw him pull his bloodied hand away from his side. "Adam, oh God. Y-You're bleeding."

His mother, huddled behind a nearby sofa with Cordelia and Viola, looked like she was about to drop into a dead faint when she also spied the blood. "Adam," she cried.

"I'm all right," he gritted out, pushing himself up into a

sitting position behind a leather wing chair. "I'm sure it's only a graze."

By this time Jackson had managed to wrestle the curtains closed with the help of Fitz, the other footman on duty.

"Fitz," Adam called. "Find Quigley. Get him to check that all the doors are locked and manned and all curtains are drawn throughout the house. Snuff out as many candles and lamps as you can. In here, too. The less light there is inside the house, the harder it will be for the assailant to turn anyone into a target."

"I'll need some light so I can examine your wound, Adam, so let's not extinguish any in here just yet. The curtains should shield us from view for now," said Catherine. Her face was pale, but her voice was steady. "Do you think you can get your jacket off?"

By God his wife was brave. If Adam wasn't in so much pain and needed desperately to keep his head, he'd hold her tight and give her a massive kiss. "All in good time," he said. "I need to make sure that whoever just fired a shot isn't going to fire anymore."

"I understand," said Catherine firmly but gently. "But you won't be good to anyone if you keel over from loss of blood."

Adam nodded. "Very well." He caught Jackson's attention. "Don't worry about the candles and lamps. Instead, I'd like you to escort my mother and sisters upstairs to Lady Dalton's sitting room. Make sure the curtains are shut with a minimum number of candles burning. Then check on my son and stand guard outside the nursery. You'll be able to keep an eye on my wife's rooms at the same time. Guard them with your life."

Jackson bowed. "Yes, my lord."

"But, Adam—" began his mother, but Adam held up a hand.

"Please just do as I ask, Mother. I'm fine and I need to

know everyone is safe. After Jackson leaves you, lock the door to Catherine's suite and only open it if you know who's on the other side. And stay away from all the windows. Don't be tempted to look out to see what's going on. Of course, I'm assuming there's only one attacker outside. He might have even absconded by now. But at this stage it's better to err on the side of caution."

"Yes, Adam," murmured his mother. To Cordelia and Viola who were white-faced but stoic she said, "Come girls, we'll do as your brother bids. What he says makes sense."

As soon as the drawing room door shut, Adam eased off his evening jacket with a muttered curse. Catherine then helped him to remove his ruined silk waistcoat. Just below his ribcage, his cambric shirt was stained with blood and the fabric was torn.

"I don't think the damage is too bad. The bullet just nicked my flank as it whistled past." He leaned to the side to make it easier for Catherine to tug his shirt free of his trousers, but hissed when she did so.

Catherine tutted as she lifted the hem. "I'll be the judge of that," she murmured. She frowned. "I'm no physician, but I think you're right. The wound seems superficial. It might need a few stitches..."

"I don't have time for that. I need to make sure the house is secure before I head outside." He began to loosen the elaborately knotted folds of his muslin neckcloth. "Here, use this to make a bandage to staunch the bleeding." He gave a snort. "I'm glad my valet insisted that I wear this ridiculously long cravat this evening, otherwise we'd be tearing up your petticoats."

"Don't you want me to clean the wound first?" asked Catherine as she slid the fabric from around his neck. "There's a pitcher of water on the sideboard. Or I could use alcohol. I promise I won't use your precious Cordovan Amontillado."

"I wouldn't object to you using my mother's Bristol Milk sherry," said Adam with a grim laugh. "It's quite vile, but there's no time. Just wrap the muslin about my middle. I'll live. We'll summon the physician in the morning if he's needed."

"You're a terrible patient, do you know that?" Catherine muttered as she proceeded to bandage him up.

He smiled even though his side was smarting like hell. "No doubt. But you know, as we Englishmen like to say, 'stiff upper lip and soldier on' and all that."

Catherine gave small snort. "Bravado is all well and good... up until a certain point, my dear husband." She tied off a secure knot then looked him in the eye. "There we go. Promise me you won't do anything foolhardy."

"*Ma belle*"—Adam cupped her jaw—"I will be careful. And while I don't want to alarm you, you and I both know that that bullet may not have been meant for me."

Catherine drew a shaky breath. "I know," she whispered, her voice catching. Guilt and fear chased over her beautiful face like clouds drifting over the sun. "And that's what scares me the most. Someone really hates me, Adam. So much so that they wish me dead. And whoever it is, they don't care that you or perhaps even our son might get hurt. If it's Lord Makepeace..."

"I'll catch him," Adam said fiercely. "Whether it's Makepeace or one of the Fortescues—whoever it is—I will catch him, and he will know my wrath."

"Thank you," Catherine leaned forward and placed a quick yet soft kiss on his lips.

Adam felt a sudden lump of emotion jamming his throat. "You don't need to thank me. I'd do anything for you, you know that, don't you?"

Catherine's blue-gray eyes grew bright with tears as she

nodded. "I know. But I don't want you to risk your life for me—"

"Shhh. I'll be fine, my love. I'm going to arm myself with my dueling pistols—they're in my private study—and then I'll take several men with me to hunt around the grounds. Mr. Kerr is a good shot—he used to be in the navy. And the groundsman, too. The guards at the front gate—they're men who've all had military training according to Lord Maxwell—would have heard the gun's report so I suspect they've already begun a search."

Catherine helped Adam to his feet then he headed for the door.

"I'll summon one of the footmen to escort you up to the nursery to check on our son," he called over his shoulder. "Wait there until—"

A distant scream rent the air followed by a faint cry of, "My lady, my lady."

Catherine rushed across the room to Adam's side. "Oh God. That sounds like Lizzy," she cried, reaching past Adam to grip the handle of the drawing room door. He swiftly stopped her from opening it.

"It might be a trap," he warned. His own gut had tightened with dread. He'd sent his mother and sisters upstairs to that part of the Abbey, though at least they'd been accompanied by Jackson. "You stay here. Let me go first."

Catherine's eyes were wild with fear. "I-I don't care if it's a potential trap. I must go with you. Louis—"

Adam gave a curt nod. "Very well. But stay behind me."

He bade Catherine stand to one side of the door, then he opened it a fraction to check the long gallery outside. It was cloaked in deep shadow—only a single lamp was burning—but there was enough light to discern the curtains were drawn against the night and everything looked as it should.

Lizzy's wail came again. Louder this time. "My lady! Oh, my lady. Come quickly!

That was enough to spur Adam into action. Disregarding the pain in his side he raced down the gallery, Catherine following him closely.

By the time they reached the Great Hall, Quigley and Fitz had appeared while Mrs. Beckett, the housekeeper, and a group of ashen-faced maids were huddled by the banked fire at the far end of the vast chamber.

"Everything is secure, my lord," called out Quigley as Adam began to scale the stairs with Catherine. "All the doors are locked and guarded."

"Good man—stay with the ladies. Fitz, come with me and Lady Dalton."

The three of them were only halfway up the stairs when Lizzy appeared on the landing. She was sobbing frantically and wringing her hands. "Oh, my lady. My lord...I can't find him anywhere."

Adam's heart plummeted to the floor as he began to take the stairs two at a time. "Who?" he demanded even though his gut knew the answer. "My son?"

"Yes, your little Lord Rosemont," wailed Lizzy. "I don't know where he is. He's disappeared. I wasn't gone from the nursery for long. Just a few minutes, I swear. And I was just doing as Jackson told me—"

Adam reached the landing. He gripped Lizzy's arm. "Are you sure my son isn't hiding somewhere?"

"I-I don't think so, my lord... I've searched and called... And Pippin is still sound asleep on the bed. Unnaturally so. I can't seem to rouse him."

Catherine reached Adam's side. She was breathless from rushing but managed to ask, "Lizzy...try to tell us exactly what happened."

The young woman nodded, her head bobbing frantically.

"Yes, my lady... I heard a commotion downstairs. A crash and screams and shouts so I stepped out of the nursery to listen. I was...I was frightened. Hetty came out of your suite, too. Then a minute later, Jackson appeared with your mother and Lady Cordelia and Lady Viola. He told Hetty and me that Lord Dalton had been wounded—shot, but he would be all right—and that we were all to go into your sitting room and to lock the door, draw the curtains, and not to look out the windows in case the shooter was still outside. And then he said that he would stand guard outside the nursery while keeping an eye on Lady Dalton's rooms at the same time. I waited in your sitting room, my lady, for a minute or two...but then I was worried Lord Rosemont might wake up and I didn't want him to be all alone. So I quit the room and..." She closed her eyes and drew a shuddering breath. "When I came out, I couldn't see Jackson anywhere in the hall. I wondered if he'd gone into the nursery to check on Lord Rosemont, but when I entered the room, I saw his bed was empty."

Fresh tears began to spill down the nursemaid's cheeks. "Jackson wasn't in the nursery either. And Pippin wouldn't stir and I began to feel like there was something terribly wrong. So then I called the young master and checked under the bed and in the wardrobe and behind the curtains—even though Jackson had said to stay away from the windows, but Lord Rosemont wasn't anywhere... I'm so scared. I don't know what to think."

Catherine's eyes locked with Adam's. "Do you think Jackson could have taken Louis? Maybe somewhere he thought might be safer? Maybe Louis woke up and was asking for me so Jackson thought to bring him downstairs to the drawing room? I know I'm grasping at straws, but the hallways are so dark, perhaps we somehow missed them?"

Adam scrubbed a hand down his face. Anger and fear burned like acid through his veins. What the hell was going on? And what the bloody hell was Jackson up to? Lizzy was right, something was terribly wrong with this whole situation. But he needed to stay calm. To think. "I don't know, *ma belle*," he said, his voice grim. "Maybe. Do you trust Jackson?"

Catherine's nod was emphatic. "Yes. I do. He was already working for Edward when I married him. He dotes on Louis."

Adam nodded. "All right... Rest assured, we'll conduct a thorough search."

He turned to Fitz. "Check every room on the floor above." After the young footman raced off toward the next flight of stairs, Adam called down to Quigley. "My son is missing from his bed. He might be with Jackson. Can you mount a quick search of the downstairs rooms and then the south wing? Check with the guards on all the doors if they've seen anything. My wife, Lizzy, and I will search the north wing on this floor. Everyone report back here in ten minutes."

The butler gave a quick bow. "Yes, my lord."

"We've seen nothing untoward, my lord," called out one of the footmen posted by the Abbey's main entrance. "The last time we saw Jackson, he was escorting your mother and the Ladies Cordelia and Viola upstairs. That must have been only five or six minutes ago. But we'll keep an eye out."

Adam nodded his thanks, then took Catherine's hand as they rushed down the hall toward the north wing. "You, I, and Lizzy will check the rooms on our floor. I'll ask my mother and sisters and your lady's maid to search too. At this point, time is of the essence, and I'm relatively certain that everyone one will be safe as long as they don't go near any uncovered windows." He gave her hand a reassuring squeeze. "I promise you, we'll find Louis."

But after ten minutes the search proved fruitless, at least on the second floor of the Abbey's north wing. Neither Jackson nor Louis could be found in any of the rooms. Lizzy was crying again, his mother and sisters were as pale as ghosts, and Catherine looked like she was on the verge of breaking down, too.

Adam couldn't say that he blamed her. He was gripped by such a powerful sense of foreboding, he barely noticed the pain in his side anymore. "We'll return to the Great Hall. Perhaps Quigley or the others will have some news," Adam said to Catherine even though he had a horrible feeling that they wouldn't. "All the doors are guarded so Louis must be inside the Abbey somewhere."

But his wife shook her head. "I don't think he is," she said, dashing away a tear from her cheek. "I can feel it in here." She placed a fist on her chest. On her heart. "He's been taken. And I can't help thinking that the attack on the drawing room and Louis's disappearance are both connected somehow. And *where* on earth is Jackson?"

Adam felt a muscle tick in his jaw. "Perhaps he's not as loyal as you think—"

At that moment there was another scream. Adam's gaze shot to the end of the corridor and he spied Hetty standing by the door to the servants' stairwell. "I've found Jackson, my lord, my lady," she called out, her voice quivering with fear. "He's been injured. Hit over the head." She screamed again and stumbled back, her hands fluttering about her face and neck like she was batting something away. "Oh God, I hope he's not dead!"

Adam bolted down the hall and flung the door wider. Sure enough, the footman lay sprawled at the bottom of the stairs. His periwig had been knocked off and there was blood trickling from a gash on the man's forehead. But he wasn't dead. Adam could detect a steady pulse in his neck.

"He's just been knocked unconscious," he called out to Catherine who was hovering behind him in the open doorway. "Can you procure some smelling salts? My mother normally has some."

At that moment, Jackson began to stir. His eyelids fluttered and he groaned. He raised a hand to the gash. "My head," he mumbled. Then his eyes flew wide open and his gaze connected with Adam's. "Oh God! Lord Dalton—your son—"

"What about him? Where is he?" demanded Adam. He didn't care if his tone was too brusque. Desperation and anger and fear were clawing at his insides, making him rougher then he would normally be.

Catherine entered the stairwell and knelt down beside the footman. "I know you've been hurt, Jackson, but if you can, please tell us what's happened. Where's my Louis?" She couldn't hide the hitch in her voice or the anguish in her eyes.

Jackson groaned and pushed himself up to a sitting position. "Oh Lord... I feel dizzy..." His head dropped forward into his hands which were resting on his bent knees. "My head is splitting... I'm so sorry..."

"Adam, let's get Jackson out of the stairwell," said Catherine. "There's a settee nearby in the corridor." She turned back to the footman and touched his shoulder. "Do you think you can get up if we help?"

Jackson raised his head and gave a small smile. "I think so, my lady."

Once the footman was installed on the settee, he confessed the news Adam had been fearing all along. That someone—a strange man—had taken Louis from his room. That after Jackson had made sure Lady Dalton, Lady Cordelia, and Lady Viola were locked up safe and sound with Lizzie and Hetty, he'd returned to the nursery to stand guard as he'd been instructed, only to discover that Louis was not in his bed. "But my memory is hazy, my lady," he said to Catherine, his expression woeful. "I think the blow to my head has knocked some of my thoughts clean out of me."

Adam was beyond frustrated. "But you recall that you saw

a man—a stranger making off with Louis. What did he look like? Do you recall anything about him at all?"

Jackson frowned. "It was hard to see much in the way of detail because it's so dark down this end of the corridor. But the man was cloaked—or wearing a greatcoat. I only caught the briefest glimpse of him carrying young Lord Rosemont before he disappeared into the servants' stairwell. That's why I followed... Then I don't remember anything else."

Catherine, who was sitting beside the dazed footman, looked up at Adam. "But there are guards posted at every door. This man can't have gotten far."

"I shouldn't think so. Unless the cur has attacked one of them as well." Adam's voice was harsh with barely suppressed anger. "I'll head back to the Great Hall and mount a search with Quigley. I'll also send for the guards at the gatehouse. Maybe they've seen or heard something. There's only one road that leads to the Abbey and it goes through Little Godstow."

"But there's also the Thames," whispered Catherine. "What if...what if the kidnapper or kidnappers had a boat waiting?" Her breath hitched and she swallowed. "They could be long gone by now."

Fucking hell. Catherine was right. Adam's hands clenched into fists as he raced back toward the Great Hall.

What a monumental idiot he'd been, underestimating his wife's enemies. Why hadn't he doubled the guards on all the doors and had men patrolling the grounds of the Abbey, including all along the river? He should have an army of great hulking guard dogs roaming about the house and estate too, not just a small Cavalier spaniel like Pippin.

If anything terrible befell Louis, his little boy...

If Louis was hurt in any way. Or worse...

No, he couldn't think like that. He would get his son back. Louis would be all right.

Adam suddenly had the terrible sense that everything that

had happened tonight had somehow all been pre-meditated. By all accounts, Louis hadn't woken or struggled or cried out. Of course, young children could sleep soundly.

But then there was also something wrong with Pippin. What if Louis had been drugged? He'd fallen asleep so quickly tonight...

Was there a traitor in their midst?

If there was, whoever it was, could expect to die a long, slow, and painful death...

That was one thing Adam was absolutely certain about. That, and no matter what, he was going to rescue his son.

CHAPTER 21

C atherine couldn't believe it.

Her darling Louis, her precious little boy, had been kidnapped. *Kidnapped.*

She must be caught up in some sort of horrendous nightmare.

But she wasn't. She was very much awake, and even though Adam had bade her to stay in her suite with his mother and sisters while a search was conducted about the Abbey and its grounds—while pouring rain and freezing air nipped outside—she couldn't seem to sit still, let alone retire to her bed.

Of course, Adam's reasoning made sense—he would not let her put her own life in danger by roaming around outside in the dark when there still might be a would-be-murderer and kidnapper on the loose—but it also meant she didn't know what was going on. Adam had already been shot once tonight. What if the assailant was still out there, just watching and waiting for another opportunity to injure or even kill her husband? Or kidnap someone else?

Drusilla had ordered tea and coffee and a little supper, but

Catherine couldn't bring herself to eat or drink anything at all. All she could do was pace back and forth, back and forth across the Aubusson rug in her sitting room, willing herself not to watch the clock on the mantelpiece. Willing herself not to think the worst. Willing herself not to wail and scream like a banshee.

Louis will be all right. He'll be all right. He'll be all right... And so will Adam. That was what Catherine chanted to herself over and over again as she wrapped her hands about her churning middle and paced and paced and paced.

But *was* her son all right? If the Fortescues had kidnapped Louis, would they treat him well? Or did they mean to do away with him, so Benedict and then Gerald could inherit the earldom? It would be madness if they thought they could get away with something like that.

Then again, if Lord Makepeace had taken Louis to hurt Catherine—some sick sort of revenge for pointing the finger at his traitorous father, Albert Makepeace, all those years ago —who knew what the man would do? The threats he'd sent Catherine—because the baron *must* be the author—were deranged. And she knew from experience that Frederick Makepeace's father had certainly been a violent man...

Oh, God... Catherine stopped by the fire and stared into the leaping flames. She was so beside herself with worry and bone-deep dread, she felt sick with it.

It was clear that Louis had been drugged. The milk on his bedside table had a bitter aftertaste to it and Adam suspected it had been laced with laudanum by someone in the house...or someone who'd managed to sneak into the house undetected —a stranger—at some point during the evening when staff were distracted with dinner preparations. That same someone had also apparently slipped laudanum into Pippin's food. The dog was routinely fed in the yard, just outside the kitchen, right before Louis took his dinner in the nursery.

Whoever that someone was, Catherine and Adam could *not* work out. Lizzy tearfully and ardently professed it was not her. That she would never hurt little Lord Rosemont. That she loved him like he was her own child.

Jackson, who'd been serving the Rosemont family for years, had been bludgeoned by the kidnapper—in fact, Catherine suspected the poor man would be unfit for duty for at least another day or two. Given the extent of his injuries, logic dictated it couldn't be him. Besides, Edward had always trusted the man—apparently Jackson had grown up in Briarcombe—and Catherine believed her first husband had been a shrewd judge of character.

Hetty had been with Catherine, arranging her hair and helping her change into her dinner finery during the time Louis's milk had been sent up from the kitchen. Adam was certain his staff would not take part in such a heinous crime either.

But *someone* had drugged both Louis and Pippin. That malicious someone had stolen into the house and lain in wait until he'd seen an opportunity to kidnap her son.

Catherine picked up the poker and jabbed at the logs, sending bright sparks up the chimney. She was so angry, so filled with ire just thinking about it, she knew she'd shoot the evil swine herself if she ever came face to face with him.

"Catherine, dear. Come and sit," called the Dowager Lady Dalton from the silk-upholstered sofa. "Have some chamomile tea."

Catherine turned to face her mother-in-law. "I don't think I can." Her voice sounded so strained and brittle, it might shatter.

Lady Viola approached, much like one would approach a deer that might bolt at any moment. "At least put down the poker. Your hands are shaking," she said gently.

The young woman was right. As Catherine placed the fire-iron back in its stand, her vision misted with tears. Drusilla, Viola, and Cordelia had been so lovely to her, so kind, she almost couldn't bear it.

"Maybe I'll sit. Just for a minute or two," she conceded, then took the spot beside the dowager countess. Her gaze drifted over the supper things on the low table before her and her stomach grumbled in protest. "Maybe I'll try a cucumber sandwich. And a small glass of barley water."

"Good girl," said Drusilla. She poured a drink for Catherine then handed it to her. "You won't do anyone any good if you collapse from exhaustion and lack of sustenance. Especially when your little Louis comes home. He's going to need you. Just like my Adam needs you."

Catherine couldn't bring herself to even contemplate the idea that Louis might be home any minute. She didn't want to lose hope, but the waiting and worrying were excruciatingly painful. She was trying to swallow down all her panic while balancing on a knife edge, not knowing if she would teeter over into the arms of relief or into a deep abyss of dark anguish.

Tamping down a sudden surge of despair, Catherine instead focused on Drusilla's last remark. "You really do think Adam needs me?"

"Pfft." Drusilla waved a hand. "Of course he does. Take this evening, for example. The girls and I were cowering behind a settee while you were the Rock of Gibraltar. You talked Adam into getting his wound checked. You tended to it. I am most impressed. You're not squeamish or the least faint-hearted."

"Thank you," murmured Catherine. She sipped her barley water and nibbled her sandwich...but then her eyes filled with tears again as she imagined Louis waking up in a strange place. How frightened he would be. How groggy and disoriented he would feel from whatever opiate he'd been given. How he'd call for her and she'd never come.

The dark thoughts seemed to multiply, squeezing the air from Catherine's lungs. Would his kidnapper feed him when he was hungry? Would Louis be given blankets and a bed? Or would he be treated cruelly? Would he be cold and hungry? Bound and gagged?

Would his captor deliberately hurt him in ways she couldn't even bring herself to think about?

Catherine suddenly couldn't take another sip or bite of anything. She put down her glass and prayed with all her might. Another chant began in her head. *Adam will find him. You know he'll find him. He has to find him.*

Two hours later, at ten minutes to ten, Adam returned to the Abbey. Catherine, who'd asked Quigley to send word as soon as his master returned, raced down to the Great Hall.

Her husband was soaking wet, his face as white as parchment, and his lips were almost blue with cold. "You were right, Catherine, the kidnapper used a boat," he said as he shrugged off his wet and muddy greatcoat and passed it to Fitz. "Mr. Kerr and I found the place where the boat had been tied up. Not far from the old abbey ruins. The ground was all churned up."

"Which way do you think the kidnapper went?" asked Catherine.

"South, I expect, with the flow of the river toward Oxford. But as to how far they've gone downstream..." Adam scrubbed a hand through his sopping hair. "I couldn't say. I've sent one of the guards at the gate to summon the parish constable in Little Godstow and to alert the constable in charge of the night watchmen in Oxford itself. The more men we have on the lookout, the better."

Catherine bit her lip to stop herself crying. She couldn't bring herself to remark, *"And what if no one sees anything helpful?"* Instead she asked, "How is your side? Should I send for the doctor in Little Godstow?" At least the bloodstains on Adam's wet shirt didn't look fresh.

Adam shook his head. "There isn't one. We'd have to send for the chap we use in Wolvercote or even Oxford." He grasped Catherine's arms. "I'm sore but I'm fine. Your bandage has held up, but you can check the wound shortly if you like. I'm going to change into something warmer and drier, then I'm going to head to Oxford myself. On horseback."

"You're going to scour the riverbanks, aren't you?" Catherine swallowed as dread gripped her heart. "You don't think the kidnapper threw our son into the Thames, do you?"

Adam's jaw tightened. "I hope to God that hasn't happened. But no, I'm going to look out for the place they might have landed. It's only been a few hours. I don't want to leave you, but I need to keep searching for Louis. You'll be safe here. I really do think the shot that was fired into the drawing room was a crude distraction to create chaos, and nothing else. There's no sign of anyone else on the grounds and everything is locked up and well-guarded. The groundsman, Cowley, is patrolling the estate with our neighbor's hunting hounds."

Catherine sighed. Adam spoke sense, but it was so very hard to stay in the background when she wanted to join the search too.

Adam stroked her cheek. "I know it's hard, my love. Terrifying, in fact. But I need to go on horseback, and you don't ride. And I need to know you are safe, not wandering the dark canals and streets of Oxford in the rain. As soon as there's any sort of news, I'll send word. Try to get some rest."

She nodded. "I will."

It was a lie. The only thing which gave Catherine any sort of comfort in the long hopeless hours of what seemed like a never-ending night was the fact that Adam had called her "my love" twice this evening.

It might mean nothing, but those two tiny words were enough for her to hold onto for now. They were the small flickering light in the dark that got her through to the dawn of the next day when Adam returned to St Clair Abbey.

CHAPTER 22

Adam didn't have any news when he arrived back at St Clair Abbey just before dawn. None at all. The person who'd taken Louis hadn't left any sort of trail. Not a single breadcrumb of a clue as to where he'd taken or Louis —or why.

He still believed that the Fortescues were the prime suspects, so he'd made sure that the local constabulary was on the lookout for Benedict, Lilith, and Gerald. If any of the Fortescues were in Oxfordshire, they would be found. And that *might* lead them to Louis. If Adam's assumptions were correct...

Even though Adam prayed a lead might come to light in the next few hours—there were men still scouring the local area with a fine-tooth comb—he'd also dispatched a courier to Maxwell in London to secure further assistance. The Scot's Home Office connections would be enormously useful at a time like this, especially if Lord Makepeace's whereabouts could be tracked down. Adam's instincts told him the baron was also involved somehow.

He would do whatever he could to find his son.

When Adam dragged his exhausted, aching body upstairs, he found Catherine in her sitting room, dozing in a chair by the fire. He suspected she'd been up most of the night, waiting and fretting.

His heart ached for her and their son. His chest was being crushed by a leaden weight of despair and a great deal of guilt. Guilt he hadn't put better protections in place to keep Louis safe.

But self-recrimination and mental flagellation wouldn't bring his son back. Only decisive action would. He had to be strong. He mustn't give up hope.

Catherine and most of all, Louis, were counting on him. And he wouldn't fail them.

He approached the fireside and his heart cramped when he saw Catherine was still in her finery from the evening before, although her elegantly arranged hair had begun to slide free of its pins and the loosened locks had tangled about her shoulders. He imagined that she'd run desperate fingers through it countless times during the night.

Kneeling down beside her, he gently touched her shoulder. "Catherine, my love..."

She started and her eyes flew open. "Adam... You're back... Tell me you have news."

Adam's gut clenched. "I haven't any, I'm afraid..." He brought her pale hand to his cheek. "But everything that can be done to find Louis *is* being done. Both the Oxford Watch and Ward force have been marshaled. Even the University's own private constabulary joined in the search once they heard it was a missing child." He also told her about the courier he'd sent to rally Maxwell. "Our son is an earl and this is not an insignificant crime. The Home Office should be involved."

Catherine nodded and tears filled her eyes. "I know... I know you'd move heaven and earth for our boy. But maybe that won't be enough. I think we need a miracle, Adam. And I don't know if I believe in those."

Oh, dear God, she was breaking his heart.

"Come..." Adam took her hand and she docilely followed him into her bedchamber. He slid the pins from her hair before gently removing her clothes until she was dressed in nothing but her chemise. He tucked her into the bed, then removed his coat and filthy boots before sliding beneath the covers with her.

"Rest now, my love. For just an hour or two. Rest." Adam cradled her in his arms until she fell asleep.

～

Adam started awake.

Christ. He didn't think he'd be able to fall asleep, such was the violence of his inner turmoil and the pain in his injured side, but he had. Like Catherine, he had been exhausted.

As he slid away from Catherine—which was no mean feat considering his side was sore as hell—she stirred...then sat bolt upright as though she'd just emerged from a bad dream. Sadness flooded his chest at the thought that she'd simply moved from one nightmare straight into another.

"What time is it?" Her voice was husky with sleep as she pushed her tangled hair out of her eyes.

"Half-past nine." Adam grimaced as he tugged his shirt from his breeches and investigated the bandage around his hips. No blood had seeped through the linen, so he took that as a good sign that the wounded flesh was knitting together on its own and he wouldn't need stitches.

Catherine made a similar observation. "I'm glad your search last night didn't worsen your injury." She hopped out of bed and rang for her maid. "After we've dressed, do you have any suggestions about what we should do next?" she asked. "I don't think I can sit around all day waiting for news. I have to do something. I'll go mad otherwise."

"I understand," said Adam, crossing to the door that connected their bedrooms. "I'll get changed and then we can repair to my study. I don't have much of an appetite, but I think some strong coffee wouldn't go astray while we discuss a plan of attack for the day ahead."

Catherine's mouth twitched with the ghost of a smile. "I agree with you about the coffee. I'll be ready in ten minutes."

The coffee helped clear Adam's head a little, even if it did nothing to relieve the grittiness in his eyes or the ever-present fear in his heart.

"I'm hoping Walsh will arrive back here today," he said as he poured himself another cup of coffee. He was so tense he couldn't make himself sit, so he stood on the hearthrug before the fire. "He might be able to help us to locate the Fortescues. If they haven't taken Louis, at least we'll be able to rule them out."

"Hmmm." Catherine was seated in a wingchair, her legs curled up beneath her skirts, her chin resting in her hand. Bruise-like shadows of fatigue shaded her blue eyes. "Unless they've hired someone to do their dirty work to distance them-selves from such a despicable act. For instance, the man who was watching me the night of the fire at Rosemont House... I still don't know who that was. It might have been Lord Make-peace. But what if it was a hired thug? Despite Mr. Walsh's recent intelligence regarding the Fortescue's reduced income, the family still has substantial financial resources at their disposal."

Catherine was right, of course. "You make a good point." Adam blew out a sigh. "Despite the fact I'm down a footmen after last night, I've doubled the guards on the doors and there'll be regular patrols around the Abbey grounds. Gardeners have stepped forward, and a few tenants I trust have volunteered. It will be virtually impossible for anyone to enter the estate or leave without being challenged."

Catherine pulled at a thread on her shawl. "How is Jackson this morning? Have you heard?"

"Quigley mentioned that he's sporting a sizable bruise and has a headache. But no other ill-effects have been reported. Even so, I think Jackson should have the day off to recuperate. He's lucky he wasn't killed." Adam glanced at Catherine's cup which sat on a nearby occasional table. "Would you like more coffee? Or fresh toast?" Despite the fact that Adam had only ordered coffee, the cook had sent up a tray that included pastries, rolls, and buttered toast with a variety of preserves. Adam had managed to force down a currant bun, but Catherine had barely touched her marmalade on toast.

But his wife shook her head. "No. I know I should eat something, but I truly have no appetite."

Adam approached, captured her hand, and kissed it. "We'll find him. I swear to you we will. When you're ready, we can travel into Oxford together. I've already arranged for the carriage to be brought round."

"Won't that slow you down? It would be faster if you rode..."

Adam gave her hand a squeeze. "Not that much faster. And I'd value your input when I meet with the head watch-man. Your observations are astute."

A short time later, he escorted Catherine down to the Great Hall. He was glad to see that Pippin had woken from his drug induced slumber and was nosing about the flagstones. Upon spying Catherine the spaniel trotted over to her, tail wagging, then gave a little yap as if to say, "Where's Louis?"

She bent down to stroke the dog's head. "I know, boy. We're all feeling a bit lost and confused and dismal too."

When the footmen-cum-guards opened the front doors, it was to reveal Adam's four-in-hand carriage ready and waiting.

The sun, which had made a brief appearance during their hurried breakfast, had disappeared behind a large bank of bruise-colored clouds. The scent of rain was in the air and a chill wind whipped through the beech trees that lined the drive, sending swirling flurries of dark golden leaves to the ground.

Catherine shivered and hugged her pelisse about her as she stepped onto the stone portico. Her eyes glistened with tears and Adam rather suspected it wasn't only the biting cold wind that had provoked them.

"Perhaps we should fetch you a cloak—" he began but then broke off. He could hear the unmistakable sound of hooves and carriage wheels crunching on gravel. Whoever it was, they were approaching the Abbey at pace. The guards at the gatehouse wouldn't have let anyone in who was intent on anything nefarious. Nevertheless, Adam stepped forward slightly to shield Catherine. He wasn't taking any chances.

Then he saw that one of the armed guards was riding postillion, escorting the plain black carriage to the front door. The man raised his hand in greeting. And he was grinning. "Good news, my lord, my lady," he shouted. "Your son, Lord Rosemont, is back!"

What?

Adam couldn't believe it. Catherine stepped forward and clutched his arm. "I must be dreaming," she whispered. "Any moment I'll wake up and discover this is all a dream."

But it wasn't. As the carriage slowed, drawing to a stop before the stairs, little Louis's face appeared at the window. He was jumping up and down and waving madly. Seated next to him was a middle-aged man who Adam did not recognize.

"Oh, our boy! He's all right!" Catherine picked up her skirts and raced down the stairs. Adam followed, reaching the carriage in a handful of strides. His chest was flooded with joy and sheer relief, so much so, he could barely breathe.

He had questions, so many questions tumbling through his head, all clamoring to be answered—especially when the gentleman opened the carriage door and lifted Louis down. But right at this moment, all he cared about was the fact that Catherine was holding their son in her arms, tears of joy streaming down her beautiful face.

At least Adam presumed so... It was a little hard to see clearly because his vision was blurred by tears too.

~

Louis was home. Louis was safe.

Catherine could scarcely believe it. And it was Benedict Fortescue, of all people, who'd bought her boy home.

Benedict...

Catherine didn't know if she should thank him or string him from a yardarm and demand answers as to why Louis was with him.

But for the moment she was simply overwhelmed with gratitude and relief and joy as she hugged her son. She could barely speak. Her face was steaming with tears as she clasped Louis tight and pressed her wet cheek to his golden head. Adam had dropped to his knees and encircled them both with his strong arms and Pippin was leaping about them all, barking excitedly.

When she at last stood with Louis still in her arms, Benedict regarded her from the beneath the brim of his beaver hat. Even though his eyes were in shadow, she couldn't mistake the odd expression in his gaze. He seemed guarded. Perhaps even apprehensive.

"No doubt you have questions, my lady," he said quietly, "about what's gone on." He bowed to Adam. "Lord Dalton, I take it? I'm Benedict Fortescue. Your son's cousin. Or should I say, first cousin once removed? Second cousin? I'm never sure about these sorts of things." He didn't offer his hand and Adam didn't extend his.

Catherine got the sense that both men were sizing each other up. Taking their measure. Tension hung in the air alongside the threat of rain.

"Yes, I am Lord Dalton," Adam replied. His tone was serious, his expression wary. "And yes, both my wife and I have many questions. I trust that you can explain just how and why my son is with you."

Benedict's lips compressed into a thin line. "I can."

"Mama, Papa, I've been on a grand adventure," cried Louis cheerfully. "Like Nimble and Longtail and Brighteyes and Softdown. And Cousin Benedict has brought me home."

"So he has, my darling boy. So he has," murmured Catherine, pressing a kiss to Louis's forehead. He was still dressed in his flannel nightshirt and his nightcap. One of his socks was missing. "Let's get you inside where it's nice and warm. I'll have Lizzy set up a lovely bath and Cook will get you something to eat. Anything you like. You must be hungry."

"Only a little bit," said Louis. "Cousin Benedict gave me some barley sugars in the carriage. He said you wouldn't mind even though it's not my birthday…" His forehead dipped into a frown. "Do you mind, Mama? I don't want you to be cross."

"No, I'm not cross, darling. Not at all." Catherine hugged him tight as she carried him into the Abbey. Adam and Benedict followed close behind. When she reached the stairs, Lizzy, Hetty, and Mrs. Beckett all appeared on the landing. They were closely followed by Lady Dalton, Cordelia, and Viola.

Lizzy squealed and rushed down to greet her charge.

Louis held out his arms to her. "Lizzy! I've been adventuring!"

Even though everything inside Catherine told her not to relinquish her hold on her son, she passed him to the nurse. Adam was going to interrogate Benedict about what had happened last night and who was responsible for Louis's kidnapping, and she was *not* going to miss out on that intelligence. Beneath her joy she was angry. So angry she could smash something or someone into a million little pieces.

Whoever had taken her son, that person would pay.

She gave instructions to Lizzy and promised Louis that she would see him in the nursery very soon. While she was doing that, Adam spoke in a low voice to his mother, and the dowager countess nodded sagely.

Then Drusilla addressed Catherine. "The girls and I will watch over Louis. Take all the time you need to do what you need to do, my dear," she said. The light in her eyes was nothing but kind and full of understanding. "He'll be well looked after. We won't let him out of our sight."

Catherine cast her a grateful smile. "Thank you," she murmured. "Your support means a lot."

Benedict's expression kept shifting between solemn and anxious once they were installed in Adam's study. Adam didn't offer the man any sort of refreshment and Catherine suspected Benedict wouldn't have accepted anything anyway.

Adam sat behind his desk and Catherine settled upon the window seat, just as she'd done the day before.

The day when the unthinkable had happened.

Benedict took the chair in front of Adam's desk. He sat stiffly, his hat resting in his lap. He hadn't even removed his coat or gloves—evidently Quigley did not consider him respectable enough to request them. It was almost as though he were expecting to be leaving at any minute.

Adam cleared his throat. "I think you'd best tell me everything, Mr. Fortescue. From the very beginning. And don't leave anything out. Do not obfuscate. My wife and I have been through hell. And while we both appreciate the fact you've returned our son to us, that in no way excuses that someone—

whether it was you, your wife, or son Gerald—took him from us in the first place."

"Lord Dalton, I promise you that I will be honest and forthright. I will keep nothing from you or from Lady Dalton." He glanced at Catherine. "You both deserve to know the unadulterated truth...as far as I know it."

"And what is the truth, Benedict?" asked Catherine. Her voice was tight with anger. "Who attacked my husband last night? Who drugged Louis and then stole him from his bed? Where did they take him? And why?" She thumped her fist on the cushion beside her. "Why take my little boy?"

Benedict's eyebrows shot to his hairline as his gaze whipped to Adam. He truly looked incredulous. "You were attacked?"

The light in Adam's eyes grew hard. "Yes. I was shot. The attack occurred last night, only moments before Louis was kidnapped. But it could have been anybody who was in the firing line. My lady-wife, my mother, my sisters..."

Benedict shook his head. "I...I had no idea. And needless to say, I'm truly shocked and appalled. I honestly don't know who fired at you, my lord... But I digress, and as I said, I want to be forthright." His narrow shoulders rose as he drew a deep breath. "I suspect you might have already guessed that my son, Gerald, and my wife, Lilith, are behind your son's kidnapping."

Catherine released a breath as Benedict at last confirmed her suspicions. "Tell us why—" she began, but then Adam interjected.

"Yes, tell us why. But also tell us why we should believe you. How do we know you weren't an active participant in Louis's kidnapping? You might have seen him safely home, but perhaps you got cold feet..."

"You have every right to be suspicious of me and my motives. But I urge you to hear me out." Benedict blew out a sigh. "To be perfectly frank...ever since my cousin Edward died, my wife and son have coveted the earldom. In fact, given the rumors that have been flying around about young Lord Rosemont's parentage..." The tips of Benedict's ears grew ruddy as his gaze lit on Catherine. "I apologize, Lady Dalton, I mean no offense, you asked me to explain... But ever since Louis was born, there's been speculation that he was...ahem, a by-blow. Lilith, in particular has always believed that to be true. And"—Benedict's blush deepened, spreading to his cheeks and down his neck—"on occasion she has spread gossip amongst those of her acquaintance with more elevated connections to gain their favor. She might have even sold lies to the newspapers... Not for the money, mind you. More because she doesn't like you, my lady. She feels like she should have been Lady Rosemont, not you."

Catherine bristled with anger. She couldn't say she was surprised. "And you, Benedict? Have you coveted the earldom? Have you spread hurtful rumors about me to defame me?" She couldn't say they were *all* lies because Louis wasn't actually Edward's son.

"The answer is no, to both of your questions," Benedict said, lifting his chin and meeting her gaze directly. "I've never wanted to be the Earl of Rosemont. Not ever. I'm a quiet man. I have enough in my life to keep me occupied. My marriage to Lilith afforded me with all the creature comforts I could ever need. But Lilith, she's always been ambitious and has never been satisfied with her lot in life. She's always wanted to elevate her rank, status, and wealth. I do believe the only reason she married me to begin with was because I was the cousin of an earl. I suspect she's always wanted to be the next Lady Rosemont. And Gerald wants that title. More than anything."

Benedict turned his attention to Adam. "When we heard that Catherine had wed again, Lilith suspected that you, Lord

Dalton, would become Louis's guardian... I think that was the trigger for Lilith and Gerald to take action. Why they hatched this mad plan to take Louis..." Benedict winced and his gaze flitted to Catherine before returning to Adam. "And to make him disappear... One way or another..."

Oh, my God. Catherine was relieved she was sitting down. She'd been worried for so long that someone was trying to harm Louis—to perhaps, even end his life—but to hear it confirmed out loud was brutally shocking.

Adam's hands clenched into fists on the desk blotter. When he spoke, his voice was eerily soft but laced with an undertone of deadly, steely strength. "Just so we are perfectly clear, you are telling me that your wife and your son were going to murder my son, a four-year-old child—"

"They hadn't quite decided— "

Adam's fury erupted. He smashed his fist on the desk, rattling the crystal ink wells and scattering papers. "What do you mean, they hadn't quite decided? How long have you known about this diabolical plan of theirs? Speak plainly before I take justice into my own hands and shoot you myself."

Benedict paled. "I knew nothing about the plan to take Louis and do him harm until late last night, my lord. I swear before God and all that's holy, that is the truth. While it *is* true that I had known for some time that my wife had been intentionally harming Lady Rosemont's reputation—over the years, Lilith had voiced the idea that perhaps one day, we could challenge Catherine's right to be Louis's sole guardian on the basis she was an unfit mother. Because of her...past..." Benedict's blush returned as he looked at Catherine. "Forgive me, my lady, because of rather salacious rumors about your past profession...which I'm sure are nothing but calumny.

Catherine snorted. "Of course."

Benedict cleared his throat, evidently embarrassed. "In any

event, while I agree that I failed to curb my wife's scandalmongering tendencies—and I, in fact, never wished to challenge your right to be your son's sole guardian—I couldn't condone what Lilith and Gerald were discussing last night. Or should I say, in the early hours of this morning."

"Why should I believe anything you say, Fortescue?" Adam scoffed. "You have yet to convince me that you played no part in this crime."

Panic flared in Benedict's eyes as he sat forward in his seat. "My lord, I swear I had no idea what they were up to. A few days ago, Lilith told me that she wished to travel north to spend some time with her extended family in Yorkshire, and that Gerald wanted to accompany us. She said we wouldn't take the Great North Road as we usually do, but instead take a different route at a leisurely pace, stopping at various places she'd always wanted to visit. Gerald too. He expressed an interest in seeing Oxford and its university."

"You didn't think this was at all suspicious behavior, given that St Clair Abbey is only five miles from Oxford?" demanded Adam hotly, impatience flashing in his eyes.

"No, I didn't. But I should have," admitted Benedict. "Especially when instead of taking rooms at an inn in Oxford itself, Lilith hired a cottage beside the Thames—Millcote Cottage—not far from Wolvercote village, so that she might enjoy the 'country air'. The place has a small boathouse because Gerald purportedly wanted to go rowing—even though it's November, freezing and raining." Benedict's mouth twisted, his expression rueful. "Little did I know that Gerald intended to use the boat to kidnap little Lord Rosemont last night...until I was awoken to discover him carrying your sound asleep son in from the rain. Gerald was soaking wet, but Louis was relatively dry. He was wrapped up in a moleskin cloak. Even so, I was alarmed because the boy looked so pale and wouldn't rouse until Gerald told me that he'd been fed laudanum so he wouldn't struggle and fall out of the rowboat and drown."

Catherine's stomach lurched at the very idea of her boy drowning in the cold rushing river. How dare Gerald and Lilith do this! But she bit her tongue to stop herself railing aloud. She needed to hear everything, no matter how terrible the truth might be.

Benedict continued. "Lilith took Louis and placed him in a bedroom at the back of the cottage and locked the door. I, of course, demanded to know what was going on, but all Lilith would say was that she and Gerald had taken your son from St Clair Abbey because, at long last, she'd decided to do what needed to be done. She wouldn't elaborate when I began to ask questions about how Gerald had managed to get into the Abbey and steal the boy and effect an escape without getting caught. Or how they thought they could get away with it. But Gerald got angry with me and told me to go to bed. That the less I knew, the better. But I couldn't sleep. I was wracked with worry and guilt. After a few hours, when Lilith hadn't come to bed, I crept downstairs, and I overheard Lilith and Gerald discussing the best way to conceal Louis until they worked out what to do with him next...to make him"—Benedict swallowed—"d-disappear. They were also talking about how to keep me quiet. Gerald asserted that I was a weak link that they would need to deal with. To be eliminated if needs be. He asked his mother if she would be prepared to go that far—to get rid of me—and when she replied, yes, she would, I was both horrified and angry."

Anguish transformed Benedict's features. "I couldn't believe... My wife and son were plotting to kill me too. I had to act. Not just for Louis's sake, but for my sake as well. But I had to be just as stealthy and clever as Lilith and Gerald had been. I had to outwit them. I'd spotted Lilith's bottle of laudanum in the cottage's kitchen. She'd left it on the mantel. So when I rose—it was early—I dressed quietly then went downstairs and made a pot of coffee and a pot of tea and laced them both with the laudanum. I also checked on your son—Lilith left the key in the kitchen too—and he was still asleep."

Catherine frowned. "Wouldn't Gerald and Lilith think it odd that you'd made pots of coffee and tea? Not a maid?"

Benedict shrugged. "I had to take that chance. There's a maid-of-all-work who comes to the cottage for five or six hours each day, to clean and cook, but she isn't expected until half-past ten or thereabouts. If my son or wife questioned me, I had a legitimate excuse for making my own hot beverage... I hadn't slept well and I needed the coffee. In any event, Gerald heard me and came downstairs. He looked quite haggard, so I suspect he hadn't slept well either. He accepted the cup of coffee I gave him without question and drank it in a few short gulps. Then he went back upstairs. I took a tea tray up to Lilith and she also drank a cup without question. Within half-an-hour, both of them were snoring in their beds like boar pigs. Then I roused our coachman who'd accompanied us on our trip and made him ready the carriage, posthaste. By that time, Louis was beginning to stir. Of course he was upset and confused at first—it had been some months since he'd last seen me. But then I reminded him about the book I gave him for his birthday—the one about the mouse and his adventures— and I bribed him with some sweets that I had in my coat pocket. So in the end, he was quite happy to come and hop in the carriage with me...especially when I promised I would take him back home to his Mama and new Papa." Benedict let out a great shuddering breath." And you know the rest..."

Adam pushed to his feet and leaned across the desk. "So what you are telling me is that your swine of a son and despicable Lady Macbeth of a wife are still blissfully sound asleep at this cottage on the outskirts of Wolvercote? That my son's kidnappers are both less than three miles from here?"

Benedict nodded. "Yes. You'll find the rowboat Gerald used last night still moored at the small dock beside the boathouse. I suspect they will be still asleep because of the laudanum. I gave them a decent dose. I didn't want to take any chances."

"Christ." Adam ran a hand through his hair. He glanced at the longcase clock in the corner of the study. It was almost half-past ten. "Won't your maid-of-all-work will be arriving at the cottage soon?" he asked through gritted teeth.

Benedict nodded. "Yes, but I doubt even she'll be able to wake them, even if she began smashing plates and clanging pots and pans." His nervous swallow was audible, almost a gulp. "What are you going to do, Lord Dalton?"

Adam caught Catherine's gaze. Knowledge flashed between them: without words, without movement. She drew a breath. "I'll stay here with Louis while you summon the local constabulary."

Adam gave a curt nod and his attention returned to Benedict. "You're coming with me, Fortescue. I'm not going to let you out of my sight..." He narrowed his eyes. "Are you ready for what will happen next? That your wife and son will be arrested and will go on trial for kidnapping and attempted murder? That your family's name will be forever mired in infamy?"

Benedict's countenance grew as pale as the starched white collar of his shirt and neckcloth. But his gaze was unflinching and his voice as solemn as a judge's as he spoke. "I am. I'm willing to live with public censure. I wouldn't have been able to live with myself if Lilith and Gerald had gotten away with their mad plan." Then he gave snort. "If they'd let *me* live, of course."

As the men left the room Catherine followed, intending to head to the nursery. But then she called after Benedict. "Mr. Fortescue, you didn't tell us about all the accidents and the threatening letters. What of those? Who was responsible for all of that, Lilith or Gerald? Or both of them?"

Benedict halted his steps and swung around. His brow furrowed into a deep frown. "What accidents, my lady? What letters?"

"You know, the frozen pond near miss and the broken axel on my carriage. The broken saddle strap on Louis's pony and the fire at Rosemont House. I know you are aware of the swing accident a few weeks ago."

Benedict still looked confused. "Yes, I know about the swing accident. Everyone in Briarcombe was talking about it. And the fire was reported in the newspapers. But I don't know about anything else. Especially the bit about the threatening letters..."

Catherine sighed. Even though frustration nipped, she said, "Never mind."

Adam returned to her side in a handful of strides and gently grasped her arm. "I'll be sure to question Lilith and Gerald about all that," he said in a low voice. "Don't worry, my love. We'll get to the bottom of everything. I promise. You just look after Louis and get some sleep when you can." Then he kissed her and whispered, "Give our boy a big hug from me. I'll be back before you know it."

CHAPTER 23

A dam waited outside Millcote Cottage as Lilith and Gerald Fortescue were arrested by the Oxford constabulary.

As much as he wanted to enter the small, thatched dwelling himself, and to mete out his own form of justice, he wasn't foolish enough to let his own rage take over. He would not swing from the hangman's noose for murder. He had too much to live for.

He had a wonderful sweet son and a beautiful wife. And last night, he'd failed them both. What had occurred at St Clair Abbey should never have happened and he would forever regret that his own hubris had been responsible for the nightmare that had unfolded. He'd grossly underestimated his wife's and son's enemies and hadn't put enough security measures in place.

If it weren't for the fact that Benedict Fortescue had come forward—and part of Adam believed the man had only done so to get justice on his side—only God knew what fate would have befallen Louis.

But Louis is safe. Catherine is safe, he reminded himself as

Lilith and Gerald Fortescue were hauled out of Millcote Cottage—half-dressed and still half-drugged—and unceremoniously thrown into the back of a heavily manned prison coach. *And that evil, unscrupulous pair shall feel the full weight of the law.*

Though there was still the lingering question about those terrible letters Catherine had been sent, and the numerous accidents that had occurred. Even the shot last night—who'd fired the weapon and who'd been the intended target—none of that had been explained, either.

Adam still wasn't convinced that Lord Makepeace wasn't involved in this vendetta against his family. It was clear, at least in his mind, that the dog had had something to do with the letter that had been handed to Louis at Gunter's Tea Shop. The man *had* been spotted in Hyde Park with Pippin. There was no doubt that he despised Catherine, given the insults he'd spewed about her that night at the Cockspur Tavern. But did Makepeace's campaign of hate have anything to do with the Fortescues?

One thing Adam intended to do was question Gerald Fortescue himself. It hadn't been hard to convince the governor and head warden at the Oxford Castle Prison that he needed to do so. Despite the notoriety of Stephen St Clair, the previous Earl of Dalton, Adam and his family were generally well-regarded in the city of Oxford.

Hours later, once Lilith and Gerald had appeared in the local magistrate's court and had been charged with kidnapping, a felony crime, they were transferred to cells within the forbidding and inhospitable Oxford Prison. In Adam's opinion, the place could be as inhospitable as the fiery pits of Hell itself, and he still wouldn't be satisfied.

It was the head warden himself who escorted Adam down to the fetid and ice-cold holding cells within the bowels of the prison. Mold grew in dank shadowy corners, and the screams and wails and cries that echoed through the dark and narrow corridors were almost enough to chill one to the bone.

Even though Adam was wearing a superfine riding jacket and a thick wool Garrick coat with his hands encased in fleece-lined leather gloves, he still felt half-frozen. When he exhaled, his breath misted in the air.

He had not one shred of pity for Gerald Fortescue when the warden stopped in front of a heavy, iron studded door, and he spied the man through the small, barred window. Indeed, Gerald was a miserable sight to behold. He sat upon a narrow stone bench, manacled to the wall, wearing nothing but a flannel nightshirt, trousers, and one leather slipper; the other foot was bare. It seemed he wasn't just devoid of stockings and a coat but all hope, considering the way he was hunched over, cradling his head in his hands.

Good, thought Adam. *I hope he's reflecting on what brought him here and the future that awaits him...at the end of a hangman's noose.*

When the warden unlocked the door and hauled it open, Gerald lifted his head and eyed Adam with suspicion when he stepped across the threshold into the cell.

"Who are you, then?" he asked gruffly. His eyes were heavy-lidded, as though still fighting off the aftereffects of the laudanum. "Some solicitor my useless father has hired to defend me?"

"No..." said Adam quietly. "Actually, I'm surprised you don't recognize me, Fortescue... I mean, didn't you have me in your sights last night? Take a shot at me? Or was it my wife you were trying to murder?"

Instead of looking startled at Adam's accusation, Gerald Fortescue's gaze narrowed. It combed over Adam from the top of his head to the toes of his hessians. "I don't know what the fuck you're talking about. I've never seen you before in my life."

Was he bluffing? Adam couldn't be sure. He took a step closer. "Well, you should know who I am," he said, in that same soft but menacing tone. "I was at Millcote Cottage when you were arrested. I watched you standing in the dock of the magistrate's court but an hour ago... I'm the father of the little boy you kidnapped. I am the Earl of Dalton."

"*Fuck!*" Gerald's face paled beneath the dark stubble shading his jaw and his panicked gaze darted to the warden who waited in the corridor outside. "Why the hell have you let this man into my cell, you bastard? He'll kill me!"

Adam couldn't contain a snort of laughter. "Oh, I'm not going to let you get off *that* easily, Fortescue. Not that anyone would blame me if I did take matters into my own hands, considering the magnitude of your crimes, and your mother's."

"It's all lies," declared Gerald. "It's my father who's responsible. Whatever he's told you about the kidnapping of your son, it's not true. He's made it all up to save his own skin."

Adam cocked a brow. "Really? That's going to be your defense?"

"Why not?" Gerald Fortescue thrust out his chin and the belligerent gesture was somehow vaguely familiar. "My father has a stake in this too. Why would a jury believe he didn't want the earldom just as much as me? If not more so, considering he's next in line for the title."

"Yet he's the one who returned my son to me," returned Adam hotly.

Gerald sneered. "That's because my father is a lily-livered coward," He scratched his stubbled jaw and the shadow of a memory suddenly stirred in Adam's mind. He had the sudden and peculiar sense that he'd seen this man before today, but he couldn't quite place him... Perhaps Gerald simply reminded Adam of Benedict, his father. The family resemblance was strong. Both men were tall and dark-haired with strong jawlines...

The hazy memory flickered and flared in Adam's mind eye again as he continued to study Gerald...and then realization slapped him like a bucket of cold water thrown in his face.

Bloody blazing ballocking hell!

Gerald Fortescue was the "benevolent stranger" Adam had seen at the Cockspur. The man who'd paid off Frederick Makepeace's chit.

He *knew* it beyond a shadow of a doubt. Adam wasn't sure why he hadn't made the connection until now. It was well known that both men had a taste for gaming in disreputable gaming hells... Perhaps that's how Gerald and Makepeace had first met.

But why continue to speculate when he could get the answers straight from the horse's mouth?

Adam leaned back against the wall of the cell, affecting a nonchalance he in no way felt. He removed the glove from his right hand and flexed his fingers, examining his knuckles. The abrasion and bruising which had resulted from planting a facer on Makepeace had faded. He didn't want to use his fists to get Gerald to talk. But he would if he had to.

Adam gave a small snort and slapped his glove against his thigh. No, he was lying to himself. There was a deep dark vengeful part of him that would relish taking Gerald Fortescue apart piece by piece—and slowly—until the snake confessed all...

"Tell me about Lord Makepeace," he said softly. "Your association with him. What you've both been plotting. What part he's played in this vile vendetta against my wife and son."

Gerald spat on the floor. "Who the fuck is Lord Make—"

Adam snapped. He lunged forward and pinned Gerald against the wall, his forearm pressing against the cur's throat. "Now listen here, you foul, sniveling, spineless swine," he snarled, pushing so hard Gerald's eyes bulged. He began to ineffectually claw at Adam's sleeve. "You're going to tell me what I want to know. Or I'm going to break your neck like a twig. You understand?"

Gerald emitted a strangled choking sound which Adam took to be a "yes" and he released the pressure on the man's throat.

"I met him at the cock fights once," gasped Gerald. "At the Cockspur Tavern. That's it—"

Adam applied force to Gerald's neck again. If the man's larynx was crushed, so be it. "I don't believe you," he growled. "There must be more to it. You took my son but who took a shot at me last night? Was it you or Makepeace or some hired thug? What. Do. You. Know?" Each word of Adam's last question was punctuated with another brutal press against Gerald's voice box. His anger, his thirst for vengeance was like a ferocious, ravenous beast, rearing its head. He'd let it loose, and it was running rampant. It wanted its pound of flesh. Maybe several pounds.

But then, all of a sudden, the fire inside Adam subsided. With a huff of disgust, he released Gerald and stepped back. He pulled at the cuffs of his coat and pulled on his glove while the man who'd planned to kill his son coughed and spluttered and gasped. Not even a flicker of sympathy or remorse stirred within Adam. Not one speck.

"You...bastard..." Gerald wheezed. "You could have killed me."

Adam shrugged. "No one would blame me. But know this"—he leaned forward and was pleased to see that Gerald shrank away from him—"tomorrow morning I'll be back. And you will tell me what I want to know. I'm not interested in half-truths. I don't wish to hear more of your obfuscating and pathetic denials. If you *do* own up to your crimes, if you *do* admit to your association with Lord Makepeace, I *might* be able to put in a good word for you with the magistrate, so you won't be sent to the gallows but get transported instead. Same for your mother."

Then Adam turned on his heel and strode away. He had better things to do with the rest of his day—like returning home to his wife and son.

And maybe after spending one night in a freezing cold jail cell, Gerald Fortescue might have a change of heart. Especially since his neck would be bloody sore. That should be a sufficient reminder of what his fate would be—death by hanging —if he didn't cooperate on the morrow.

CHAPTER 24

Catherine awoke from her nap with a start, then breathed a soft sigh of pure relief when she realized everything *was* actually right with her world. That she wasn't caught up in some terrible nightmare.

She was presently lying warm and snug in her four-poster bed with Louis curled up beside her. The light of the fire revealed that Pippin was asleep at their feet. Even though the curtains were drawn against the rainy day, she sensed it was early evening. A quick glance at the mantel clock confirmed that she was right. It was almost five o'clock and naturally, her thoughts turned to Adam. She was burning to know how he'd been getting on in Oxford.

At around noon, she'd received word from him that both Gerald and Lilith Fortescue had been arrested for kidnapping Louis and the pair were currently being held in Oxford Castle Prison.

To say Catherine was relieved would be an understatement, though she was still dying to know if Adam had learned who'd shot him last night. Until the perpetrator of that particular crime was discovered, she wouldn't be able to completely let down her guard. It might have been Gerald, but then again, it might have been someone else entirely. Someone like Lord Makepeace. But the guards who were now regularly patrolling the Abbey grounds had not seen anyone fitting the baron's description. If they did see a strange man lurking about, they would apprehend him on sight.

Catherine also wanted to know how Gerald had managed to brazenly drug and then kidnap her son, all without being detected by anyone at all. It was a complex crime, yet somehow he'd managed to pull it off without any help.

It was a perplexing mystery, but hopefully when Adam returned to the Abbey, he'd have some answers.

Catherine carefully pushed herself up against the pillows so she wouldn't disturb Louis, then stroked the tangled curls away from his flushed cheek. After Adam had left with Benedict—and because the protective lioness inside her couldn't help herself—she'd summoned the physician from Wolvercote. Following his examination, the doctor had reassured her that Louis hadn't been hurt or harmed in anyway, but that the laudanum might make him a little bit drowsy on and off over the next day or so.

Catherine was more than a little fatigued, too. Following the doctor's visit, she'd quite happily read stories to Louis in her room until they'd both fallen asleep. Because of everything that had happened, she suspected it would be difficult to let Louis out of her sight for quite some time to come. In fact, she'd already asked Lizzy to set up a bed for Louis in the sitting room between her bedchamber and Adam's. The nurse had also offered to sleep close by her young charge in a pallet bed. "I'll keep a warming pan under my pillow, my lady," she'd declared fiercely. "If anyone comes into the room other than you or Lord Dalton, I'll brain him then skewer him with a poker."

Catherine didn't doubt for a minute that the nursemaid

meant what she said—and she also trusted that Adam wouldn't mind. He would understand why she was so nervous about sleeping too far away from their son.

~

By the time Adam arrived home, night had completely fallen and he was completely spent. But he was both relieved and heartened when he found Louis and Catherine in her sitting room...which had been turned into another makeshift nursery. And he thoroughly approved.

Louis was eating his supper before the fire—a simple repast of toast and a boiled egg—but as soon as he saw Adam, he dropped his spoon and bolted across the room.

"Papa!" he cried, hugging him about the legs. "Mama said you'd be back soon! Will you read me a story when I go to bed? I'm not tired yet though. Mama and I had a big afternoon nap in her room."

Adam picked him up and hugged him tight. "I will, my boy, I will. And I'm glad you and your Mama are well rested." He smiled at Catherine over their son's head. "Are you feeling a little better?"

"Very much," she replied softly. "Especially now that you're safely home. But you"—she reached out and stroked his cheek—"must be utterly exhausted."

His mouth slid into a wry grin. "Just a little. But it doesn't matter. I'm with you and our son. *That's* all that matters."

Catherine's eyes glowed with a warm light. "Shall I ring for something to eat? I have no idea what's on the menu for tonight's dinner, but I'll ask for trays to be sent up. Your mother and the able Mrs. Beckett have taken care of all that. I suspect that like me, you've barely eaten a thing since this morning."

"I still have some egg and toast soldiers left," said Louis brightly. "Would you like some, Papa?"

Adam smiled, kissed his son's temple, then put him down gently on the hearthrug. "No, you finish your dinner. And then I'm sure Lizzy will have some pudding for you."

Lizzy, who was hovering nearby, grinned. "I do, my little lord. It's treacle pudding."

Louis clapped his hands. "Hurrah! My favorite!"

Adam wound his arms about Catherine and gave her a soft kiss. "I'll certainly enjoy my dinner tonight. And then when Louis has gone to bed, we can talk, *ma belle*, about all the things I learned…or didn't learn."

"Oh…" Catherine's face fell. "It sounds like a certain someone wasn't very forthcoming this afternoon…"

Adam grimaced. "No, he wasn't. But I'm rather hoping that a night spent in a cold-as-hell prison cell will loosen his tongue."

Two hours later when dinner was over, Adam at last led Catherine into her bedchamber and closed the door. "I hope you don't mind, but I thought we could do with some privacy while we discuss everything that needs to be discussed." Louis was tucked up in bed and sound asleep while his nurse watched over him. Quigley had assured Adam that the Abbey was locked up tight and everyone inside was being guarded like they were the Crown jewels.

"No, I don't mind," she said. "Some topics are best discussed behind closed doors. But are you sure you're up to this? You've had no sleep at all. And of course, your side—it must still pain you."

"It's tender, but I'll be fine." Adam wrapped his arms around Catherine because he couldn't seem to help himself. He wanted her near. Wanted to revel in the fact she was safe. He could have lost her yesterday too. "The bullet missed anything vital and there's no sign of infection. My valet

315

checked it when I dressed this morning. You can check it again after we've talked if it makes you feel better."

"It would." Catherine brushed his hair away from his brow as though surreptitiously testing that he didn't have a fever. She must have been satisfied as she said, "Can I get you something to drink? There's a decanter of brandy in my sitting room..."

Adam smiled and tucked a loose lock of silken blonde hair behind her ear. "No. All I need is you right now, my sweet wife." He kissed Catherine with lingering tenderness. She meant so very much to him.

"Heavens," she murmured when he at last drew back. "I wasn't expecting that."

"Weren't you?" Adam's gaze searched hers. "You know how much you mean to me, don't you?"

"I..." Catherine blushed and her own gaze fell away. "I know you care. You always have."

Adam frowned. There was something about Catherine's voice—a note of uncertainty perhaps—and the way she avoided looking at him directly that worried him. "Yes. Always," he said solemnly. "And that's why I'm doing everything in my power to protect you and our son. With my very life if I have to."

Catherine's eyes lifted to meet his again. There were shadows in their blue depths. "You almost paid that price last night," she whispered.

"I know." Adam was unable to disguise the harsh edge of frustration in his voice. "And I'm still not sure who pulled that damned trigger. Or how Gerald Fortescue managed to get away with everything that he did."

"You said he wouldn't tell you anything of import."

"No. The only thing I learned was that he does know Makepeace." Adam explained how he'd seen Gerald at the Cockspur Tavern. That he'd been the stranger who'd smoothed things over with the doorman who'd thrown Makepeace out. "Of course, Gerald wouldn't admit to any sort of close acquaintanceship. But as I said earlier, he might be a tad more cooperative after he's had a night to stew in his own juices."

"I hope so," said Catherine with a sigh. "I certainly found Newgate most unpleasant. I just want all of this awfulness to be over with."

"So do I, my love."

Again, his wife's gaze slid away from his. Adam frowned. He'd called her his "love." Did that particular term of endearment bother her? He'd only begun to use it recently because...

Because he loved Catherine.

Christ. He was in love with this gorgeous, intelligent, brave, simply amazing woman in his arms. The mother of his child. The embodiment of his every dream and desire. The woman he'd let go but had never been able to forget... If truth be told, he'd loved her then too.

He'd *always* been in love with her. But he'd been too much of a dolt—no, too much of a stickler and a coward who was willing to come up with pathetic excuses about his "noble" duty—to admit that he loved her. Not just to Catherine, but to himself.

But no more... Tonight he would tell her. Whether or not she loved him in return, she had to know the truth. Either one or both of them could have been killed last night. They'd almost lost their son. Life was precious and fragile, and he and Catherine had already spent too many years apart.

Come what may, he couldn't hide from his feelings any longer.

"Catherine..." Adam captured her chin and ever-so-gently tilted her face so she couldn't escape his gaze. "We've known each other a long time. Shared every sort of intimacy imaginable in the bedroom. Shared countless hours reveling in each other's company. We've supported each other through the most difficult, even harrowing times. We've found endless comfort in each other's arms. Yet, I can't help but feel that there's a wall between us. I've sensed it for a while now. Especially when we make love..."

Catherine's cheeks turned a deep pink. She swallowed. "I'm...I'm not sure what you mean," she whispered.

Adam frowned. She was blushing. She was uncomfortable. She felt vulnerable...he'd stake his life on it. Which *might* mean that she loved him too. But—just like him—she was too afraid to admit how she felt. "Yes, you do know what I mean," he said with gentle gravity. "You know *exactly* what I mean. For instance, whenever we make love, you won't look at me."

Something hot flashed in Catherine's eyes. Indignance or fear that he'd fathomed the truth? She shook her head. "That's not true."

"Yes, it is, my love." he said in a velvet-soft voice. He brushed a thumb across her flushed cheek. "I know you're hiding from me."

She closed her eyes, confirming his suspicions. Triumph flared.

"Look at me now," he commanded softly.

She wrenched her chin from his grasp and angled her head down. "I can't."

"Why?" Adam caressed her cheek with a feather-light touch. Brushed his fingers against her neck where her delicate pulse fluttered rapidly like the wings of a trapped butterfly.

She opened her eyes and almost glared at him. Her body seemed to be vibrating. Trembling. "Because... Because I'm..."

So many strong, conflicting emotions were tumbling around inside her. Adam could almost feel them. *See* them. So much passion. Such stubbornness. Oh, how he loved her. "You're afraid?" he finished gently. "Because of what I might see in your eyes?"

"Yes, damn you, Adam," she returned hotly. Her tone was defiant and her gaze fairly blazed now. "I'm terrified you might see how I feel about you. How I've always felt about you from the very start—" Her voice cracked and she broke off. Her breasts rose and fell with her quickened breathing. Tears shimmered in her eyes. But that wasn't all. Adam unabashedly searched her gaze and saw other things. Aside from fierce anger and pride, he also saw yearning and hope and fear and... His breath caught. There was love. So much love. Oh, how had he never noticed that before? What a blind idiotic fool he'd been.

He drew a deep breath. "I think that tonight, we *both* need to be brave, dear heart... Would it help if I went first? If I told you that I love you?"

Catherine clutched his arms tightly. "Is that true?" she breathed. "Please don't jest. If you're jesting or lying, I might expire on the spot."

Adam held her gaze. The fact that she doubted him was his fault. But he would make this right. He *would* convince her. "Yes, my darling wife, my *love*, it's true. Undeniably so. I love you so much it almost hurts. I love you so much, I can't imagine my life without you in it. And if I could go back in time and change the choice I made five years ago, I would. In a heartbeat. Because I have always loved you. It's why I could never forget you. I've...I've just been too scared to acknowledge my feelings. I let who I was and what I thought was my duty get in the way of what we could have had. What we *should* have had. I should not have forsaken you. I should not have denied what I really felt inside my heart, in my blood, indeed, in every fiber of my being, right down to the depths of my very soul. Without you and the precious son that you've given me, I'd be an empty shell of a man. I just pray that you can forgive me—"

Catherine gripped his head and pulled him down for a brief but passionate, almost fierce kiss. "Of course I forgive you. I love you too, Adam. I've loved you for the longest time. Forever, in fact. And I've been a coward too. I thought that if I played a part—if I relied on my practiced role of seductress—if I hid myself away, then maybe you wouldn't notice. More than anything, I didn't want things to become strained between us if you learned that I loved you, but you didn't feel the same way. It was my fear of rejection, and of being hurt, which made me dishonest. And I'm sorry."

Adam captured her beloved face between his hands. "You have nothing to be sorry about. I understand the need to protect one's heart. But no more. We will be open and honest and vulnerable with each other from now on. We will be our true and authentic selves. There will be no secrets. No lies. Just us and our love laid bare."

"Yes..." Catherine smiled. There were more tears in her eyes, but this time, Adam suspected they were borne of joy, not frustration or anger or fear. "More than anything, I want that for us too."

~

Catherine's heart was singing. Her soul was flying. Soaring high.

Adam had just professed his love for her in the most beautiful and profound way—and she believed him. It wasn't only his words that had convinced her. It was the way he was looking at her, his gaze touching her face as though his soul was speaking to hers. He'd seen through all her artifice. He'd stripped away all her defenses. He *knew* everything about her. She no longer had to hide. She wasn't afraid anymore.

Last night had been the darkest of Catherine's life. But tonight was undoubtedly the best. And she would rejoice in it. What she and Adam had was precious and there was no time like the present to celebrate.

"Perhaps it's not only our love we can lay bare," Catherine whispered as she slid her fingers beneath Adam's coat and flexed them against his chest. "Perhaps we could make love. With care though. And slowly. I don't want to make your injury worse."

Adam's mouth tilted into a heart-stopping but tender smile. "It's like you read my mind. Slow lovemaking sounds perfect."

"We'll have to be quiet too," murmured Catherine as she slid Adam's coat from his wide shoulders and down his arms. "We don't want to disturb anyone next door."

"I can be quiet," said Adam as he worked on the fastenings of Catherine's gown. "You, on the other hand..."

She gave his arm a playful swat. "Are you saying I'm loud when I'm in the throes of passion?"

Adam kissed her. "I love the sounds you make when you come," he whispered against her lips. He slid her gown off her shoulders and it fell to the floor. "Never hold back on my account."

Within minutes, they were both naked...well, except for the bandage around Adam's hips. Catherine reached out and gently touched the white linen. "You mustn't overexert yourself," she murmured.

Adam gave a low chuckle. "Look at my cock, woman. Does it not look like it's primed and ready to go?"

He wasn't wrong—it curved upward in a proud fierce arc toward his taut stomach. Catherine wrapped her fingers around the thick shaft and gave him a gentle squeeze. "I could go down on you..."

But Adam shook his head. His hands cupped her breasts as his thumbs swirled over her nipples, making lazy circles around the taut aching points. "No. Not tonight. Not this time. I want to be inside you. I want to look into your eyes and watch your face when you come."

Catherine felt her cheeks heat. She felt suddenly, inexplicably shy. It was almost like they were making love for the very first time. And perhaps they were. Because it was the very first time since both of them had admitted their love for one another.

"I want to do that too," she whispered huskily. And she meant it.

Adam took her hand and drew her over to the curtained bed. "I'll lie back against the pillows, and you can ride me..."

"Yes..." Catherine pushed between the partially drawn damask drapes and knelt upon the pale lilac silk counterpane. She plucked at her own nipple while between her thighs, she could already feel that she was slick and aching for Adam's attention. She suddenly couldn't wait for her husband to be inside her. To be at one with her.

For Adam's delight as much as her own, she traced a finger along the seam of her damp sex and when she withdrew it, it was glistening with the glossy evidence of her arousal. When she tasted her own dew with a delicate flick of her tongue, Adam groaned and fisted the thick shaft of his cock; the head was already swollen and ruddy, weeping in anticipation of what they were about to do.

He eased himself onto the bed, and as soon as he leaned back against the bed's pillows and headboard, Catherine carefully straddled him. As her wet sex grazed his cock, her eyes locked with his. "Feel how much I want you, my husband," she murmured. "How much I need you." She gently grasped his shaft and notched it at her entrance. "How much I love you." And then she sank down, slowly, deliberately, relishing the tight but fluid slide. The feel of him filling her and how greedily she clasped him in return.

Adam groaned and clutched her hips. His gaze, blue and burning, seemed to fuse with hers. His voice, when he spoke, was filled with raw emotion. "God, how I love you, Catherine." Reaching up, he gently cupped her face. "Kiss me, my love. I need to taste you."

Catherine leaned down and brushed her lips across Adam's in a teasing caress. Their breaths mingled, their tongues touched, and then Adam slid his hand into her hair and claimed her mouth in a possessive, hungry kiss.

As his tongue stroked hers, his other hand found her breast and Catherine moaned with unfettered delight when he pinched her nipple. Adam was deliberately teasing her, stoking the flames of her desire and she so wanted to burn.

She broke the kiss and Adam immediately seized both her breasts. He buried his face in the valley between them, inhaling deeply as though he couldn't get enough of her scent. Then he feasted on her sensitive flesh with his hot mouth, suckling on one nipple then the other, drawing on each peak deeply, sending sparks shooting straight to her sex.

She was aflame with acute need, suspended on a precipice of exquisite agony. She adored Adam's erotic caresses, but they weren't enough. She had to move. Had to ease the throbbing ache deep inside her. Find the all-consuming pleasure he never failed to give her.

She began to gently rock her hips, undulating back and forth. Adam's hot thick length pulsed inside her. He rocked with her, increasing the delicious friction of their joining. Releasing her breasts, he sought her gaze then quite deliberately sucked two of his fingers into his mouth. When he withdrew them they were slick and wet, and Catherine moaned at the wickedly erotic display. She knew what he was going to do even before he reached between their gently working bodies, searching for the apex of her tender slit.

Even so, she gasped when he found her throbbing clitoris and began to work her, delicately rubbing her swollen aching nub with his wet fingertips. Fretting and teasing and circling and pinching until she was almost mindless with the tension building inside her.

All the while she moved with him, grinding into him, using his cock to rub some special secret place deep inside her feminine core. His eyes bore into hers and she couldn't look away. Didn't want to. She'd never experienced such a deep connection with Adam. They'd had fulfilling sex countless times, but not like this. Never like this.

"That's it, Catherine my love," he growled, his gaze fierce yet somehow soft at the same time. "Use me and find your pleasure. Take me with you and I will follow. We are two souls bound by love. Two hearts beating together as one. Two bodies meeting and finding heaven."

"Yes," Catherine moaned, her body rocking frantically. "God yes."

She gripped his shoulders. Stared straight into his eyes. His soul. "Tell me you love me, Adam."

"I love you." His voice was thick with emotion. One of his hands clasped her neck. "I'm yours. You are mine. We belong together."

"Forever," she whispered.

His smile lit his eyes. "Forever."

Oh, but this was coupling was bliss. Catherine had never felt so wanted and adored. Her body pulsed around Adam's straining, gently pumping cock. They were rising and falling in perfect unison. Like the tide lapping the shore. Like the sun and the moon ascending and descending in the heavens. Their lovemaking was powerful and rhythmic, and Catherine never wanted it to end. But it must. Her orgasm was building, building, rushing toward her in a great wave. "I'm going to come," she whispered hoarsely. "Come with me."

"I will," Adam ground out, working her clitoris harder, using just the right amount of pressure to drive her wild. His face was flushed, his eyes ablaze. "But let me watch the pleasure break over you first. Let me feel and see it all. Don't hold back."

Catherine whimpered. "You can have it all. Every little piece of me. I've nothing to hide..." Her feminine muscles were quivering now. Her whole body was trembling. She was going to come completely undone. She was going to fall. She couldn't resist the overwhelming pull toward release—

"Look at me," Adam groaned. "Love me. Come, Catherine."

And she did. As sublime, thought-robbing pleasure swept through her body, Catherine couldn't contain her soft cry of joy. To muffle the sound, Adam captured her mouth in an ardent kiss. His hands were in her hair, his tongue in her mouth when she felt him let go too. He groaned hoarsely as the sweat-slickened muscles of his powerful body convulsed and twitched, as his cock swelled and pulsed. Catherine could feel the rush of his hot seed, the gust of his warm breath, the way his mouth curved into a smile as he nuzzled her neck.

When she lifted her head, she caught his drowsy, heavy-lidded gaze. "I love you, Adam," she whispered, looking deeply into his eyes. The blue depths glowed with satisfaction. And love. So much love. Catherine imagined she looked much the same.

"I love you too," Adam returned softly and then he kissed her with such sweet and tender reverence, she thought she might cry.

As they lay down together, their limbs entwined, Catherine never thought she could be happier or more content than she was right now. She had the gift of Adam's love, and she would treasure it forever.

CHAPTER 25

The next afternoon, after Adam had set out to "speak with" Gerald Fortescue at the Oxford Castle Prison—Adam hoped the man might be fearful and miserable enough by now to confess all—Catherine took Louis to his grandmother's suite in the south wing of the Abbey for a bit of luncheon. As the dowager countess was pouring tea and Cordelia and Viola were plying their young nephew with sandwiches and tiny cakes, Quigley knocked on the door.

"I'm so sorry to interrupt, my lady," he said to Catherine, "but Mr. Walsh, the inquiry agent, is waiting in the Great Hall. He wanted to speak with his lordship, but as he's presently engaged in Oxford..."

"Oh..." Catherine frowned and put down her tea. "Of course, I'll see him. Perhaps you could show him to the library?"

Quigley bowed. "Yes, my lady."

Drusilla arched a brow. "Isn't he the inquiry agent Adam employed?"

"Yes. He's been checking on a few details about this and that at the Rosemont country estate. We wondered if there might have been a break-in at Briarwood Park at some point—"

At that moment, there was an unceremonious clatter of china and silverware, and Catherine jumped. Jackson—who'd insisted on resuming his duties despite the fact he was still sporting a sizable purple bruise on his forehead—had almost dropped a tray of pastries as he'd deposited them on a nearby sideboard.

The dowager countess frowned at the man. "Jackson, is it? Are you certain you are fit for duty?"

The footman turned around and bowed. An uncharacteristic flush had spread across his lean cheeks. "My apologies, my lady," he said to Drusilla. "And to you too, Lady Dalton," he said to Catherine.

"That's quite all right," replied Catherine. "I suspect we're all still a bit out of sorts given the events of the last few days." She observed the young man as he tidied up the minor mess he'd made. He really wasn't looking all that well. There were lines of strain bracketing his mouth and shadows beneath his eyes. "Once you've finished service here, why don't you go down to the kitchen and have spot of lunch yourself?" she added. "I'm sure Cook has some pastries or sandwiches left over."

Jackson bowed. His expression had returned to pleasantly neutral rather than flustered. "Yes, my lady."

Catherine stood then bent down to kiss Louis on the cheek. "Don't eat too much now, will you?" she said to her son. "Sandwiches first. Then you may have a pastry or two. *Then* cake."

Louis pulled a face but nevertheless he said, "Yes, Mama."

"We'll make sure he eats well," said Viola with a smile.

"I should be back soon."

When Catherine entered the library, it was to find Mr. Walsh standing by the roaring fire, warming his hands. She didn't blame him. The November day was gloomy and cold and misty. No doubt the poor man was half frozen.

As soon as he saw Catherine, he snapped to attention and bowed. "My lady," he said. "My apologies for taking so long to return to St Clair Abbey. The weather"—he gestured toward one of the mullioned windows and the gray day beyond—"rather hampers speedy travel."

"Yes, I can well imagine," agreed Catherine. "Can I ring for you anything? A pot of tea or coffee? Some luncheon?"

"No, that's quite all right, my lady. I'll stop off at a local inn for pie and an ale when I reach Oxford." The man frowned. "I've just learned from your butler that his lordship is currently at the prison, interviewing Gerald Fortescue..."

"Yes, that's right," said Catherine gravely. She filled in the inquiry agent on what had taken place over the last two days —how Adam had been shot, Louis had been kidnapped by Gerald with support from Lilith, but that Benedict Fortescue had returned Louis home, safe and relatively sound, the very next morning. "Since their arrest, Gerald and Lilith have been refusing to explain how they managed to pull off such an elaborate kidnapping plot without some sort of help from inside the Abbey—or who took a shot at Adam in the drawing room shortly before Louis was taken. But so far, my husband and I have been unable to identify who might have betrayed us in such a heinous way. Everyone we employ seems loyal but there are certain things, small but important details such as: How did Gerald Fortescue know his way around the inside of the Abbey? How did he manage to slip laudanum into Louis's milk? All the answers to those questions remain a mystery." She sighed. "One thing both Lord Dalton and I *are* certain about is that Lord Makepeace has *something* to do with all this. The only thing Gerald has confirmed is that he *does* know Makepeace." Catherine explained how Adam had seen Gerald at the Cockpit Tavern the night the baron had been thrown out. "They must be in league in some way, shape, or form."

"Hmmm." Mr. Walsh looked thoughtful. "That might explain Lord Makepeace's monetary windfalls every now and again... If Gerald Fortescue is a friend, maybe he's bailing him out whenever things get too bad."

"Perhaps," agreed Catherine. "Did you find out if anyone had surreptitiously broken into Briarwood Park and conducted a clandestine search?"

Mr. Walsh lifted a dark brow. "I did. Your housekeeper remarked that early one morning, she found an unlocked door into the house. About a fortnight ago. But she didn't report the occurrence to you, your ladyship, as you'd only just married. She said she didn't want to worry you unnecessarily, especially since nothing had been taken. As far as she could tell, at any rate."

"Had my rooms been searched?" asked Catherine. She was suddenly feeling rather cold, even though the fire was blazing.

The inquiry agent gave an apologetic grimace. "Yes, it seems they had. Cupboard doors and drawers in your dressing room, bedroom, and sitting room, had been left slightly open. Items had been moved or subtly rifled through. But nothing of value was reportedly missing. The housekeeper had even wondered if it might have been a lax maid-of-all-work who she'd recently hired from Briarcombe village. When I questioned the girl, she denied ever doing anything so underhanded. She was most upset, and I got the feeling she spoke the truth."

Catherine shivered and folded her arms about her middle. She hated the idea of a malevolent stranger—or perhaps Frederick Makepeace himself—searching through her personal things. It was disturbing. "I wonder if it was Lord Makepeace or someone he hired. There's no other explanation for all these break-ins at my properties. But this rare blue diamond he might be after... I don't have it. I'd never even heard of it until recently."

Mr. Walsh nodded. "It's hard to say who it was at this point. Perhaps your husband might be able to prize some more information out of Gerald Fortescue. If he *is* friends with Makepeace, he might know what the baron's been up to. And why..." The inquiry agent paused and glanced at the door to the library, as though he wanted to make sure it was shut. "There is one more thing I learned when in Briarcombe that may or may not be pertinent to everything that's been going on, my lady. It relates to what you said about your staff... whether they are all loyal...or not."

Catherine's curiosity was immediately piqued. "I'd be grateful if you could share it."

"When I was having dinner at the Rose and Crown Inn in Briarcombe the night before last, I overheard the publican lamenting how much he missed one of his best barmaids, a woman by the name of Mary Jackson. Apparently she retired a year or so ago due to ill health. She lives just outside the village with her..."common-law" husband, shall we say? The publican also mentioned her son was a footman up at Briarwood Park."

"Mary Jackson?" repeated Catherine. "I've never heard of her. But then, the villagers in Briarcombe never really warmed to me for...for one reason or another. Jackson has certainly never talked about her."

Mr. Walsh nodded. "After a few discreet inquiries, I discovered that many years ago—over twenty-five years ago in fact—Mary Jackson actually worked as a maid at Briarwood Park."

"I see," said Catherine. "I didn't know that."

The inquiry agent shifted his weight from one foot to the other as though he was suddenly a little uncomfortable. "I also got the feeling that Mary Jackson wasn't only a barmaid when she worked at the Rose and Crown... That she provided other sorts of services for various gentlemen passing through the village"—Mr. Walsh cleared his throat—"for the right price. That might explain why your footman doesn't talk about her."

"Oh... Yes I suppose it would..." Catherine frowned. "Jackson is in his late twenties. He was in my first husband's employ before I became Lady Rosemont but..." She caught the inquiry agent's eye. "Did you discover why Mary Jackson stopped working at Briarwood Park?"

"I believe she was increasing, my lady..."

A tight knot of tension twisted Catherine's stomach. "And...and did you also hear any rumors about who the father of that child might be?"

"No," said Mr. Walsh quietly. "The publican wouldn't tell me anything, and neither would your housekeeper, even after I offered her a few guineas. Mary Jackson slammed the door in my face. I suppose the father of her child could be anyone really. Another servant at Briarwood Park. A stable hand. Someone in the village. But still. It makes you think."

Yes, it certainly did. Could Jackson's father have been Edward, the Earl of Rosemont? Catherine suddenly felt ill. Not like herself at all. She pleated her fingers across her belly and drew a deep breath in an attempt to calm her riotous thoughts.

If Edward had fathered Jackson but then cast Mary aside —if Jackson *knew* that—he might be harboring some sort of deep grudge. Ergo, Jackson might be jealous that Louis now bore the title of Lord Rosemont instead of him. Even though Jackson was Edward's by-blow.

But then Louis wasn't Edward's son at all... Maybe that made it even worse.

Had Jackson been the traitor in their midst all along? But he'd worked for Edward for years. He'd served him faithfully and Catherine too. Jackson seemed devoted to Louis...

Didn't he? But he'd also been present every time Louis had been involved in a near-miss or accident over the past year...

Jackson had also been a victim two nights ago when Louis had been kidnapped. He'd been bludgeoned unconscious in the servants' stairwell while chasing after Gerald Fortescue... Hadn't he?

Catherine wasn't sure what was real and what wasn't any more. Oh, how she wished Adam was here right now.

"Are you all right, Lady Dalton?" asked Mr. Walsh. His tone was gentle, his expression concerned.

"I'm...I'm not sure," she said. "Your news makes me concerned that my footman, Jackson, is a wolf in sheep's clothing. That he might mean my son, or even me, harm. But maybe he doesn't..."

"I had planned to head straight to Oxford, my lady" said Mr. Walsh. "To see your husband. I can be there in less than half an hour. But I could stay here and question Jackson instead...?"

Catherine bit her lip, suddenly undecided. She couldn't ignore Mr. Walsh's intelligence. But perhaps it would be better if she and Adam questioned Jackson. "No, I think it's best if you continue on to Oxford to see my husband. Please tell him to come home straightaway." In the meantime, she'd ask Quigley to summon the armed guards on the gate. They could hold Jackson in the gatehouse until Adam returned. It might be unfair, but Catherine would *not* take any chances when it came to the safety of her son. Or herself for that matter.

The inquiry agent bowed. "I'll see myself out, my lady."

"Thank you," she replied. "If you cross paths with my butler, please tell him I'd like to see him. I'll meet him in the dowager countess's sitting room."

Of course, she could ring for Quigley and wait here in the library for him. But she wasn't sure where Jackson was at this minute. He might be in the kitchen eating lunch just like she'd asked him to do, but then again, he might not. He might be up to anything right now. Maybe he was lurking nearby, watching her. Listening at keyholes. Maybe he was watching Louis... Plotting something else nefarious. The man *had* been oddly jumpy when he'd brought that tray into Drusilla's sitting room...

Catherine didn't want to distrust her footman, but she'd be foolish not to. And she wanted to be close to Louis. To make sure he was safe.

She quit the library and hastened down the hall toward the south wing and the dowager countess's rooms. Her pulse was racing, her stomach churning. Perhaps she was starting at shadows. Perhaps the last few days had made her overly suspicious when she didn't need to be. Perhaps, perhaps, perhaps...

One thing she wouldn't do was panic. She needed to be sensible. Logical. Maybe she should summon the carriage and spirit Louis away from here. She only needed to travel into Oxford. Yes, she could even encourage Drusilla, Viola, and Cordelia to come too. They could all pretend they'd decided to go on a jaunt into town. Just for fun. Fitz and one of the other burly young footmen or even a groom could accompany them. And on the way out, she could talk to the guards on the gate herself. In hindsight, she could have asked Mr. Walsh to send the gatehouse guards to the Abbey. But she really *wasn't* thinking straight.

Catherine changed her direction, retracing her steps toward the north wing and her suite. More than anything she wanted to get Louis as far away from Jackson—from danger— as possible. She'd fetch her cloak and bonnet and gloves. A coat for Louis, too.

Oh, Lord, she was panicking. She felt short of breath and almost dizzy by the time she reached her rooms. Maybe she should just go down to the Great Hall. There were more footmen at the front door. Adam's footmen. Quigley might even be there. There was safety in numbers.

She pushed into her sitting room. She was here now so she may as well grab her cloak from her dressing room just in case she did decide to call the carriage round. She'd be quick. She wouldn't even bother about a bonnet or gloves.

She opened her mouth to call Lizzy, then snapped it shut again. Her breath caught in her chest as she froze in the middle of the room. Through the open doorway that led into her dressing room, she could see Jackson. He was pawing through something on her dressing table. Her jewelry box?

Why was he going through her jewelry? How dare he!

Anger rushed in to replace Catherine's shock. Ice-cold fear quickly followed. She took a step back, then another...and then she crashed into the corner of Louis's makeshift bed and cried out before she could stop herself.

Jackson whirled around. In one hand he held the exquisite sapphire and diamond necklace Adam had recently given her as a wedding present...and in the other he held a pistol.

"Don't move, my lady," he said in an ominously quiet voice that made the hair on Catherine's nape stand on end, "or make another sound."

"Or what?" she whispered.

Jackson cocked the pistol. "Or I'll shoot you."

CHAPTER 26

A night in Oxford Prison had done wonders for Gerald
Fortescue's level of cooperation. Which certainly suited
Adam because, by all accounts, he wouldn't get any useful
information out of Lilith. She was reportedly a sobbing hyster-
ical mess, ranting and raving in the style of Lady Macbeth.
While she might be able to shed some light on certain things,
Adam had a feeling she didn't know anything about Lord
Makepeace's role in the events which had taken place at St
Clair Abbey two nights ago or everything that had been going
on in recent months. No, it was her son who had orchestrated
this evil campaign against the two people Adam loved most in
the world.

When Adam was let into Gerald's cell the man was
huddled on the stone bench, still manacled, still only half-
dressed. His knees were drawn up to his chest and he was shivering. Adam almost felt sorry for the man...but not quite.

*He was going to kill your son. He might very well have tried
to kill you or Catherine. You have the bullet wound to prove it.
He deserves not one iota of your sympathy.*

"Wh-What do you want to know?" Gerald said without

prompting. "I'll t-tell you everything if you'll just g-get me a b-blanket."

"Whether I show you any sort of mercy will depend on how valuable your information is, Fortescue," said Adam. "Because I'm absolutely certain you would not have shown my son any mercy."

Gerald leveled a hollow-eyed look at Adam. "I hadn't d-decided what to do with him, exactly," he said. "My mother suggested that we c-could just give him another name and sell him off to someone. M-Make him disappear into anonymity. After seven years, he would be declared d-dead."

Adam clenched his teeth and fists as he struggled to rein in his anger, when all he really wanted to do was slam Gerald Fortescue's head against the cell's filthy stone floor again and again, or strangle him with the rusty iron chain that secured him to the damp and moldy wall. "And then you could claim the title after you'd killed off you father." Adam's jaw was so tight, he barely managed to get the words out.

Gerald's mouth twisted into a cold smile that was more of a grimace. "Something like that. The earldom *should* be mine one d-day. F-Fortescue blood runs through my veins. It's not easy seeing your title go to a child who is another man's b-bastard. *Your* bastard I take it, Lord Dalton? I know C-Catherine was your mistress before you married the Marquess of Winthorpe's daughter. Even you must acknowledge that it was pretty spiteful of old cousin Eddy to wed a pregnant whore—"

Adam was across the room and gripping Gerald's neck before he could stop himself. "Enough, Fortescue. I'm not here to listen to you spew vitriol about my wife and son," he snarled. "You see yourself as hard done by. That you've been cheated. But guess what? I simply don't care. So stop whining and tell me what I want to know. Who shot me? Who did you employ to help kidnap my son? How is Lord Makepeace involved? Because I *know* he is."

"All...bloody...right..." gasped Gerald, scrabbling at Adam's hand. "I'll tell you...everything. Just...let go."

Adam released him with a hard shove that bounced the head of his son's would-be-murderer off the stone wall. "So talk," he demanded in a voice edged with steel. "Don't leave anything out."

And Gerald did. He told Adam everything.

By the time the dog had finished making his confession, Adam wanted to kill him. But he didn't have time. Catherine was in mortal danger and he had to get back to St Clair Abbey. Before it was too late.

CHAPTER 27

Even though a pistol was trained on her, somehow Catherine made her voice work. "Jackson, what is going on? If it's money you want or need, I can give you that. Quite a lot actually... Or....or take my necklace. Or even the whole jewelry box. The only thing I ask is that you don't sh— "

Jackson raised the weapon higher—now pointing it straight at Catherine's head—as he strode toward her. "You don't understand anything, my lady. It's not just about money. God, I wish it were that simple."

Catherine closed her eyes for a moment, trying to stay calm. Panic was squeezing her chest and she couldn't seem to catch her breath. "Then tell me what I can do to help," she whispered. "Help me to understand why you're doing this. If you're in trouble—"

Jackson emitted a short bark of bitter laughter. "It's too late for that. I'm in trouble so deep, I'm drowning."

Catherine forced herself to meet Jackson's gaze. "Are you going to kill me?" Her voice was a mere thread of sound.

A muscle worked in the footman's jaw. "It was never supposed to end like this," he said, his voice edged with desperation. "I just...I was just angry, you know? Angry because Lord Rosemont gave your son—another man's child—everything that should have been mine. Why did he decide to marry you and not my mother? What makes you better than her?"

Catherine ignored his last question because she honestly didn't think she could come up with any answer that would satisfy Jackson. Instead, she asked, "Mary? Is that your mother's name? She worked at Briarcombe Park, didn't she?"

The muscle in Jackson's jaw flickered again. "Yes... That bloody meddling inquiry agent just told you that, didn't he?"

"Yes," said Catherine. "He did. I'm so sorry Edward treated you and your mother so badly—"

Jackson gave a disgusted huff. "*Are* you sorry? You agreed to marry him. You went along with his outrageous plan. You've hurt so many people, *my* lady."

"I-I didn't know about you, Jackson. At the time when Edward proposed, I had no other choice—"

"You and your son have everything, yet my mother and I had to be happy with the scant breadcrumbs Lord Rosemont threw our way," rejoined Jackson, his voice laced with acid. "When he arranged work for my mother at the Rose and Crown, she was thankful. When I was old enough to work at Briarwood Park, I was grateful too. And then you come along—a pregnant whore—and he gives you the world! How is *that* fair?"

"I-I know. It's *not* fair. I see that now... It must have been difficult holding in all of your anger and resentment all this time. I...I never realized you hated me and my son so much."

Jackson's gaze grew haunted. Almost remorseful. "I'm not a bad person, my lady. I wasn't going to do anything at all. I swallowed my bitterness and served you and your son faithfully for nearly four years...and then Gerald Fortescue came along. He told me that he'd heard talk in the village about

Lord Rosemont and my mother. He told me that he also felt cheated out of a title. All because of what you and Edward had done. He asked me if I would consider helping him to claim the earldom for his family. That he would share the wealth with me when the title and estate *were* his one day. And what he asked me to do—what he paid me to do—seemed harmless...at first."

"What sorts of things?" Catherine knew the answer to her question before Jackson even answered.

"He asked me to play *saboteur* every now and again. To upset the apple cart. To make it seem like you were an incompetent mother and couldn't take care of your 'little Lord Rosemont'. That way, the Fortescues could wrest away Louis's guardianship and seize control of the estate. So, I lay traps—I broke the ice on the lake at Briarwood Park after Twelfth Night so it would seem like you were endangering your son's life when you took him sledding. I tampered with the saddle when he started riding lessons. I sawed through the rope of Louis's swing. But I didn't tamper with the axel on your carriage. I think that *was* just an accident."

Catherine's stomach was flooded with nausea. "You were deliberately trying to hurt a little boy, Jackson. How could you?"

Jackson's cheeks grew red. "But he *wasn't* hurt. Not badly. And...and whenever I tried to stop, whenever I voiced doubts or misgivings, Gerald Fortescue would tell me that I couldn't back out because then he'd be forced to go to the authorities and tell them what *I'd* been up to. And I would be blamed for it all. It would be my word, the word of a lowly footman against his, a gentleman of means who could hire expensive lawyers. Gerald was...he was blackmailing me. He's *still* blackmailing me. I *have* to do what he says. And...and I also have to do what Lord Makepeace says..."

Lord Makepeace... Ha! Catherine *knew* that horrible man

had a hand in all of this. "Has Frederick Makepeace been paying you to do his dirty work too, Jackson? Did he get you to set the fire at Rosemont House? To pass me all those terrifying notes? And why? For what purpose? Just to frighten me?" She inhaled a short breath and her heart stuttered as another shocking thought occurred to her. "Did Lord Makepeace shoot my husband? Or was he trying to shoot me?"

Oh, God...

Jackson was stuffing the necklace which he'd been holding all this time into the pocket of his liveried jacket. "I don't need to answer any more of your questions, my lady. We've been talking long enough. I need to end this." The footman was clearly worried Hetty or Lizzy might wander in. Or another housemaid. He took a few steps closer to Catherine and grasped her arm. The muzzle of the pistol, cold and hard, pressed into her side. "Get a cloak or coat," he ordered in a tone that brooked no argument. "You and I are going for a nice little walk outside."

"Where to? And why?"

"I think that's the least of your concerns right now."

Catherine rather thought it was very much her concern. But what could she do?

Ice-cold terror trickling down her spine, she grabbed Adam's old greatcoat which hung on a peg in her dressing room. For comfort and perhaps for luck. A talisman of sorts.

If she was about to die, at least she could pretend that Adam was somehow with her.

As soon as she'd thrown it on, Jackson gripped her elbow and marched her across the room. Through her clothing she could feel the pistol prodding into her side.

Jackson opened the door a crack and peered out. Then he opened it wider. "Walk. We're going to take the servants' stairs at the end of the hall. If we see anyone, you're going to tell them you need fresh air. That you're going for a stroll and I'm accompanying you for protection. And don't even think about screaming or creating a fuss. If you try to alert anyone"—Jackson gave her ribs another sharp jab with the pistol—"it will be the last thing that you do."

"But it's misty and freezing and looks like rain," Catherine protested faintly as they headed for the servant's entrance; it was a jib door neatly secreted into the wall panels. "No one will believe me. And what about the guards stationed on all the doors? Won't they be suspicious?"

"We won't encounter any," said Jackson. "Halfway down the servant's stairs, there's a priest's hole and a secret passage that leads into the family crypt by the Abbey's chapel." The footman smirked. "So much for all your husband's careful planning to keep his family safe... It seems he forgot about *that* secret entrance. It's unguarded."

Catherine's heart faltered. "How did *you* find it then?" she had to ask. Lady Dalton hadn't mentioned it during Catherine's tour of the Abbey...

Jackson shrugged. "By accident. Call it luck. A stray draft in the stairwell blew my candle out one night, and when I bumped into a wooden wall panel in the dark, it just opened."

They were at the servants' entrance now. Catherine glanced frantically down the hallway toward the main stairs, but it was deserted. A sob gathered in her throat but she pushed it down. She must keep her head. It was the only way she could survive this.

Jackson opened the jib door and forced her into a darkened stairwell. A narrow turret window was the only source of light. "Move," he ordered. "I'll tell you when to stop."

Catherine complied. She really had no other choice. As she descended the spiraling stairs, she ventured, "This is how Gerald sneaked into the Abbey, isn't it? You let him in via the priest's hole. But was it you or Gerald who put laudanum in Louis's milk and Pippin's food?"

"I dispensed the laudanum."

"And who hit you over the head? Or was your head wound self-inflicted to disguise the fact you've been in league with the enemy?"

Silence.

"Whatever Gerald Fortescue and Lord Makepeace have been paying you, I'll pay you double. No one has to know, Jackson, this can all end—"

"Shut it," growled Jackson. "I don't want to hear any more... Right, stop here."

He reached passed Catherine, pressed on a dark wood panel and it creaked open. It was pitch black beyond.

"I can't go down there," Catherine breathed. "I'll fall."

"At this point, do you think I really care if you break your neck, my lady?"

"Well, you must. To some extent," Catherine muttered as she carefully stepped into the dark suffocating space and felt for the next stone stair. "Why else are you going to all this trouble to sneak me out of the Abbey?"

"Maybe I'm just planning to use you as a hostage in exchange for my freedom if I get caught."

"Caught stealing my necklace?" Catherine asked. "Or for all the other terrible things you've done for Gerald Fortescue and Lord Makepeace?"

More silence. In fact, the only sounds in the stairwell were the scuff of their footsteps and Catherine's panicked breathing. When she reached the bottom, she thought she might cry. If Jackson snuffed out her life in the St Clair family crypt... She shuddered. No, she would not think that way. She would find a way out of this mess.

She could hear Jackson breathing heavily by her ear as he fumbled around in the dark. There was a harsh scraping sound of stone against stone, then a narrow aperture of light appeared. A doorway into the crypt.

Yet again, the footman poked Catherine with the pistol and demanded that she move, and of course, she did. She squeezed through the gap in the stone wall and found herself stumbling down a step into the gray stone sepulcher that Drusilla had briefly shown her during their tour. She didn't have time to take much in because Jackson was relentless. He frog-marched her past tombs and carved stone effigies to the tomb's entrance—a pair of wrought-iron gates—and then they were outside.

Maybe the guards on patrol will see me, thought Catherine as Jackson propelled her across the lawn, away from the Abbey. *Lady Dalton will notice that I'm gone. Louis will ask for me. Mr. Walsh will alert Adam that he's needed at home. Someone will come—I just need to keep Jackson distracted. Keep him talking.*

Within a few minutes, Catherine was shivering, not just with cold but with terror. A stand of trees loomed up ahead and beyond that, she thought she spied the crumbling ruins of the original abbey through the shreds of drifting mist. Were they heading toward the dower house? Or maybe the Thames? Did Jackson have a boat that would spirit her away?

And then Catherine saw a movement near the copse. A guard! With a pair of hounds! It appeared to be the Abbey's groundsman, Mr. Cowley. Catherine had met him at least twice before. Would he notice that anything was amiss?

Jackson hauled her behind a nearby oak tree. "Don't move a muscle. Don't even breathe," he growled.

But the footman hadn't been quick enough. The hounds bayed and the groundsman changed course and started heading toward them.

Thank God. Catherine nearly fainted with relief.

The sound of the pistol cocking was loud in the frigid air. "Wave. Smile. Pretend there's nothing wrong," said Jackson, his voice like flint. "Nothing at all."

Catherine raised her hand. Affected a wave. Cowley waved back but he continued his approach.

"Are you all right, my lady?" he called.

Jackson's whisper was harsh in her ear. "Answer. Tell him what I told you to say."

Catherine waved again and pasted a false smile on her face. "Yes... I'm just taking a walk. It's good for the constitution," she called back. "You know. One needs one's fresh air."

"Of course." The groundsman paused. Catherine estimated he was about thirty yards away. One of the hounds whined, but the other was wagging its tail. "I'm glad to see you have an escort," the man added. "Very sensible. But I wouldn't go too far..." He gestured at the lowering clouds. "It looks like rain."

"Yes...it does," agreed Catherine, far too brightly. Her smile was such a rictus of false gaiety, she thought her face might crack. Would the man notice she was wearing a gentleman's greatcoat? Surely he would think that was odd....which might lead him to believe that something was amiss. "I'm grateful for the warmth of my coat," she said, raising her arm again, "but silly me, I should have brought an umbrella. I expect I'll be heading back to the house soon for a warm cup of tea."

The groundsman's gaze shifted to Jackson but then returned to Catherine. "Very good, my lady," he said with a bow. "Enjoy your walk."

"Yes... Thank you..." Catherine's heart plummeted to the pile of dead, damp oak leaves beneath her feet as the man moved on. But underneath her fear, she was also seething with frustrated anger. Turning her head, she hissed at Jackson. "I am not taking another step until you tell me *where* we're going."

"The dower house," he returned. "All will become clear when we get there."

CHAPTER 28

The dower house, while in a picturesque location, looked desolate and neglected and only added to Catherine's sense of dread and foreboding. She couldn't imagination that Drusilla, Viola, and Cordelia would be happy living here.

Then again, it probably didn't help that the two-story, slate-roofed house was shrouded in mist with a backdrop of a crumbling ruin and a leaden sky. The surrounding garden was sodden and leaf strewn, and the front door and window frames were horribly weathered. The bare windowpanes looked like dull, sightless eyes.

And of course, she was regarding it all while a pistol was pressed into her side.

As Jackson forced Catherine up the front path, their footsteps crunched on the gravel. If anyone was inside the house, they would be sure to hear their approach.

"You're taking me to Lord Makepeace, aren't you?" said Catherine. Her voice trembled while her stomach churned. She had no idea how he'd managed to get onto the estate undetected...

Unless Gerald had brought him here in his boat the night Louis had been kidnapped...

Oh God. Had the baron been hiding out in the dower house for two days? Waiting for Jackson to bring her to him? "He wants to kill me, doesn't he?" she whispered.

When Jackson didn't respond, Catherine knew that she'd guessed the truth. Her legs suddenly felt as insubstantial as the mist drifting by.

The footman reached past her and knocked sharply on the door. Three short raps. To Catherine, they sounded like a death knell.

From inside the house came the sound of heavy booted footsteps, echoing on bare floorboards. "The groundsman saw you, Jackson. Where you and I were headed," she whispered frantically. "You don't have to do this—"

"Devil take me, my lady. Haven't you worked it out by now?" hissed Jackson. "Lord Makepeace wants that bloody French blue diamond of yours. The one you stole from his father all those years ago—the one I have in my pocket. He's been after it for weeks."

"But... But that's not..." Catherine clamped her lips together. Jackson thought the sapphire necklace Adam had given her contained the famous, long-lost diamond? The footman might be fooled, but surely Lord Makepeace wouldn't be. "Why on earth does he think that I have it?"

Before Jackson could say anything, the door flew open and there stood Lord Makepeace in the flesh. Catherine studied him, sizing up the man who'd been tormenting her for weeks. The son of the man who'd murdered her friend. The tendency to do evil things undoubtedly ran through the Makepeace family's veins.

She'd never seen the baron up this close before, only from a distance when he'd been in Hyde Park—the day he'd taken Pippin and waved at her and Louis from afar. The prickle along her skin and down her spine also told her that he was the stranger who'd been watching her from the shadows on the night of the fire at Rosemont House.

He was tall and thin with an aristocratic blade of a nose and dark unkept hair. Stubble shadowed his jaw. His coat was creased, his cravat was rumpled, and his dark eyes gleamed at her from beneath heavy lids.

"My dear Lady Dalton," he said as he sketched a mocking bow. "How lovely of you to come calling. Do come in."

Jackson gave her a little prod with the pistol and Catherine crossed the threshold. Unlike Dante in *Inferno*, she wouldn't abandon her hope. Not yet.

"Y-You won't get away with this," she stammered as Jackson forced her to follow the baron into a nearby room—a parlor perhaps—that contained a bare fireplace and furniture shrouded in dustsheets.

"Get away with what, pray tell?" Lord Makepeace tossed his overly long hair out of his eyes and then sprawled in negligent fashion on the window seat overlooking the dead front garden.

"This mad plan of yours to avenge your father's death."

The baron crossed his arms over his chest and arched a sardonic brow. "I mean, you did ruin my life by labeling my father a murderer and a traitor. I do feel a *little* bit of retribution is in order for destroying my family's good name. And my plan has been working rather splendidly so far, thanks to Jackson here and my friend Gerald Fortescue. Pity Fortescue got caught though. And that his father, Benedict, had a conscience." He gestured at the footman who'd remained by the parlor door. "Yes, I'm all up to date. While I've been squatting here for the past few days, Jackson's been filling me in on all the details."

Damn Jackson to hell for his betrayal. Catherine shot the man a venomous look before returning her attention to Makepeace. "Well, Jackson also would have told you that your bullet failed to kill my husband two nights ago when you shot into the drawing room."

The baron smirked. "No, that bullet was meant for *you*, my dear. It's just that... Well, I'm afraid that I'm a bad shot. And really, it was just a bit of fun. My goal was to simply create a diversion while Gerald stole your son." Lord Makepeace's grin widened. "But I wouldn't worry. Jackson, who's a far better shot, won't miss his target today. Especially after I've at last got my hands on what I want. You know, a certain priceless stone that *you* stole from my father five years ago. On the night he died..."

Catherine narrowed her gaze as anger flared. "You mean, the night Sir Louis Fortescue died because *your* father, a traitor to King and country, stabbed him to death?" she returned heatedly. "And I *don't* have the French Blue if that's what you mean." Makepeace was clearly mad! "It's you who's been breaking into all my properties and looking for it, isn't it? Why do you even think that I have it?"

Makepeace gave an impatient huff. "Are you really going to pretend you don't? Because Gerald *told* me that you do. He said that he saw you wearing it countless times in London and when he visited you at your country house. That you used to brag about it when you were lording it over him and his parents like the pretentious, money-grubbing, social-climbing slut that you are." His gaze transferred to Jackson. "Did you find it?"

"Yes, my lord." The footman pulled the necklace from his jacket pocket and tossed it across the room to Makepeace who deftly caught it.

Catherine's head was spinning. Her, lord anything over the Fortescues? Was the man deranged?

"At long bloody last." The baron raised it to the light and examined the deep blue sapphire in the center. "It's certainly large...and stunningly beautiful... But *is* it what I want?"

He glanced at Catherine as he pulled a small magnifying glass from his coat pocket. Then he held the necklace closer to the window and examined the sapphire in detail in the light.

Catherine held her breath. If Lord Makepeace realized the stone *wasn't* the diamond he coveted, what would he do then? Would he be angry? Would he lash out at her? But if he couldn't tell the difference between a blue diamond and a sapphire—if he thought this *was* the famed French Blue—he would undoubtedly kill her because he now had what he wanted...at least in his own mind.

Either way, she could probably count how long she had left to live in the space of a handful of ragged breaths and unsteady heartbeats.

No. She wouldn't give up. She wasn't going to lose her life on a dusty wooden floor in an abandoned dower house full of shrouded furniture that looked like ghosts. She wouldn't leave Louis, or leave Adam. Not when they'd truly found each other.

She would buy some time. She'd talk her way out of this. Appeal to whatever was left of Jackson's decency. While he'd betrayed her and Louis over and over again, he still kept referring to her as "my lady". That *had* to mean something.

If she could just get outside. There might be another guard patrolling the grounds... She could catch his attention. At this point, screaming and even making a run for it seemed liked viable options. She had a beautiful son and a husband who adored her.

She would do whatever she could to survive.

Lord Makepeace finished his examination of the necklace then looked up at her. His triumphant smile told her everything she needed to know even before he spoke. "Good news!

For me, at least. The jewel is real and not paste. But I'm afraid it's not such good news for you, Lady Dalton."

"Take the necklace. Have it. I don't care," said Catherine in the strongest voice she could muster. She couldn't afford to show any sign of weakness. "If you let me go, I won't breathe a word—"

Lord Makepeace let out a short bark of laughter. "Oh, my lady. You really think I'd let you go? No, no, no. I'm an 'eye for an eye' sort of man. I want my pound of flesh. My father is dead because of you. So you must die too." He nodded at the footman. "Jackson..."

"No!" Catherine whirled around to face the footman who still stood in the doorway. His pistol was aimed at her, but indecision clouded his gaze. She would take it as a sign he could be reasoned with. "Jackson. Please... Think about what you're about to do. You're about to commit cold-blooded murder."

Jackson's face contorted. "I have to, my lady. I've done too many things. Bad things."

Catherine drew a shaky breath. "I know but...but if you shoot me, in here, there'll be blood and a mess to clean up. Others might hear the pistol's report and come to investigate. There'll be evidence I *was* murdered. But maybe if we all went outside...if we went down to the river. Perhaps..." She glanced at Lord Makepeace who was studying her with a half-amused expression before returning her attention back to the footman. "Perhaps if you hit me over the head with something... knocked me unconscious and...and then my body was pushed into the Thames, it would look like an accident. Like I'd tripped and fallen and bumped my head and had then drowned. Then you wouldn't be blamed, Jackson. No one would know. You could...you could get away."

Jackson dragged a hand down his face. He was clearly conflicted. He looked at Lord Makepeace. "What say you, my lord? The last patrol was only ten minutes ago. There shouldn't be another one passing by for another hour or so..."

The baron smirked and shrugged a shoulder. "Why not?" he said. "I'm gentleman enough to allow a lady to decide the manner of her death. If she wishes to be bludgeoned then drowned in the Thames, rather than shot, so be it."

Catherine couldn't believe she'd convinced these terrible, murderous men to agree to her plan. Once she was outside, she would make a run for it. She'd head for the abbey ruins and take cover. She'd scream and scream and scream. She'd throw broken bricks and stones...

Jackson marched her outside onto the damp grass, Lord Makepeace following. She wrapped Adam's coat tightly about herself. As tight as she could. She fancied she could feel her husband's warmth and his strength. Even hear his deep voice whisper in her ear, "Courage, my love."

Up ahead was the dark swollen river and the abbey ruins were behind her. There was a small expanse of woodland to her left. The main entrance to the St Clair estate was off to the right...but that was at least a half-a-mile away.

She had to decide which direction to take...and quickly.

It started to rain. A thick stinging veil swept toward her. Catherine picked up her skirts. Thoughts of Louis and Adam filled her head. How much she loved them both. With her entire heart and soul.

She inhaled a deep breath and she ran.

Adam thanked God that he'd chosen to ride his horse into Oxford because it meant he could ride like the wind on his return journey to St Clair Abbey.

Fuck. Catherine was in danger.

Gerald had told him everything. How he'd befriended

Frederick Makepeace a few months ago, then manipulated the man into tormenting Catherine just to create more chaos in her life. How he'd lied to Makepeace and told the baron that Catherine had stolen the French Blue diamond out from under his father's nose on the night of Sir Louis Fortescue's murder. And Gerald, the despicable swine, had done *all* that just to destroy Catherine's peace of mind, to unsettle her and make her seem even more unfit to be Louis's guardian. To make it easier for the Fortescues to take her son away.

Gerald had also confessed that he'd manipulated Jackson, Catherine's supposedly loyal footman. How he'd learned that Jackson bore the Rosemont family a deep grudge because he was really Edward's bastard. Gerald had then used that knowledge to his own advantage. He'd essentially recruited the young footman to become a *saboteur* for both him and Frederick Makepeace. To disrupt Catherine's life by setting up accidents and passing her poison-filled notes. By helping Makepeace and Gerald onto the St Clair estate and assisting them to carry out their attacks.

Gerald had been the puppet master, pulling the strings. Making everyone dance to his tune. All to destroy Catherine and Louis.

And Lord Makepeace was still apparently at St Clair Abbey. Squatting in the dower house, waiting for his chance to steal a priceless jewel Catherine didn't even own. And he'd kill her. There was no doubt in Adam's mind that the baron meant her harm.

He was more than halfway home when he came upon Mr. Walsh, the inquiry agent.

The man waved him down. "My lord," he cried. "My lord, I have news."

Adam reined in his horse impatiently. "If this is about Lord Makepeace and my wife's traitorous footman, I already know," he called out. "I must get back. Her life might be in danger."

Walsh swore beneath his breath. "I *knew* I shouldn't have left her. I hope you can forgive me for doing so, my lord. But after hearing my own intelligence about her foot-man, Lady Dalton asked me to summon you straightaway. She too feared that Jackson might be a wolf in sheep's clothing."

Double fuck. There was no time to lose. "Walsh, could you head into Little Godstow and rouse the local constable? It's less than two miles away. I'll continue home."

"Of course, my lord. Godspeed!"

Adam kicked his horse into a full gallop. As he thundered along the muddy road at a breakneck pace, he prayed he would get to St Clair Abbey before something catastrophic happened to his wife. The love of his life.

If Jackson or Makepeace harmed even a single hair on her head...

No, Adam couldn't think like that. Everything would be all right. Everything would be fine.

His fears only increased tenfold when he reached the gate-house. The groundsman Cowley who was talking to the guards turned to greeted him. "My lord, welcome back. If you're looking for her ladyship, she's not up at the house."

Adam's blood ran cold. "What do you mean?"

"She's out for a walk. I saw her not ten minutes ago, not far from the dower house. But don't worry. She had an escort."

"Who?" Adam demanded hotly.

The groundsman blinked in surprise. "Why, her footman, Jackson."

Bloody blazing hell and shit. "Jackson is a traitor," growled Adam. "He's been in league with my wife's enemies. I have reason to believe that one of those enemies—the man that shot me—Lord Makepeace has been squatting in the dower house."

Cowley looked horrified and the two guardsman on the gate snapped to attention. "We'll all follow you to the dower house, my lord," declared the groundsman.

"Keep up if you can." Adam flicked his reins and he was off, just as the heavens opened and it began to rain.

~

Catherine ran as though she was being chased by the hounds of hell. She didn't look back, she bolted straight for the shelter of the abbey ruins and a nearby stand of trees.

She heard a shout but kept going, even though her thighs were burning. Even though her heart was crashing against her ribs and her lungs were on fire. Her ragged breaths puffed out like frozen smoke.

The abbey, with its disintegrating towers, cracked walls, and window arches like broken ribs, loomed before her. Adam had warned her that the few remaining window arches were the sections most likely to collapse, but she didn't care. She needed to take cover before Jackson or Lord Makepeace took a shot at her.

There was another shout and a sound like thundering hooves. She heard someone calling her name. A familiar most beloved voice.

Adam?

Hope surged in Catherine's breast and she whirled around... Yes, it was Adam. Her husband was on horseback and rounding the dower house, riding toward her pell-mell, hot on the heels of Jackson and Lord Makepeace.

Oh God. She shouldn't have stopped. Her pursuers were so close—not twenty yards away—and gaining ground. But as she picked up her skirts again, preparing to flee, Jackson slipped and stumbled. He went flying, his body sprawling across the wet grass...and then there was an ear-splitting crack as a gun discharged. The footman's body convulsed before he went completely still.

Catherine gasped. Had Jackson just accidentally shot himself?

She wasn't going to go back and find out, not with Lord Makepeace charging at her like a red-faced, murderous bull. And, oh God save her, he was reaching into his coat.

He had a pistol of his own. And he was extending his arm, aiming the muzzle straight at her.

Catherine spun around and ran. But instead of heading for the abbey, she changed course and veered for the nearby copse. The trees were slightly closer and would hopefully provide more places to hide.

She plunged into the copse as she heard Adam shout, "Stop, Makepeace! Drop your weapon!"

If death was approaching, she would face it head on. She skated to a stop behind a beech tree then, heart in her mouth, peered around its thick trunk...just in time to see Adam, still on horseback, reach Lord Makepeace. Like an avenging Norse god or a Viking warrior of old, her husband leaned down and grabbed the baron by the scruff of his neck, then hurled the man forward.

The powerful momentum of the throw, combined with Makepeace's forward trajectory, sent the man hurtling through the air...until he struck the abbey's wall. As the baron crumpled onto the grass, his pistol discharged...and then in the next instant, the already fractured stone arch above his head began to crumble like a soggy pastry that had been left out too long in the rain.

"Look out!" Catherine cried as great chunks of disintegrating limestone began to rain down. The whole wall was collapsing on top of Lord Makepeace and Adam was far too close.

His mount reared up, but Adam maintained his seat and quickly brought the terrified beast under control. He expertly wheeled the horse around and within seconds, he was bolting toward the copse. Toward Catherine, and safety.

As soon as Adam reached the tree line, he smoothly slid from the back of his still moving horse. Catherine ran straight at him.

"Catherine." He caught her and pulled her close, wrapping her up tightly in his warm arms and his love. "Jesus Christ and all his saints. I thought I was going to lose you."

"I'm here. I'm safe, I'm whole." Catherine looked up into her beloved husband's handsome face. It was wet with rain and tears, just like hers.

Then his brow furrowed in a puzzled frown. "You're wearing my old coat."

"Yes... I wanted to feel as though you were with me if..." Catherine bit her lip. She couldn't complete the awful thought as a fresh rush of tears threatened to spill.

"God, I love you." Adam's voice was raw and brimming with heartfelt emotion as he gripped her tighter. "The idea of spending my life without you..." He shook his head.

"You'll never have to," whispered Catherine. "I'm yours, just as you are mine. We belong together."

"Yes..." Adam caught the side of her face with a gloved hand, then he lowered his head and his mouth covered hers. His kiss was hot and searching, almost desperate, yet also sweetly tender. Catherine could taste the salt of their mingled tears and feel the strength of their mutual ardor.

This kiss reaffirmed that at long last, everything was right with their world, and God willing would be so, forever.

When they drew apart, Adam rested his forehead against

Catherine's. "I should get you away from this Godforsaken place and out of this infernal rain."

"Yes..." In the distance, Catherine could see a small knot of men and hounds racing toward them on foot. The afternoon, much like the entire year, had been full of darkness and danger, but now it was all over.

She smiled up at Adam. "Let's go home, my darling husband. Let's go home and see our son."

EPILOGUE

St Clair Abbey, Oxfordshire
Summer 1821
Five years later...

"He's so fast asleep, there could be a riot outside and he wouldn't stir, my lady," Lizzy said softly as she gently rocked the cradle of her youngest charge. A smile warmer than the afternoon sun shining through the nearby window broke across the nursemaid's face. "He's such a good boy."

"He is indeed," said Catherine looking down at her four-month-old son, William George Adam St Clair. Her third son with Adam. A warm rush of tender emotion filled her heart as she regarded the soft down of Will's fair hair, his rosy chubby cheeks, and the way his delicate lashes fluttered as though he was dreaming. If he didn't look so content, she'd pick him up just for another cuddle, just so she could inhale his delicious baby scent.

The sound of disgruntled voices suddenly filtered through the wood panels of the closed nursery door, disrupting the peaceful hush within the room. Louis's original "makeshift" nursery had become the official nursery long ago.

As Lizzy scowled, Catherine released a tiny huff of laughter. "Speaking of riots," she murmured in a tone lightly laced with ironic amusement.

The new under-nursemaid, Annie, who was quietly picking up the toys scattered over the rug at the other end of the room, placed a pair of tiny wooden elephants on the deck of a miniature ark. "I can investigate, my lady," she offered as she made to rise to her feet.

"No need," said Catherine. "I'm sure it's just a case of youthful exuberance, nothing too serious." She nodded at Lizzy. "Call me if you need anything." She was still nursing Will herself, but as he'd just had an enormous feed, she suspected he wouldn't stir for ages. Will was a wonderful sleeper just like Louis had been. Unlike her rumbustious twins…

Stepping out into the hallway, Catherine found her two *enfants terribles* in the midst of an "animated" discussion. Lady Cordelia who was hovering nearby gave Catherine an apologetic smile and nine-year-old Louis, who was holding Pippin in his arms, rolled his eyes as if to say, "They're at it again, Mama."

And indeed they were.

"It's my turn to count!" cried four-year-old Phillip Adam Drusus, Adam's heir.

"No, it's my turn!" countered Phillip's equally vocal twin, Grace Catherine Madeleine. She stomped her slipper-clad foot for emphasis. Tilting her chin up to look at Catherine she said, "Tell him it's my turn, Mama. He can't have all the counting turns. I can count to ten too."

"I can count to twenty," returned Phillip with a self-satisfied gleam in his blue eyes.

Grace poked out her tongue at him. "Cannot."

Louis put down Pippin on the hall rug and the spaniel gave his hand a lick. "It doesn't matter, you two. Whoever counts, only has to count to ten."

"I take it we're playing hide and seek?" said Catherine to twenty-one-year-old Cordelia.

The young woman smiled. "Yes. Or trying to! We seemed to have reached an impasse."

Since Catherine and Adam's "scandalous" marriage five years ago, Drusilla had wisely decided that it would be best to delay her daughters' come outs for a few years. "They are so very young. There's still plenty of time for them to be introduced to Society," she'd said to Adam and Catherine. And they'd both agreed with her reasoning. As Lilith Fortescue was no longer feeding fuel to the salacious gossip fire about Catherine's past—an impossible feat given the fact the contemptable woman had been transported to Australia to serve a life sentence, alongside her equally despicable son Gerald—the notoriety of the "Courtesan Countess" was bound to lessen over time.

While Viola had initially been a trifle miffed that her Society debut had been delayed, she'd subsequently decided —at the start of the year in fact—that she didn't want a Season at all... Just after Christmastide, she'd fallen head over heels in love with the son and heir of Viscount Wolvercote, a local nobleman, and the young man, Robert, most happily felt exactly the same way about Viola. A wedding proposal had been issued and accepted in the spring and a wedding was planned for the middle of July. As the Wolvercote estate was only three miles from St Clair Abbey, Drusilla was especially thrilled that her oldest daughter would never be far away.

In fact, Drusilla and Viola were currently visiting Wolvercote Hall, taking luncheon with Lady Wolvercote while they discussed the finals plans for the upcoming nuptials. The ceremony would take place in the St Clair Abbey private chapel in a few weeks' time.

As for the ever-patient Cordelia, she was looking forward to having her Season next year. She was a sweet-natured young woman who doted on her nephews and niece so much, Catherine suspected that when she did eventually wed, she'd want to start a family straightaway.

Catherine responded to her sister-in-law's last remark over the heads of her glowering four-year olds. "I think your assessment is correct, dear sister." She knelt down on the floor and caught the defiant, blue-eyed gazes of Phillip and Grace. "I think that *I* should like to join in your game. And I also think that we should move away from the nursery so we don't disturb your baby brother's nap."

An expression of delight immediately transformed Grace's flushed round face. "Oh, yes, Mama. Do join in," she cried, clapping her hands while Phillip looked equally as pleased.

"Huzzah, Mama!" he all but shouted which earned him a rather loud and rebuking, "Shhhh," from Louis.

"May I join in the game too?" A deep, much-loved voice resonated down the hallway.

Adam. He was back from attending various business matters in Oxford.

As Catherine rose to her feet, her effortlessly handsome husband advanced toward them all. His top boots might be dusty and his navy-blue tailcoat a little rumpled, but in Catherine's eyes, he was quintessentially perfect.

Before he reached the small group outside the nursery, Grace and Phillip bolted toward their father and attached themselves around his legs like gleeful limpets, all the while crying, "Papa, Papa!"

Adam laughed and hoisted Grace up into his arms as he drew closer. Upon arriving at Catherine's side, he feathered a kiss across her cheek. "How goes it, my lovely lady-wife?"

"Boisterously," she replied with a smile, her own heart tripping with sweet delight. After five years of marriage to Adam—indeed, after knowing and loving him for ten years—the sight of him and the way he looked at her, never failed to warm her from head to toe.

"*Are* you going to play, Papa?" asked Louis, stepping forward.

"Yes, the more the merrier, dear brother," added Cordelia.

"Do you have time?" Catherine knew how busy he'd been of late.

"I do," Adam said with a lopsided grin. "I take it our Will is behaving himself even if these two rapscallions are not?" He gently ruffled Grace's flaxen curls before putting her down beside Phillip.

Catherine laughed. "Will is currently wallowing in a deep postprandial milk haze."

"Ah," murmured Adam softly by her ear. "Does that mean I can play with his mother for a little while?"

Catherine felt herself blushing and she was tempted to playfully swat her husband's arm. "I think hide-and-seek is the game at hand, my lord," she said.

Adam's grinned widened. "That's sounds perfect for what I have in mind."

He really was incorrigible. But perhaps so was Catherine, because she would readily admit that as soon as her husband had intimated he'd like to "play" with her, she couldn't deny she should very much like that too.

It was decided that Cordelia and Grace would count to ten, while Louis helped Phillip to hide. "Pappa and Mama" were instructed by Grace to "go off and hide somewhere too."

Adam entwined his fingers with Catherine's as they rushed off down the hallway like a pair of children themselves. Adam tried to pull her toward their bedchamber—they'd ceased maintaining separate bedrooms years ago—but

Catherine steered him toward Adam's private study. Once the door snicked shut behind them, she tugged him into the deep window embrasure and they both yanked the blue velvet curtains shut.

Then, they collapsed, laughing and breathless, onto the sunlit cushioned window seat.

At this time of year, the grounds of St Clair Abbey—the manicured green lawns, the bright flower beds, the verdant woodland of oak and beech trees—were breathtakingly beautiful. Catherine always fancied that she was glimpsing heaven whenever she took in the view as she did now. In the far distance, she could see the Thames and the cupola of the Palladian temple folly which had been built in place of the now demolished abbey ruins.

Since that terrible afternoon when Lord Makepeace and Jackson had tried to take Catherine's life—since those awful men had both perished at the site—Adam and Catherine had endeavored to expunge the painful memories by replacing them with happy ones. And Catherine believed they'd succeeded by rejuvenating that part of the St Clair Abbey grounds rather than shunning it. The banks of the Thames were now a site for family picnics, and in the warmer summer months, there were often rowing jaunts upon the river. Even horse and pony rides. Catherine, under Adam's patient and expert tutelage, could now ride too.

And sometimes, it was a place for Catherine and Adam to be alone in their very own *Le Petit Trianon*...

The slate roof of the riverside house which was no longer called the "Dower House" (or "Dour House" as Drusilla had once termed it) was also just visible above the trees. After the dowager countess decided that she would permanently reside in her apartments at St Clair Abbey, the house had been lovingly renovated by Catherine, and upon completion, she'd jokingly dubbed it *Le Petit Trianon* after the "pastoral retreat" in the grounds of Versailles Palace.

How her own mother, Madeleine, would have laughed at that.

The house had become a romantic hideaway—a retreat from all distractions for both her and Adam—which they took advantage of on the odd occasion. Glimpsing it through the mullion-paned windows of Adam's study filled Catherine's head with all kinds of amorous ideas.

She suspected her husband's thinking had drifted the same way too. Especially when he pushed a lock of her hair behind her ear and murmured huskily, "So, my love, what shall we do while we wait to be found...?"

Catherine quite deliberately snagged her lower lip with her top teeth. It was a coquettish affectation that never failed to drive her husband wild. "Well..." she began, her fingers flirting with the folds of Adam's cravat, "even though I know what *you* really have in mind, I suspect we won't have time for a full banquet..."

"You'd be surprised..." Adam's hand slid behind her nape. Bending his head, he began to nuzzle her neck. His mouth was warm as he brushed light teasing kisses along the line of her jaw until he arrived at the sensitive hollow beneath her ear. "I'm starving for you, you know. And you smell delicious. I can be ruthlessly efficient in the pursuit of pleasure..."

Catherine sighed and melted into his intimate embrace. "We should visit *Le Petit Trianon* later this afternoon. I'm sure we can both spare an hour or two... I also think that we both deserve to indulge in a leisurely feast rather than a hurried mouthful or two."

Adam gave her earlobe a playful tug and emitted a low growl. "Agreed."

Drawing back, he studied her face. "Have I told you lately how beautiful you are?"

Catherine laughed even as she blushed at his compliment. She might only be four-and-thirty, but the bright afternoon sunlight streaming through the windowpane would be highlighting every little thing that was less than perfect about her face and her hair; she was no longer in the first flush of youth. "After bearing four children I'm not quite as beautiful as I was ten years ago, my darling husband."

"Rubbish." Adam smiled, the laughter lines around his own eyes crinkling deeply. "To me you're more beautiful now and grow more beautiful every day. I love that you are the mother of my children. You've brought such joy into my life, *ma belle.*"

Catherine's breath caught. "Do you mean that?" she whispered. Over the years, she liked to think that her scandalous past hadn't given Adam cause to regret their union. At one time, it had been her greatest fear. But sometimes she needed to hear him say he had no regrets.

Adam cupped her face with one hand and gently caressed her cheek with the pad of his thumb. "Life without you would be incomplete, my love. The only regret I will ever have is that I did not have the courage to admit that I loved you right from the very start. That I was a fool not to marry you ten years ago when I could have."

And then he bent his head and his mouth claimed hers in a possessive yet worshipful kiss.

As Catherine sank into him and wound her arms about his neck, as her fingers slid into the silken locks of his hair, she realized she'd been wrong before...

Heaven wasn't outside the windows of St Clair Abbey. She'd seen it in her husband's eyes as he'd made his deeply heartfelt confession. A confession that provoked tears of happiness in Catherine's own eyes and made her heart swell with boundless joy. Heaven was in Adam's reverent kiss and the warmth of his arms.

Heaven would *always* be here. And like their love, that would never, ever change.

There was a rattle at the door and someone—or perhaps a group of someones—burst into the room. "Look behind the curtains, Grace!"

In the next instant, the drapes flew back revealing Phillip, Grace, Louis, and Pippin.

"Are you two kissing again?" demanded Phillip, his nose wrinkling in apparent disgust.

"They're always kissing," said Grace with a roll of her eyes. Behind her, Louis shuffled his feet and examined the toes of his boots, but his mouth was curved in a bashful grin.

Adam caught Catherine's gaze. There was a smile in his eyes and in his voice as he said, "I'll never stop kissing your, Mama, my children. Just like I'll never stop loving her. I'll love her forever."

And in her heart of hearts, Catherine knew this to be an immutable truth.

AUTHOR'S NOTE

Just a few quick notes for my dear readers...

Louis's favorite book, *The Life and Perambulations of a Mouse*, is an actual children's book. It was written by Dorothy Kilner and was first published in 1784.

The villages of Briarcombe and Little Godstow are purely fictional. Godstow, just outside of Oxford, was the inspiration for the latter.

According to my research into crimes tried at the Old Bailey, London's central criminal court, in 1814, kidnapping a child under the age of ten became a felony crime rather than just a misdemeanor. Felony crimes were punishable by hanging, imprisonment, or transportation.

For ease of reading, I've sometimes referred to parish constables and watchmen as the "constabulary" even though that term wasn't generally in use for domestic policing at the time.

From what I've read, the famed Tavernier Blue or French Blue diamond did actually disappear for a period of time—around twenty years—after it was stolen from the French Royal Store-house along with other French Crown Jewels in 1792. Accounts suggest it reappeared, recut, in London in 1812. Some accounts also suggest it went missing for a much longer period of time. It is believed that the famous Hope Diamond, now housed in the Smithsonian National Museum of Natural History in Washington D.C., came from the French Blue.

THANK YOU FROM THE AUTHOR

Thank you so much for reading **A Most Unsuitable Countess**! If you have the time and inclination, please do consider leaving a review wherever you bought the book. I would greatly appreciate it!

Read on to find out more about the first two books in the Scandalous Regency Widows series...

FIND OUT MORE ABOUT THE SCANDALOUS REGENCY
WIDOWS SERIES...

Lady Beauchamp's Proposal, Book 1

*A runaway countess finds love when she least expects it...
but she can't hide from her past forever.*

Elizabeth, Lady Beauchamp, fears for her life. When she
discovers her dissolute and long-estranged husband has
syphilis—and he wants to beget an heir no matter the cost—
she flees to a remote part of Scotland to begin a new life as the
widowed governess, Mrs. Beth Eliott at Eilean Tor Castle.

When Mrs. Eliott unexpectedly arrives on his doorstep, the
reclusive and recently widowed Marquess of Rothsburgh is
both irritated and intrigued. No longer in need of a governess
—his young daughter now resides with his sister's family in
Edinburgh—he proposes the beautiful widow fill a position of
a different kind...

Torn between staying true to her marriage vows and her
wanton attraction to the devilishly handsome marquess, Elizabeth struggles against the temptation to become his mistress.
But living a lie is not easy when you have fallen in love. And
secrets always have a way of coming out...

The Ice Duchess, Book 2

*The Duchess of Darby never thought she'd meet a man
who could melt the ice around her heart...until she
crosses paths with Lord Markham. But will the past
come back to burn them both?*

Georgiana Dudley—the "Ice Duchess"—has just emerged from mourning after a nine-year marriage of convenience to the Duke of Darby, her twin brother's lover. Deeply hurt by a scoundrel a decade ago, Georgie swore she would never turn her head for any man, let alone another rakehell. But then she encounters the wickedly handsome and all too charming Rafe Landsbury, the Earl of Markham and against her better judgment, her interest is reluctantly aroused. An affair may be impossible to resist but dare she trust Lord Markham with her most intimate secrets...and her heart?

Society believes Rafe to be a diplomat but for many years he has been working on the Continent as a spy for the Crown. Leaving the shadowy world of espionage behind, he returns to London with the intention of finding a wife. When he is paired with the frosty yet fascinating Duchess of Darby at the piquet table during a ton ball, he is intrigued. Do-or-die man that he is, he's certainly not going to let her cool demeanor dissuade him from pursuing her.

When Rafe's dark past returns to endanger Georgie, he is determined to protect her at all costs, even if that means hiding who he once was. With the stakes so high, both Georgie and Rafe must decide if love is a risk worth taking...

DON'T MISS AMY ROSE BENNETT'S OTHER ROMANCES

Visit www.amyrosebennett.com to find out more...

SCANDALOUS REGENCY WIDOWS

Lady Beauchamp's Proposal, Book 1
The Ice Duchess, Book 2
A Most Unsuitable Countess, Book 3

≈

IMPROPER LIAISONS

An Improper Proposition, Book 1
An Improper Governess, Book 2
An Improper Christmas, Book 3
An Improper Duke, Book 4 (Out Jan 2024)

≈

THE BYRONIC BOOK CLUB

Up All Night with a Good Duke, Book 1
Curled Up with an Earl, Book 2
Tall, Duke, and Scandalous, Book 3

≈

THE DISREPUTABLE DEBUTANTES

How to Catch a Wicked Viscount, Book 1
How to Catch an Errant Earl, Book 2

How to Catch a Sinful Marquess, Book 3
How to Catch a Devilish Duke, Book 4

❧

STANDALONE TITLES

All She Wants for Christmas
Dashing Through the Snow
The Duke Who Came to Christmas Dinner
My Lady of Misrule
Long Gone Girl

❧

COMING SOON...

HIGHLAND ROGUES
The Master of Strathburn, Book 1
The Laird of Blackloch, Book 2

LADY MEETS ROGUE
The Lady and the Libertine (**FREE** for newsletter subscribers)
The Lady and the Privateer (Out July 2023)
The Lady and the Duke (Out January 2024)

ABOUT THE AUTHOR

Amy Rose Bennett is an Australian author who has a passion for penning emotion-packed historical romances. Of course, her strong-willed heroines and rakish heroes always find their happily ever after. A former speech pathologist, Amy is happily married to her very own romantic hero and has two lovely, very accomplished adult daughters. When she's not creating stories, Amy loves to cook up a storm in the kitchen, lose herself in a good book or a witty rom-com, and when she can afford it, travel to all the places she writes about.

Sign up for Amy Rose Bennett's newsletter via her website at www.amyrosebennett.com to receive all of her latest book news! When you subscribe, you'll also receive an exclusive FREE copy of her hot but sweet novella, *The Lady and the Libertine!*

When bluestocking Lady Angelina Pembroke decides the only way out of an impending but unwanted engagement is to ruin her reputation, she approaches London's most notorious libertine —a former naval officer dubbed the "Tattooed Viscount"—to ensure her plan is a resounding success. But sometimes, the road to ruination isn't all plain sailing...especially when love gets in the way...

www.ingramcontent.com/pod-product-compliance
Lightning Source LLC
Chambersburg PA
CBHW020907040125
19912CB00042B/326